Looking for Mrs Dextrose

Nick Griffiths

Independent Book Publisher

Legend Press Ltd, 2 London Wall Buildings,
London EC2M 5UU
info@legend-paperbooks.co.uk
www.legendpress.co.uk

Contents © Nick Griffiths 2010

The right of the above author to be identified as the author of this work has been asserted in accordance with the Copyright, Designs and Patent Act 1988.

British Library Cataloguing in Publication Data available.

ISBN 978-1-9077564-9-8

All characters, other than those clearly in the public domain, and place names, other than those well-established such as towns and cities, are fictitious and any resemblance is purely coincidental.

Set in Times
Printed by CPI Books, UK.

Cover designed by Gudrun Jobst
www.yotedesign.com

All rights reserved. No part of this publication may be reproduced, stored in or introduced into a retrieval system, or transmitted, in any form, or by any means electronic, mechanical, photocopying, recording or otherwise, without the prior permission of the publisher. Any person who commits any unauthorised act in relation to this publication may be liable to criminal prosecution
and civil claims for damages.

Independent Book Publisher

PRAISE FOR LOOKING FOR MRS DEXTROSE

'IF you like *Alice in Wonderland* or *Fear and Loathing in Las Vegas* then you will love *Looking for Mrs Dextrose*. Nick Griffiths latest novel combines the fantasy of Carroll with the grime of Thompson to make something special, if slightly nauseating.'
Julie Shennan, Strathclyde Telegraph

'By the end of the book I had laughed, had a little lip quiver, checked under the bed for errant puppets and been put off my food twice – a feat very few novels can achieve... For pure escapism, for belly laughs, for twists and turns, *Looking for Mrs Dextrose* is the ideal read.'
Caroline Tecks, The Cambridge Student

'Charming and witty, packed with sharp observations and banter... like a literary version of *The Mighty Boosh*.'
Tom Fordy, St Mary's University

'I found myself snorting with laughter...clever, slick and enticing.'
Iyanu Onalaja, Spaghetti Junction, Birmingham City University

'Amazingly well-written dialogue... every page reeks of invention.'
Libby Holderness, Reading University

'*Looking for Mrs Dextrose* is puerile, at times revolting, and utterly unmissable... The book's spectacular energy speaks for itself and your life won't feel complete without it.'
Carol Williamson, Fuse magazine, Sheffield University

'For the first time in my life, I found myself wanting to punch a book. I then proceeded to punch the book...'
Paul Dunn, Le Nurb, Brunel University

'Fluidly written, filled with un-literary references and cheap gags... It ends up being a comedy in spite of itself.'
Alistair Todd, The Courier, Aberdeen University

'Griffiths is true to form... A masterpiece of bizarre, expect-the-unexpected type writing which has been compared to Douglas Adams and maybe hints of Ben Elton. I can't wait for the third instalment of the Dextrose saga.'
Rob McDade, Borders Australia

'I don't think anyone would take Nick Griffiths for forty-five. I am sure that most people would take him for at least seven or eight years younger...I found him rather dishy.'
C. Richardson

'If you like the absurd and the unpredictable, you'll like this book. I read this book whilst commuting and... was pretty horrified when a snort escaped from my face whilst reading Nick Griffiths' work of comic genius.'
Charlotte Chase, charlottepaperchase.blogspot.com

PRAISE FOR IN THE FOOTSTEPS OF HARRISON DEXTROSE

'Funny, hilarious even… Can't wait for the sequel.'
Matthew Reid, goodreads

'Highly imaginative, entertaining and addictive.'
Jo Burn, Facebook

"If Michael Palin had an insane lovechild…"
Magda McHugh, Facebook

'Minking fantastic! I won't beat about the bush – you need to buy this book. Think of a tryst between Terry Pratchett, Bill Bryson and *The Hitchhiker's Guide To The Galaxy*…'
Martyn Goodman, Facebook

'For a rather irreverent, but silly, banal outing, this might just be a work of genius. Oh and it is HIGHLY comic – his use of language and weird descriptions reminded me of Tibor Fischer. Couldn't recommend it more.'
Andy Walker, Facebook

'Wow – this is the kind of book I'd love to be able to write. Surreal crazy characters, odd events and make-believe but somehow familiar places! The interludes from the Dextrose text are about as snigger-inducingly funny as a deep rolling fart in church!'
Graham Sedge, Facebook

'Can I please spend all my holidays in High Yawl!'
Debbie McGlashan, Facebook

'I was hooked from the start. Beware reading this in public if you are of a sensitive disposition - you will laugh out loud. A lot.''
Laura Gahan, Amazon

'Comfortably one of the most poorly written books I've ever read.'
Dick Dashwood, Amazon

'*In the Footsteps of...* is one of the most entertaining and funny books I've read since finishing my last Douglas Adams.'
Lee Duddell, Amazon

'One of the most imaginative and original writers I have come across in a long time. Definitely buy this book. You will love it.'
Nicky Beards, Amazon

'The outward silliness is underpinned with a razor sharp intelligence that raises this novel way above an enjoyable but transient read to an intellectually challenging piece of work. And it's funny! Properly funny, laugh-out-loud-on-a-train funny – people may move away from you on public transport, but you won't care.'
Mairi-Claire, Amazon

'This book is hilarious – full of grotesque characterizations, surreal situations and lots of hidden references to decipher. It had me laughing out loud, and I cannot wait for the sequel.'
Vicki, Amazon

'Accessible, clever and downright funny. Immerse yourself in an intelligent and humorous novel and enjoy the ride. Just be

warned that life may be a little dull afterwards.'
A Copson, Amazon

'I challenge anyone to read this book and not enjoy it.'
Daniel Parsons, Amazon

'His whole writing style and voice is brilliant! Witty and entertaining, this unique book will have you laughing out loud. I will be recommending it far and wide.'
EC Alexander, Amazon

'A really fun, funny book which is both well-written and entertaining (fancy...!).'
JP Clarkson, Amazon

'The one downside? The twist in the last chapter was cringe-worthy. But the first 23 chapters are lots of fun.'
R Selby, Amazon

'I smiled all the way through.'
Colin, Amazon

Also by Nick Griffiths:

In the Footsteps of Harrison Dextrose
(Legend Press)

Who Goes There (Legend Press)

Dalek I Loved You (Gollancz)

www.nickgriffiths.co.uk

www.twitter.com/mrsdextrose

For Sinead, a mindful wife

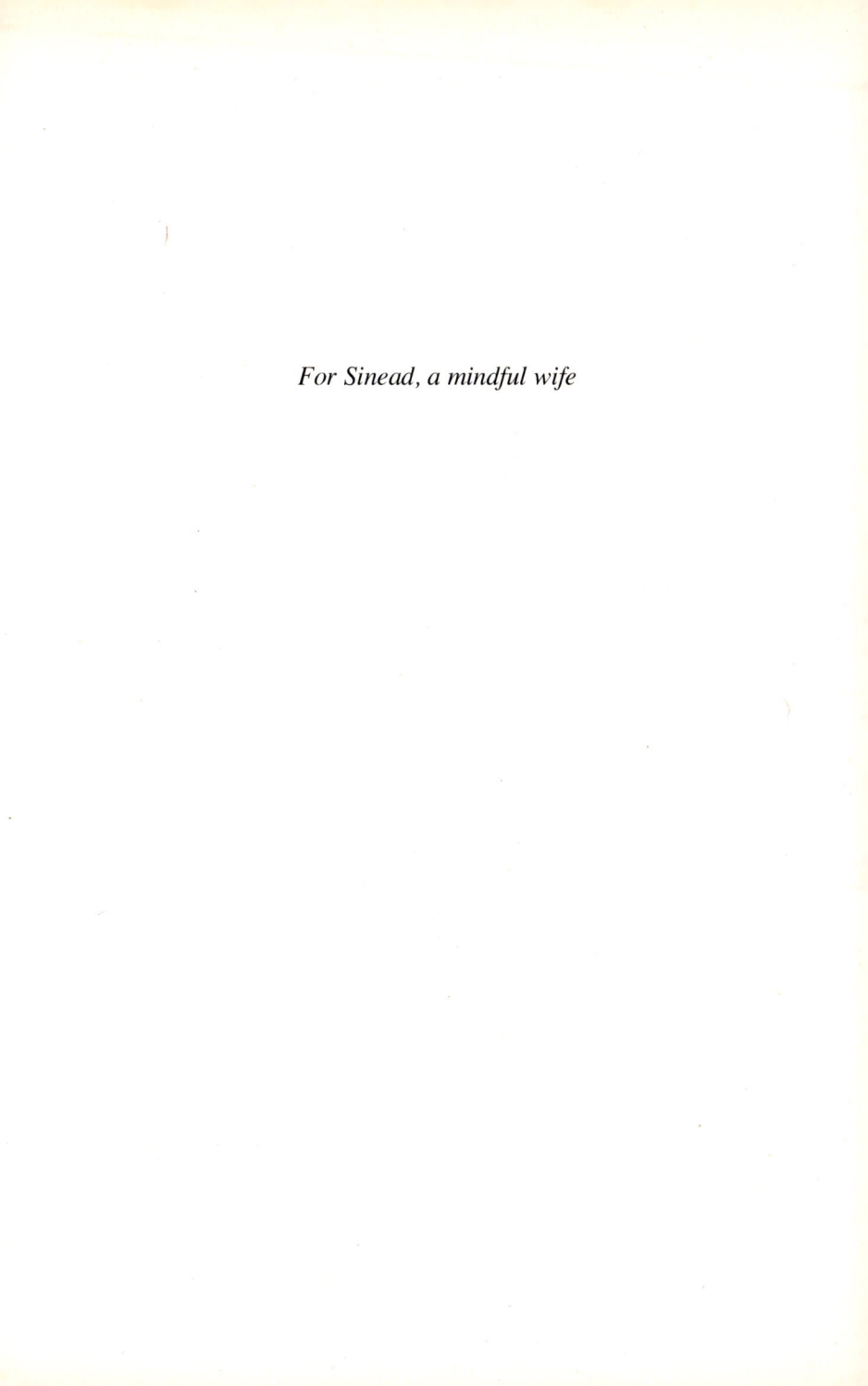

Gossips wine bar, Mlwlw, Saturday, 1.15 am

So I had been adopted and my real father, the man who had sired me, was Harrison Dextrose. Yet to gaze upon him now... Were there anything active left in those aged walnuts, I imagined a lonely sperm wheezing on a fag, shouting obscenities to itself at some sort of ball-bag bus stop.

The imagery made me bring up a small amount of sick.

Still I should have been delighted. My father – a renowned explorer! For 15 years I had lapped up the exploits in his book, *The Lost Incompetent: A Bible for the Inept Traveller*. Those exploits were the reason I was here, in this tired and tatty bar in a rainforest, many miles from what less adventurous souls might term 'civilisation'. Dextrose's seedy, rampant, exotic travels had seemed such an antidote to my suburban lethargy that I had been drawn to follow in his footsteps, only to chance upon the great man himself at my journey's end.

I should have been delighted. But I wasn't.

The star of *The Lost Incompetent* slumped before me in Gossips was a mess. Flushed and decaying, beaten by the booze. He had once explored foreign lands and their womenfolk as diligently as my fingers had explored the crevices of crisp packets – but no longer. How could he have fallen so far down? His dark grey hair and beard, silver-streaked, were so much tumbleweed. His vast gut seeped like lava from beneath a khaki shirt, buttons stretched to near pinging point, and hung down over a pair of pink velour tracksuit bottoms. He wore a tweed overcoat – in a jungle – that was torn and interestingly stained.

And there he existed, barely, making indiscernible noises as his eyelids flickered and froth gathered at the corners of his mouth.

My so-called father.

There had to be some mistake.

The owner of the Mlwlw nightspot was one Livingstone Quench, a friend of Dextrose's since way back when. I called to him as he mock-beavered behind his bar, my thoughts spinning like smalls in a tumble-dryer.

"Mr Quench? Could you help me, please?"

He smiled. "Yes, son?" And came over to our table.

Quench was not remotely the alcoholic landlord I might have expected. He wore an old dinner suit with bare feet. His skin was absurdly tanned and his face deeply lined, in the manner of one who laughs easily. His long, whitening hair was pulled back into a ponytail and his nose was splattered against his face, as if he had once boxed, or sleep-walked into an elephant. He was burly and toned: a presence, despite his advancing years.

"'Ow can I 'elp?" he asked, gravel-voiced.

When he had pulled up a chair, I explained about the photographs.

Barely 15 minutes ago I had entered Gossips as Alexander Grey, son of the middle-England Greys of Glibley – or so I had believed. The only other customer in the bar had turned out to be, to my amazement, Harrison Dextrose, holed up with his old mucker in the middle of nowhere. Sozzled and morose, he had lurched at me clutching two battered, browning photographs from his wallet: one depicted his wife in a headscarf, gaily clinging to the mast of a yacht; the other, his baby son, bawling, adopted shortly after the shutter had clicked.

Down to the dust flecks from the lens, the latter picture matched the one I carried around in my own wallet. Dextrose's adopted son and I were one and the same.

What was it he had exclaimed?

"Me son! Pilsbury! I found him!" As if he had put in the legwork.

Which made me Pilsbury Dextrose, which would take some getting used to, and one third of the Dextrose family, a wandering cock-up. It was all rather much to take in.

(Concerning the poor woman in the headscarf, Dextrose had mentioned in passing that he'd lost her while exploring and that her whereabouts remained a mystery.)

Yet at no point during my recounting of the tale did Quench look perplexed.

"You don't seem surprised," I said.

He shrugged. Big shoulders. "Why would I? The way 'e put it abaht – back in the day when it worked – I'm surprised there ain't more of you!" Quench winked. "'E's shown me that photo before, a few times. When 'e gets really drunk and mitherin'. 'Ere, show me yours, son."

I pulled out my dog-eared old snap and handed it to him.

"Yep, one and the same," he said. "And, y'know," he went on, peering at me keenly, "I reckon I can see the family resemblance. Same eyes, same nose."

I glanced at Dextrose's nose, pock-marked, crimson and bulbous, the overripe strawberry that everyone leaves in the punnet. As I did so, his right nostril blew a bubble of snot that might fascinate a small child.

Quench must have caught me grimacing. "Well, maybe not the nose," he chuckled. "But why not? Every lad's someone's son an' plenty of folks 'ave been adopted. Stranger fings used to 'appen in *Dynasty*, right?"

Barroom logic, it made some sort of sense.

"Did he ever say why his son... why I had been adopted?"

"Not that I recall." He pondered for a moment. "Nah, sorry. Anyway, when 'e gets in that sort o' state 'e generally talks a load o' shite."

"You really think I'm his son, Mr Quench?" Could it really be true?

He put his hand, twice the size of mine and extensively signet-ringed, on my knee. "Yep. An' call me Livingstone, son. Reckon it calls for a celebration, don'chew? Beer?"

"YES! BEER!" barked Dextrose, waking up.

I considered engaging this new father figure in conversation while we sat there, just the two of us, but could not begin to think where to start. He avoided my gaze, possibly on purpose, and I wondered whether he had forgotten who I was.

It was a relief when the barkeep returned clutching three bottles in one mitt, placing them on the table. Dextrose grabbed the nearest and upended it into his gob, then did the same with mine before I could snatch it away.

Quench raised an eyebrow and passed me his. "So," he said. "'Appy families at last!"

As far as I could tell, he wasn't being ironic.

He held up a finger. "Although, I s'pose, you'd really need 'is missus 'ere to be a proper 'appy family."

"Yeah, maybe," I replied distractedly, still suffering from the swirling smalls.

"Yeah, *course*!" averred Quench, apparently having made up his mind.

"Well, I have only just found my..." – Dextrose was

excavating his nose with a pinky – "father."

Quench eyed me less than benevolently. "What, you're prepared to leave 'er aht there, *somewhere*? Now you've found 'im, you're not goin' to find 'er as well?"

In that moment, with his wonky conk and watery, piercing eyes, he looked like an East End gangster (who are notoriously loyal to their mothers). Indeed, thinking about it, nowhere in *The Lost Incompetent* had it mentioned what Livingstone Quench did for a living, though he had never seemed short of a bob or two.

I was torn between fear and indignation; that Mrs Dextrose was missing was hardly my fault. "It's all a bit sudden…"

Quench cut me dead and leaned in. "Nah listen 'ere, son. I've been tryin' to get 'Arry 'ere off 'is arse to find the old girl for a while nah. But look at 'im. 'E ain't up to it! 'E couldn't find a bird in a… bird zoo. But you. Strapping young lad like you…"

Quench was staring at me. Even Dextrose was trying similarly to focus his gaze.

"Well. I…"

The barkeep slapped my back, causing me to go "Oof", and announced: "Good! That's sorted then!"

Was it? "But…"

"More beer!" cried Dad.

Dextrose's appraisal of his wife's situation had been succinct: "Minking[1] lost her!" That was it. No place names, no directions, not even a description. Hardly food for thought for the budding Holmes.

Still, buoyed by Quench's forthrightness – or too timid too demur – when he returned with refills I decided to show willing. "Any idea where she is, Mr Quench?"

"I told you, son, call me Livingstone. You don't fink I've asked before? 'Ere, watch…" He patted the table in front of

---

[1] The Lost Incompetent's editor had censored the author's multiple profanities with the word 'mink'. Interestingly, it appeared that Dextrose had adopted the affectation.

him. "Oi, 'Arry, what 'appened to the missus? Where'd'you lose 'er?"

"Only ever minked her once!" Dextrose slurred, then tried to wink but managed more of a disturbed squint.

"Couldn't she have just made her own way home?" I asked.

"You'd 'ave fort so. But no. 'Arry's got some special explorer's passport – gets 'im frew dodgy borders, stuff like that – an' 'e put her on that. Mrs D don't have no normal passport, son. So she can't go nowhere wivaht 'im. She, as they say, is right royally stuffed."

"Right. Oh dear."

"Y'see what I'm sayin'."

He then spoke to Dextrose, enunciating slowly, as if to a visiting foreigner. "Your boy 'ere is gonna 'elp you find your missus, 'Arry. So you need to 'elp 'im aht. One more time, for old time's sake: Where. Did. You. Last. See. 'Er?"

Dextrose seemed suddenly to notice me. "Who's this nod-cock?" he sneered.

We were getting nowhere.

From what I'd read, Quench had opened the 'wine bar' (I'd seen no sign of the grape) having done a runner from England some decades hence. Why Dextrose had returned here – and how long ago – I did not know.

"How long's he been here?" I asked Quench.

The lapsed explorer had once again fallen asleep, mid-interrogation, and a slime-trail of drool was snaking its way down the bird's nest that passed for his beard.

"You mean 'ow long's 'e been sat there today, or 'ow long since 'e arrived 'ere in Gossips?"

"Since he arrived in Gossips."

The barkeep looked around, as if that might jog his memory, and whistled. "Couple o' weeks? Could be more. Time flies in a place like this, y'know?"

I could imagine. "But you haven't seen anything of Mrs Dextrose?"

"Not a sausage."

I asked him when Dextrose realised she was missing.

"When I said to 'im, 'Where's the missus?' and 'e looks startled and goes, 'Not a minking clue!' and starts lookin' under the tables."

"And when was that?"

"Not long after 'e got 'ere."

"So she could be absolutely anywhere!"

"Don't give up so easy, son. Livingstone Quench 'as a cunning plan!"

He repaired behind his bar, clinked around among glass and reappeared clutching a bottle shaped into the form of a horned devil's head, containing a liquid the colour of blood. Six inches high, it bore no labelling of any kind.

"I've 'ad this for years," he said. "Never used it before."

"What is it?"

The local shaman had given it to him, he said, in return for a favour (on which he declined to elaborate). "'E called it demon juice, told me it 'ad magic powers." Quench leaned in close. "Told me it works like a troof serum, y'know, taps into the soul? Like good old-fashioned torture, but wivaht the pain! Might just 'elp old 'Arry 'ere to remember."

He handed me the bottle. The liquid was viscous and clung to the insides of the horns. There was a small cork stopper in the top of the head. The devil leered.

"It looks toxic," I pointed out.

"Shaman reckoned it might work if you jus' blew the vapours over someone. 'E reckoned only the well stubborn'd need to actually drink some of the muck."

We looked at each other pointedly.

"So what's the plan?" I asked.

He took the demon juice off me and removed his dinner jacket. "We should at least try just blowin' it over 'im first."

I heard a quiet 'sqnk' as the bar owner eased the cork from the top of the bottle. A cloud of russet vapour rose instantly from the open neck, reminding me of bromine experiments in school chemistry lessons. It lingered, swirling, like a genie.

Quench held the bottle close to the slumbering Dextrose's face and blew.

The effect was instantaneous. My biological father lurched upright in his seat, eyes filled with unseemly desire, and lunged at the brew.

"No-no-no!" went Quench, whipping the bottle outside of his reach.

Dextrose, too pissed to shift his bulk, sat with his arms flailing wildly towards the concoction, like an infant strapped into a pram. "Want it!" he drooled.

"Not till we've talked abaht the missus, 'Arry," said Quench.

Dextrose actually shook his fist. "I told yer – I don't minking remember!"

"Think, Dad, think!" I urged him, daring to use such familiarity.

He glared at me as if I were rodent-shit that had found its way into his bar snacks.

No, mere vapours were not going to suffice.

Neither Quench nor I had the heart to administer the potentially damaging dose and so we spent valuable time debating our justification, while Dextrose tried repeatedly to shift his butt from his chair to reach the bottle.

It was during our quandary that he finally managed the feat, much to our surprise. With a stupor-defying lurch, he swiped it from Quench's hand.

"GOTCHER!" he exclaimed, clasping one glass devil-horn and tipping, a fabulous red goo flopping glutinously onto his extended, dishcloth-textured tongue. Only the viscosity of the liquid prevented the fool from downing the entire volume before Quench could wrest it from his grip.

"'E'll overdose!" cried the barkeep. But there was nothing we could do.

We watched, alarmed but rapt, as his body launched into convulsions. Dextrose gurgled, twisted, writhed, his hands pulling the shapes of a demented shadow-puppeteer, jaws furiously masticating.

"Quick! Ask 'im nah!" cried Quench.

Why me? "Mr Dextrose, where is Mrs Dextrose? Where did you leave her?"

He regarded me like a wounded animal, his eyes bloodshot and fearful. "*Nggggddgggnnngggddddggggg*," he moaned, tongue lolling out. "*Hhhhhlllllllmmmmmmmnnn*."

"What's 'e say?" demanded Quench.

How would I know? "It's just a noise. He can't talk properly on that stuff!" An apparent flaw in the Shaman's plan.

"So what do we do?"

I had no idea.

Dextrose's face had become the colour of an exquisite bruise and he was clawing at his gums, seemingly scraping away at the toxins.

As we watched helplessly, Quench clicked his fingers. "Got it!"

He snatched a beermat off the table and scrabbled around in his jacket on the floor, muttering, before retrieving a pencil. "If 'e can't speak it, 'e can write it! Right!"

Brilliant!

Dextrose had now become quite still but was breathing heavily, chest heaving, clinging to the arms of his chair, neck stiff, eyes focused at infinity. Quench put the pencil in

Dextrose's right hand and closed his fingers around it, then put the beermat in the other.

"Ask 'im again," he told me.

I spoke clearly. "Mr Dextrose. Where is Mrs Dextrose?"

No reaction.

Quench leaned in. "Where is she, 'Arry? Tell us!"

"*Nggggddgggnnnggddddg...*"

"Nah, mate! Write it dahn!"

The mouldering old buffer only obeyed. Without once looking at what he was writing, Dextrose brought the pencil and beermat together and scribbled.

Moments later, he stopped abruptly and dropped both. The pencil rolled with a dampened buzz from the table to the floor. Pink foam, bloodied bubbling bile, started oozing from his mouth. He felt for it, rolled it in his fingers. Then he threw his head back and groaned, a groan that I pray I never hear again.

It was Jacob Marley times ten, it was deepest despair and purest purgatory, and it rolled like fog around a graveyard.

"Quick! Get him some water!" I yelped.

Quench hurtled away and dashed back with a glass, tipping its contents over Dextrose's upturned face. The water cascaded around his mouth as the orifice hissed and bubbled, coming across all Charybdis. He juddered and shook, until finally he was still. Too still. Lifeless.

We waited, mouths open, eyes trained, everything rigid.

"'Ave we killed 'im?" whispered Quench.

Then suddenly Dextrose shuddered. Spluttered. Wretched. Projectile-vomited a mess I will not, could not, describe.

He evil-eyed Quench. "Poison us with minking water, would yer, yer brownbagger?" he spat, showering him with dastardly germs in suspension.

It was some time before we could calm him down and return to the task in hand.

What had Harrison Dextrose written? Would it solve the Mystery of the Missing Mrs Dextrose?

I sought the fateful beermat, which was obscured rather within a puddle of the most unpleasant consistency. Clutching it gingerly between fingernail and thumbnail, I turned it upside-down, rotated it one way then the other, attempting to identify Dextrose's scribblings from another dimension.

"It's not writing. It's a drawing," I concluded.

"What of?" asked Quench.

"It can't be this. All I can see is a cow jumping over the moon, which doesn't make much sense."

"You sure?" said Quench, grabbing it off me. "Hmm," he hummed after some deliberation. "Might be a very big dog lyin' beside a plate?"

He handed it back.

Here is what Dextrose had drawn:

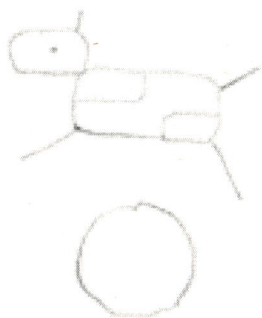

"It's meaningless," I sighed.

But Quench wasn't so easily defeated. "Can't be," he said. "'Cordin' to the Shaman, the demon juice never fails. No bugger's immune."

"Well, you explain it, Mr Quench... Livingstone. How can a cow – or very big dog – jumping over the moon – or lying beside a plate – in any way relate to the whereabouts of Mrs Dextrose?"

"'Ere, let's 'ave anuver look."

"I do see your point," he said eventually. "What if we try it upside dahn?"

So we did:

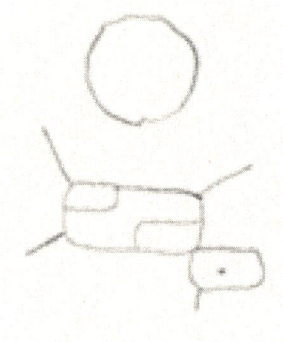

After some deliberation Quench began thinking aloud. "If that is a cow – an' I'm not sayin' it is – maybe that's not the moon? Maybe we're assumin' it's the moon 'cos of the nursery rhyme? In fact, if that is the moon, where's the craters? So if it ain't, what else is rahnd? What if it's a ball? A cow jumpin' over a ball makes more sense..."

"Than a cow jumping over the moon, yes. But..."

He ignored me. "You ever 'eard of cows playin' football?"

I couldn't tell whether he was serious. "A bovine XI, you mean?"

"Mmm," he muttered, at least sceptical if not dismissing

the idea out of hand.

While Quench might have been a model of alcoholic restraint given his profession, there were many years when he had been Harrison Dextrose's closest drinking buddy – which must have taken its toll.

"Perhaps we should ask Mr Dextrose?" I suggested.

Mr Dextrose had been staring glassily-eyed into space while mumbling to himself.

Quench thrust the beermat drawing in front of his face. "'Ere, 'Arry," he said. "What's this you've drawn?"

However, being asked a question was too much for Harry's system, which promptly packed up for the night and all his lights went out.

"P'rhaps we'd better ask 'im tomorrer. Come on, Pilsbury, you've 'ad a long journey. You can sleep in one of me guest huts aht back."

"What about him?" I asked.

"Don't you worry abaht 'im. I'll take care of 'im," said Quench, and winked. "Not for the first time."

As I settled down to sleep inside a bamboo-walled hut with dried palm fronds for its roof, wrapped in a sheet against the jungle's night-time chill, I tried to get my head around this new family I had stumbled upon, wondering whether I had missed any glaring signs to my adoption. The ales I had drunk did not help.

I had been raised by Father and Mother – being what I called them and how they referred to each other within my earshot – in the event-lite, chintz-heavy town of Glibley in Surrey.

Father had been a teacher and a strict disciplinarian; Mother pandered to his whims and was often flustered. Everything was at arm's length and there hadn't been many laughs. Fun had been practically frowned upon. Was that the action of proper parents?

At Christmas we'd make our own crackers, Father being always 'careful' with his money, and he would traditionally write the motto/joke. So, at the festive dinner table, we'd pull on these silent novelties – Mother being scared of loud bangs – and Father would gleefully hand me the emergent slip of paper.

Instead of the usual, 'What's yellow and black and goes 'Zzub-zzub?'' I'd get, 'What's yellow and black, of the order Hymenoptera and genus Vespula?'

Yes, fun had been low on their agenda.

When they had perished together in the same gardening accident during my final term at school, I had felt sadness though no enduring grief. My sizeable inheritance had arrived, bankrolling the lethargic existence in which I had indulged for the previous 15 years, and I had put them out of my mind. It had been all too easy.

But how could I not have realised that I was adopted, that Father and Mother weren't my real parents? I guessed there was a clue in the names. Who else was obliged to call their parents Mother and Father in the late 20th century?

I had always felt it, deep down inside: that distance between myself and them. Yet I had glossed over it, put it down to their being old-fashioned. Now the truth was dawning.

And, of course, they had called me 'Alexander'. Never 'Alex'.

"Come here, Alexander."

"Do this, Alexander."

"Do that, Alexander."

Alexander. Not even my real name.

Mind you, which idiot calls their son Pilsbury?

New ties. Abandonment. Lies, deceit, years wasted. The

journey I had made. Loss and gain. The memories flitted past and the sounds of the rainforest – caws, hoots, cackles, howls – swirled around my eardrums. I was exhausted.

Gossips, Saturday, 12:30pm:

I entered Gossips via the back door. Quench was in there, finding stuff to do behind his bar. There was no sign of Dextrose and no customers. How on earth the business constituted a living, I had no idea.

"'Ere 'e comes, the man of the moment! What time d'you call this?" he quipped. "'Ow you feelin'?"

"Confused."

"Well, never mind," he replied, hardly Samaritan-standard.

Quench produced a mug of coffee and a plate of exotic fruit, and sat beside me while I scoffed in fast-forward.

"I've 'ad an idea," he said.

"Really?" I wished I hadn't sounded so surprised.

"We'll go an' consult the Shaman," he said. "If anyone can tell us what 'Arry's drawing means, it's 'im."

I wasn't so sure; it felt like compounding an error. "Really? You think that's a good idea?"

"Course it is!"

I smiled half-heartedly.

"Come on then! No time like the present!"

We were going *now*? "What about your bar?"

"What about it?"

"What about Mr Dex… Dad?" That would take time.

"'E'll be sleeping off that 'angover for a while now. Come on! Chop-chop! You *can* trust me, y'know, Pilsbury."

26

"Yes. Yes, I know I can. Thanks, Mr Quench."

"Livingstone, son. I've already told you. Call me Livingstone."

The humidity outside enveloped me like a sodden duvet. Within seconds, my happy-tortoise tanktop was drenched with sweat.

"Woof!" I went, as we began walking.

"You get used to it," said Quench. "When I first came 'ere I 'ad to buy a mangle an' wring aht me clothes, lit'rally. But your body adjusts. No idea where the sweat goes to, mind. Don't really bear finkin' abaht."

It didn't, so I moved the subject on. "Why did you come here, to Mlwlw, Livingstone? There's a story in *The Lost Incompetent*..."

He chuckled. "That old cobblers. Wilson Niff an' the Sodastream wee, yeah? I'm s'posed to 'ave been so upset that Niff don't notice his beer's my carbonated pee, I take off to anuver continent? Cam on, son! God love old 'Arry – I can never tell if 'e believes 'is own stories. No. I'll tell you why I came 'ere. It was supposed to be an 'oliday. 'See the Jungle – Cheap'. 'Arry'd arranged it. I turn up at the docks, 'e ain't there. Should I go wivaht 'im? Seemed daft not to. Long story short, I end up 'ere."

"So the Niff story isn't true?"

Quench roared with laughter. "What do you fink nah you've seen 'Arry? 'Is 'ole system's shot to shit. I don't even remember a Wilson Niff."

"Then his book..."

He stopped walking. "Look. I don't mean to do 'im dahn, Pilsbury. Put it this way: I'd be prahd if old 'Arry was my Dad. Well, maybe not prahd. Not the way 'e is nah. 'Ang on, let me start again, this ain't comin' aht right. Look. I've known 'Arry longer than I care to remember. And we're mates. Always 'ave been, always will be. An' that says it all. Right? There's more to 'im than 'e lets on. I swear to you. That man's been arahnd the block a few times, 'e's got stories. An' if they ain't all funny stories, or interestin', 'e spins 'em, y'know? So 'is book, it's true in parts. Uver bits 'e exaggerates and uver bits is complete bollocks. 'S fair enough, ain't it? Like, if you wrote down your life story – 'ow dull would that be?"

"Cheers."

He slapped his forehead. "I'm sorry, son, I didn't mean it like that! I'm sure you've 'ad a really interestin' life."

"Not really." There was no escaping it.

"No? Oh." He started walking again. "Better get a move on, eh?"

Mlwlw's main drag in daylight was like nothing I had ever experienced. Individual buildings concocted from wood with palm fronds as roof material, raised up off the ground a couple of feet on stilts, I imagined as protection against the torrential rains when they finally came. Boy, could I have killed for a cool drenching.

Behind the buildings, the forest loomed: a sense of chlorophyll and insects on too many legs.

There were clothes lines stretched across the roadway, from which Western-style clothing hung. Shorts and T-shirts, socks and pants, in vibrant colours. "Today's wash day," explained Quench, as if he'd read my thoughts.

Through the odd open doorway I glimpsed adults busying themselves inside, among the shadows. One lady came out onto her porch and waved; when I returned the greeting, she made it clear it was Quench she had been waving to.

Out on the dry-dirt road a few children, cropped-haired and lithe with muscle, ran around in shorts and Manchester United tops, kicking a football. They stopped playing and stared at me as we walked past.

Quench hailed them in the local tongue and they began to

follow us, dancing in our wake and laughing, until the barkeep turned around and told them to, "Leave it aht, lads." They ran off.

We were on a mission. It felt good.

By the time we had left the village behind, the persistent animal calls that had kept me awake at night no longer troubled me. Instead they drifted into the background, like the sound of traffic back in England.

Where vegetation had been cleared away for the development of the village, the sun had felt oppressive. As the dwellings dwindled the trees began to take over, their broad-leafed foliage forming a high canopy, casting welcome shadows about the ground.

The smells were of vegetation and earth, rammed up singed nostrils by heat. Something about the sensation seemed strange, and it took a while to realise why: there was no pollution here, only unbastardised nature.

Vines slithered up pole-straight trunks, taking the shortest route from seed to sun, and often I found myself double-taking, checking for snakes. If there were one creature's path I most feared crossing, it was that of the serpent. I had only ever seen them on television, but that was enough: generally featuring a fool in shorts holding one by the tail, chatting to camera, while the writhing beast lunged, hoping to inject said fool with enough venom to make his head turn black and fall off.

"Are there snakes in Mlwlw?" I asked Quench, already fearing the response.

"Sure," he replied. "The locals go an abaht the bang-bang viper – packs enough poison to fell a rhino. Watch aht for that one!"

I glanced around, paranoid. "What's it look like?"

"Y'know, I never fort to ask! Don't worry 'baht it, Pilsbury.

Them's more scared of you than you is of them."

Were that true, I wondered how they functioned on a daily basis.

Shaman's hut, Saturday, 4.40pm.

After about half an hour we reached the Shaman's hut, in a clearing set back from the vague path we had been following.
It was cylindrical in shape with a conical roof, all natural materials. Coconuts hung from its eaves.
It struck me suddenly that all the animals had become silent, their cackles and caws replaced by an eerie whistling that came from within the hut.
Quench sensed my unease. "Nuffing to worry abaht," he said. "'E's more of a mystic than a witch doctor. Jus' let me do the talkin'. Come on."
As we were about to enter through the hanging-reed curtain that formed the door, I yelped and stumbled backwards. "Those... those coconuts. They're not coconuts. Aren't they... shrunken heads?"
Horrible, leathery, pocket-sized heads, with dark hollows for eyes and mouths that moaned in silence – perhaps a dozen of them – hung by their gathered hair, greeting visitors like pickled ghouls.
"Don't take no notice of them," said Quench. "'E buys 'em in from up-river. They're just for show. 'E's quite the showman, the Shaman." He chuckled at his own sense of poetry.

Against my better judgement I entered the hut, wondering when to commence grovelling. At once the weird whistling stopped.

In the light of the lofted door I caught sight of two figures seated against the far wall, one man-sized with perhaps a tall hat; the other, much smaller, appeared to be sitting on the taller man's knee. As the curtain dropped behind me the image fell into gloom. I felt Quench's arm around my shoulders, pressing me down, and we dropped to our knees. There I stayed, listening to my own breathing, uncertain. The smell of the dry-earth floor mingled with something acrid, seeming to emanate from a pot hanging over a dwindling fire across the way. Fresh sweat joined stale sweat under my top.

I waited for someone to speak. No one did.

Then I heard movement. The Shaman and his colleague had risen. Padding feet approached, slowly. Something touched my shoulder from behind and I flinched, barely containing a squeal. Next the other shoulder, then the same two light taps came from in front of me, as dark shapes passed by. I suspected I was being circled and anointed with a stick.

On the third circuit the movement stopped and at once a hideous apparition took shape just inches before me in mid-air: a countenance of rotting stumpy teeth and burning widened eyes, with thick white stripes, like a tiger's markings, dragged across glowing dark flesh.

I flung myself backwards, exhaling my fear, and would have fallen head-first out of the door had I not missed it and cracked the back of my skull against a wall.

"Hahaha!" went the apparition.

Then I realised: it was the larger of the two figures – the Shaman, no doubt – shining a pocket torch under his chin.

Oh yes, very effective, very funny, I thought, part pissed off, part petrified. If this little ritual were for my benefit, it was working.

Next, a blind was lifted at the rear of the hut and sunlight flooded the space, the sudden glare causing me to shield my eyes. The figures now sat illuminated from behind, drenched in shadow. Even in such awkward lighting I could tell there was something odd about the smaller fellow. The way he sat, bolt upright like a meerkat, back on the Shaman's lap.

The Shaman spoke, in a language that was all deep consonants and contorted tongue, rising and falling, the effect not that dissimilar to the sound of a didgeridoo. I glanced toward Quench for advice, but he remained kneeling, head bowed.

The smaller figure's head turned to face me. "I an great Shaman son," he said. "He not skleak your tongue so I translate thor you his great oo-ords… his great skeakings… things he say. Stek ford."

What did he mean, "Stek ford?" And something about the voice. So unnaturally pitched, and strangulated. Though my senses were disoriented by the entire experience, something was niggling at the back of my mind.

"Go on!" hissed Quench.

"Go on, what?" I hissed back.

"Step forward!"

I had to remind myself why we were there – Dextrose's crazed sketch – having become more concerned about remaining sane. What could I say that might resemble decorum? How did one even address a shaman?

I rose and walked forward. The closer I approached the shamanic duo, the more I could make out. The Shaman himself was dressed in a skirt-type garment made of animal skin, into which multi-coloured beads had been stitched in seemingly random shapes. His torso was bare, his nipples both run through with an ivory hook, and he had a pot belly. Garlands of dried leaves hung around his neck. His face, painted with those white stripes, looked haggard but hard. He wore a conical hat, like a wizard's, with sun and moon designs set in beading, another of his precious shrunken heads hanging from its peak.

And... Bugger me, if my suspicions about his son weren't correct.

"Hmmn!" went the Shaman, thrusting out his hand.

"See!" translated his son.

Among the shafts of sunlight I saw the Shaman's bony index finger held out towards me. Running through it appeared to be a bloody nail; however, the red-paint job was poor and there was no blood on the digit itself, which was a dead giveaway. In fact, I'd once bought the same 'Nail Through Finger!' trick as a child.

The Shaman quickly withdrew his hand into his lap and returned it with a flourish, his now nail-free finger miraculously 'healed'.

"Klowerthul nagic!" declared the son.

"Sorry?" I said.

"'E means 'powerful magic'," Quench explained from the back.

"I see. That is powerful magic indeed," I lied. "Listen. Would you mind if I had a quick word with my friend?"

The Shaman started. The boy regarded his father then me, and his mouth dropped open, incredulous.

I didn't bother waiting for their answer.

"Who's the nutter with the ventriloquist's dummy?" I hissed in Quench's ear.

"Be careful what you say!" he hissed back. "That's the top dog round 'ere you're talkin' abaht."

"With the lame nail-through-the-finger trick?"

"Well it fools everyone else."

"Did it fool you?" I snorted.

He changed the subject. "'Ow did you spot the dummy?"

"What, you mean his son made of wood?"

"Wood, yeah."

"Wearing a monocle, top hat and three-piece suit?"

"That's right."

"You did know it was a dummy?"

"Course! After a little while."

We debated very hastily the point of continuing with the plan, while the Shaman sat mumbling with his son in tongues, clearly put out. I was all for leaving, until Quench pointed out that if we quit now we only had Dextrose to fall back on. It was a deal clincher.

Bar my dignity, I had nothing to lose. And how many times during my travels had that remained unscathed and intact? I was reminded mercifully briefly of my abduction on Emo Island, by the madman Borhed and his minions, when to win my freedom I had been obliged to choose the winner of an 'Insect Race to Death'. And I had actively cheered on a dung beetle.

I returned to the Shaman and knelt (playing along). "Great Shaman, I wish for your wisdom."

His son spoke: "You hath angered great Shaman. Thery dangerous. Cun closer. Oo-otch!"

The Shaman beckoned me forward with a bony finger until I was within a metre of his face. His lips were terribly chapped and the madness resulting from power danced in his eyes.

He held out the palm of his hand – the one that wasn't up his son's bum – between our two faces. On it was laid a small pile of brown powder. He looked at it, looked at me, and leered, all fucked teeth and gum disease. Then he blew it in my face.

Immediately I sniffed, sniffed again, then could not hold it back. As I sneezed violently, I ducked just in time to avoid covering the Shaman in snot.

Sneezing powder.

"Klowerthul nagic!" declared the son.

At that range I could see his daddy's lips move.

I showed the Shaman Harrison Dextrose's sketch, which had become rather limp in my sweat-drenched back pocket. He studied it closely, turning it this way and that, as Quench and I had done previously.

Eventually he said something in that didgeridoo language of his.

I addressed the dummy. "What's he saying?"

"He say there is klace where the cattle klay thootgall."

The Shaman and wooden boy both stared at me.

I stared back. "There is a place where the cattle play football?"

The Shaman laughed, a deep, rumbling, laugh – "Hrr-hrr-hrr-hrr-hrr" – while his son's mouth clattered woodenly up and down, red tongue flashing on and off.

The Shaman reached forward and patted me on the shoulder, now wheezing at his own wit.

"Shanan idea oth joke," said the dummy. "Gut he does know neaning oth your riddle. Thirst oo-ee nake deal. Yes?"

Outside the Shaman's hut, Saturday, 2:20pm:

We had cut a deal, the Shaman and I.

He needed to travel deep into the jungle to pick up some "nagic sucklies" – "magic supplies" – from a "lost tribe", as the Shaman called them. I happened to be in possession of a motorbike and sidecar.

The Shaman claimed to understand Dextrose's sketch, and would explain it to me once I had chauffeured him into the interior of the jungle. Though I was convinced he had by far the better end of the deal, I was too polite to say so.

Then we were back out in the sunshine, among the non-talking heads. Immediately, a wooziness hit me.

"Wow!" I said, as sky became orange and purple. "I feel unusual."

"Me too," said Quench. "Did you notice the smell in there?"

I nodded, which only made me feel dizzier.

"Psychoactives. The Shaman brews 'em. From roots an' leaves an' suchlike. 'E uses 'em to visit uver spiritual planes. Least that's what 'e says. I reckon 'e jus' loves gettin' wasted! But dahn't you worry, son, you've only breaved in a few fumes. 'E drinks the stuff!"

I began choking, feeling nauseous.

Quench went on: "So. I reckon that went pretty well."

I regarded him from my bent-double position. "Did it?"
"Sure!"
"Really?"
"Well. Last time I visited the Shaman 'e give me some soap, an' after I used it me face turned black!"

Gossips, Saturday, 3.30pm

As I followed Livingstone Quench into the bar, knackered and drenched after the walk back, I fully expected to find Dextrose in his usual spot. He did not disappoint.

Already his table was covered in empty bottles and he looked half-cut, staring morosely into the latest glass neck. I felt a pang of self-pity take shape in my gut. What chance did I have of getting through to such a sorry mess?

"Alright, 'Arry!" called Quench, quite jovial, no doubt used to the sight.

Dextrose noticed him. "More beer!" he called back.

He didn't even look at me.

"Brought your boy, Pilsbury," said Quench. "Maybe it's time you two got to know each uver, yeah?"

"No, it's OK, Livingstone. But thanks for trying," I mumbled. "I think I'll go and lie down."

"Bollocks!" said the barman, manhandling me towards Dextrose's table. "You take a seat and we'll all 'ave a nice chat. Beer?"

I wasn't convinced. "I might have something soft, thanks." I'd seen what alcohol could do to people.

"'Ave a beer," he persisted. "I might 'ave a few meself tonight."

It struck me that Quench had not yet taken any money from me, which led to me recalling my financial situation: £175 in travellers' cheques. Enough for bed and board, I imagined, though hardly sufficient to get me home.

Home: England. Familiarity, stability and sweet ennui. What was I even doing in Mlwlw, I wondered, sitting opposite this propped-up dolt?

I dropped my head into my hands and rubbed my eyeballs so hard that shades of crimson and purple lolled around inside my eyelids.

A voice broke into my self-absorption. "Cheer up," it slurred. "Might never minking happen."

Dextrose, of all the cheek! He was staring at me, elbows on table, half-sneer on his chops.

"It already is happening!" I snapped back. "And you're causing it!"

"Is I?" He looked baffled. "How?"

By being revealed as my father – and a useless drunk – frankly. Yet what should I have expected? I'd read his book. I knew what he was like. Had I never picked up the thing, become so drawn into it, I would never have met him. Then again I'd still be a sofa-sloth back in Glibley. His book had opened my eyes; was it his fault I now wished I could close them? Cause and effect.

In the end, the best I could reply was: "You're supposed to be my father."

"Is I?" He blinked. Or tried to; the right eyelid refused to open and he prised it apart with filthy fingers. He peered at me, as if through specs. "Yer know, that rings a minking bell."

Rings a bell! And so it all spewed out: the confusion, the fear, the righteous indignation. "Mr Dextrose, I have spent the last month following in your footsteps. I've been trussed up and imprisoned, I've been hung over the edge of a volcano, I've been drugged, I've been shot at. I feared for my life. But I made it. Which amazed me. Believe me, it did. And when I arrived here I met you. Out of the blue. *My hero*. And just to put the icing on the cake, you turn out to be my father! And you know what?" It was obvious from his expression that he didn't. "I'm gutted. You don't remember me, do you? What's my name, Mr Dextrose? What's the name of your son?"

He licked his lips, rested a hand on my forearm, spoke slowly and soothingly. "Would yer like us to sign a book for yer?"

"You smug bastard, I..."

"Now-now," cut in Quench, banging three bottles down on the table. "That's no way to start, is it? 'Ere, 'Arry, tell us abaht that time you met them fat lasses in that place... Enzo Island? Elmo Island?"

"It's not Elmo. It's Emo," I huffed. "Emo Island." That place with that bloody dung beetle.

Dextrose took a few swigs of beer and wiped a forearm across his mouth. "So. Yer wants a few stories, does yer?"

My rage vanished like a bloodstain bleached at the prospect of hearing Dextrose's adventures from the author's own mouth. How well I knew his own tales of Emo Island. And those 'fat lasses' Quench referred to, so indelicately – surely they couldn't be the lusty Frihedhags, those aged sisters uneasy on the eye, who had helped to save me from Borhed?

I'd slept with Piggy Frihedhag, by accident – being rather drunken following the celebrations of Borhed's demise – and had woken up with an arm trapped in the terrible vacuum between her voluminous buttocks.

But of course, it was I who had vanquished the malevolent Borhed, no one else, and it was I who should take the credit. This, I realised, was an opportunity for a little showboating of my own; Dextrose's braggadocio could wait a moment.

This'd floor them. Earn me a little respect.

"Livingstone," I said, "have you ever killed a man with a dead penguin?" Because I had.

I'd expected him to regard me with manly pride, shaking his head in mute disbelief. But no – he actually stopped and thought for a while, as if he had often considered employing an arsenal of viciously pointy taxidermy.

By the time he replied, "Nah, son, I don't believe I 'ave," my moment had passed. "Why? 'Ave you?"

"Yes. But don't worry about it," I replied sulkily.

Dextrose butted in. "Good. Cos I were gonna tell yer…"

"No, 'old on, 'Arry, let the lad speak," said Quench.

That appeased my pride. Alright, I would tell my tale, after all. But where to begin? With the salty skipper, 'Mad Dog' Mahaffey, who was supposed to have taken me from England to Emo Island aboard his patchwork vessel, the Unsmoked Haddock, but who had let his dog steer the boat one night and, amazingly, we had ended up miles off course?

Or with my journey through the Unknown Tunnel, from Frartsi to Emo Island, by pony and cart, at the end of which I had stumbled upon Borhed and the dwarf, Detritos?

Which tale captured best my bravado and derring-do?

"Give me a second, I can't decide where to start," I told my audience.

They were becoming restless. Quench was drumming his gold-laden fingers on the table, while Dextrose was attaching crown caps to his forehead using saliva, and had begun to resemble some sort of homeless Roy Wood.

Remembering Detritos had started the pangs of guilt. I had tried to put him out of my mind since his untimely death, concerning which I felt – wrongly, I hoped to convince myself – at least some degree of culpability.

The frustrating, lascivious, daring, delusional, fiercely loyal little fellow had popped up at the beginning of my adventures and, whether I had encouraged his company or not, he was there at the end. He had saved my bacon on more than one occasion. Indeed, had Detritos not appeared from nowhere – or rather, from inside a hobby horse – toting an Uzi at the end of the Insect Race to Death, I might not have survived long enough to perform the *coup de grâce* with that deceased penguin.

That's where I would start my tale, I decided: just after Detritos and his Uzi, grab a little limelight for myself.

"Right, mink this!" declared Dextrose, the instant I opened my mouth. "Here's the one about I and Paloma Slaver!"

Quench actually had to stop himself from clapping like a delighted child.

"I thought I..." I began.

But no one was listening.

Gossips, Monday, during the wee hours:

"...then I turned her over and the minking smell disappeared!"

Twin streams of frothed ale shot from Quench's nostrils, his face the colour of a boil forming. He roared with laughter, clutching the table for support though he was seated. My stomach muscles ached, such had been the night's hilarity, while my brain drained and the hours evaporated.

Dextrose, in his element, had come alive. Raconteur, adventurer, *bon viveur*, egotist, dirty, arrogant bastard.

Tale after tale, some I had known off by heart – though the author's live intonations and new embellishments (gross exaggerations, some might have contended) added so much – others plucked from expeditions he was yet, probably ever, to bequeath to the history books. I prayed I would remember them all come daybreak. Or was it already daybreak?

Inside Gossips, time stumbled around in circles looking for the exit and odours thrived. Whenever one of us opened the back door to visit the outside loo, foul vapours visibly escaped the place, and we briefly breathed in deeply the sweetness of the jungle. One other potential customer had entered the bar, however Dextrose had instantly bellowed, "Mink off!" and he had done so.

As we three lost ourselves in communal alcoholic reverie, I

learned to love the infamous lapsed explorer all over again. And I wondered how different my life would have been, had he and Mrs Dextrose raised me as nature had intended. One time I pushed my luck, referred to him as "Dad" – and he did not correct me.

Every one of his stories was a gem. The Flatulent Ghost of Framingham (actually Dextrose, somehow stuck inside his bedsheet, driven out of town by locals once his unintentional deceit was discovered); The Fetid Milkmaid of Nozvodrogost (the conclusion of which can be found above); The Repeated Defiling of Crewman Skink (Dextrose and crewman Shark, vastly inebriated, dressing a comatose Skink as the back end of a pantomime horse, at the Shah of Arovia's stud farm)... nor was he yet finished.

"I've another!" he announced. "Me dubious relationship with the well-bottomed socialite Nadia of Bujina!"

I chanced pointing out the obvious. "Weren't you married to Mrs D..."

He thrust his face towards mine, bloated and blinking. "What? Were *you* gonna tell her?" Then he calmed down and continued. "She were a lusty minker, that Nadia, décolletage on display and a goer's gait. Little did I know how it would end... Ah, maybe I shouldn't say. No sense making meself look foolish."

Quench slapped my knee, well-oiled. "I know this one. Go on, 'Arry, tell it!"

I sensed he knew them all.

Dextrose wiped a hand across his mouth, inadvertently dragging with it a strand of phlegm and attaching its other end to his right ear. It sagged gradually as the story continued, the effect quite mesmerising.

"Ah, what the mink! Got us a few shags, dinnit!"

And so he began. "I'd settled for a while in Bujina, tired of wandering and abandoned by me crew, the spineless bunch of carrot promoters. At me usual hostelry – a wine bar, if yer will – I'd become something of an attraction, on account of the clientele hearing tell of me daring travels. Mainly because I kept shouting about them until some minker paid me some attention!" Dextrose chortled, a hacking creation with gurgles. "This were in me younger days, when I were deemed a catch... Not that I's no catch now. But yes, young man, Mrs Dextrose were already on the scene. Many hundreds of miles away!

"A clutch of hangers-on develops, who buys us cocktails laced with precious stones so one's plip-plops sparkle the following day, in exchange for stories. The boys is minks and their ladyfriends is minxes. One in particular – this were Nadia – has her eye on us. Fancies a bit of rough, I doesn't doubt. Always brushing us with a buttock or two as she excuses herself fer the powder room."

Quench nudged me and winked. I winked back.

Our pie-eyed narrator went on: "Course, we ends up minking and an infatuation develops – on young Dextrose's side of the relations, the fool. I had me brain in me ball-bag and a strumpet on me pillow. I curse meself looking back. In the end I only ask her minking father – some lord or somesuch, a toad in tweed – for her hand in marriage! On bended knee, can yer believe? The whifflegig I were!

"'No problem,' says Lord Twot. Believe us, Dextrose should have smelled a rat. He worshipped that girl just as much as I, might have minked her too for all I know. So he disappears into his pile and returns. Nadia on one arm, box in the other, glint in his minking fat eye. 'Here,' he says, handing us the box. 'Take it.' Now, I thinks, what's all this about?

"So I opens it and finds... This rotting grey claw, stinking like a bluebottle's banquet. Turns out his daughter, the duplicitous little mink, has an artificial hand, result of a childhood disease, and that's the one that got chopped off, boxed and stored by the family, being the sort of thing the aristocracy do. Minking perverts. 'You wanted her hand – now yer got it!' he bellows."

Dextrose studied my expression, a mixture of disgust, distrust and bewilderment. "Well?" he concluded. "How was I to know she had a plastic hand? She'd always pulled us off with the other one!"

He and Quench embraced each other, such was their delirium. I was left uncertain whether the entire story had been an elaborate, fabricated springboard for that one punchline. The point, I supposed, was that it failed to matter. This must have been like the days of the Vikings, when the warriors sat around blazing fires, inebriated on grog, and told their tales. I felt privileged to be hearing them, if just a little disturbed by their content, though I dared not show it in such manly company.

So there we were, we three, belly-laughing until it burned, gasping for air and inhaling only pestilence. Dextrose beckoned me towards him and pressed me onto his pink-tracksuited knee while Quench, the intermediary, looked on with pride. Dampness immediately seeped through my underwear, but I did not mind.

I studied him, at closer ranger than ever before. The nasal blackheads that had been such a feature of *The Lost Incompetent*'s cover seemed to have bred since that portrait was snapped, and his wrinkles were noticeably deeper. But that monochrome photograph had so failed to do justice to the fire in his eyes.

He slapped an arm around my shoulders and hugged me in, my face becoming enmeshed in his greasy, sodden whiskers.

"Y'know, I've decided I like you, young'un," he said, and my heart skipped a beat. "What did yer say yer name were?"

Gossips guest room, Monday, 1̵0̵.2̵0̵am:

My eyes flickered open. Individual rays of sunlight streamed through gaps in the walls of the dusky, windowless guest hut. I was aware that I was being watched. I lifted my head, which immediately turned cartwheels as my temples protested in the strongest terms. Then I yelped and propelled myself backwards.

At the end of my bed was a glowing head with an evil stare, cheeks crudely, obscenely rouged, chiselled jaw like an ostentatious ironing board, its eyes too large to be real, alive yet dead, sporting a monocle... Hang on... It was that fucking dummy and the Shaman's torch. *Jesus*. My bpm fluttered barely downwards.

"Time to go," said the wooden boy, mouth clacking.

Gossips, Monday, 10.25am:

I was still pissed and well over the drink-driving limit, though I imagined the region was hardly troubled by wave upon wave of traffic cops. How dearly I wanted Dextrose to come with us following last night's partially successful bonding exercise. I had even convinced myself that he would have remembered me at the end, had he not been so sozzled.

There would be room enough behind me on the bike, if he could cling on, with the Shaman and son in the sidecar. If I could somehow just persuade him to do so he would surely sober up during the journey, and then what might happen? Although I did not dare become carried away.

Pushing open the back door to Gossips, I heard snoring. Livingstone Quench, slumped over last night's table, was fast asleep, his ponytail soaked in dregs. Dextrose was still conscious, if barely. He swayed in his seat, drawling drivel at a bottle he was holding up to his face.

As he heard the three of us enter, his head turned by increments. I imagined I could hear his mechanism attempting to focus.

"Whadz thish?" he slurred.

"This is the Shaman," I said, as if to a toddler.

The village quack had painted a sinister skull shape over his face in white, and had donned a snazzy cloak of iridescent feathers.

"I knowoo e-is!" Dextrose replied, then began giggling uncontrollably.

I decided against completing the introductions, no sense the Shaman discovering we were related.

Quench woke up, toppled sideways off his seat, crawled across the floor and stopped at the Shaman's feet, hiccoughing violently.

The Shaman – or rather his son – said nothing. A flicker of a smile suggested the human half of the outfit found the inebriation amusing.

"Hoi!" went Dextrose suddenly. "Let Harrishun Dextroshe buy zhaman a jrink. Eh? Liddle jrinkie? Whazhuafter zhaman?"

This was news: Dextrose offering to buy someone a drink. He must have been pissed! Or was there some ulterior motive?

The Shaman pretended to hear nothing. "Oo-ee go!" the boy said to me.

I faltered. I so badly wanted to take Dextrose with us – but in that state? Perhaps I could lash us together on the bike and...

"Oi! Zhayman! Wodjuafter? Eh? No, angon. Ledme guess..."

What was his game here?

"Goddle-o-geer! Eh? Zatride zhaman? Goddle-o-geer! Goddle-o-geer!"

The Shaman flounced towards the door, the dummy's legs flailing, pursued by Dextrose's mocking slur: "Goddle-o-geer! Goddle-o-geer!"

I surveyed his bedraggled form with disdain and muttered, "Idiot".

He belched, a reverberating mouth-fart that occupied the room.

As I held my hands out to take the dummy from the Shaman, so he'd have both of his free to climb into the sidecar, he pulled the wooden boy away and hissed at me, spittle bubbling between the gaps in his horrible teeth. Instead, he clambered in by himself, squashing the boy's chest against the hard steel of the sidecar in the process. I was on my own with the lunatic.

I stood astride the bike, an old warhorse of a machine painted gun-metal, wondering what I had got myself into. The Shaman had assured me that the lost tribe he was visiting were "not thar" away – but where exactly? How far was "not thar"? What sort of terrain would we encounter? Was there enough petrol in the tank? I really hadn't thought this through. And what about the Shaman's side of the bargain? I only had his word that he could solve Dextrose's pictorial puzzler.

"Great Shaman," I said. "As a token of trust between us, could you perhaps tell me the meaning of the drawing before we set off? I'll still keep my side of the bargain, of course." (Could I have sounded any more English?)

He glowered at me.

Discomforted, I added in a French accent: "Just a wafer-thin hint?"

The dummy's head poked out from the cloak of iridescent feathers and stared at me. A silence descended.

Eventually the Shaman spoke to the boy, who translated: "Do not thorget klowerthul nagic."

That old chestnut. "No. Of course not. But if I'm to drive you all the way to wherever it is, I do need some proof that you can explain the drawing."

"Hnn," went the dummy, pondering. (I noticed that the Shaman sometimes couldn't be bothered with the charade of 'translation'.) "Thery oo-ell. There is a nak. That is the key."

I didn't get it. "A knack? A nifty way of doing something?"

"No, a nak."

"A knack?"

"No! A *nak*! Like an atlas gut snaller."

"*Like an atlas gut snaller?*"

"That is oo-ot I said."

"Like an atlas gut snaller? ...Like an atlas *but smaller*!"
"Yeah! A *nak*!"
"A *map*!"
"Gingo!"

So there was a map and that was the key. It was enough to be going on with.
"Which way?"
The Shaman pointed straight ahead, the same route Quench and I had followed the previous day to the Shaman's hut. I turned the key in the ignition, kicked the starter, gunned the throttle and the engine thrummed into life first time. Surely a good omen!

We followed the dirt track out of Mlwlw as the sort of birds I'd previously have seen only in pet shops flew up and away from our motorik din, and dark shapes beat hasty retreats among the canopy. Our movement through the air offered a welcome breeze and the engine noise thankfully negated the option of conversation. Whenever we needed to make a turn, the Shaman elbowed me in the thigh and gesticulated. Thus was my mind left largely to its own devices.

It could not help but wonder what on earth I thought I was I doing. My own journey was over: I had followed in Dextrose's footsteps to his own conclusion, at Gossips. Job done, mission accomplished. Really, I should have been returning home. To what, though? No job, no girlfriend, my stylus stuck in suburbia's lame groove?

If I were to remain abroad, there would have to be some point. And that had to involve my new family. This discovery of my real genealogy had to be a sign.

So that was it, the plan: I would sober up Dad, make him see sense, and together we would find my mother. Thus reunited, the Dextrose family could fly back to England, to an idyllic life of hugs, home baking and affectionate mirth. Yes, that would do it.

A blur appeared in front of my eyes, replaced swiftly by the arrogant gaze of some form of irate primate – baboon? gibbon? – now sitting on my handlebars, having dropped in from an overhanging branch. I slammed on the brakes and stared back, frozen in fear. I was sure I had heard that monkeys can rip one's head off. This one's pink nostrils looked like a strange new human sex-part and its opened gob revealed fangs, top and bottom, like something off a vampire.

"Oo-oo aa-aa!" it went, performing that aggressive bobbing/loping-arms dance familiar from nature documentaries.

Cries from above echoed its agitation and I looked up to see various of its kin, glaring at us like morons glued to a soap.

"Hoi!" went the dummy.

The Shaman pushed out a red plastic rose attached to his feathery cloak. The primate on the handlebars bent in to look and the Shaman hit it with a long squirt of water. In shock it somersaulted backwards into a heap among dense shrubs, howling as it sailed.

I lofted a thumb at the Shaman. "Powerful magic!"

I swear he smirked back.

"Go!" hollered the wooden boy.

En route to the lost tribe, Monday, 2.10 pm:

I'd been riding for quite a while, my inner thighs noticeably chafing and my bottom indelibly numb, when the Shaman signalled for me to stop the bike. My stomach rumbled. Though the route had become increasingly bumpy, over creeping vegetation and barely formed trackway, we were yet to encounter anything previously untouched by human progress.

"Get oth gike!" snapped the boy.

I did so without question, no doubt a result of my Englishness.

"Are we nearly there yet?" I enquired.

The Shaman pushed the boy's head towards me and the top hat fell off. He retrieved it with a harrumph. "Yes!" barked the boy. "No nore koo-estions!"

I'd only asked one!

The Shaman then took my place on the motorbike, arranging his son in his lap, and motioned for me to get into the sidecar. For several minutes he sat there looking rather proud of himself, occasionally urging it forwards with a thrust of his thighs, but of course we did not move.

Eventually the boy asked: "How nachine oo-erk?"

We stalled more than a dozen times in as many yards before the

Shaman got the hang of puttering gradually forwards in bottom gear. Such was his trepidation, his arms and neck were rod-stiff; even the dummy somehow looked more horrified than usual.

Quite why he'd demanded to take over the driving bemused me. Were he trying to show off he was greatly mistaken, show-offs not generally wearing expressions of exquisite unease. Who, anyway, would he be showing off to?

That question was shortly answered when two figures in animal skins, clutching spears, appeared from among foliage. They stopped before us, dropped to their knees and kissed the ground before the oncoming Shaman. We, inexorably, carried on going and ran over one of them.

Reaching across hastily, I managed to apply the brake.

As the tribesmen rose to their feet, the one who had been run over checked his body-parts for damage and looked distinctly put out. He was the taller of the two and had a scar running diagonally down his torso, from right nipple to navel. Probably accident-prone. He did not smile. The other, more compact, wore a broad grin the width of his face and was sporting a pair of dead scorpions as ear-rings.

The three locals spoke among themselves in a new language I failed to understand, sounding similar to the Aghanaspan I had heard, with added clicks of the tongue and the occasional guttural snort. From their body language, it was plain that the Shaman was much respected.

Greetings dispensed with, the tribesmen led us through a gap between clumped trees, like some makeshift guard of honour, though they stole regular backward glances to ensure we were at a safe distance behind. The scarred chap was limping badly and kept inspecting his elbow.

The ground opened out into an expansive clearing. It was like stepping into a Tardis. Circular wooden huts with palm-frond roofs – similar in construction but smaller than those back in Mlwlw – were dotted about, and adults and children stood rooted to the spot, staring, focused upon our arrival. Some looked concerned, most aghast – at myself or the motorbike, it was hard to tell. The only movement came from pigs, snuffling among them for unseen morsels. Flies buzzed my head and nipped at any exposed flesh. Though I swatted at them, their numbers were so great it was a war I could not win.

So this was the lost tribe. I might feasibly have been the first white man on the planet ever to witness them. How thrilling! *This* was genuine exploration, such as Doctor Livingstone practised, or Magellan and Columbus, the doyens of the history books. Might I even have one-upped Harrison Dextrose, I wondered?

Happily, the Shaman managed to brake before we maimed anyone.

One by one the villagers edged forward until they were crowded around the motorbike, muttering to one another, tentatively reaching out to touch the metal machine. One small boy foolishly pressed a palm onto the hot engine, squealed and withdrew his hand, shaking it violently while everyone around him, besides one woman I assumed to be his mother, chuckled enthusiastically. To my surprise, they didn't seem remotely impressed by me, their first ever Westerner.

The women were all bare-chested, which might have been titillating had I not assumed the responsibilities of a pioneering anthropologist, and wore skirts made of skins or woven natural materials. The men, also bare-chested, wore either loin-cloths, or something like a skirt made of animal skin, and the children were all naked.

Both sexes sported jewellery and bodily adornments: beads, sparkling stones, small bones and carved ivory, dead insects and creepy beasts. One gentleman appeared to be wearing a bright green, red-spotted frog as a jaunty beret.

The Shaman had donned his tall wizard's hat with the

celestial designs, and had his nose in the air. Whenever anyone went to touch the dummy, he pulled the boy away and growled.

Suddenly everyone fell silent and the crowd parted.

A thick-set man, his chest draped in layers of beading, sporting leather chaps and a codpiece made from something's shell, had appeared in the doorway of the largest of the huts. Their leader, I assumed. He raised a hand to acknowledge the Shaman, spotted me and cocked his head to one side. He then began walking towards us.

It felt like an historic occasion and I wondered whether I should say something, break the ice. But how should I address this man? What was the name of his tribe? Come to think of it, where was I?

Whatever the facts, this was surely all about me, the benign conqueror.

I stood up in the sidecar, causing a couple near me to giggle behind their hands, which was off-putting. "Great leader," I began. "My name is... My name is Pilsbury Dextrose." The giggling couple snorted with laughter and tears began streaming down their cheeks. Sniggers rippled out within the crowd.

I continued, only partially undaunted: "I have come from England, a land in the West, to discover your tribe for all mankind." It sounded portentous enough.

The leader opened his arms. "Calm down, mate," he said. "We have been 'discovered'" – he actually made the 'quotes' gesture with his fingers – "a dozen times. And if you are so white, where is your camera crew?"

Hang on. "My what?"

"Your camera crew. You know: 'people with cameras'." Again the 'quotes' thing.

The villagers hooted with laughter and I noticed the shaman's bloody dummy had only joined in, bobbing its stupid head as its gob opened and closed. I could see its broomstick neck and wanted to wring the fucker.

Someone had exaggerated the 'lost' bit in 'lost tribe'.

"Look," said the leader, wafting his wrist at me. "The last one gave me a Rolex."

It was true: a huge, garish, sparkly thing that took 'gauche' to new dimensions.

He went on: "Tk-tk, tell Pilsbury" – I could swear he stifled a snigger – "who has been here before."

Tk-tk, a gangly teen with outrageously brilliant teeth, however at all sorts of angles, took up the story. "OK, from the Discovery channel we have had Chipmunk Simmers – Dad beat him at table tennis – and Tent Guy. From Australia we had The Jungle Foodie and Davina Galumph. Her catchphrase was: 'Sheilas can survive too, you know', but she said it so often that we asked her to leave. Britain sends well-meaning anthropologists. There was a large man, even though he only ate ants and leaves... What was his name?"

One of the kids piped up: "Sonny Lakeman! He was my favourite!"

A few of the other children lofted their hands and chorused: "Mine too!"

Tk-tk went on: "Then there was that little man who arrived with his own penis gourd and we had to convince him that he would not have to wear it."

The leader butted in: "He was great. Really gullible..."

Having had quite enough of their reminiscences, I butted in. "Your English is very good. Do all your tribe speak it?"

"Most of the people, yes," replied the leader. "One TV explorer left a Linguaphone English Language course, many years ago, and we play the cassettes to the children. But some of the elders choose not to learn. They feel it offends our ancestors."

There came an almighty shriek, the sound of a mother discovering her pram empty. A figure flew in among the crowd, scattering onlookers. Seeing the interloper, the villagers dropped to their knees, revealing a sinister-looking man painted in mud. It had dried and cracked and so he resembled old china. On his head he wore a headdress of coloured feathers and twigs, and he carried in one hand a big stick with a dead raven tied to it by its neck. His modesty was only covered at the front, by a red-painted crocodile's head suspended through its nostrils from string tied around his waist.

The Shaman hissed and revved the motorbike. This new fellow, visibly unhinged, tried to pull him off the machine. The Shaman produced a blowpipe and blew powder at the man, who staggered backwards and began sneezing.

"Klowerthul nagic!" declared the boy.

The crowd gasped.

The new fellow produced a pack of chewing gum and offered the Shaman a piece, which he dubiously accepted. As he pulled out the stick, a tiny mouse-trap spring thwacked him on the thumb. He howled, more at the outrage than the pain.

Applause broke out.

Eyes narrowed, the Shaman held out his hand, looking for the shake; the new fellow pulled out a knife and stabbed him in it.

The Shaman yelled in pain, shaking his hand vigorously so the buzzer he had palmed within it fell to the ground. As he was about to launch himself at his attacker, several men of the village fell upon him and the two were pulled apart.

It really was most unbecoming.

Village guest hut, Monday, 5.45pm:

The Shaman and I had been shown into the same hut, occupied by two makeshift beds (rug-covered wooden frames on the floor) and a hearth containing cold ashes. The assumption seemed to have been made that we would be staying the night and, though I didn't fancy it, I wasn't about to exacerbate the tense atmosphere by saying so out loud.

The Shaman sat there cradling the dummy, stroking its hair with a bandaged hand, sulking.

I wondered, should I stay there with him – basically hide, until we could leave – or venture out and try to make friends? Why were we still in the village, anyway? I thought he had come purely to pick up some magic supplies, an in-and-out mission? And what had that scene with Crocodile Thong been all about?

"Who was that man you fought with?" I ventured.

No reply.

"Was he another shaman?"

Still nothing.

"Is he a more powerful shaman than you?"

That roused him. He was across the hut and beside me, on all fours, like a well-motivated crab, dragging the dummy along with him. I felt his body heat and smelled his breath: an aroma of compost heaps.

"Mnnmk hnnmn, nngl," he said (or words to that effect).

"Oo-otch it, nister," translated the boy. I noticed his monocle had become cracked.

"I just wish someone would tell me what's going on," I protested.

The Shaman and his son conferred. Eventually the boy said, "Oo-ee oo-ent to shanan school together. He is ny grother."

"He's your brother!"

"That is oo-ot I said."

"So what happened?"

The Shaman shifted the boy in his lap. "Once I oo-oz shanan in this thillage. Ny grother gecane jealous and he cane here one night, nany years ago. He clained he oo-oz a nediun, that he could channel our ancestors. The kleokle listened as he klut on these silly thoices, saying that he should gee shanan here, not nee. And the kleokle geliethed hin!"

"The people believed him?"

"That is oo-ot I said."

"So you don't believe in mediums?"

"As if! Oo-ot a load of gollocks!"

"In Britain we had this lady called Doris Stokes..."

But he wasn't interested in my stories. "Helk ne to gecun shanan here once again," he said.

"Help you to become shaman here once again?"

"Jesus! Do I hath to keek rekleating nyself?"

"Is that why you brought me here, me and the motorbike? Thought you'd try to make an impression, boost your reputation?"

The boy opened his mouth in horror. The pair of them looked at each other then back at me. "No!"

I wasn't convinced. "So what do you want me to do?"

"Kill ny grother."

What? "*What?*"

"Ith I did it, I'd get in truggle."

"*You'd* get in trouble? And what do you think they'd do to *me*? Put it down to me not understanding tribal ways – some quaint English custom – and offer me the freedom of the village?"

"Nayge."

"There's no 'nayge' about it. There's *no way*! Are you *insane*?"

"Nayge."

Q tse village, Monday, 5.50pm

I decided to try to make friends. Outside the hut the light was failing, a welcome chill had developed and out among the shadows the jungle's twilight creatures were becoming excitable. Firelight glow flickered dimly in hut doorways and someone had lit a big fire in the middle of the village, around which a smattering of onlookers had gathered. Over the fire a pig was roasting; other pigs glanced at it occasionally and continued snuffling.

A small boy, aged perhaps seven, spotted me, ran across and hugged my leg. Looking up he said, "Hello. My name is Nzonze. What is your name?"

"My name is Pilsbury," I replied, patting him on the head.

The kid snorted and ran off, giggling so helplessly that he fell over and lay there twitching.

"Cheeky monkey!" I admonished him, hoping to show that I was a good sport.

I had never found it terribly easy to make friends, and this would be one of my more challenging situations. I was reminded of the time in my early teens when Father had hand-picked a small selection of his brightest pupils – he taught science and maths at Glibley Secondary – to visit our house, hoping that I might forge a bond with one or more. Visiting contemporaries being a rare treat, I had acceded to the idea, albeit warily, and Father had corralled us around the dining table to play games.

There were four boys and one girl, as I recall it. Father would have been the last person to encourage my hormonal development, and that single white female had terrible breath, thick specs and made me think of camels. The boys wore an assortment of ties and stiff collars. One smelled keenly of cheese, which I mentioned to my neighbour with a nudge in a whisper, but he only eyed me sternly and pressed a finger to his lips.

The first two 'games' involved a spelling bee and an algebra test. When I came easily last in both, Father led the competitive persecution. Finally, a memory game. Mother tiptoed in, all politeness and platitudes, and placed a tray covered in a tea-towel in the middle of the table. When Father said, "Now, Mother!" she whipped off the cloth and he timed us on a fob-watch for two minutes, while we tried to memorise every item on the tray. I came last in that as well, and had to endure one of the boys telling us the provenance and value of the Royal Doulton teapot, as Father glowed with pride and Mother clapped theatrically.

As the children left, each declaring that they'd had the most marvellous time, I was sent to my room. At least I wasn't expected to see them again.

Memories of home.

Two little tribe-girls were now clinging to my tank-top hem, pigtailed and grinning broadly.

"My name is Elza," said one.

"And my name is Knka," said the other.

"What is your name?" they chorused.

I detected a game devised among the smaller children, so told them it was "Dan" and they slunk away dejected.

Then I stood watching the pig being rotated by a crouching chap, who winked at me every time I caught his gaze. I was starving and the crisped-up creature, glazed to a deep russet finish, looked succulent. It was all I could do to stop myself from hopping into the flames and sinking my teeth into a buttock.

Someone tapped me on the shoulder. It was the wonky-toothed teen from earlier.

"I'm Tk-tk," he said, extending his hand.

We shook. "Yes, I remember your name," I lied.

"I am the son of Gdgi," he said.

He could tell I didn't know who Gdgi was. "He is the leader of our tribe," he explained. "My father."

"Absolutely!" I replied. "Tell me, what exactly is the name of this tribe?"

"Exactly, the name of this tribe is the Q'tse." He waited for me to say something.

"Right. Only no one had told me."

"Then everyone is remiss."

"Yes. Yes they are."

"So."

"Here we are!"

I noticed we were still shaking hands and gently pulled away.

The silence hurt. "You have nice weather," I blurted out. "In England, where I come from…"

Tk-tk interrupted me. "My father wishes you to be guest of honour at the feast tonight, with your friend the Shaman."

"Oh, he's not my friend!"

The boy's face betrayed suspicion.

"Well, I suppose he is really. We're all friends here, aren't we?"

"Are we?"

I really didn't know what to say.

Fortunately he broke the silence again. "You might wish to prepare yourself for the feast, Pilsbury."

"Well, I…" I thought better of explaining that I had nothing to change into. "Yes, that's a good idea. I'll see you later."

"Yes. Goodbye for now."

"Bye."

I wasn't desperate to go back to the hut and the Shaman, but then I'd just said I would prepare for dinner and Tk-tk might be watching me. What if I wandered towards the hut and doubled back at the last moment? No, it was all too fraught with potential social ineptitude. Easier to face the madman.

"Hello!" I chirped as I pushed back the door, trying to sound positive.

The Shaman was kneeling with his back to me, trying to get the fire going. "Oh. You're gack. Great," he went, even though the dummy was lying on his bed, flattened and forlorn.

"Charmed, I'm sure," I said. "Look, can we pretend that last conversation never happened? You know, just forget about it? We've been invited to a feast as guests of honour."

The fire caught. "Oh yes?"

"Don't get any ideas. I'm not doing any dirty work for you. And if you try anything, I'll…"

He turned to face me, the shrunken head hanging from the tip of his silly hat singeing gently in the licking flames. "You'll oo-ot?" he said.

I ignored it. Let him get out his dead-head trinkets – his joke-shop magic didn't scare me. The tit was all talk.

In the absence of any clothing options, I did my best to brush myself down and tug out the multiple creases stiffened and salted with dried sweat. When that didn't take long, I sat on my bed wondering what to do next.

The hut heated up quickly and smoke began billowing up towards a hole in the apex of the conical roof. The shaman was applying red face-paint: short lines perpendicular to his eyes and two fang-shapes beneath his mouth. He opened up one side of his feathery cloak and I noticed for the first time that the lining was covered in pockets of all sizes. From one he withdrew something scrunched up and unfurled it to produce a new headdress, similar in design to the current one, only twice as tall. He swapped the two, rolling the other into a pocket.

The Shaman picked up the wooden boy, inserted his arm and sat him on his knee, jiggling him until he was comfy.

The boy came alive. "You know you'll need a gift thor the leader?"

I hadn't thought of that. "Really?"

"It is custom for all guests of honour."

Shit. "But I don't have anything. I didn't pack... I mean, I didn't think we'd be staying."

He brushed imaginary dust off the boy's velvet jacket, saying nothing.

"You haven't got anything I could give him, do you?" Worth a try.

The Shaman stared at me and sniffed. "No," snapped the dummy.

"I could pay you."

This piqued his interest. "Hoo nuch?"

"I don't have any money on me here – but I do have travellers' cheques back at Gossips. I could pay you back there."

"Hoo nuch?"

I hoped he didn't have much of a grasp of the value of Sterling. "Ten pence?"

His eyes lit up. He opened one side of the cloak enough so he could peer in, without me seeing what he was up to. After some deliberation he picked out a cigar and held it out towards me.

"You can hath this," he said, but snatched it away as I reached out. "For *20* of these klennies!" The Shaman cackled dryly, like a hyena choking on Ryvita.

He held out the stogey again, a thin, long thing and inexpertly wrapped, half whipped it away, then let me take it, leering.

"You drive a hard bargain," I said.

A tse village feast, Monday, 6:25 pm:

I was surprised to see, beyond the cooking fire, tables, arranged in two rows of three, seating a dozen or so on individual stools. All the furniture was made from natural materials, bound with twine, but sturdy.

Many of the seats were already taken. Children played around the edges and were regularly shooed away.

I inhaled deeply as the scene sunk in. Here I was, privileged to be among this community so very many miles from home. Birds and monkeys, painted faces, flaming torches dotted about like fairylights, nature unburdened, freedom. Stresses slipped away. While my previous adventures had all been against the clock, here there was no time constraint. I was on the craziest, most intoxicating holiday of my life. And I would drink it in.

The leader, Gdgi, was seated centrally on one side of the far middle table, in the largest chair of all. His torso, arms and head were painted yellow, his hair whitened. On his head he wore a coiled snake, poised to strike, hood extended, which was dead enough but still threatening. He spotted the Shaman and I, and beckoned us towards him.

"Welcome!" he said, standing up. He had swapped to a golden codpiece, I noted. "Please, you must join our table," he said, waving towards two spare stools next to each other and opposite him, though I had hoped to avoid sitting near the Shaman.

"This is my wife," said Gdgi, helping the woman to his right to her feet.

It was all I could do to avoid looking perplexed. Grey haired, thin and toothless, hunch-backed, half his height and twice his age, her breasts hung like unoccupied hammocks beneath a thick golden neck-chain. Hanging from her waist, covering her privates, was some sort of mini armadillo.

I waved at her gormlessly. The Shaman bowed; his son said nothing.

As I took my seat, I said to Gdgi, "I see you have tables here."

"Yes," he replied, shrugging.

Then I remembered: "Ah yes. I brought you a gift."

"How kind. You should not have."

I held out the cigar.

His eyes lit up. "How wonderful. Cigars are one of my favourite things. How did you know?"

Should I come clean? "Always do your homework – that's my motto!" I laughed falsely and avoided looking at the Shaman.

The other occupants of our table clapped in appreciation and I bowed. They were more elderly than most attendees, and boasted the shiniest jewellery. I nodded at the gentleman to my left. He looked at me as if I had just shat in his lap and I wondered whether nodding had negative connotations in these parts.

"My name is Pilsbury," I said, extending a hand.

He stared at it, wrinkling his nose, and said something in his native tongue.

"Do you speak English?" I asked.

He nodded.

"Thank goodness for that! Could have been an awkward dinner party otherwise!"

Gdgi called across. "That is Ekoto. He is one of the elders

who refuses to learn English. He is a bit of a grumpy old sod, I am afraid."

Then the leader clapped his hands and the sound of drums began to echo through the jungle as masked dancers, their masks representing jungle animals, their waists wrapped in red sashes, began to circle us, losing themselves in the tribal rhythms.

A middle-aged woman, wearing earrings the diameter of dinner plates, brought around a tray laden with drinks and popped one in front of each diner. I hoped it might be cold beer, however it turned out to be an insipid creamy brew that tasted bittersweet and on the cusp of unpleasantness, at least with an alcoholic aftertaste that suggested perseverance might prove worthwhile.

I called the earring lady back. "Excuse me, what is this drink?"

She raised an eyebrow and clicked her tongue. "It is ch-ch. It is made from root swallowed by woman then collected later when shat into pot."

I retched, barely managing to keep the terrible concoction down.

The earring lady spotted this, looked quizzical then tutted to herself. "I am sorry. I meant spat, not shat. Your language, it is very complicated."

Somehow her revision felt like an improvement.

Food began to appear on the table. Piles of pork meat and crackling; the pig's head stripped of its ears, which had been sliced up and placed beside it; its tail, blackened and in one piece; way too much stuff that looked like offal; a pile of what looked like roasted rodents; fruits and vegetables – tubas, squashes, nuts and greens, in shades of browns, reds and yellows – the like of which I had never seen; plates of flat bread and bowls of honey; and – ah – reed dishes filled with fat, writhing grubs trying desperately to escape over the dish rims. Aside from the horrors, the crackling alone made my stomach kiss my heart. However, I was aware that no one had yet dived in and I feared breaking with protocol by doing so first.

I dared to nudge the Shaman, hoping for advice. Both he and the boy glared at me. Before I could speak, Gdgi clapped again. The drumming stopped and the tribe fell silent.

The leader rose from his stool to address the crowd. I tried to make sense of his speech, but the sounds were impenetrably alien. At one point he must have cracked a joke because everyone laughed. When I joined in obsequiously, everyone's eyes fell on me and the laughter grew louder.

"We welcome our guests of honour tonight," said Gdgi, thankfully switching to English. "The Shaman you already know, and with him our new friend, Pilsbury." More chuckling, which he silenced with a look of reproach. He turned to me. "When a white stranger accepts our hospitality, he must take a test, to show he is worthy."

My buttocks tightened, my teeth clenched. Had I known, there is no way I would have stayed.

Gdgi continued: "We call this test Ymze Lysta and it has been taken by all before you who passed this way and asked for our help" – I didn't recall doing so – "It is simple, you will come to no harm. Probably. It is for our amusement. Pilsbury, are you hungry?"

"I suppose I am *quite* hungry," I replied warily.

"That is good, because we have some food for you."

A great "Ooooooooh!" arose from the crowd and he grinned knowingly.

I inspected the potential monstrosities on the dinner table before me. What could they have in mind? The offal soaking in a brown liquid, like a discarded rug sample in a full chamber pot? The bowl containing two things that looked horribly like pig's testicles? No, it had to be those grubs, those animated, stuffed, ribbed condoms.

Still, I was so ravenous that even they looked possibly enticing. No sense prolonging the agony, I decided. Lowering a hand into the dish, I pinched one around the midriff and felt its creamy insides pulse past my fingertips.

"No, no, no!" interjected the leader. "Not the grub. How could we gain amusement from your eating such a delicious treat? No, we have something else in mind. Clnde and Yntha, bring Pilsbury his test!"

Two figures, one male, one female, got up from the table to my right and disappeared into darkness towards the huts. As I watched them go, I noticed the other shaman seated on the far corner of the table furthest from us, no doubt to keep the warring siblings apart.

His head turned slowly. He rose and pointed at me, staring. On his face he had painted a white beetle and he wore a suit made of, well, fish. Dead silvery flat fish strung together. And there was me finding my shaman disconcerting.

Clnde and Yntha returned in a state of breathless excitement, each holding a cardboard box. Yntha, the girl I assumed, had a tuft of hair perched centrally atop her scalp and a tapering jawline, which made her head look a bit like an onion. Clnde, like Yntha in his late-teens, wore a necklace comprising millipedes threaded end to end.

The pair held out their boxes towards me. A hush had descended upon the audience, broken by the odd stage whisper.

Gdgi spoke: "Pilsbury, you must choose one of the boxes, and you must eat its entire contents while we watch. Choose now!"

I dreaded to think what lurked beneath those lids if grubs were deemed too easy on the taste buds. Spiders? Flies? Maggots? A grilled snake? What to do? How to choose, minimise the hideousness?

I studied Clnde and Yntha's expressions, hoping for a clue, but they wore the same studied look of eager expectation. I could only resort to eeny-meeny-miny-mo.

Yntha's box.

Should I change my mind?

No. Trust to eeny.

Inhaling deeply, I took the box. Yntha squealed and clenched her thighs, perhaps trapping an escaping modicum of wee. Clnde looked dejected.

The tribe began chanting, building towards hysteria. Some were now standing on stools and tables for a better view. Was this really a spectator sport? How low on genuine entertainment their daily lives must have been.

I closed my eyes and opened the lid.

Everyone whooped. I opened my eyes and looked into the box...

A *burger*?

I lifted it out and peered underneath, checking for something crawling or crisped, with legs. Nothing. I lifted the bun to check the burger itself. Nope. Seemed perfectly normal.

"Eat! Eat! Eat! Eat!" chanted the crowd.

With pleasure, I thought, and began chomping almightily.

Some in the crowd chewed on fingernails. Others watched open-mouthed, ecstatic in their revulsion. I caught several cries of "No!", a smattering in the native tongue and a single "Uncivilised!"

One woman fell to the ground vomiting, which set off a chain reaction of heaving and ejected bile among her neighbours.

Beside me, the Shaman's dummy cackled.

I was finished in moments, bulging cheeks contracting to force meaty, breaded goo between eagerly masticating gnashers. Sweet, sweet burger.

Swallowing the last morsel, smacking my lips, I asked, "Got

any more?"

Oh, the delirium. I could not have been more popular in that moment had I died dramatically of food poisoning.

"Clnde, open your box!" cried Gdgi.

And guess what? Another burger! Practically identical, the cheats!

I chewed that one with gusto, rather than wolfing it down, playing to the crowd, limp lettuce, pickle and all, as the villagers failed to control themselves. Never before had a meal tasted so sweetly of victory. This was the life, lost in the tropics among celebrating strangers. I thought briefly of home, of returning to Glibley one day to drink tea on a carpet; the prospect simply didn't measure up.

The leader held up his hands for order and his people gradually calmed down.

He spoke to me again. "Pilsbury, thank you. You have entertained us greatly, though I do not know how you can eat such a thing with such relish. You are indeed brave – and very strange!"

Cue catcalls and cheers.

Two can play the humour card, I thought. "Great leader. Our cultures are very different. Your burger is my grub." I waited; no one laughed. "Grub as in fat wriggly thing. Your burger is my fat wriggly thing... It's a pun." Silence/bewilderment. "Where I come from, people *like* burgers. Our tastes are different. Here you eat animals' testicles!"

"What do you think your burgers are made from?" replied Gdgi.

Q tse village feast, Monday, 1:00 pm

I was sordidly full. So full I could feel that final roasted rodent breast sitting at the base of my throat. Eating constantly had also made me look too busy for conversation, though a succession of well-wishers had patted my back and congratulated me on my performance in the Ymze Lysta.

Once I could not face another morsel I was trapped in a social hell, between the Shaman and sour-faced Ekoto, obliged towards small talk as the guest of honour.

I tried Ekoto first, with a little sign language. "Lovely food," I said, rubbing my stomach with one hand and miming eating with the other.

He looked right through me.

I could think of nothing more to say, so I sat there, rictus grin, while he stared at me, nodding furiously.

"Hoi, Klilsgury!" came a voice behind me.

The wooden boy's company suddenly felt like a welcome respite.

I swivelled to face the Shaman, who had opened one side of his cloak, exposing to me the rows of secret pockets. What was his game?

As I scanned through them my eyes were drawn to rolled paper protruding from one pouch. A network of lines was printed over it in black, among which was typed writing. Could it be?

"Is that the map you spoke of? The key to the sketch?"
I snatched at it, but he closed the cloak too quickly.
The boy said, "Yes, that is the nak. Do you oo-ont to see it?"
"You know I want to see it."
"Thirst you do sunthing for us."
Hang on! "But I've already done something for you. I drove you here! And I've stayed far longer than I intended."
"Thirst you do sunthing for us."
"We had a deal and I kept my side of it."
"Thirst you do sunthing for us."
I sighed. "What?"
He opened the cloak once again, reached in and pulled out a wooden cup. "This sklecial drink I nake thor ny grother. You take it to hin for nee."
So he'd made a 'special drink' for his brother, whom he had not hours earlier asked me to murder. He must have considered me stupid. Yet... if I refused, let him know I was onto him, would I ever get to see the map?
Could I not just pretend to hand over the dubious brew? It *might* work.
"OK," I said. "But you have to show me the map first."
The shaman wagged his finger and the boy cackled. "Thirst you do sunthing for us."
Fuck it. I had a plan. "Alright. Give me the drink."
It was hard to tell what colour the liquid was, in the depths of the dark receptacle, but it smelled rank, like rotten vegetables. Now, how to pretend to give it to the other shaman without arousing this one's suspicions?
I started walking, cradling the cup, which felt like death. There were other wooden cups, similar in design to this one, on other tables. If I could somehow swap them without the Shaman noticing...
With my back shielding my hands from him, I dropped the cup onto the ground and kicked it under a table, in one fluid

motion picking up an unused wooden cup. I didn't dare turn around to see whether the Shaman had noticed.

The other shaman had seen me coming. As I confronted him, he stood. His fish-suit had begun to rot and a few of the fish had fallen off, exposing portions of his body. It had also begun to smell bad.

I handed him the cup. "This is from your brother," I said, uncertain whether he would even understand me.

He did something unexpected. He smiled. Not a friendly smile, granted, more pitying, but a smile nonetheless. As he did so, the legs on the beetle painted on his face moved, as if the creature were walking.

He took the cup, drank the contents down in one, threw it to the ground, pushed me away and sat down. Was he supposed to clutch his throat, gasping, stagger around a bit and die in agony? Or was the poison more subtle than that? I hoped so. And if so, how long did I have before the Shaman realised I had switched cups?

I turned to walk back. The Shaman was laughing, the gloating Machiavellian. At least he couldn't have noticed the swap.

Sleight of hand. Too easy. Anyone could play the magic game.

A tse village feast, Monday, 10:45 pm:

Gdgi beckoned me towards him as I returned to our table. His wife had gone walkabout, mingling with the hoi-polloi, and I took her seat next to him, warily eyeing the dead snake coiled on his head.

"First I must apologise to you, Pilsbury," he said, chewing some berries open-mouthed.

"Oh really? What for?"

"The test. I made it up. We do not really ask guests to perform such things."

I felt embarrassed.

"Please do not feel embarrassed. We have fooled guests far cleverer than you." Suddenly he looked concerned. "I hope I have not offended you."

How to reassure him? "We had a television show in England, called *Beadle's About*. The host played pranks on people."

"Yes?"

"He was called Jeremy Beadle... The host, I mean."

Gdgi shrugged. "Why is this interesting?"

It was a fair point. "He had a withered hand?"

It was the death of the art of conversation.

Gamely, Gdgi ploughed on. "Tell me, Pilsbury, which lands have you travelled to?"

That was an easier one, and I told him of my previous

adventures, England to Mlwlw, embellishing only slightly. Gdgi raised an eyebrow here and there, interjected with the odd "My goodness!" and looked suitably impressed.

"What do you know?" he asked, when I had finished.

Odd question, I thought. "How do you mean?"

"You have been to all these places. What have you learned?"

Blimey. I'd never really thought in those terms. "I've learnt never to get drunk at the Frihedhags' celebration party!"

"Hmm," he said, frowning. "Do you not feel that the more you discover, the less you know?"

"Yes. No. Maybe." He had lost me. "So how did you become leader of the tribe?"

"Aha. That is a long story," said Gdgi, and he must have spotted my involuntary grimace because he added, "But I will tell you quickly. The honour is passed down from father to son. If there is no boy-child then a new dynasty is chosen. But a new leader must always prove himself worthy. He must go into the forest alone with his spear and he must bring back a wild boar to feed his people. If he does not kill such an animal, he cannot return, or it will bring shame upon his family."

I didn't know much about wild boars. Weren't they just pigs with tusks?

Gdgi went on: "My brother, Mkki, who was older than me, was killed by a boar during such a test. That is how I came to be leader. I tracked down the creature that took his life, I killed it and ate its heart, and my people stripped its bones."

He looked around him. "What do you understand of my people?"

"A little," I hazarded.

"The truth is you understand less than that, Pilsbury. Though we seem happy tonight, tomorrow we shall be sadder. Many times we return from hunting trips empty-handed. Our forest is being destroyed by companies who bring bulldozers and tear down the trees, encroaching upon our lands. We have sent delegations to speak with them and they make promises, but bring only destruction.

"And as they destroy the forest they kill many animals and drive others far away. If we "Q'tse die, Pilsbury, our ways and our language will die with us. And who will know and who will care? I wonder this often."

I didn't know what to say.

"One of your TV explorers came here some time ago and we talked when the cameras were not working, about our histories. He told me that there had been two world wars. I was shocked. My people had not heard of these. I said to him, 'How could they have been world wars if we were not invited?'"

"Right," I said.

Conversation-wise, he had waded out of my depth.

Gdgi must have cottoned on to this, because he smiled and stopped talking about himself. "I notice, Pilsbury, many times while we have talked, you have looked at your Shaman. I wondered why. I have never asked how you became friends."

It was true. I'd been desperate to keep an eye on both shamen. What would happen when mine suspected his dastardly poisoning plan had been somehow foiled?

"We aren't exactly friends," I said. "Really I'm helping him out."

"Oh? Why is that?"

"Well, it's a long story. He has a map I need to see."

"He will not show it to you?"

"No..." How much should I tell Gdgi, I wondered? Perhaps if I gave away enough he would offer to help me out. Might indiscretion be the better part of cowardice? "To be honest, I'm finding him rather devious."

Gdgi laughed. "You do not surprise me! What has he promised you?"

Tread gently. "He told me he'd show me the map if I brought him here. But he didn't. And then" – How to word this one? –

"...there was a funny thing with his brother..."

"His brother?"

"Yes. Your shaman."

"Our shaman? But that is not his brother. Indeed the shaman you bring here is a classic only child."

Really? "So he doesn't have a brother?"

"No."

"They didn't go to shaman school together?"

Gdgi slapped his thigh and roared with laughter. "Shaman school! That is very funny. Oh dear. Shaman school. Goodness me!"

I wasn't finding it funny. "He said they were big rivals."

"Goodness me, no. They are great friends!"

"But. That fight when we arrived?"

"Oh, it is for show. They are always doing that. The people love it." He noticed my deepening concern. "Is something wrong?"

"Do you trust him?"

"No. Of course not." This time he didn't laugh.

My mouth opened but nothing emerged.

Gdgi spoke: "Did you trust him?"

I didn't dare explain. "He wouldn't want to harm your shaman, then?"

"He would be more likely to harm me, Pilsbury. He enjoys power. I am sure he would love to become leader. That is why I would never accept anything from him. He is a true shaman. He understands the powers of all the plants and trees in the rainforest. There is no poison he could not make... Is there a problem here, Pilsbury?"

The cigar. How easily that could have been laced with something. And I had pretended it was from me. Had Gdgi smoked it? I hadn't noticed, but then I had hardly watched him throughout the entire feast. I scanned the table for it, for a scrunched-up butt. Checked the ground. Saw nothing. Should I ask him if he had smoked it? But then, what if he had? If I said anything now, I could drop myself into a whole heap of trouble. What to do? Shit. Shit-shit-shit-shit-shit.

Think positive. "No, no trouble," I replied, smiling weakly. "Tell me, where do you get your delicious honey?"

One can only take so much apiculture when one's mind is firmly elsewhere. At least it took his mind off our shaman chat, and eventually he seemed to bore himself and announced that he had to answer nature's call. Seizing the opportunity, I zipped back to my seat. The Shaman was there, his bastard dummy dead-eyeing me through its cracked monocle.

"You're coming with me," I said, tunnelling fingertips into his bicep.

O tse village guest hut, Sunday, ①①.⑤⓪pm:

"What did you do to the cigar?" I demanded, still gripping him by the upper arm.

He shrugged me off. "Oo-ouldn't you like to know!" went his puppet.

I grabbed the dummy round its scrawny neck. "Did you poison the cigar?"

The Shaman's eyes flared. He wrenched the boy away and, pulling back, I tore its fucking head off.

The Shaman screamed, snatched it from me, thrust the wooden neck back into place. Now even the dummy's eyes seemed aflame. "You klay dangerous gane."

Rubbish. "I was buying your 'klowerthul nagic' from joke shops when I was six years old. You don't scare me."

The Shaman peered at me over imaginary specs, dirty grin spreading. "Thery thoolish oo-ords," he lisped. Not even attempting to speak through the dummy now.

Fuck it, I thought, and punched him, hard, in the face. It surprised even me. I wasn't a violent person. In my defence, the Shaman wasn't a nice man.

He saw it coming too late and went down like a gigolo on a client. The dummy flew backwards into the wall of the hut.

I pulled open his cloak while he groaned, found the map, snatched it out and folded it into my back pocket. That still didn't seem enough payback, not after all his double-crossing and lies. An idea came to me. Striding to the back of the hut, I picked up the dummy.

"Think I'll take this with me!"

Prone and groggy, the Shaman craned his neck to see what I was doing and howled, though pitifully, like a crone all out of newts' eyes. He tried to grab my ankle as I made for the door but I kicked his hand aside. As I walked outside, breathing in the jungle and wood-smoke, he croaked after me: "You oo-ill klay thor this."

I made straight for the motorbike and sidecar, fortuitously parked near the village's entrance/exit, away from the ember glow of the feast.

No time for second thoughts or guilty concerns. No time for goodbyes. Time to scarper.

As I reached the bike a commotion came from the direction of the feast: voices rising and a woman's shriek, then more screaming. People were gathered around a prone form – at the table where I had been seated, the head table. It could mean only one thing. Gdgi had gone down.

I had to keep telling myself: it's not your fault. It's not your fault.

I threw the wooden boy into the sidecar and straddled the saddle. Unnoticed still, my heartbeat in my eardrums, I desperately patted down my pockets for the key. From nowhere, a boy appeared beside me. The last thing I needed: attention. And I recognised him. What was his name again?

"Hello, my name is Nzonze," said the kid.

With a surge of relief I felt the key in my back pocket.

"What is your name?" he said.

Ramming it into the lock, I turned the ignition and ripped back my right wrist.

"Forget it kid," I replied.

That joke wasn't funny anymore.

Somewhere outside a tse village, Monday, midnight:

The flight had been all about adrenalin. Now, as I steered along a barely existent track, illuminated by a headlight with all the candle-power of a firefly drowning in beer, back – I hoped – towards Gossips, paranoia was setting in.

If the cigar had been poisoned and assuming Gdgi was indeed lying dead, who would the people blame? Not the Shaman, who could lie his way out of a locked trunk. They would blame me – and who could blame them?

Why on earth had I claimed the cigar as my own gift? How could I have been so stupid as to trust the Shaman? Was I even going the right way? Surely I was low on petrol? What would happen if the fuel ran out in the middle of the jungle? Were the tribespeople already on my tail? What if...

Stop it, I told myself. Panic wasn't helping. I needed a little perspective...

Did something just *touch my arm*? Not possible.

My senses were alert. Was that pressure I felt, on my other shoulder? Did it really feel like... a *hand*? I twisted my head but saw nothing. Tension coursed through my bones like liquid calcification. Then... No. Not. Possible.

Something was crawling over my back, something large.

As I turned to look, my gaze whipped past the sidecar.

Double-take. The passenger seat was empty. The wooden boy had disappeared... No. Not. Possible.

Breathing, in my left ear. *Breathing.*

A shape entered my peripheral vision. A head, beside mine.

Rouged cheeks, chiselled jaw, monocle. We stared at each other, the devil-boy and I, nose-tips touching, flesh on wood. Dead, malevolent eyes.

"Ny Daddy skliked your drink," he whispered in my ear.

The dummy threw back his head and laughed and laughed and laughed and laughed and laughed and laughed and laughed.

The laughter would not stop.

Hell:

The world exploded.

And fire rained down on me.

Faces, places, memories and shapes, swirled outwards. Out towards a pinprick placed in unreality, stationed at infinity.

Time shifted, rose, fell, billowed in a heat haze. Lasted a full lifetime or vanished in a vacuum.

Within the vortex a shadow appeared. The shadow expanded. Developed features. Called a name. "Pilsbury?" Shifted, replaced by red.

Something wicked this way came, hurtling towards the distance between my eyes.

Wind. Burn. Collision. Speed.

I screamed. You screamed. We all screamed.

Then void.

Lucidity:

"Pilsbury?"

"Pilsbury?"

The voices pricked my subconscious, eventually rousing me awake. Other noises joined the repetition of my name: familiar animal calls, the sounds of humidity.

My head felt furry and my spine hurt like hell. I was lying on my back with hard ridges digging into my flesh. What had happened? And where the hell was I?

I opened my eyes, which baulked at the sunshine. There were twisted branches and broad, verdant leaves above me, though not as high above me as I might have expected. As I shifted a shoulder, my right side began to drop, sharply. I threw out an arm, grabbed at a handhold and looked over my shoulder.

What the fuck was I doing halfway up a tree?

I puked, the matter tumbling to the ground where it splattered noisily, and instantly I felt a little better.

People were looking for me – people with local accents, whose voices I failed to recognise, but who knew my name. Why? Who could they be? While arteries around my scalp throbbed, recent memories began to filter through. When they reached the point where I had inadvertently poisoned Gdgi, my head cleared in an instant. Wonderful what fear can do.

At once it became obvious who these people were. Trackers.

Hunters from Gdgi's tribe intent upon bringing his killer to justice. But I didn't kill him – that wasn't my cigar! I had lied, to make myself look better! (And, oh, how that had backfired.)

The Shaman was the guilty party. But who would believe me, the interloper?

The voices had been getting closer. Too close. I focused upon them.

"Pilsbury?"

Different male voice: "Pilsbury?"

The name came again and again; as far as I could make out, there were only two of them. Only two. It was a start. But who was I kidding? A single one of those hard-as-nails tribesman could have taken me down, even if he were half my size... And what if they were armed?

They were bound to be. What self-respecting hunter would travel without some form of weapon? I imagined myself being picked off up here, in this sodding tree, spears or arrows whistling past my ears, until the inevitable.

Oh Jesus Christ. What was I going to do?

As I assessed the situation, I could not help but wonder again: what was I doing halfway up a tree?

How on earth had I got up here?

Though I strained my brain, it offered only so much, then dug in its heels. I remembered getting on the bike after decking the Shaman. I remembered rifling through my pockets for the key. I even remembered that little kid's name: Nzonze. After that, white-out. Not a clue.

I might as well have beamed here via Mars.

"Pilsbury?" That jolted me back to the instant. Not 20 yards away, at most.

How was I going to persuade them that the Shaman was the real killer?

"Pilsbury!"

"Pilsbury!"

I could hear their footsteps now, heard them stop to sweep a hand through dead foliage, talk to each other in their own tongue. Then carry on.

I tried to curl myself up at the sides, to roll myself like a rug, so that I might hide behind mere branches, never once daring to look down.

So close now, I swore I could hear their hearts beating. Again they stopped. I screwed my eyes tight shut and dared not to breathe. Every muscle tensed.

"Hey! We see you up there!"

I waited for the spear shaft to lance my heart, praying for just a flesh wound.

"Pilsbury. Please come down. It looks very dangerous up there."

"Yes, Mr Quench will not thank us if we return you broken."

Their names were Benzani and Hagadro and they were friends and occasional customers of Livingstone Quench. Like myself, Quench had expected my trip with the Shaman to be a swift return journey and, knowing how temperamental old bikes could be, he had sent out a search party when I had not returned by nightfall, just in case.

They had followed my tracks out until coming across the vehicle, some yards off the path, its sidecar crumpled into a significant tree, yet with no sign of myself thereabouts. Tracking my footsteps, they had traced a haphazard route well into the jungle, until they had spotted me up the tree.

"You were lucky," said Benzani. "There were many signs that you were bouncing off trees on your way, which would have scared off predators. But you would not have lived for long without water, had we not found you."

"Yes," agreed his compatriot. "And many are the tree snakes."

Heading for Gossips, Monday, noon:

Though I had assured my two saviours that they had done enough already and that I was quite capable of walking, they had insisted upon taking it in turns to give me piggy-backs home. What surprised me was that the journey did not take that long. Whatever had happened during my bike ride back from Gdgi's 'lost' village, I had somehow almost made it back.

Bobbing along thus – frankly uncomfortable, given both Benzani and Hagadro's boniness – did I return to Mlwlw to find Quench sitting outside his bar, reading a cigarette packet. He leapt to his feet when he saw us and came to greet me, arms outstretched. No sign of Harrison Dextrose.

"What 'appened to you?" asked Quench. "You look like shite!"

Cheers. "I'm not entirely sure," I replied.

"By the way," Quench said. "There's someone here been looking for you."

"For me?" I felt my face blanche. Had the Q'tse come straight here? Had I not eluded them after all?

Quench continued: "Yeah. Called you by your old name: Alexander, weren't it? Took me a while to work it aht."

I breathed again. It couldn't be any of the Q'tse, who knew me only as Pilsbury, nor the Shaman himself. But if it weren't them, then who could it possibly be? Someone from my old life?

I could think of only one possible candidate... Surely not? *Suzy Goodenough*?

My motivation to follow in Dextrose's footsteps, I should explain – it wasn't purely about self-improvement. That wasn't the whole story. There was also a woman. (Isn't there always?)

Back home in Glibley I had two long-term friends: Benjamin Grebe and Suzy Goodenough. The latter, I had lusted after since schooldays. 'The goddess', Benjamin and I called her, though she remained off-bounds to us sex-wise, an unattainable angel, an ache.

There had been one incident: her 16th birthday when she had demanded I help her lose her virginity (coincidentally involving mine also), and we had both become naked in her bedroom. Fabulously nervous, I'd tried to think of something romantic to utter and had blurted out, "I like your vagina." It had gone downhill from there and the prospect of anything carnal had trailed off into obscurity.

So, when she'd offered to sleep with me should I complete the route of Dextrose's Quest in a faster time than the great explorer himself had managed – knowing I couldn't possibly turn the chance down – I had leapt at it like an adolescent on a pogo stick.

Had she come out here to find me?

My hopes were piqued.

I dusted down my tanktop, ran fingers through my hair (which emerged covered in dust, twigs and four dead beetles), cleared my throat and followed the bar owner into his den.

My first surprise was that Dextrose was not present, draped over a table. My second was that there were no women in the bar at all, let alone Suzy Goodenough, elated and flying into my arms like a bird into a window. No, there was just one chap, looking tall even seated, returning my quizzical stare.

He started getting up as I moved into the bar, and he kept on growing and growing. He must have been well over seven feet tall, with legs and arms as thin and long as his tanned face. Had he not ducked at full height, he would have put his head through the ceiling.

"Senor Alexander?" he asked.

I furrowed my brow. I had never seen him before, yet he knew of me. "Yes?"

"My bruzzer, he say I must to come to find Senor Alexander here. He say I must to help Senor Alexander."

The stranger wore long, baggy shorts, satin white, and a matching vest top with the number 57 on his chest in blue with red trim. Above that was a black-lined illustration of a chap in a sombrero chewing a cigar and toting a pistol. Below the number was a name, 'Los Desperados'. He was rather handsome in a chiselled, sporty way, if a bit tall.

His 'bruzzer'? I'd heard that pronunciation before, from the dwarf, Detritos. And hadn't there also been vague talk of a sibling? A sibling who played basketball?

As we met in the middle of Gossips, he held out his hand. "You are Senor Alexander?" His hair was very black, short, spiked and greased, and he wore unkempt, dusty stubble. His eyes were duck-pond green.

"Yes, yes I am," I said, shaking warily. "Are you Detritos's brother?"

He beamed, nodding. "Si! Is me! How is he, my bruzzer?"

Christ. He was dead at the bottom of a volcano. "He's…" – Think fast, you fool – "He's fine. I think. I haven't seen him for a while." I just couldn't bring myself to tell him the truth. What if he took it badly? Or decided to blame me?

He regarded me quizzically. "When he return?"

Shit. "Well, you know what Detritos was… is like – there one minute, gone the next! Haha!"

He began pumping my hand enthusiastically. He did know what his brother was like! "For sure! He is one, as you to say!

My name Importos! I am your friend!"

"Great!" I replied, feeling godawful.

"Detritos, he will to turn up, zen we all be friend! Yes?"

Well, no, actually.

"Beer!" It was Dextrose arriving for hopefully his first drink of the day, and he couldn't have timed the interruption better.

I ushered Importos towards the table where the lapsed explorer had plonked himself. "Importos, this is my father, Harrison Dextrose. Harrison Dextrose, Importos."

Dextrose ignored the tall man's outstretched hand. "Mink off!" he snapped.

"He doesn't mean it," I cod-chuckled.

"I minking do," demurred Dextrose.

The last thing I needed was a scene. Thinking on my feet, I called to the barkeep. "Livingstone, three beers please! And one for yourself – do come and join us! Haha!" I really would have to cease the false laughter.

My hastily hatched plan was to maintain a mixture of inane small talk and boyish banter, avoiding any mention of the dead dwarf.

Dextrose prattled on about himself as usual, which I only encouraged, and we filled the conversation with that sort of thing until Quench just had to go and ask Importos how he came to be in Gossips.

"My bruzzer, he to call me," Importos explained. "He to say, 'You to come help Senor Alexander – he to go to Gossip, you to meet zere. Come now!' I ask him, 'But where you to go?' He will not to tell. I to worry…"

"So you're a basketball player?" I asked, before he could concern himself further.

"For sure!" he said. "Basketball is family business – but Detritos, he too small! Yes!"

I laughed far more heartily than was necessary, causing

Quench to look at me strangely. "How'd you get 'ere, son?" he asked Importos. "Where you from?"

"From Green Golan, you to know?"

No one did.

Importos added: "It many mile, but I to jog here, for to be fit. OK?"

"You jogged 'ere? 'Ow far is it?" asked Quench.

"Maybe 200 mile?"

"*You jogged 200 miles?*" the barkeep spluttered.

Neither of us could quite believe it (Dextrose had stopped listening).

Importos shrugged. "When my bruzzer, he to call, I zink must to be import."

If I couldn't stop him talking about Detritos soon, the truth was bound to emerge, and then I'd be hard-pressed for an explanation. Why hadn't I simply admitted everything to start with? The dwarf had killed himself in the interests of world peace... hmm, perhaps that was why.

Suddenly I remembered the map I had stolen from the Shaman and whipped it out of my pocket. "We forgot all about this!" I announced.

"What is it?" asked Quench.

I was only too happy to explain.

It was an A5 street-map, printed on both sides in black-and-white. A furry uneven edge suggested it had been ripped from a book and, judging from its condition, it was pretty old.

The barkeep picked it up. "I recognise that design," he said, and hurried back behind the bar. He emerged with a book titled, *Pocket Map of Pretanike*, and began riffling through its pages. "Gotcha!" he said as he took his seat. "Look!"

A thin jagged line of paper nestling in the spine of the book indicated a page had been ripped out, exposing page numbers 146 and 149. He picked up our piece of the puzzle. On either side were printed the numbers 147 and 148.

"Where did you get that book?" I asked.

Quench shrugged. "Visitors leave 'em and I collect 'em, case they ever come in 'andy."

"So how the hell did the Shaman come to have this page?"

"No idea," he said. Then, wishfully, to Dextrose. "Any idea, 'Arry?"

Dextrose said nothing.

Importos only looked confused, which was ideal.

More to the point, how did the double-sided map solve the puzzle of Dextrose's crude sketch? I withdrew that from my pocket for reference. Between us, Quench and I pored over the map, seeking, hoping for something to fit. Its streets were densely packed, Gossips' lighting was poor, and we were both losing heart when the bar owner snatched up the page, held it close to his face, and declared, "Got it!"

He slammed it back down on the table and poked a fingertip at the bottom right-hand corner of page 147. "Look! See it?"

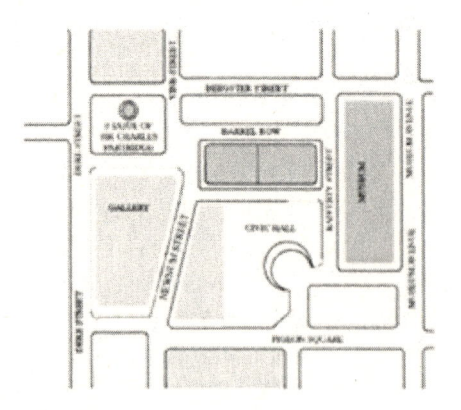

No, frankly, I couldn't.

"Alright, give it a turn," he said, twisting the page 90 degrees anticlockwise. "Nah put 'Arry's sketch beside it…"

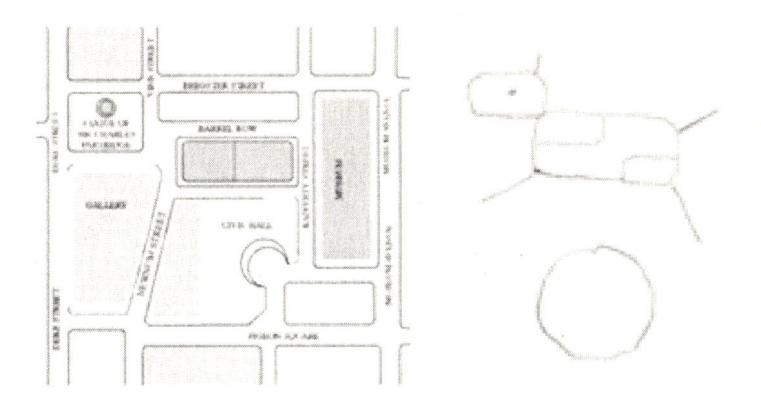

"See it nah?" He traced an outline with his finger. "See the blob where that Statue of Charlie Partridge is on the map – imagine that's 'Arry's cow's eye. See the shape the road system makes? On the map an' the drawin' – same shape!"

Well, maybe. "What about the moon? Where's that?"

"It's that rahndabaht fing at City 'All!" he cried excitedly, jabbing repeatedly at the map.

The Shaman had kept this torn out page of map from me, which he had said held the key to Dextrose's sketch. And the street patterns did look pretty much the same.

"You could be right," I said.

"Course I'm right! It's the same shape. Somewhere wivin this road system – that's where you'll find your muvver!"

The more I compared the two, the more it seemed to fit. Livingstone Quench had only gone and cracked it.

Importos interrupted our shared triumph. "And my bruzzer?"

Quench slapped him on the back. "Sorry, son, I've clean forgot me manners in all this excitement. You must be knackered after runnin' all that way. 'Ere, let me find you a guest room then I'll sort you some nosh. Sound good, yeah?"

"Absolutely," I concurred.

Gossips, Monday, 1.15pm

"What the 'ell's this all abaht wiv the lanky bugger?" demanded Quench, when he had returned from housing my new friend. "What you 'iding from 'im?"

He'd even spotted it. Thanks heavens for language barriers, I thought.

I told him as much as he needed to know. How Detritos had accompanied me for much of my journey in Dextrose's footsteps and had more than once saved my life. How we had ended up on the crater of a volcano and the dwarf had thrown himself in, believing that in doing so he would be saving the world from destruction.

At that point, he butted in. "*Savin' the world?* Come again?"

"Well, he was convinced he was."

"So why didn't you jus' tell his bruver that? That 'e killed 'isself, bein' a bit loopy?"

"I know," I wailed. "I know. But he caught me unawares. And I might have been able to stop Detritos."

"Really?"

"Well, probably not. He was pretty single-minded."

"So there you go!"

"But I can never be 100 per cent certain, and there's the guilt."

The back door of the bar opened and a figure stooped inside. "Where is food?" Importos called out gaily.

Quench stood up. "'Old on, son!" And he winked at me.

I loved that guy. He made everything feel better.

Gossips, Monday, 2.55 pm:

While Importos tucked rabidly into a hunk of cold meat and Harrison Dextrose fine-tuned his artless belligerence, Quench and I pored over maps from the bar's collection and worked out a route from Gossips to Pretanike. It looked like a hell of a hike, through a vast area of land emptier than the high-slung half of Hitler's scrotum sac. Indeed, the map showed but one road, the Nameless Highway, featuring only the odd, brief offshoot, and no more than half a dozen named landmarks in some 1,000 miles – among them Lonely Bush, Flattened Hat and Call-That-A-Hill?

At the far end of the Nameless Highway, the sprawling city of Pretanike appeared, nestling on a jagged coastline. And somewhere within that ostentatious conurbation, hopefully, was my mother. More than once I sought out Sir Charles Partridge on the map cutting. I imagined a tiny speck lunching at the statue's base, wearing a headscarf and sunglasses, the image lifted directly from her husband's one treasured snap. In my mind she had bright red lipstick and a faraway look in her eyes, as if she were consciously waiting for someone. Waiting for me.

Importos joined us, his hunger sated. "You are to look map, I see," he said. "I to be your guide. In zis way I to help, for my bruzzer."

Well, if he were to join us – and I doubted he would be dissuaded, having jogged 200 miles to get here – then he might as well be of some use. I showed him our route along the Nameless Highway.

"No. Have not to been zis place," he said, then to Quench: "Is zere pudding?"

With the others distracted elsewhere, I took the opportunity for a one-to-one with Dextrose. He had to come with me, no question. Only he would be able to recognise Mrs Dextrose, to grasp a sense of *déjà vu* as we hunted around Pretanike's back-streets. He had to do the right thing.

I chanced the direct approach. "We're leaving soon," I said, fixing him with my hardest stare.

"Good!" he said, which surprised me, until I realised from his tone he hadn't included himself in the 'we' bit.

I tried again. "No, *Dad*. I meant you and I are leaving soon. To find Mum."

He forced a little finger into his right ear, wiggled it and inspected the tip on extraction. Then he harrumphed, looked away pointedly and swigged beer in profile. Side-on, his head resembled a frog's in a hippie wig.

"I mean it," I persisted. "You have to come with me."

Another swig.

"Does Mrs Dextrose mean nothing to you?"

That got his attention. He actually stood up, as he did so hauling up the waistband of his pink velour tracksuit bottoms – in which the elastic had no doubt perished decades hence. Upright and yet to become completely arseholed, he cast a figure of some authority; for the first time since meeting him I felt that I could see past the grime and degradation to the explorer of yore, to the man I had once respected.

"Son," began Dextrose. "And I mean that in a patronising 'young boy' sense, not the minking family one. Son, what dear Mrs Dextrose means to me is between Mrs Dextrose and me-minking-self. The great Harrison Dextrose hasn't spent 39 years wedded to the walking megaphone without knowing full well what she means to him, because she told him every minking day he was with her. So don't you dare come the concern with me, you little mink." He shook his head. "Don't you minking dare."

The way he had spoken to me – the condescension, the spite – it reminded me of Father. Though I surely had every right to express my concern, my conviction had vanished. I sat there, mute, while Dextrose guzzled his remaining booze in one, hand shaking.

Then he was off, on a drinker's ramble. "Do you remember our wedding day? Cos I does. Eighteen, she were, eyes like emeralds, hair spun from gold and mammaries a gent could snorkel between. I weren't Mrs Dextrose's only suitor, mark me words, but she only ever had eyes for young Harrison. Twenty-third of October. I may have forgotten most other dates, but I shall never forget that one. The bride wore white, her mother wore black." He clenched and unclenched his fists. "Don't start me on that minking sow's bedpan!"

Dextrose caught himself, ceased his reminiscing. "Anyway, what's all this to you?"

"Mrs Dextrose is my mother. You're my Dad," I pointed out.

He blinked furiously. "I thought that's what yer said earlier, but imagined I'd misheard yer. So I'm yer *Pa*, yer say?" The spite had gone from his voice, the frustration and ire had seeped away. He sounded almost… vulnerable.

It was now or never. "Yes, I'm your son, Pilsbury. Remember the photos?"

As I scrabbled in my pockets for my snapshot, I caught Quench and Importos in my peripheral vision, arriving with fresh beers.

While Dextrose was muttering to himself – "Yer know, that does ring a minking bell" – a fresh glint inhabiting his eyes, and I was pleading, "Don't give him more beer", in slow motion the bar owner plonked down four green bottles, frothing at their tops. My father reached for his as I tried to swipe it away, but it was out of reach, and he lifted the bottle to his lips, he glugged and he glugged, and that glint in his eyes flickered and was extinguished.

Dextrose shook himself, glared at me and growled, "As I were saying, what the mink is it to you?"

Gossips, Monday, 3.55pm

Shortly before 4pm, while Importos was showering, Dextrose passed out.

"That should do it!" chirped Quench, slapping his hands together.

I was non-plussed. No way had my father reached his alcoholic capacity. I prodded his head, prone on the table, thumb in his mouth, as he gurgled away in la-la-land. No reaction.

"'E was never gonna come wiv you, Pilsbury," said Quench. "So I knocked 'im aht wiv some shaman-quality sleeping drops. 'E'll sleep like a baby for hours."

It sounded a bit dodgy. A bit like kidnap. "But…"

"Don't you worry. Jus' tell 'im I did it, for 'is own good. Right? Nah all you gotta to do is load 'im into the sidecar."

"Sidecar?"

"Aht the front. Benzani wheeled the bike in just nah." He grinned, pleased with himself. "You were out of petrol, that's all. Well, that and wrapped arahnd a tree. But 'e's knocked the dents aht as best he could an' filled her up wiv gas – by my reckoning you're good to go!"

"How much do I owe you?" It was all I could think of, though I owed Livingstone Quench far more than mere cash.

He held up a finger. "'Old on," he said. "I'll get your bar bill."

This was going to be painful. I couldn't recall Dextrose handing over money for a single drink, and particularly on that second night, when we had become tangled up in the lapsed explorer's deftly spun yarns, there were many times when I, the willing gimp, had cried all too blithely, "My round!"

Quench returned with a till receipt. "£231.82!" he declared.

"Ah," I went, knowing full well that my wallet contained just £175 in traveller's cheques.

"Well?" demanded Quench, his usually benign features narrowing to something more schoolmasterly. But he could not hold it for long and burst into raucous laughter, patting me on the cheek like a well-rouged aunt. "As if I could charge you, young Pilsbury! Any son of 'Arry's is a son of mine – an' jus' you remember that! 'Ere, 'old on a minute," he said, and left by the back door.

When he returned he was lugging a battered tan leather suitcase in one hand and had a khaki suit draped over the opposite forearm. "'Ere'" he said, thrusting the suited arm towards me. "This'll make you look the part, if you're gonna be accompanying a world-renowned explorer."

"What is it?"

"It's a safari suit," he said. "Left behind by some tourist. Reckon it'll fit you jus' fine." He smiled. "An' this is 'Arry's stuff. We'll 'ave to strap in on the back." As he heaved the suitcase upright, it tinkled like an early-morning milk float.

If we hurried, I thought, we could sneak off before Importos realised we had gone.

Outside Gossips, Monday, 4.30pm.

Dextrose – quite some dead weight, requiring the strength of myself and Quench to shift – had been stuffed into the sidecar. His arms were lolling out of the sides, his gut had become caught on the tiny windscreen and his head was tipped backwards so that his mouth gaped open, snoring at the sky.

I had quickly donned the safari suit, having dumped my stinking casuals in a bag and thrust that into the recesses of a half-empty rucksack. So few possessions – but I didn't care.

"'Ere," said Quench, pushing a roll of banknotes into my hand and closing my fingers around it. "You'll need this. Long way to where you're goin'."

"I can't…" I faltered.

"Course you can."

I wondered out loud: "How can you afford all this?"

He narrowed his eyes at me. "Ask me no questions, I'll tell you no lies." Then he chuckled. "Ah, what's the 'arm in tellin' you? Bank job, '72."

Not all gangsters are unlovable, I decided.

"Nah, go on, quick, 'fore that lanky fella catches up wiv you!" (And Gdgi's people, and the Shaman, I thought, glad I had failed to mention them to him.)

Dextrose belched in his coma. Livingstone Quench and I shook hands, mine feeling so much smaller than his.

"Good luck, lad," he said. And he turned, walked back into

Gossips and shut the door behind him. Not a sweat patch on his back.

Boy, was I going to miss him.

As I gunned the engine, on the verge of getting away with it, Importos came haring outside, his gangling limbs waving around like windsocks in a squall. "Hey! Senor Alexander! You to forget Importos!"

On the road from Mlwlw, Monday, 5.30pm

There had been one road out of Mlwlw, left towards the southern coast instead of right into the jungle. It was strewn with nature's debris, causing Dextrose's head to jerk up and down violently. Importos clung on behind me, towering over my head. Anything he tried to say to me was swept away by the rushing air or drowned out beneath the engine's thrum.

I felt happy to be on the road, welcomed the miles strewn before us. This was freedom and let it last, cutting through the breeze, between the verdant sentries guarding the roadside, as we... not exactly hurtled along, though it was progress... out towards new lands, fresh experiences.

Let the Shaman come after me. And all of the villagers! They would not catch us, not while I was in this mood!

The trees became shorter and more sparse, the further from Mlwlw we travelled, as the rainforest began to peter out. The route became smoother. Occasionally we would pass people on the road: women with bundles or baskets on their heads, men carrying tools, shooting us uncertain smiles, children jumping and waving excitedly.

I held my face up to the sky, let the sun's rays rain down on me, took my hands off the handlebars, flung them out wide and opened my mouth to pour out my joy. I spotted the black blob hurtling towards me too late, swallowed the large flying insect, heard its panicked buzzing inside my head as its wings beat dementedly on the roof of my mouth. Jamming my hands back onto the handlebars, I spat violently while retching and, when I was sure the dastardly bug had been ejected, felt around my mouth with a doctorly tongue, paranoid that I might have been stung. Behind and above me Importos laughed with abandon, his stomach pulsing against my spine.

After an hour or so I spotted our first sign up ahead, partially concealed by vegetation to the left of the track. As we drew closer I saw it was a hefty wooden construct nailed between two poles. On it was written, in two languages:

NTHULU HNKUTA TMBALA

YOU ENTER NAMELESS HIGHWAY

And as we chugged past it, I noticed that someone had sprayed a graffiti figure beneath:

Which hardly inspired a satisfying dollop of confidence.

Still, here we were. I was in one piece, there was no one on our tail, as far as I could see, and we had sufficient supplies, Quench having packed sarnies *ad infinitum* as well as a vast water can. As we approached a bend in the track beyond which I hoped the Nameless Highway would come into view, my heart was beating like a cantering nag. What would it look like?

Our home for the next few days, its name evoked in my mind's eye scenes from Clint Eastwood movies, cowboys in hats chewing on tobacco, toting pistols the length of savaloys, bar brawls and prostitutes in petticoats. But were names deceptive?

Then we turned the bend and the answer lay spread before me: the Nameless Highway looked like nothing on earth. *Literally* nothing on earth. It were as if a god with a giant vacuum had sucked up every last feature, from one side to the other. Desolation. Sand, sand, sand, as far as the eye could see, deep orange in colour. This could have been the surface of Mars. And bisecting it, fashioned in pristine tarmac, the road. The Nameless Highway, as straight as a python eating a pool cue, stretching out towards the far horizon.

Sand and a road. Not a bush nor a cactus nor another soul in sight. Certainly no Clint.

Just sand. And a road.

The Nameless Highway.

Our home for the coming days.

I stopped the bike, exhaled deeply, and stared. "Fuck."

Beside me, Dextrose continued to doze. Behind me, Importos moaned.

"We in big shit," he said.

At least there was a breeze rolling in over the sands from the south, from an unseen ocean that I imagined I could taste. It calmed the intensity of the sun dipping behind us and tousled my blonde hair, overgrown and untended since the start of my travels. When had I last shaved,'I wondered? When had I last even looked in a mirror? Vanity and real travel functioned poles apart, I realised, running a hand over the curves of my face and through patchy bum-fluff. Any self-respecting 33-year-old back home would have been ashamed to call that a beard. I wore its untidiness with honour – to me it said 'explorer'.

According to the map, the first stop on the Nameless Highway would be a settlement imaginatively named First Stop. It was about half an inch in, on a road that went on for roughly five. According to the scale, that meant a journey of perhaps 250 miles before we would hit civilisation. We dared not even consider roadside camping, so would have to make First Stop that night, which was pushing it given our top speed of 45 miles per hour. (On heart-stopping occasions, when the motorbike and sidecar seemed possessed by a devil-may-care spirit, the speedometer needle would crawl over the 45 mark, like a pensioner negotiating an obstacle course, then oscillate wildly either side of 46, dancing on hot coals, appalled and elated by its own temerity. Then it would backfire – the machine version of shitting itself – and normal service would resume.)

I checked my watch, the lovely Timeco Z112.2 XG, too many buttons and space-age face, purchased in High Yawl. It was sold to me, in that Utopia for the commercially minded, by the delightful Mimsy Flopkins, who had mourned my leaving her emporium with the phrase, "Your premature departure has left a hole in my soul." I hadn't necessarily believed her, though it did stick in my mind. The Timeco Z112.2 XG was a lovely watch, which she promised would flash red if I stopped breathing.

It was 18.42. Time to get going. Importos and I glugged down some water, and I managed to tip some into Dextrose's upturned gob without him stirring.

"Hold on to your hat!" I called over my shoulder and upwards to Importos, though of course he wasn't wearing a hat. "Next stop, First Stop!"

"To whoppy-do!" he called back drily.

Meanwhile, Dextrose snored: a crackly, hacking sound.

The ride quickly settled into a rhythm, with the engine as soundtrack. With no features to speak of, not even a white line down the middle of the road, it sometimes seemed we weren't moving, so I had to trust to the speedometer's insistence and the blurred rotation of the front wheel. It was as if we were perched atop a rotating drum.

I could sink into it, my mind wandering, picking up random signals from the cosmos and turning them over. Inevitably, though, my thoughts veered towards family.

Harrison Dextrose was my father, that much I had accepted; however, the implications had not fully sunk in. The situation felt true yet unreal. My only memories of him came second-hand, from the contents of *The Lost Incompetent*. That was how I knew him, though the boorish drunk I had encountered in the flesh bore only a minor resemblance to his own recorded take on himself – which tended to gloss over the negatives and blame everyone else. I had to assume that encroaching old age – more spare time and the alcohol to fill it – had narrowed his mind, and that the Dextrose of his writings, the curmudgeonly but playful character, had he existed at all, lay dormant. Just needed a nudge or two to emerge, I hoped... Nay, felt certain.

As I gazed around me, witnessing the sheer expanse of sand on every side, I realised how far I had come – physically and mentally – and was reminded of my childhood beach holidays.

Our family breaks were invariably a disaster. Father and Mother refused to go abroad – allegedly too concerned about the dangers of sunburn; in reality too tight – so we had endured a variety of homegrown resorts, once a year in August. The old family photograph albums were packed with shots of miserable people sheltering from thunderstorms under plastic hats and umbrellas.

It hadn't helped that I had been the only child, that Father was such a killjoy and Mother his lapdog. It was he who had told me, aged five, that Santa didn't exist, and who had squashed a moth on my pillow one night, claiming in the morning that I had rolled over and killed the tooth fairy.

There were times when I sensed that my very presence annoyed him. Rarely on those seaside holidays would he join in with my building of sandcastles, so I remember being surprised when he once offered to bury me in the sand. One is supposed to leave the head showing but Father just kept on shovelling, until I spluttered and Mother urged him to stop. When he did, he was breathing heavily and his face was flushed.

Another time I had made a little friend named Timothy, and we'd played in the hotel grounds together. Timothy had guns that fired caps, friction-driven racing cars and a cowboy outfit; I had a hoop that could be rolled along the ground with a stick. Timothy's parents showered on him the usual seaside treats: fish and chips, sticks of rock, outsized lollipops, the sort of fripperies of which Father disapproved. He actually mocked up candyfloss using cotton wool and a stick, so that I could wander the promenade without looking neglected of confectionery to passers-by.

Whenever tension arose between myself and Father, I would retreat into Mother's bosom, where she would silently stroke my hair. He taunted me as "Mummy's boy", which seemed to him the worst of insults.

Though she sometimes dared to call him Humphrey, he always referred to her as 'Mother'. I was knocking on puberty before I discovered she had a name, too: Mildred. (There had been an awkward moment during one school holiday, when I had been unable to sleep and had overheard my parents indulging in what I imagined was a rare night of passion. In between rhythmic squeaking, Father had clearly said, "Not there, Mildred".)

I knew nothing about their past together, because the subject was off-bounds. What drew them together, I could only assume, was the attraction of opposites. What had possessed such a stiff, soulless couple to adopt a child, I doubted I would ever know.

Nameless Highway, Monday, 6.00pm:

Importos had been tapping repeatedly on my bonce, and when I stopped he informed me that he needed a wee. As he loped off to the side of the tarmac, grumbling to himself, I noticed that Dextrose's face was looking rather red, and I wondered whether I shouldn't have left it angled directly towards the sun.

Panicking mildly, I found an oily rag among the ancient toolkit beneath the saddle, soaked it in water and laid it over his face. Once I could no longer see his damaged skin, I felt much better.

"I been to zink of my bruzzer," said Importos, when he had concluded his business.

"Uhuh?" I replied warily.

"When he to call Importos, say I to help Senor Alexander, he to tell will call also Gossip, for to say OK. This call, it does not happen…"

"Maybe he's just not near a phone?" I suggested, quelling a facial tic.

"Maybe," said Importos.

I could tell that he wasn't convinced.

Nameless Highway, Monday, 7pm:

The sky had changed colour, from the watery blue of a baby's eyes to the red of blood dripped in water; the deepening tones of the sand and the sky merged almost as one. The sun was directly behind us but I was keen to witness its setting, so turned the bike 180, switched off the engine and sat there in silence. I believe even Importos was taken aback, because he too said nothing.

Clouds had appeared in strata above the horizon, in so many burnt orange hues. I stared at the sun, unable to resist its lure, until its white glow became tinged with blue and it seemed suddenly to become a perfectly circular window, through which one might gaze into the outer reaches of space. Focused thus, my mind expanded. It might have been the end of the world we were witnessing.

The sun dipped gradually further, the sky turning shades of purple, until just the tip of an arc of whiteness remained, then the lights went out. Importos exhaled a whistle.

In that moment I was aware just how insignificant we were, we humans perched on a pebble among the heavens.

Nameless Highway, Monday, 9.00pm:

I had been driving in a trance, locked into the dim thrown cone of light of our wonky old headlamp. Above us the sky was pitch black, and I had never seen stars shine so intensely; indeed, I'd had no idea that there were so very many of them. Occasionally, in the periphery of the headlamp's glow I spotted a spiny blotch of vegetation, as if there might be actual features among the landscape, this far along the Nameless Highway. Once, I swore I saw two pinprick glows up ahead that turned to black and were gone – perhaps the first sign of animal life?

Dextrose remained unconscious, Quench's potion having more than done the trick, and I encouraged myself to believe that we'd kidnapped and drugged him for his own good.

By my reckoning, we were tantalisingly close to First Stop when suddenly the engine coughed violently. The bike juddered, the noise ceased and we ground to a halt. According to the petrol gauge the tank was full, which was impossible. Its pointer had previously languished either at zero or full, nowhere in between, perhaps offering an expression of the machine's mood rather than the fuel situation in its tank. Ignoring it, I faced the fact: we had run out of petrol.

No panic. Quench (again) had foreseen the prospect and had lashed to the rear of the sidecar a jerry can of petrol.

As I climbed off the bike, Importos cursed in his native tongue before demanding to know, "Is zere yet?" His voice emerged crystalline from the silence, then was obliterated by the vast emptiness.

"Shhh!" I replied, and in a hoarse whisper, "You'll wake Dad!" The longer he slumbered, the easier our progress would be. Indeed, I was absolutely dreading him waking.

It was pitch black around the back of the bike, which made finding and removing the spare fuel can – as quietly as possible – tortuous. However, I managed it eventually, while Importos monitored me as if he were conducting a time and motion study.

As I filled the petrol tank, the fuel glug-glug-glugging, quelling the urge to whistle, I swore I caught movement up ahead. Importos must have sensed it too, because he suddenly stared towards the headlamp's beam. Dust and insects were lit up in the glare as tiny random flares, like the imperfections in yesteryear's celluloid.

Neither Importos nor I dared to breathe as we directed our eyes and ears towards the hazy, dim extent of the glow, some 20 yards ahead, sensitive to the slightest movement or sound.

Stillness. Silence.

Nothing to worry about.

Pretty sure.

By millimetres I eased my fear-frozen limbs back into action and resumed filling the petrol tank, the echo sounding deeper as the volume rose, until I could tell the liquid was near to overflowing and the jerry can was half its original weight.

It was while I was reattaching the can to the sidecar that we heard it: a shuffling – as if someone were dragging a corpse. Coming from up ahead. And the sound was getting closer, travelling down the Nameless Highway towards us.

"Shit," I whispered.

"To get fucking out!" snarled Importos, through clenched teeth.

I slid my right leg over the leather seat and felt for the key.

That was when we heard it: "GBL-GBL-GBL-GBL-OINK!"

It was a sound like no other and it struck fear into my heart. "GBL-GBL-GBL-GBL-OINK!" Closer still.

And then something appeared at the far reaches of the headlamp's glare. A shape, crossing the road.

Importos' teeth chattered.

The creature was a mutation, an abomination, a sin. It had the head of a turkey, the body of a flat fish and the tail of a pig. As it moved, its fishy body curved into a wave, propelling it forward and making that disturbing dragged-corpse noise. It was big: larger in size than any of its respective elements as nature intended. I'd say it was about five feet long, three feet wide, and its head stood four feet off the tarmac. It was a monster.

Forgive my lack of artistry, but it looked a little bit like this (only far more vicious):

"W-w-what ze to fuck?" stuttered Importos.

It stopped and stared right at us, its beady eyes boring right through me as its horrible, dangly, red beard-thing wobbled like disturbed entrails.

"GBL-GBL-GBL-GBL-OINK!" it went.

Then it shuffled off the side of the road and into darkness.

The last we heard of it was its receding cry: "GBL-GBL-GBL-GBL-OINK!"

I breathed a sigh of relief and continued towards First Stop, wondering what other horrors might lurk out there.

Nameless Highway, 10.39pm:

I hadn't been able to decide whether the distant, faint lights were the headlights of another vehicle coming towards us, or stationery lights from some kind of building; such was the disorientating perspective of this strange, lonely road. But, as we drew nearer, I became convinced: First Stop.

When we pulled off the road I will admit that I had expected more: somewhere to stock up with supplies; a petrol pump, perhaps; soft-lit accommodation, in which to rejuvenate travel-sore limbs; even a caravan selling tea and burgers wouldn't have gone amiss.

Instead, First Stop comprised just one building: Socks 'N' Sandals Bar. And 'Bar' was pushing it. Socks 'N' Sandals Glorified Shack would have troubled the Trades Descriptions people less. Which isn't to say that I wasn't delighted and relieved to have made it thus far, and for the chance to unwind. I was just a tad underwhelmed.

My watch read 22:39 – prime drinking time, even in a place as remote as this, yet ours was the only vehicle out front. Was the dive even open? The lights were on in the two unusually small windows either side of the entrance, and from somewhere around the back there came the ugly moan of what I assumed to be a generator.

Importos was looking worryingly contemplative, so I tried

cheering him up.

"Looking forward to a lovely cold beer?"

He wasn't interested. "I to make phone in bar. Maybe Detritos home."

"Oh, don't worry about him. He'll be fine. He always is," I said. However, the lies were beginning to pain me. My friend was dead and there I was trying to convince his concerned brother otherwise. It wasn't healthy.

"Maybe," he replied. "I to phone. For to be sure."

I could only hope this remote hovel was unacquainted with telephony.

Dextrose remained blissfully asleep, the oily rag undulating at low frequency in time with his breathing. He would hardly want to miss a bar trip… But would such delights be in his best interests? Not remotely, I reasoned. Leave him be, let the cleansing processes of slumber continue their nursing.

Socks 'N' Sandals was constructed of vertical wooden planking, desert-dry and cracked, distressed by the sun. The entire structure looked as if it might have been washed up on a beach, years ago.

When I tried to peer through one of the windows, grab a sneak preview of what I was in for, I couldn't: it was at least a foot too high for me – some seven feet off the ground. For perhaps the first time on the trip, Importos came in useful.

"Zree men sit at bar," he reported, stooping to look.

There came a voice from inside: "Christ, mate – a floating head!"

Then another: "Where?"

By which time Importos had moved away from the window, and a third voice said, "You're seein' things, mate. You wanna lay off the sauce."

There was a pause, then a chorus of, "Nah!" then raucous laughter.

Crazy times beckoned.

I stepped inside, followed by Importos. You could have heard a zygote drop into marshmallow. Three men were on stools at a red Formica bar, with a barman behind. All hovering around middle-age, all staring at us, besides the one chap furthest away who had fallen asleep into his folded arms.

There were two tables, and built against the far wall were two cubicles, which I assumed had something to do with sanitation. Behind the bar was a single shelf, stacked with just three bottles of whisky and one with no label containing a mouthwash-green concoction. Attached to the bar were two pumps, selling the same brew: YYY. Beside the bar was a back door, which I assumed led outside, given the general dimensions.

The overall colour scheme hadn't progressed far beyond brown. It was a dingy, soulless place, the bare minimum required to dispense and consume alcohol. It smelled of booze slops and urine.

Each of the customers was wearing shorts and brown leather sandals, with knee-length socks, a short-sleeved shirt and bush hat. They were weathered and grizzly, and whoever supplied their shaving materials must have died some weeks ago.

The barman was a fat chap with chipmunk cheeks, in a filthy white T-shirt and crotch-hugging shorts. He also sported socks and sandals. I wondered which came first: the fashion statement or the name of the bar.

The burliest of the customers, nearest us, and staring with exaggerated boggle-eyes, spoke first. "What the fuck is *that*?" he exclaimed. He had a ginger beard.

Assuming he was referring to my unusually tall colleague, and anxious to present an amenable front, I began to explain. "This is my friend, Importos. He's a basket…"

He interrupted me. "Not him, mate. You!"

Everyone awake laughed (including Importos – the first time on the trip I had heard him express any emotion much above 'gloomy'). I fear I flushed.

The barman spoke next: "You're a sight for sore eyes, boys." His forearms were covered in scraggly tattoos, which looked as if they had been inked by small children during a sugar rush.

"Hold on," said the burly bloke, patting his pockets. "I got some eye lotion here somewhere!... *For sore eyes*, see?"

This time only the chap next to him, a short, untrustworthy-looking fucker, laughed. I noticed that Burly Bloke had used condoms hanging by strings from his hat brim. Had there been another hostelry within the next couple of hundred miles, I would have got back on the bike. But there wasn't.

"I'm Bri," said the barman, waving.

Burly Bloke held out a hand, then pulled it away when I stepped forward to shake it. "The name's Kai. This here," he slapped the hat off his neighbour, "is Si. And that drunken bozo passed out at the end is..."

I took my chance. "Guy?"

Blank look. "No, mate, his name's Duane."

"Where is phone?" demanded Importos.

Bri, Kai and Si laughed.

"You're joking, mate," said Bri the barman. "We don't want no one contacting us in here, and we have no desire to contact them. Not when we're drinkin'. Same reason as I built them windows too high to see through." He raised his eyes at my basketball-playing acquaintance. "At least for normal folks."

I exhaled quietly. My secret was safe. For now.

We would have pulled up bar stools, but there were only the three so we shuffled closer and stood.

"You haven't introduced yourselves, boys," said Bri.

"I'm Pilsbury," I said, flinching in advance.

"Wow!" said Bri.

"Genius!" went Si, whose mouth had dropped so far open I could see that only two front teeth occupied his lower jaw. His eyes were tiny, dark and glinting, like a rat's.

"Mate, let me shake yer hand," said Kai, this time actually doing so.

The barman's eyes had misted over. "Never come across it before. Pils. Actually named after beer..."

"It's Pilsbury, really," I said.

"Pils. Jeez. Lucky bastard," sighed Si. "And who are you, tall fella?"

"Bill," said Importos.

"Funny name for a foreigner," noted Si.

Importos glared at him so Bri said hurriedly, "What you boys having?"

"No, no, Bri, allow me." Kai motioned towards the pathetic selection of alcoholic products available and asked, "So what are you boys having?"

"That's very kind of you," I smarmed. "I'll have a pint, please."

"I too," said Importos, not yet in enough of a huff to turn down refreshment.

We stared in quiet desperation as the barman poured a succession of cool ales, first for the regulars, then for himself, and finally our own two glasses. How I had earned that.

"Cheers!" I chirped, raising my glass to the natives, who raised theirs back (except Duane, who was still asleep). I had worried that Socks 'N' Sandals' wares might be as insipid as its décor, however the hoppy, fizzy concoction really wasn't bad at all, if a little watery.

"That'll be ten eighty-six," said Bri.

"Er." I looked at Kai, but he was engrossed in a point on the bar surface.

After I had paid, and ordered a fresh round for all (cursing myself), Kai seemed to notice us again.

"How tall are you, mate?" he asked Importos.

"How stupid is you, mate?" Importos replied.

This seemed to get Kai's back up.

He stood up, all gob and beer-stain, rolling his shoulders menacingly. One of the condoms hanging from his hat swung onto his cheek and stuck there. He peeled it off. Burly as he was – reasonably over six feet tall, with biceps like large loaves – and wearing a vulpine sneer, he remained noticeably shorter than Importos. The fact must have dawned on him, for he sat down again and said in a too-loud voice: "Sciatica playing up again, boys. Must be this bloody stool. Needed a quick stretch."

Importos picked up his beer and made for one of the tables, evil-eyeing Kai all the way.

Socks N Sandals, Monday, 10:55 pm

How much closer to the middle of nowhere could I get, I wondered, as I sipped and savoured the second pint? This was proper travelling, with yours truly in the driving seat. Maybe I'd had this sort of thing in my blood all along, and it had been quashed by Father's narrow-minded parochialism? Maybe...

"You got a girl, mate?" It was Si, leering at me.

Should I lie? Upgrade Suzy Goodenough from mere 'tease'?

"Cos Kai'd fuck her!" went Si, before I could decide.

"He's not wrong, mate. I would too!" agreed Kai, assuming I required confirmation.

"He would, y'know!" laughed Si.

"I'd fuck anything!" chortled Kai.

"You'd fuck his girl's mum, wouldn't you, Kai!"

"I would!"

"He would! And her gran, right?"

"Yep. Her too, Si."

"And her gran's dog!"

"Yeah, well, I don't know about that, mate." Pause for effect. "*What colour is it?*"

Brilliant!

Kai and Si were complete morons.

There I had been, chastising my younger self for not having

the temerity to leave Glibley behind for fresh horizons; here they were – in Socks 'N' Sandals. Where did they even live? I hadn't seen any vehicles out front.

Bri plonked a fresh round of beers on the bar and threw in a bar snack for me from under the counter. "Try these," he said. "Sheep Shavings."

Crispy brown curls, of fat and singed wool, they were a lamb version of pork scratchings, my bar snack *du jour* back home, and I took to them effortlessly enough to order three more bags; two of which I jammed into my safari suit pockets for later. Stock up on supplies. Me, the seasoned explorer.

While I crunched away an awkward silence reigned, until Si piped up: "Here, Kai, tell us who else you'd fuck."

Before he could reply, I piped up: "Bumped into a really weird animal on the road earlier."

"Lot of really weird animals round here, mate," pointed out Bri. "What'd'e look like?"

I described the creature that had confronted us on the Nameless Highway, the turkey/fish/pig concoction, exaggerating how fearsome it had looked and the bravery with which I had faced it off, which seemed to suit the tenor of the place.

Kai said, "Jeez, mate, you should consider yerself lucky. That's the gobble-beaked flatpig. Only a dozen of them left in the entire country."

"How dangerous are they?" I ventured, hoping it might be generally feared and loathed.

Kai snorted. "Dangerous? The gobble-beaked flatpig? Might give yer a nasty peck I suppose, if yer got too close!"

Kai, Si and Bri laughed. Then Si said, "That's about the *least* dangerous critter we got round here. Fact, pretty much anything else out there'll bite you, eat you, poison you or make off with your kiddies."

There followed a competition between Kai, Si and Bri to recall their most death-defying animal encounter, during which I became increasingly paranoid. Spiders, snakes and birds, big cats, small cats, bears, armadillos, 'gators and the sticklebacked buggerfish. There was a tiny millipede that made its home in your ear and during winter dug towards the brain to hibernate, forming a network of tunnels in the tissue until the human host one day started dribbling and didn't stop.

There was the rat-faced house bat, which slept in crevices of homes during the day and by night would urinate in the mouths of unsuspecting sleepers, attracted by the ultrasonic tones in their snoring... which would have been bad enough, had the bat not also numbered among its favourite snacks the googleberry, which contained significant traces of cyanide.

Then there was the so-called Walt's kitten – actually a lizard from the chameleon family – which killed and skinned kittens, wrapped themselves in the fur, affected a miaow and wandered into town, preying on, ripping to shreds and devouring female shoppers susceptible to cuteness.

Naturally Kai trumped the lot. "Want to know the scariest, most psychotic creature out there?"

Bri and Si did; I didn't.

Kai went with Bri and Si. "And I lived to tell the tale, right? The twinkle-toed toad!"

There was a pause. "No way, mate!" gasped Si.

"You *met* one? *Where?*" asked Bri.

"Just out here!" declared Kai. "Right outside the back door!"

"Jesus," I mumbled, feeling the colour drain from my face.

"What happened?" asked Si.

"Maybe save that story for another day?" I suggested.

"Well," began Kai. "I'd nipped out the back door to get away from Si, who can be quite boring."

"I can't!" protested his alleged buddy.

"Trust me, mate, you can. Anyway, I'd nipped out back, grab some fresh, take in the stars, and I think to meself, might as well take a piss."

Bri and Si nodded.

"So I've flopped out the old man, gushing away, and I can swear I hear this scuffling. So I stop the flow and listen. Nothing. Start again. Scuttle. Stop. Listen. Nothing. Now I'm getting nervous, but I've started so I'll finish, if you know what I mean?"

We did.

"So I'm holding the old man with one hand and fumbling for me torch with the other. I'm thinking everything's OK cos the scuttling sound's stopped. But just to be on the safe side, I turn on the torch – and I spot it straight away…"

"Hopping up your piss stream?" suggested Si.

"Hopping up me piss stream! Like your twinkle-toed toad is wont to do."

I will admit I was caught up in the tale. "Is that bad?" I asked, despite knowing the answer.

"Is that *bad*? Is that *BAD*?" went Kai, exchanging glances with Bri and Si. "Mate, have you any idea what would have happened if that toad had reached me old mucker?"

I shook my head mutely.

"Mate, here's how the twinkle-toed toad works. It hops up unsuspecting blokes' piss streams, as previously discussed. When it's got to the top, it flicks its tongue into the little hole and there's a teeny-tiny barb on the end of its tongue, so it sticks there. Then, slowly but surely, it pulls its way into your old man."

My crotch region shrunk for cover. "How big is it?"

"Bit personal – *eh, boys?*" quipped Kai.

I was in no mood for frivolity. "The toad, I meant."

"Yeah, I knew that, mate. I'm not an idiot," he kidded himself, before addressing Bri and Si. "How big would you say the twinkle-toed toad is, boys?"

"About so long," suggested Bri, holding his fingertips barely a centimetre apart.

"Yeah, that's about it," agreed Kai.

I breathed out again. "That's painful, but it's not fatal, surely?"

"Mate," said Kai. "I haven't finished."

"So the toad's now pulled itself inside your old man, which – as you rightly suggested – would be bloody painful, but it might not kill yer. This is when, for reasons best known to itself, the twinkle-toed toad decides to commit harry-karry. By inflating, and inflating, and inflating its throat. Preparing for its final croak. Literally. So you're watching as the old man gets bigger and bigger and bigger – but not in a good way. Like a balloon, mate. Terrifying. And then suddenly: BANG! Your..."

But Kai never finished his sentence, because there came an almighty crash followed by a roar. We turned in unison towards the commotion, and there in the doorway was the silhouette of a man in the pose of an ogre. Hairy head down, eyes forward, muscles tensed, arms ready to strangulate, fingers shaped into claws.

"KIDNAP!" it bellowed, then stood there breathing heavily.

I knew only too well who this was. And he wasn't happy.

"What the fuck is *that*?" I heard Kai gasp for the second time that night. "Bri, get yer gun, mate! Quick!"

"No-no-no!" I yelped, raising my arms in a gesture of surrender and hurrying towards the figure in the doorway. I grabbed him by the arm and pulled him into the light. "Bri, Si, Kai – may I introduce my Dad. Mr Harrison Dextrose!"

"What. The. Fuck?" went Bri.

"Jesus," gasped Kai.

"Huh?" gulped Si.

They were no oil-paintings themselves.

Then I saw Dextrose's head and realised what they were on about. Oh, it was hideous. His previously sunburned face had erupted into a swollen mass of blisters and pustules. They covered his eyes and mouth and made a mockery of his nose. Barely a single patch of flesh one might have termed 'normal' remained. Vivid reds and purples, dotted with yellow heads, and around those billowing blisters, in all shapes and sizes, packed with rusty-coloured liquid; the one on his right cheek, just below the eye, looked a touch like a sideways map of Britain and made me feel briefly homesick. And all that... pollution, trapped within Dextrose's habitual explosion of greasy, matted, greying hair.

"He's barred!" shouted Bri, cowering.

Dextrose was staring at me, or at least his face was pointing in my direction. I could just make out one pupil, the one not obscured by sideways-Britain, blazing with righteous indignation.

"You!" he growled. "You minking mink!" A boil burst in the corner of his mouth and pus dribbled over a blister on his chin.

He hit me, hard in the face, and I went down.

The next thing I knew, I was being hauled off the floor with one hand by Kai, while Bri and Si restrained a spitting Dextrose from assaulting me further.

"Don't hurt him!" I wailed.

"Why not?" asked Bri, wheezing. "He wants to kill you!"

"He's my Dad!"

During the scuffle several of Dextrose's blisters had burst, so that his face had become more shapely, if now covered in off-white, ragged, seeping flaps of skin. His pink velour tracksuit bottoms were around his knees – at least his shirt hem overlapped his modesty – and one of his arms was bent backwards, trapped in the sleeve of his half-removed overcoat. Though he struggled and snorted, he was high on rage but low on energy, and gradually his shoulders slumped.

Finally, I heard him sigh quietly and wonder aloud, "How did it come to this?"

"You sure this is your father?" said Kai.

"You sure he's even human?" said Bri, his voice rising higher with each successive word.

I explained about the journey we had undertaken from Mlwlw and the exposure to the sun, stating that Dextrose had fallen asleep in the sidecar rather than being drugged unconscious.

The lapsed explorer did not play ball. "Minking lies!" he railed, offering a renewed but fruitless struggle. "That minker kidnapped me!"

"What's a minker?" asked Bri.

"Long story," I said.

"I still think we should throw him out," asserted Socks 'N' Sandals' patron.

"Agreed," said Si and Kai.

"I too," added Importos, from the safety of his table, having not lifted a finger to help.

But Dextrose had ceased paying attention and was sniffing the air. "I know that smell!" He inhaled with relish. "Booze! Lovely minking booze!" He swiped aside his captors, at once superhuman, flung himself at the bar, tumbled over it, landed in a heap on the other side and was up in a jiffy, pouring himself a pint. Once content with the head he walked around to the customers' side of the bar, pushed Duane off his stool and occupied it himself. Though Duane's head hit the floor with a thud, he uttered not a peep and lay at Dextrose's feet in the shape of a homicide-department outline.

Far from being appalled, Bri, Si and Kai's expressions became sunnily dispossessed.

"Hold on, fellas," went Kai. "He's only one of us!"

"So who the fuck is this?" demanded Si, pointing a twiggy finger at me.

"Yeah, go sit with your ladyfriend," snapped Kai, nodding towards Importos.

"Bloody nerve," grumbled Bri. "Taking up our valuable time like that."

Importos was tapping an empty pint glass on the table when I pulled up the chair opposite. He glared down at me with those murky green eyes. "Where my beer? Why you to buy zem beer? Zey stupid."

"They're not!" I riposted without thinking it through. Anyway, how dare he? "Why should I buy your drink? Why don't you buy your own drink?"

"Because," he said, in the tone of one addressing the intellectually challenged. "I. To. Have. No. Money."

"You mean you've come all this way *without money*?"

He shrugged. "So?"

"So I'm expected to pay for you?"

Importos looked gobsmacked. "I to come all zis way. For to help you." He jabbed me above the breast. "Is most little can to do."

"But you haven't actually helped!" I thought for a moment, hoping to speak fairly. "Besides when you looked through that window just now."

"See? I to help!"

"Well it's hardly Sherpa Tensing, is it?"

"Who she?"

I was about to become infuriated when I remembered Detritos and my lies. Could guilty parties buy off their guilt with alcohol, I wondered? In my slightly inebriated state, those cold ales having gone straight to my head, I decided it was worth a shot. "Don't worry about it," I told Importos. "What are you having?"

"I to have two beer. To say sorry."

My crimes, I suspected, would require considerably more than two.

Socks N Sandals, Tuesday, 12.10am:

Having bought another round for the entire pub, including Duane, who was quite possibly dead, I retook my seat opposite Importos, cradling four fresh ales (if Importos needed two, so did I). As Bri had poured, I had overheard Dextrose launching into that old chestnut about Nadia of Bujina, his audience already rapt.

The tall man chugged on his first pint. "When last time you to see bruzzer?"

He wasn't ever going to let it lie, as I had feared. I was going to have to tell him something to put him off the scent – but where to start? How to wheedle around Detritos's demise while making my tale seem palatable?

The facts, as I had experienced them, were these:

Detritos was a member of a worldwide network of secret agents, named Secret Heroes Ho! (SHH! for short). He had become convinced – here I stress that he was very probably delusional – that a terrorist group was plotting to fire a laser at the moon, dragging it out of earth orbit to crash into our planet, unless a ransom was paid. The dwarf had stolen the ruby at the heart of the laser, and the terrorists wanted it back. The events had culminated in a showdown beside the crater of the volcano, Monserratum.

Now, how much of that was Importos likely to believe? The dwarf had made me an honorary member of the network, complete with my own 'SHH!' button badge – still attached to my tank top, in my baggage – and as such I could hardly come out with, "Did you know that Detritos was a spy?" which didn't feel terribly Mata Hari.

No, I would have to play it subtly.

When had I last seen his brother?

"He comes and goes," I replied, then winked. "As well you know."

Importos leaned away from me. "Why you to do eye zing?" he spluttered.

Interesting, I thought: he hadn't taken my hint. Perhaps he knew nothing of Detritos's secret activities? How best to phrase such a question without giving too much away? I settled on: "What do you know of your brother's secret activities?" instantly wishing I had left out 'secret'. It struck me that I was quite drunk.

The tall man looked quite taken aback. "What ze to fuck? What zis secret active?"

That was the clincher: he knew nothing of Detritos's spying, I felt certain. So, could I now use the secretive nature of the dwarf's alleged profession to my advantage? Before I could think of a reply, however, Importos spoke to me conspiratorially: "Wait. For many time, I have zink Detritos hide from Importos somezing."

Don't reveal your hand too soon, I told myself. "Yes?"

"Zis secret active. Is very secret?"

What sort of a question was that? "Er. Yes."

"He to do in dark?"

Quite possibly. "Yes."

"He to do alone? Maybe one uzzer person?"

I had joined Detritos on his final mission, otherwise I imagined he acted alone. "Yes."

"He in, out, zen gone?"

SAS style? Pretty much. "Yes."

"He to make up name, not to use real?"

Of course! Detritos had had a codename: Green Sparrow. "That's right!"

Importos nodded sagely, grinning. "He is homosex man prostitute!"

What? *No!* "Yes!" Shit. (It had just sounded better than: "He is dead spy!")

Importos clapped his very large hands together and laughed. "Haha! Zis bruzzer, he crazy!"

I appeared to be compounding the error.

At least that seemed to appease him and he began opening up, telling me about their childhood in Green Golan. He was the elder of the two, he said. Only when Detritos was ten years old had their parents begun to accept he was unlikely to join the family business (being professional basketball).

As a result, Importos had become the golden boy and Detritos was increasingly shunned. "One Christmas," the tall man told me, "parent zey to give Importos many zing: basketball short, basketball shirt, basketball sock, basketball shoe, basketball hoop, basketball ball, television for to watch basketball, Harlem Globe Trotter calendar. Parent, zey to give Detritos leg of chair. To tell him: you to get next leg year later, and so on. Detritos very sad."

Poor bugger. Though he hadn't been overly giving himself, he had always been generous with his actions. There was no doubting that I would have been dead were it not for him. What had been his last words to me? "We beeg friend, yes?"

Yes, we had been big friends.

"Hey! Meester Alexander! Importos to tell good story. At least fucking to listen!"

"Sorry," I said. "Miles away." I noticed we had finished our drinks.

As I got up to buy more beers, I stumbled and nearly took a fall. The long day, the sun, my exertions, and now the booze, had all taken their toll. I also realised that I needed the toilet for the first time since entering Socks 'N' Sandals, no doubt a result of dehydration and the previous night's unusual diet at the feast with the Q'tse. Importos' next free beer would have to wait.

Bri, Si and Kai were lost in Dextrose's latest tale – one I recognised from *The Lost Incompetent*, concerning crewman Shark's conviction that he had seen the Holy Grail in a vision – as I hovered behind them, pathetically holding up my hand like a schoolboy, hoping to gain their attention.

"Which way's the toilet?" I asked, timidly.

Bri, Si and Kai burst into laughter as Dextrose reached one of his inevitable punchlines.

"Which way's the toilet?" I tried again, louder.

"Mink off!" snapped Dextrose, not even looking at me.

"Yeah, mink off!" went Si, turning and sneering.

"Yeah, you minker!" went Kai, to renewed guffaws.

I gave up. "I'll find it myself, shall I?"

No one replied.

Well, it couldn't be that tricky: there were only those two cubicles to choose from.

I made first for the one on the left.

"Not that one," came Bri's raised voice. "That's my room."

Did he mean that he actually *lived* here: in this crapfest, in that tiny space?

As I pulled on the wobbly door-handle of the other cubicle, I was hit by a wave of acrid fumes that made me recoil. Twin urinals, stained and leaking, side by side – fairground attractions for touristic germs – and sodden wooden flooring, nothing else. No sit-down.

Could I hold it in? I hovered for a moment and decided that I couldn't. What to do? That which had begun as a desire had elevated to desperation.

I returned to the bar and closed the door behind me, gratefully gulping in the comparatively fresher air. "Excuse me!" I said with feeling.

"*What now?*" wailed Bri, as if I had been pestering him with sanitation-based enquiries all night.

Dextrose slammed a fist on the bar, Kai put his hands on his hips and glared at me, then Si did the same.

"Is there anything more than a urinal?" I ventured.

Kai slapped his knee. "Oh that's lovely! D'y'hear that, Si? He wants to know if there's '*anything more than a urinal?*' That is priceless!"

"Yeah, that's priceless," agreed Si, slapping his knee.

Kai tapped Dextrose on the arm. "D'y'hear that, Mr Dextrose? He said he wants…"

"I heard what he minking said," growled Dextrose.

The idiot looked put out. "Yeah, well I was just going to say, you should put that in your next book. That's all."

As if there would be a next book, given the state of him. Were any member of the Dextrose family likely to document their travels, it would have to be me. In fact, I decided there and then, I might even do just that. If he could do it, I was damn well sure I could. The conviction gave me strength.

"Hilarious as my query was, I do need 'more than a urinal', so if you'd point me to the sit-down I'd be very grateful."

Kai winked at Bri. Then Bri said, "Yeah, listen, mate. I never got round to plumbing one in. So we *go* out back, if you get my drift. There's a hole out there, mate." He pointed at the back door.

Socks 'N' Sandals' patrons hooted derisively.

"Mind your pee while you poop, mate!" wheezed Kai.

"Wouldn't want you attracting one of them toads!"

I swallowed, hard, and stared at the back door.

They were all watching, stifling glee with hands to mouths, as I lifted the catch and pulled.

"Go on, mate," called out Si, the weasel. "It won't bite – *or will it?*"

The comedy genius.

I had no intention of letting them witness my nerves shredding as I wept freely, so I dived outside, slamming the door shut behind me. Instantly my heart stopped and my senses came alive.

It was quiet out there, disconcertingly so, though the dry, cool night air provided some comfort. My eyes darted from side to side, scanning what ground I could make out under the faint illumination of a crescent moon. I stood rigid, straining my ears to detect the presence of even the tiniest movement – because one thing was certain out there: I was not alone.

Any fool knows that night-time equals party time for the unconsciously inhuman. Earthly abominations on four, six, eight, ten legs and more, I feared them all. They were all going about their dastardly business under cover of darkness, smelling the air keenly, seeking person-flesh.

As I feared I imagined the sounds, so they came. A tiny footfall here, a shuffling in the sand over there, the Doppler-effected buzz of insect wings cavorting around my ears. Or was my mind playing tricks?

…What was that? Over there, perhaps a hundred yards up ahead, out into the gloom. Had that been… a scuttle? It had. What scuttles, I wondered. Rodents? Yes, rodents. Rodents with their teeth bared, rife with the diseases of carrion. Or lizards: they might easily scuttle. All nasty-scaled and venom-fuelled, with their creepy crests and pensioner-skin. *Arthropods*. The family of fuckers including the scorpion. Anything with an exoskeleton was not pissing about. Arthropods would surely scuttle.

I backed towards the door, already only a few inches away, shuddering, and marched on the spot, which kept each alternate foot off the ground for a small amount of time. My intention was to confuse ground-based attackers.

But, wait a second. Hadn't that sound been more of a scamper? It had. Hadn't it? A scamper was surely less sinister than a scuttle. Stars of Disney cartoons scampered. Yes, it had been a scamper, I convinced myself.

Hauling down a deep breath, I relaxed very slightly. Fact-wise, I hadn't actually seen anything, even with my night vision starting to kick in. I had *thought* I'd heard movement, but the sozzled paranoid mind is apt to play tricks.

Just maybe I could do my business real fast, if I found Bri's hole? "Come on!" I told myself out loud.

And then I heard the tiny, high-pitched 'Ribbit' – at least, I could have sworn I did. I'd been so worried about non-amphibians that the twinkle-toed toad had completely slipped my mind. No longer. Thumbnail-sized, the sadistic critters might feasibly have been gathering around me as I cowered in the doorway. Tens of them, perhaps hundreds, barely burrowed into the sand, only their beady eyes above the surface, gazing longingly at my fly region. 'Pull down the zip! Pull down the zip!' I imagined them urging me in toad thoughts.

Or... Sweet Jesus, what was that? Directly to my left, and close enough that I might be able to touch it. I darted my gaze towards the sound, saw nothing. There it was again! Was that... toad *frottage*?

It was the final straw.

I turned on a penny, grabbed the catch and hurled myself back through the door with such abandon that I tripped on the step and was launched into Socks 'N' Sandals, arms and legs flailing, like Gene Kelly via catapult. As my internal instrument panels went haywire and my gyros worked to right me, I heard the joyous whoops and catcalls of the guys at the bar. I burned with indignation.

Now I really had to go. The fear had exacerbated my need.

As I picked myself up off the floor, Kai taunted me: "Brought any toads in with yer, Pils mate? If yer know what I mean!"

"Yes, I know what you mean, Kai," I said. "I'll use the toilet in here, if that's OK with you?"

Bri piped up: "Hey, you can't use that if…"

I cut in: "Don't worry, Bri. The moment has passed."

It hadn't.

Inside Socks N Sandals toilet, Tuesday, 12:15am

I would have to work quickly, since Bri would be suspicious, but I had a plan.

Pulling a bag of Sheep Shavings from my jacket pocket, I emptied the contents onto the floor. Peeing into a urinal with one hand, I held the opened bag beneath me with the other, trousers around my ankles. The bodily functions were such a blessed relief that I almost failed to hear the footsteps on floorboards – someone was approaching. There was no time to think.

I dropped the filled bag into my trousers, yanked them up and was zipping up my fly as the door swung open and Bri stood in the doorway, brow furrowed, gob agape despite the smell. "Are you done yet?"

"Sure," I said, praying the bag had closed by itself. "All sorted!"

He looked down at the floor. "Where'd these Sheep Shavings come from?"

"Those?" I thought fast. "Already there when I came in."

It confused his tiny mind and he mulled it over while seconds ticked by. Finally he decided: "Yeah. Sounds reasonable."

Great. Now leave me alone. *Go!*

But Bri didn't go. With the mannered gait of a detective cross-examining suspects on sofas, he walked to the next-door urinal and began very slowly to grapple with his own fly. Though I felt sure his need was not genuine, what could I do?

So I smiled at him and edged gingerly towards the door, hoping he would not spot me mincing unnaturally. And when I sat down very gingerly opposite Importos, having exchanged nods with the chaps at the bar, wearing a fixed grin, I made sure my thighs were very far apart and just prayed I wasn't perched on anything untoward.

"Where beer?" demanded Importos. I noticed he was slurring.

How was I going to get rid of the bag?

When I failed to respond, Importos persisted: "Where beer? You to buy beer."

What if the contents were already seeping out?

"Hey!" he banged his empty glass down on the table.

It did feel warm down there, but it also felt dry. I reckoned I'd got away with it. Reached a stasis.

"I to talk!"

"Yes, I know you're to talking! Look, why don't you get the drinks for a change?" I chucked some cash at him.

He shovelled it up in his great mitts. "OK," he huffed. "Zis one only."

I could try to work the bag down my trouser leg and ditch it on the floor, like they did with all that soil in *The Great Escape*. But what if it got stuck? Or someone spotted me shaking my leg vigorously?

Importos returned with four more beers. My head swam. The alcohol, the wankers at the bar, the tension, the confusion: they were all getting to me.

I made a snap decision, rose and headed for the toilet. I'd extricate the bag and just get rid of it. Anywhere.

But Bri's voice emerged, among my swirling plans. "No you don't mate! Bog's out of order!"

I didn't even protest. I just turned on my heel and sat down.

Importos' long, happy face was there in mine, as he lofted his glass toward me. "Hey! As to say in Green Golan: 'Pingu!'" He had free beer. He was smiling.

I clinked my glass against his. "Yeah, Pingu."

"I to tell more story," he said. "You like."

Dextrose swivelled his corpulent bulk around on his stool – or rather, Duane's stool – and stared at me. I wondered what was in store: drunken abuse or the genial ranting of the contented sop?

"Come join us," he called out.

Wonders would never cease.

He swayed on the stool, reached for his glass and downed the contents. "Got some good news for yer, boy. Harrison Dextrose is preparing 'imself to forgive yer. Anyone who chauffeurs him to this gent's oasis can't be all bad." He was arseholed, so the 'this' came out more like 'thizzz'. Mind you, I was probably as bad. Like father, like son.

"Come on, boy, come and join us," he persisted. "I'll tell yer about the whorehouses of High Yawl! Priscilla Split and Phoenicia Splay! Feet on the ceiling and baby-oil by the bucket. I'll never forget 'em. Or those other ones." He nudged next-door Si in the ribs. "You're gonna minking love this one!" he told him, blinking furiously like Icarus approaching the sun.

I'd read the High Yawl story more often than I cared to remember. Good old Dextrose, rogering his way around the globe. All harmless fun. But things had changed. "You know, *Dad*" – I stressed the word though no one seemed to notice – "I do have your book. I've read it many times." (Yup, that had sounded like 'timezzz'.)

His blistered, burnt, buggered face somehow lit up. "There! See!" he announced to the room. "A fan! An' where is we? In the middle of minking nowhere. See? Can't escape 'em! Is that what yer've been after all this time, yer young codger's coccyx: an autograph?" He nudged Si again. "All he had to do were ask!"

He, Bri, Si and Kai roared with laughter, as if a fabulous joke had been cracked.

Over the din, I tried to explain: "No, *Dad*, I don't want your autograph. I want..." But it was pointless. He had lost interest.

Importos reached across the table and enveloped me in an extensive hug, smelling of ale, sweat and manliness. "You friend!" he announced.

In my alcoholic haze I decided I was warming to him, though he went on to dominate the conversation. He told me how Detritos had left home at 16, neglected by his parents and dejected, though the two brothers had supported and loved one other. In the ensuing years their contact had been only sporadic, as the dwarf wandered about the globe finding work and solace here and there.

Importos still lived at home with his parents – I sensed he was a bit of a mummy's boy – and Detritos returned only rarely, always unannounced, and would flit away unnoticed in the wee hours of a morning.

By that stage of the tale we were on a fresh set of pints. Importos' nose was running and he started banging on about basketball. After a while his hoop-based monologues entered my one ear, wandered around listlessly for a while, humming to themselves, then exited through the other.

I do remember one of his stories, about some coach who came to town to look after his team, Los Desperados, then made poor decisions and the community turned against him, though it all turned out fine in the end when they won some trophy or other. For some reason my memory chose to store the coach's name. It was Dale. Norman Dale.

And so that early morning in Socks 'N' Sandals wore on.

With each successive gulp of frothy, lovely beer Importos' voice washed further over me, undulating with echo, like a film soundtrack slowed down, as shapes blurred and mingled before my eyes, and the beers came and went.

Until something disturbing occurred, which threatened to shatter the mood: Importos suddenly turned on me, out of nowhere.

Banging his fist on the table he snarled, "Importos to have friend. Bad friend. Yes? Senor Alexander to get?"

I fumbled to make sense of him. "Sorry? What?"

"You is to know!" he snapped. "You is to keep off somezing of bruzzer. Importos to know, yes?" He went to tap his temple but missed.

"I don't know what…"

But there was no stopping him. "You to know bad people to do people, zey to lie?" His words rather rolled into one, making him even harder to understand than normal. But when he made a slashing motion with a finger across his throat, unfortunately pulling that gesture off, I understood only too well. "They to kill. Senor Alexander to get?"

I did. But my mind was just too addled to let it properly sink in. I tried to assume that booze had got the better of him, made him aggressive and that he was talking rubbish.

I sought to placate him the only way I knew. "You wan' another beer?"

"Is. Worse. Free. Holiday. Ever," he replied, then nodded.

My final awareness of that night appeared in a snapshot: I was being carried over someone's shoulder, my head swinging, my stomach compressed. Though I tried to say something, unconsciousness retook me.

Disorientation:

When consciousness returned, my addled mind registered a heavy downward force, around the small of my back. It lifted then came again, accompanied by a grunt and stinking fumes. What the hell was happening?

I forced open gummy eyes. Darkness.

My right cheek was pressed into rough material and my arms were stretched down by my sides. I was on my front and – I felt for the safari suit with fingertips, but found only flesh – my trousers were down. Startled, I gasped, "*What th…*"

A rough, greasy hand clamped over my mouth.

I panicked and struggled, but was pinned down by a hand between my shoulders. I couldn't move.

A voice came: "Let's keep this between ourselves, eh, mate?" accompanied by more fumes. Kai's voice.

I tried to get my head around the situation. I realised what was *meant* to be happening. But it wasn't, I could tell. And I would have known.

So what the hell *was* happening?

Kai again, from above, the words slopping against each other: "Mate, I'm sorry." Drunk as a skunk. "I couldn't help it."

Clearly *he* thought he was doing *it*. But I would have felt it. And I couldn't, not that.

There was *something* going on, a short distance down my legs, between my thighs. A slick sensation, coming and going.

Was that rubber I could feel? Couldn't be. In that state Kai had more chance of trapping a goblin under a hat than he did of putting on a condom.

My head was throbbing, I was horrified and confused. What was Kai doing, if not perpetrating something very wrong? Then I heard it, very faintly, each time he wobbled up and down. A crinkling sound. And it dawned on me slowly what that sound was.

It was the sound of that Sheep Shavings packet, the one I'd been forced to store down my trousers.

He was only toing and froing inside a bag of shite.

I let out a snort, which disappeared into his hand and which he must have misinterpreted as something approaching ardour, because he bent down and growled into my ear, "Nice, ain't it?"

I tried to protest otherwise, but only "Nm ntth nt" emerged from behind his clamped hand. "Ltt be gnn!" I struggled, but could not move.

Kai was too strong and too heavy.

"Look. If I let yer gob go, you promise not to shout?" He was breathing heavily, in short, sharp bursts.

I managed a semblance of a nod.

"Right," he said, and allowed the merest gap between his palm and my mouth. When I uttered no noise he pulled his hand away further, still methodically pumping up and down.

"Where am I?" I whispered hoarsely. Though I had a headache like a bullfight in progress and could taste my booze history in the back of my throat, Kai was by necessity sobering me up.

"You passed out, mate. I carried you into Bri's room, put you on his bed. Then I sneaked back later. Hnnnn. Couldn't help it."

"So they don't know?"

"Mate, they don't know where *they* are."

That was more than a relief. I definitely didn't want this to get out.

I wondered: "Are you…"

He made an unattractive hawking noise. "Sorry, missed that."

"Are you… you know?"

"What… A gay? Christ no! Fucking fairies. Fuck off! Gnnnth. Are you?"

"No, as it happens."

"You take what you can get out here. Jeez it gets lonely."

"Right."

"Yeah, that's what I – uuuuch – thought."

Part of me hated him, a dafter part felt sorry for him. Both parts wanted him off me. If only I could get him back for this… "How desperate have you got? Mate? You know, sex-wise?"

He stopped pumping. "Hoho, mate! I couldn't!" But he was thinking about it. "Alright, if you go first."

"I fucked a gerbil once." (I hadn't.)

He fell on top of me, wheezing more than laughing. His breath was an abomination and I had to burrow my nose in the blanket. "Mate! Jeez! I thought I was bad, but you're the man, mate!"

I extracted my nose for long enough to blurt out, "So what have you done?"

He hoisted himself up and started again. "Nnnnf. Well, I've got this leatherette settee at home and whenever I…"

"Right, that'll do," I snapped. "Would you mind getting off me, please?"

He sounded taken aback. "What, is it…"

"Yes, it is a bit much, actually."

"Jeez, I'm sorry, mate, I had no idea."

"It's fine, just please, get off."

He did so with a self-satisfied, "Aaaaaaaah," and was gone.

I repositioned my attire, made sure I left the Sheep Shavings bag on Bri's bed, and marched out into the main room. It was carnage out there.

There were glasses all over the bar, some upright, some fallen, some broken, almost all empty, with shards of glass all over the floor (as well as Duane). Dextrose was talking complete garbage to Si, who had fallen asleep in the palm of his hand, propped on the bar. Bri was unconscious, only his head visible, jammed between the two beer pumps. Across the room, Importos lay sprawled face down across the table, having swiped aside the containers of everything we had drunk. Which, judging by the broken glass on the floor, was plenty.

Kai had regained his stool and was perched there precariously, swaying from one of its legs to another, trying to grasp a half-full pint in front of him but missing each time.

No one noticed me.

I strode over to Importos, kicking the glass aside, hoping he might not be too much of a handful having at least slept, and with so much body available to soak up the booze. He was snoring, which had caused a dome of frothy bubbles to form in the dregs around his nose.

"Oi, wake up!" I told him, pushing his hunched form.

No reaction.

I tried again.

"Qué? Please. No. To help," he burbled, looking up. Half of his face had gone wrinkly through sitting in liquid.

"We're leaving," I said.

"No-no-no." He slumped back onto the table.

"Yes-yes-yes," I averred, tugging at his basketball shirt. "And you're going to have to help me move *that*," I added, pointing at Dextrose.

Outside Socks N Sandals, Tuesday, 6.45 am:

Harrison Dextrose had remained stubbornly immovable, literally stuck to his stool, until I had promised him that we were heading for a different bar. Immediately he had dived for the door, but had tripped over Duane and fallen flat on his face, leaving interestingly shaped shards of glass embedded in his already disfigured flesh. I felt little pity for him and he felt no shame.

Importos and I took an arm each and dragged him across the floor, then bundled him outside, where he lay, snorting up sand.

Importos flopped down beside him. "To fuck zis for game of soldier."

We couldn't possibly lift Dextrose up, to feed him feet-first into the sidecar, so we pushed him in headfirst instead, confident he would not notice. Indeed, within seconds, the tinny echo of his deep-sleep mumbles could be heard.

The sun had already risen, a flushed-red orb hovering above our unseen destination, at the far end of the Nameless Highway. The landscape around now lit up, I could make out actual vegetation, albeit occasional scraggy-looking trees dotted about the sands, isolated and friendless. Up ahead and to the right of the road, contours appeared on the horizon, adding promise to the monotonous flatness. To crown it all, I heard birdsong. Just the one bird and, despite the barren landscape, I couldn't spot it, but it was there, and it sounded optimistic.

One final task.

"Wait here," I told Importos, and left him cradling his head in his hands, moaning at his lap.

Back inside Socks 'N' Sandals, I was amazed to find Duane up and about, busying himself with a broom, whistling.

"Hello, mate," he chirped. "What can I do for you?" Perhaps he was staff? His outfit was drenched and clung to him in funny places, and his hat was upside-down on his head.

Bri and Si remained as I had left them, and Kai, too, had succumbed to slumber, entrenched on his stool.

"WAKEY WAKEY!" I hollered

It certainly took Duane by surprise, as he ducked down and covered his head with his hands, as if under attack by something airborne. In doing so he discovered the upside-down hat, inspected it with quaint surprise and, on the verge of chastising it, nestled it onto his bonce as the milliner had intended.

Meanwhile, Bri, Si and Kai were shaking their heads – Bri extricating his from between the pumps and rubbing his jaws tenderly – and looking generally startled.

I held the door open with one hand, let natural light flood in, hoping that would confuse them into lasting consciousness.

"I have something to tell you all," I said. "I hope at least one of you remembers it."

Duane put up his hand. "I will!"

"Good work, Duane," I acknowledged. Had he been more lucid during my stay, I reckoned we might have got on.

"Wha'd'you want?" moaned Si, audibly pained.

"Ready?" I asked. "Kai fucks furniture."

My words echoed around the wooden hovel and were sucked up into the damp patches.

To ensure it had sunk in, I added: "Kai told me he makes love to his leatherette settee."

Bri looked more concerned with his jaw. But Duane appeared suitably put out and Si managed to slap Kai's side and wail, "Jeez, mate, I've sat on that sofa. Loads of times!"

As I turned to depart, Kai's voice came: "Two things, mate…"

He was peering at me over bags the colour of biblical storms. "Two things, mate," he said again. "One. I checked over the old man after our… chat. And – how do I put this delicately? – you need to brush up on your personal hygiene, mate. And two. There is no twinkle-toed toad. Made him up. Gotcha – hook, line and sinker! Now fuck off!"

Nameless Highway, Tuesday, 9 am.

People normally ride off into the sunset. I was doing the opposite: heading for the sunrise. The tarmac shimmered and the light glared off it, resulting in my permanent squint.

Elements of the previous night kept returning to me, just when I needed them least, and I hummed favourite songs to myself to ward off the memories. A smattering of Pink Floyd, some Galaxie 500, David Bowie. Then bastard *Agadoo* became lodged in there and would not shift, no doubt as its cursed writers had intended.

Even that was preferable to reliving Kai's attentions.

Importos was a dead weight on my back and shoulders, his head resting on top of mine, like we were some sort of totem pole. The first time I braked, for no reason other than boredom, he went flying off the back, having omitted to hold on, and was knocked unconscious on the road surface. I had to turn the bike around to retrieve him. While I tended to him with water and apologies, Dextrose's legs and arse remained sticking out of the sidecar, occasionally twitching, though nothing more energetic.

When I had revived him, Importos rubbed the back of his head vigorously. His dark hair, once shiny with unguents and grease, was grey with dust and windborne particles. His long face was longer than ever and his mood seemed dark. I recalled his drunken threats and hoped they were idle.

"Why weren't you holding on?" I asked gently.

"Because to try sleep!" Then he cursed in his own tongue.
"You're trying to sleep – *on the back of a motorbike?*"
"Where you to say do zen?"

He had a point. The only one of us managing their reasonable quota of shut-eye was Dextrose, through no design of his own. Or perhaps his lifestyle was all based on elaborate forward-planning, rather than the haphazard hedonism it appeared to be?

An idea came to me. The lapsed explorer was not minor of girth. We could ransack his belongings for a belt, to fasten around myself and Importos. Then, should I brake, provided I could take the strain, we would both remain on the machine.

It seemed like a reasonable idea.

I unstrapped Dextrose's mock-leather suitcase and undid the restraining buckle while bottles inside tinkled. It was strange to hold the artefact in my hands. Had that case travelled the world with him? Had it seen all the sights he had seen?

There was a crumpled old cardboard label tied to the handle and I wondered what secret it might reveal. Perhaps an airline destination – even Dextrose's home address?

Instead, it read: 'Woolworths £2.99'.

I pushed the buttons and the two catches thunked up. Importos moved closer, as anxious as I to peer inside.

Now, bearing in mind that Dextrose's recommended packing list had appeared in *The Lost Incompetent*, and included such genuinely essential items as: clothing, sleeping bag, compass, billy-can and first-aid kit, I detected a faint whiff of hypocrisy when I opened his own case and found nothing but bottles of beer and whiskey. I had expected to find something useful, even a spare pair of socks would have been a start – certainly not just booze. Even assuming a well-meaning, loyal Quench had packed for him, the conclusion was inescapable: it represented the extent of Dextrose's fall from any form of professionalism.

He had on him what he was wearing, and I hoped those overcoat pockets were deep, because if he had come without money we weren't going to be flying home to Britain once we had recovered Mrs Dextrose.

He had to buck up his ideas, and I knew where to start.

"Here, Importos," I said, "grab a couple of those bottles. We're going to empty them into the sand."

Despite his hangover, he must have rumbled the excessive spontaneity of the idea. "No-no-no," he said. "Head to pain now, no later. We to keep. I to need"

However, I was in no mood for arguing and picked out two bottles of finest Irish whiskey, walked out into the sand, threw one down beside me, unscrewed the top off the other and began pouring. Golden liquid glug-glug-glugged into the silica grains and I smiled with satisfaction.

Casting the empty aside I unscrewed the other bottle's cap...

It was as if he had smelled the fumes, even as he slept. A great hollow bellow of rage came from within the tin-can sidecar and I turned to see Dextrose's fat little legs kicking furiously in his pink togs, as if the anti-Santa had become trapped down a chimney.

"NO YER DON'T, YER MINK!" he raged, hollow-sounding, scrabbling furiously to push himself out of the compartment. "DON'T YER MINKIN' DARE!"

Then, unexpectedly, he fell silent. All anyone around would have heard would have been the dainty 'blibble-ibble-ibble ibble-ib' of the final dregs of booze departing their bottle.

Next came a blood-curdling scream. It was terrible to hear. Genuine dread.

"GETUSOUTOFHERE!" he wailed, redoubling his frantic efforts to release himself. But he was well jammed in and his general lack of fitness and blubber-buggered centre of gravity did him no favours.

Importos made a break for it, jogged up the road and sat on the kerb, where he began rocking backwards and forwards. It left me, grabbing handfuls of overcoat, to heave Dextrose out of his hellhole.

He sat up and pointed towards the sidecar. "E-e-e-e-evil," he stammered.

"What is it?" I asked.

"E-e-e-e-evil," was all he could utter.

I fully expected something to crawl out over the rim of the sidecar. Something crested or poisonous. We waited for full minutes, but nothing did.

Dextrose curled into a ball and lay on his side in the sand, sucking his thumb. Once again, it would be down to me to take charge. I couldn't pretend that the idea appealed.

I needed a weapon and had an idea. Crawling close to the ground, as I had seen SAS types do in movies, I returned to Dextrose's suitcase and slipped out the last two bottles of whiskey. He made no move to stop me. That's how shaken he was.

Rising to my feet I smashed the bottles together, sending broken glass flying and showering myself in booze. I heard Dextrose whimper, but that was the extent of his protest. What the hell was in that sidecar?

I strode manfully forward at first, then thought better of it and began crawling like a baby. The metal panelling was so hot to the touch that I could not press my ear against it, so instead I pricked up my ears and listened intently. Not a peep.

Must be something small and deadly, I imagined, clutching the broken bottles as Evel Knievel must have gripped his handlebars.

The longer I stayed there, the likelier I was to be attacked, so I knew I had to go for it. Up, peek, down.

What had I registered in that split second? Just a battered old leather seat (empty) and the gloomy depths of the sidecar.

Nothing had attacked me and that, at least, gave me heart. Perhaps Dextrose had imagined the horror or had woken from a nightmare?

I rose again, slower this time, and peered over the sidecar's rim, deep into the shadows. Then I too saw it.

Yelping, I pushed myself away and landed on the ground. Even as that happened I realised what I had seen.

Reaching down into the footwell with fingertips I just managed to grab hold of a leg. I dragged out the 'evil' and held it aloft.

Dextrose shielded his face in fear, but gradually realised his folly. "What the mink is that?" he asked.

"It's the Shaman's dummy," I said.

It all came flooding back. I had stolen the dummy in retribution and had lobbed it into the sidecar. Presumably, when I crashed, it had been sent flying forward into that dark recess. So it had been there all along, obscured to Dextrose by his gut – until he'd gone in head-first.

His footprints were all over the dark dinner suit, the top hat was missing – probably crumpled somewhere in the sidecar – the cracked glass had fallen out of its monocle frame, which remained suspended by string from the breast pocket, its face was dirtied and its nose had been knocked off. Yet, even with those injuries, it retained the power to unnerve.

Dextrose heaved himself up, dusted himself down, and said: "Get rid of it."

He was right. That *thing* carried with it all manner of bad karma. I clutched the dummy by one of its scrawny arms and tossed it as far as I could into the sands. It flew like laundry and, being so defiantly unaerodynamic, didn't travel very far, although it did land in a satisfying heap with one leg sticking up like a makeshift gravestone. And that was the end of that.

"Right, now yer can take us back to Gossips," said Dextrose.

Why hadn't I seen that coming? "But... Dad. You do know where we're going, don't you?"

"Does I look like Einstein?" he shot back.

The hair, yes. The rest of him, no. He looked fucking terrible, like something you'd discover under rubble after a nuclear war.

"We're trying to find your wife."

He didn't seem to recognise the concept, so I added, "Mrs Dextrose."

He shook his head. "Some other time."

Not now, not after how far we'd come. "No," I said. "We have to go." It was time I stood up to him.

He reached into a tweed overcoat pocket, pulled out a pistol and levelled it at me.

"I said. Some. Other. Minking. Time."

I studied the gun: an ancient-looking silver, chipped revolver, long-barrelled, perhaps a relic of the Wild West. Though still potentially deadly. Had I known he was armed, I would never have brought him with me.

I forced myself to remain calm. "Where did you get that?"

He shrugged. "Found it just then, in me pocket. Seem to recall one of them hop-sozzled cud-munchers in that bar giving it us, once I'd told them what a devious woman's mind you possessed. Pilsbury – us own flesh and blood an' all."

Wow. First time he'd remembered who I was unprompted. But he was all show, surely? He wouldn't use it. No chance, not even him, deprived of alcohol and home comforts, kidnapped, brutalised by the elements, dragged through broken glass...

I didn't dare risk it.

So that was it, then. The game was up. I was returning to Gossips and Mrs Dextrose would remain lost forever... Could I somehow disarm him, I wondered? Given his creaking reactions? Then again, could I disarm anyone?

"OK, you win," I said. "But I wish you'd reconsider. We've done enough drinking. We should find Mrs Dextrose."

A thought flitted across his eyes. "Not today." He waved the gun at me. "Get in the sidecar. I'll drive."

Having turned the bike around to pick up Importos, I didn't have the heart to tell him he was going the wrong way when he swung it 180 with an uncharacteristic whoop. As any budding mathematician will tell you, two negatives make a positive.

"Mr Dextrose, can we pick up Importos?" I asked, as we reached the tall man.
"EH?" He couldn't hear me over the engine.
"CAN WE PICK UP IMPORTOS?"
"WHO?"
Hardly spoilt for choice. "HIM SULKING AT THE SIDE OF THE ROAD."
"WHY?"
"BECAUSE OTHERWISE HE'LL DIE OUT HERE."
I couldn't have the demise of both brothers on my conscience.
Dextrose stopped the bike but kept the engine running.
"Hop on," I told Importos.
"No. He mad," he replied, and started jogging away.
I called after him: "I don't think he meant it."
Importos only jogged faster.
We caught him up again.
"You'll die of thirst," I pointed out.
He slowed down then stopped, glaring at me with intent. His basketball outfit was sand-stained and distressed. Sweat poured off his forehead.
I tapped Dextrose. "DAD, CAN WE STOP, PLEASE?"
He did so. Not only that, but I had referred to him as 'Dad' in a very loud voice and he'd neither snorted nor denied the association. More than that, I had developed the confidence unselfconsciously to do so.
While Importos took on liquid, Dextrose turned to me.

Though it was hard to tell, in a face that looked like four-cheese pizza, I fancied he was trying his damndest to look tender. "Pilsbury," he said. "Back there. I wouldn't have minking shot yer."

Now that, I thought, is proper parenting.

Nameless Highway, Tuesday, ① ⓪ ② ⑤ am:

The bike spluttered, shuddered and ground to a halt. Once again we were out of fuel. One half-can remained, which would just about fill her up. Then that was it. Death in the wilderness: a lonely business. I assumed – prayed – we would hit a petrol station soon.

Dextrose offered to attend to the tank and was as jovial as I had ever seen him. I couldn't help being suspicious. Had he a hip flask secreted in one of those deep pockets? I certainly hadn't noticed him taking surreptitious slugs, nor had he touched the beers in his suitcase, now reattached to the machine.

There was but one conclusion: that he was quite simply happy to be heading back to his good friend Quench. (Or so he thought.)

Yes, I did feel guilt, but some people need to be dragged kicking and screaming (or blindly) towards the path of righteousness. It was enough for now to see him smile, even if that did resemble more of a wonky, scabbed-over gash. We were family of sorts.

About to remount our replenished steel steed, Dextrose still commandeering the controls, I felt a hand clench tight around my wrist. It was Importos, blocking out the sun.

"More Importos to zink, more he to zink Senor Alexander to lie."

He bloody knew. Of course he did. I just stood there, mute,

trying to adopt an expression of innocence.

He went on: "Next time to stop, Importos to call zis bad people. Zey to find bruzzer. Senor Alexander to pray not to lie. Yes?" Then he grabbed me by the throat.

The next thing, his hand was swiped away and Dextrose was there between us.

"Who is this minker?" he said to me.

"It's Importos, Dad," I said. That guilt hit me once again. "He's a friend."

"Funny minking sort of friend," he pointed out.

Importos squared up to him, resembling an altercation between Little and Large. "What is problem, fat man?"

As far as I was aware, I was the only person to witness Detritos' final moment. Only I knew for certain that he was dead. So I was safe, surely?... Unless I allowed paranoia into the equation, when all sorts of unlikely though quite feasible options kicked in. What if we had been watched? What if Detritos had left details of his whereabouts with someone? Or SHH! had equipped him with some sort of tracking device? On the positive side, Importos' bad friends would have a job tracking me down, since the dwarf's brother knew me only as Alexander, not by my new name.

"D'yer want us to shoot him, Pilsbury?" asked Dad.

Brilliant, I thought. Had he never seen *Dad's Army*?

"No! God no! Haha!" I slapped the tall man's back in a lame all-guys-together gesture. "It's just a misunderstanding. Isn't it, Importos?"

Importos shot me a dark look. "Who to know? Importos to make phone after stop. We to see, yes?"

The air had turned sinister.

Nameless Highway, Tuesday 11.33am:

Having been excited for quite a while, as I watched the approach of another vehicle – the first to pass us on that desolate, endless stretch of tarmac – my tenterhooks were wantonly uprooted when we were finally passed by what turned out to be a farm truck, a rusty old contraption with three tatty chickens in the back. The driver – male, 60s, corn-cob pipe, hat – stared directly ahead as he did so, though I waved and reached across to toot the horn. I could only assume he rode the Nameless Highway as a matter of course and vowed never again to become excited about other traffic.

Nameless Highway, Tuesday, noon:

Around noon, Dextrose started to ask questions.

Why hadn't we passed Socks 'N' Sandals yet (he didn't know its name; in fact, he called it, "that hick-infested leper colony", but I knew what he meant)?

How far away was it? And how far from that would Mlwlw be?

The ace up my sleeve was the fact that he had been out cold, so would be none the wiser. In reply I exaggerated loosely: "Took a fair few hours. Don't worry, we'll get there!"

As luck would have it, moments later something black appeared up ahead in the distance and I was able to fib gratuitously: "There, bet that's Socks 'N' Sandals."

I was hoping desperately that it would be a petrol station.

Not long afterwards the sky changed colour bewilderingly suddenly. One moment it was all's-well-with-the-world Delftware-blue, the next the clouds had converged above us, like opposing armies meeting on a battleground. Electrical in nature, they pressed the air down onto our heads until we could sense it. The sun faded to grey and the world descended into gloom.

We actually saw the rain coming. A curtain of torrential drops appeared before us and we drove into it, as if entering a waterfall, covering our heads and laughing – even Importos. It was an exhilarating experience.

In milliseconds, my safari suit was sodden and clinging to my skin. I raised my face to the heavens and let their contents pour over me, wash away the dust and grime and all the tribulations of the past. Rolling up my sleeves, I used the liquid's chill as a salve on my sunburnt skin. Water collected quickly in the bottom of the sidecar; many miles away lightning strikes lit clouds up and the thunder rolled in.

Visibility dropped considerably, until I could see but 50 yards in any direction. Either side of the Nameless Highway the sand had darkened and become an extensively pitted paste, each tiny pit the grave of a raindrop.

"HOW MUCH LONGER TO THAT BAR?" called out Dextrose over the downpour's din, overcoat tails flapping behind him. His silvery curls had been battered down flat. The rain poured through them, transferring via his sideburns to his beard, which had turned pointy; the water flowed from it with the ferocity of a much-needed piss. I wondered how many tiny critters were being washed right out of his hair as it did so. He blinked repeatedly as the rain smacked into his eyes, and his sudden cleanliness only exacerbated how damaged his face was.

Poor bugger.

"NO IDEA!" I replied. "SOON!"

He nodded, smiled, turned to face back into the driving rain; the speedometer needle dared to flicker into 41.

However, despite Mother Nature's cleansing efforts, my thoughts remained troubled. Those manifold lies would catch me up, sure as dogs were dogs, and then there would be hell to pay.

Nameless Highway, Tuesday, ①:③⑤ pm:

My emotions were decidedly mixed when I spotted the short signpost – the first in several hundred miles:

**Lonely Bush
Gas Station
1km ahead
Can't miss us!**

Dextrose must have seen it, too, as he scowled at me. No, that wasn't Socks 'N' Sandals. And yes, they probably would have a phone that Importos could use.

I had to tell Dad the latest porky. "OH YES!" I shouted. "NOW I REMEMBER PASSING THAT ON THE WAY OUT!"

What else could I say? I would have to string him along for as long as possible, and hope that the truth dawned on him while he was in a very good mood. The prospect made me shudder.

"ANYWAY, WE NEED TO FILL UP! PRETTY HANDY, REALLY. WE WERE IN DANGER OF…" Shut up, you fool, stop talking! He was lost in thought anyway, no doubt weighing up the likeliness of my story.

Importos had retreated into himself. Not a word in miles, no doubt pent-up and brooding.

The Lonely Bush Gas Station comprised a two-storey red-brick house with a wooden shack tacked onto the front, serving as the cashier's office. There was one pump, Art Deco-style in faded turquoise, with pleasing curves and a recumbent white oval perched on top. This may once have been lit from inside, but no longer, with the word GAS painted on it in a kitsch typeface. It was covered by a corrugated-plastic awning on four rusty poles. Out front was a single, lonely bush. Elsewhere: sand, drenched.

As we reached the forecourt, the eye of the storm hit us and the time between lightning flash and thunder clap became negligible. A shadowy figure lurked in the doorway of the office, sheltering from the storm, monitoring our arrival. It was a scene straight out of an old B-movie.

Dextrose guided us beneath the awning, parked the bike beside the pump and turned off the engine. All we heard was the insistent patter of rain on plastic. It was a relief to escape the bombardment.

Just as I was climbing out of the sidecar a vivid flash appeared to my right, accompanied by crashing thunder that battered the eardrums. I physically jumped from the shock. Lightning had hit the lonely bush, which was now ablaze.

"Don't worry about that," came a voice. "Happens every time. We'll plant a new one tomorrow. Always do." The figure in the doorway.

He stepped towards us, rain instantly tumbling off the brim of his ancient pink baseball cap. He was in his mid-70s, I reckoned, thin-faced, with little round spectacles and silver sideburns, but very dark eyebrows. A black jacket covered his denim overalls and for some reason he was carrying a pitchfork. He looked doleful, perhaps understandably.

"Petrol, please!" I said. "And that can," pointing at the spare.
"What?" he said.
"Petrol!" I said.
"What?" He was standing beside the pump now, the nozzle

in his hand.

"Petrol!" I persisted.

"What?" he replied.

"Petrol!"

"What?"

"Petrol!"

"What?"

"Petrol!"

"What?"

Then I remembered the sign. "Sorry, I meant gas!"

"What?"

"Gas!"

"What?"

I could see that Dextrose was about to lamp him.

"You'll have to speak up!" he said. "I'm half deaf!"

Half-deaf? "GAS, PLEASE! FILL HER UP! AND THE CAN! PLEASE!"

"You don't have to shout, young man!" He went to unscrew the petrol cap, looked at the pitchfork in his hand, seemed surprised to find it there, and threw it across what passed for a forecourt.

"Stupid bugger," he muttered to himself, absent-mindedly.

An old woman appeared in the office doorway. "Guests, Eustace? You should have told me!"

Eustace didn't hear her. I had the impression she was used to this.

"Not very nice weather, is it, boys?" she called out.

At first glance I had thought she was sitting in a chair, but quickly realised it was a wheelchair. A motorised one, on four small off-white wheels, controlled with a ball-tipped joystick in her right hand.

Her hair was white, almost translucent, tied in a bun that sat on top of her head. She wore a lace-trimmed black dress, ankle-length, but which rode up slightly as she was seated, exposing thick brown tights. She wasn't wearing shoes. Like her partner – husband, I assumed – she too wore little round glasses, perched on the end of her nose.

"Where phone?" demanded Importos.

What could I do?

"Well, young man, we do have a telephone. But it's not really for the customers."

I nearly ran over and hugged her.

However, she was not finished. "But I tell you what: you come in for some of my tea and cake, when you've done with your boys' things out there, then I'll let you use it if you're quick – how does that sound?"

She turned before any of us could answer, the servo-motors in her wheelchair whirring.

Importos eyed me and smiled, not in a gentlemanly manner.

It was the first time I'd been offered tea and cake with my petrol, though I supposed that was what happened when one shopped among the inevitably lonely. Since our packed sandwiches were curling at the edges and water's thrill dulled quickly, it was an offer that would be hard to refuse. It would also put off the moment when Importos made his calls. Perhaps in that time, I could find and cut the telephone wire? It was an idea worth percolating.

Dextrose was less enamoured. "*Tea and minking cake?*" he railed. "Does Harrison Dextrose look like he drinks *tea*?"

He didn't, admittedly, although the bulging waistline did suggest a penchant for cake.

I tried to reason with him: "But Dad, it'd do us good! Warm us up! And we can get dried off."

"*You* can dry off – and you can mink off while you're doing it. Harrison Dextrose does not drink tea." He folded his arms, signalling an end to the matter.

Still I tried. "What are you going to do, then? You can't sit out here – it's miserable."

It failed to sink in. "Hey, you!" went Dextrose, tugging Eustace's sleeve as he concluded filling the tank. "How far from here to Mlwlw?"

I froze.

"What?" said Eustace.

"HOW FAR TO MLWLW?"

I prayed he wouldn't know.

"Mlwlw?" said Eustace, and thought for agonising seconds. "Never heard of it."

Yay for old people!

Then Importos pointed out, "Importos not to trust fat man. He to go wizout."

Leave without us? I hadn't thought of that. Recently contented Dextrose seemed suddenly malleable and trustworthy, but what if he reverted to type? One whiff of booze might be all it took. Indeed, his upbeat mood seemed already to be waning. I had an idea.

"Look! Over there!" I blurted out, pointing randomly into the rain. "A naked lady!"

Everyone bar old Eustace followed my finger. With Dextrose's attention thus diverted, I whipped the key out of the ignition and pocketed it. Sorted.

However, before I could stop him, he had dismounted the bike and started running – or rather, quick-hobbling – towards the entirely fictitious lovely.

"No, wait! Dad!"

He didn't stop.

"I might have imagined it!"

But it was no use – he was not for turning.

The house was entered via the cashier's office, which contained a desk and chair, a till with keys on levers, straight out of commercial history, and assorted tools hung from the back wall:

pliers, hammers, shears, machete, screwdrivers, hand-drill, the usual, all well-maintained despite their evident age.

The old lady was waiting for us at the door into the main house. Now I could see her clearly: paper-thin, grey skin with myriad wrinkles, like cats' whiskers, emanating from the corners of her mouth. A peanut-sized mole nestled on the end of her nose, and proved distracting when talking to her.

Also noticeable was the odour: a cloying indiscernible whiff, which I decided to take in my stride. In my experience all old people's houses had a distinctive, unsettling odour.

Before he fell out with them, Father used to take Mother and I to visit his Aunt Amelia and her husband, Eric, who bred hamsters. There were cages all over the house, and as I sat there in my Sunday best – since we were visiting relatives – all I heard was the drone of adult-talk mingling with the squeaking of hamster wheels rotating. Interestingly, their house smelled not of rodents but of gravy. I never did fathom that out.

Then there was Mother's mother, Grandmother, the only (supposed) grandparent of whom I was ever aware. She was a dreadful old witch who was so decrepit that I never saw her move. She just sat in an armchair staring at a clock, wishing out loud that the Lord would take her and put her out of her misery. Her house reeked of mouldy undergarments and I used to have to affect an interest in flowers so that I could escape into the garden.

I never understood why we had to visit her, since hardly anyone ever spoke. They all just sat around occasionally going, "Hmm" and "So", or Grandmother wished she was dead.

I was uncomfortably delighted when her wish finally came true.

Most embarrassing was realising that our own house had a smell: a not-nice vegetable-y whiff. I'd only notice it when I returned from boarding school at weekends, and very quickly I would become oblivious to it. It was as if Father, Mother, the house and I were melding into one amorphous pong; I wondered at times whether I carried that back to school with me, and whether that might partly explain my wanting popularity.

Matters came to head when Father one time invited his Headmaster from Glibley Secondary to dinner, planning to woo him with a roast partridge. The head was barely over the threshold when he sniffed the air and said to Father, "Hydrogen sulphide? Been bringing your experiments home with you, Mr Grey?"

That had been an awkward dinner and Father stopped inviting people round after that.

At least our new old-lady friend from the gas station was odour-aware, pre-empting any similar social *faux pas*. "Please excuse the smell," she said. "I've been boiling up some offal for the dog."

Mmm.

We introduced ourselves – her name was Hilda. When I shook her limp, bony hand it felt as if I were cradling a dead bird. She showed us into her dining room, where she had already laid out teacups and a brewing pot on a circular oak table, around which four placemats with plates, knives and forks were set in front of three chairs. Eustace followed us in.

Rain beat against the window, performing a constant drum roll, and a bare lightbulb suspended from the ceiling cut through the gloom. There were photographs pinned haphazardly around the walls, all of people, I noticed. No scenery. Many of those pictured were different, suggesting a large circle of family and friends keenly missed. However, there was one face that featured regularly on one wall, in various situations and at different ages, from birth to around his mid-twenties.

"Your son?" I enquired, pointing.

Instead of answering, Hilda eyed up Importos. "My, aren't you tall!" she exclaimed. "How tall are you?"

He sneered at her. "How stupid are…"

I cut over him. "He's almost eight feet tall! Amazing, isn't it!"

Hilda wheeled herself before the chairless table setting, the 'Vrt-vrrrrrt' of her motors the only sound, then ushered me to sit opposite and Importos beside her. He sat, comically towering over the table, though I could not find it funny.

"Eustace! Go fetch the short stool so our friend can sit at the table properly!" Hilda told him, sharply but without shouting.

Clearly he heard her fine, as he shuffled off dutifully and returned with the item while we waited in painful silence. All the while, Importos did not take his eyes off me.

Desperate to break the tension, and to divert my thoughts from Importos' bad friends, I struck up conversation. "So, Hilda," I said. "How long have you and your husband lived in Lonely Bush?"

"Well. How old are you, young man?" she replied.

I told her I was 33.

"Well we've lived here a lot longer than that," she said.

I took my first sip of tea, which was so weak I wondered whether it was actually tea-based.

Hilda turned to Importos. "And how old are you, big fella?"

He finished his cup. "Where is cake? Importos to phone. Yes?"

"All in good time," she said, patting his knee, which was sticking up.

In my peripheral vision I noticed Eustace, to my right, staring at me, his mouth hanging open.

Hilda said, "Didn't your other friend want to come in?"

I loved that: 'other friend'. "No, I said. "He didn't." I couldn't think what else to say.

China clinked on china.

The atmosphere was making me so nervous I started blurting

out polite but inane questions to fill the silences.

How long had they been married? (Longer than she would care to mention.)

What was their dog called? (Jeff/Geoff.)

Where was he? (Outside.)

What breed was he? (I don't even like dogs.)

Had they ever – wait for it – run out of gas themselves? (No.)

My *pièce de resistance*, though, was this, to Hilda: "How do you get upstairs?" How very sensitive.

Fortuitously, she hadn't seemed offended. "Oh, we live down here," she replied. "We save upstairs for visitors. And we do get a few come to stay," she said smiling, motioning towards the photographs on the wall.

"But we do get lonely," said Eustace. His cheery opening gambit that teatime.

I was absolutely desperate to leave, yet equally desperate that the repast never ended. A terrible quandary. A debate began raging in my head: should I stay, put up with the social hideousness, or should I go, and hope that Importos' bad friends were out?

During my consideration, Hilda said, "I'll fetch a fresh pot."

"No more tea!" snapped Importos.

"Actually, I'm still rather thirsty," I said. "More tea would be lovely, thank you."

The tall man glared at me. I smirked back, which would not help my cause. I just couldn't help it.

"You asked whether that was my son," Hilda noted on her return. She unpinned a photograph from the wall and flicked it across the table towards me. "Well yes, it was. What do you think of him?"

A loaded question, if ever I'd heard one. The picture, in the washed-out, slightly unreal colours of a previous printing technology, was of a young man, in perhaps his late-teens, taken on a beach. He grinned into the camera beneath a clump of blond hair, with a bare torso, red swimming trunks, not a care in the world. In his hand he held an ice-cream cone. His eyes stared straight into mine.

"He looks very happy," I said.

Suddenly I knew exactly what she was going to say next. I could have scribbled it on a piece of card, sealed it in an envelope and had a stranger open and reveal it to an amazed audience.

"He's dead," she said.

Why had I ever mentioned the boy? My mind was made up. There was no way I was tottering down that conversational path, and balls to Importos and his Mafioso. Just let them try and find me – the explorer!

"I'm very sorry to hear that," I said, pointedly downing the last dregs of my cup. "And I'm very grateful for your hospitality, but we really must be getting on."

"Don't go!" squawked Hilda, a little too desperately. Then more softly: "Not yet."

"We do get lonely," said Eustace.

"Yes, we do," agreed his wife.

No way. I stood up. "Honestly, I'd stay if I could but..."

"But you haven't had your cake yet!" trilled the old woman. "Let me fetch it now. It's Victoria sponge. Our favourite."

She returned, smiling as sweetly as her crinkly face would allow, holding aloft a sponge cake on a silver plate. She wheeled herself back before her place-setting and put down the cake on the table. Picking up a cake knife, she asked, "Right then, who wants some?"

Importos sighed impatiently. "Oh I then. To give quick."

And she stabbed him in the neck.

She stabbed him so vehemently that the blade went straight through; then she pushed the knife away, opening up his throat. I wished I had been looking anywhere than at his face during those perverted moments, but I hadn't. I'd been staring right at him.

I watched as his expression changed from annoyance to disorientation, and realisation to terror. I watched as his green eyes briefly blazed and then the fire extinguished. I watched as the blood sprayed out, covering teacups and cake, and his rattling, gurgling groan, the sound of a drain emptying, filled the room. The rain continued spattering its tribal drumbeat on the window. I couldn't move.

Hilda turned to me, still smiling sweetly, blood covering the hand that held the knife. "He won't be leaving us. Now, what about you?"

I couldn't speak.

Importos dropped sideways, like an oak felled.

Through my delirium I heard the servo-motors. 'Dvrrrt-dvrrt...' Hilda was coming for me.

No way. No. Fucking. Way.

I leapt to my feet.

"Stick him, Eustace! Stick him with your knife!" Hilda shouted.

Old Eustace, right beside me.

"What?" he said.

I took my chance. Pushed his chair over, sending him sprawling in front of his very slowly advancing wife.

I jumped over him, pulled open the door and ran out of that room, out through the cashier's office, out into the rain.

I heard her behind me: "Get out of the way, Eustace. He mustn't leave!"

Dextrose, thankfully, had returned to the motorbike and sidecar, hunched over and tinkering, beer bottle in one hand. No, *please*, I thought. Not the old Dextrose. Not now.

"DAD!" I screamed, running at him.

He looked round.
"START THE BIKE! QUICK!"
"Eh?"

I reached him, panting, adrenalin in full flow.

"She's killed him. Start the…" Wait! I had the key! But what was he doing? Wires in his hand…

I looked back towards the house, fumbling through too many safari suit pockets. No sign of the demented couple.

"What are you doing?" I demanded.

He looked up at me from his crouching position, that blistered, ravaged face with its thatch, and he looked almost apologetic. "Hot-wire the minker?"

The bloody fool. One chance: hope he hadn't damaged anything.

Felt steel, felt its edges: the key. Got it.

"Get in the sidecar! NOW!"

"But me beers," he said, looking at his opened suitcase on the forecourt, still full of bottles. Seemed he'd only drunk one or two. I might be in luck.

"GET IN THE SIDECAR!"

I turned towards the house again and saw Hilda's head through the window of the cashier's office. Not facing us, but bending down beneath the till. What was she up to?

When I turned back, Dextrose had one leg in the sidecar and, unable to lift the other, was stranded, a victim of his own shocking equilibrium. I moved swiftly around the bike, bundled him in, leapt onto the rider's seat. Key in ignition. Turn. Nothing.

Turn again. Nothing.

And again. Nothing.

Not a dicky bird.

Fuck. "WHAT HAVE YOU DONE?"

"Not sure," he said quietly.

Frantically, I pulled at the wires behind the ignition. Bare ends. Unconnected.

BANG! A ripping sound above my head.

In the doorway of the office, Hilda sat pointing a shotgun towards us; Eustace was standing behind her, a hand on her shoulder. Above us, the corrugated awning was now peppered with holes.

"Come on, boys, come inside," she called out.

"We do get lonely," said Eustace.

"We do," she echoed.

"Dad, we've got to run," I told Dextrose.

I had entered a strange state of calm that took me by surprise. The adrenalin still flowed yet the panic had subsided and it felt as though someone else, someone in control, had taken charge of my actions. An out-of-body experience.

BANG! The shot cut in half one of the struts holding up the awning, which began to tilt precariously as the others felt their age.

"Shit!" I heard Hilda curse.

As I helped Dextrose out of the sidecar, I saw she had uncocked the shotgun and was fumbling with two fresh cartridges.

I took his hand in mine. "Come on, Dad, we've got to go." As we left the shelter of the awning the rain spattered our faces. I noticed some of Importos' blood, tiny drops on my arm, watched it become diluted and roll off into the sand.

But Dextrose could not run. He could not even jog. Though I tugged at him, urging him on, it was like dragging a mattress through a hole half its size. "Come *on*! *Please!*" I urged.

Twice he fell over and I had to haul him to his feet, newly drenched and soiled, before we made the tarmac of the Nameless Highway. Behind me, over Dad's shoulder, I saw Hilda had started towards us, one hand on her steering knob, the other holding the gun; she was straining her head forward, as if that might encourage the wheelchair to go faster. It didn't.

Neither though was I able to motivate Dextrose into anything above a tortuous pace, and when we were 50 yards up the road I saw Hilda reach the road behind us, in tepid pursuit.

Suddenly I was back in my own body, all out of ideas and bravado. We could not continue like this for much longer, and she was battery-powered. A hopeless shot, she might have been, but she would soon begin to gain on us and we would be done for.

Then Dextrose stopped and would not move. He was bent over, gasping like an asthmatic jackass. "What... the... mink... is... going... on?" he went, between wheezes.

"The old woman killed Importos and now she wants to kill us!"

His brow crumpled. "Importos?"

There was no time to explain. "Look!" I said, pointing back down the Nameless Highway.

Hilda had stopped, too, not 20 yards from us. She levelled the shotgun at us. "Ready boys?" she called out.

"GET DOWN!" I yelled, screwing my eyes shut and throwing myself to the ground.

BANG!
BANG!
"Damn you!" Hilda's voice.
BANG!
"Mink you!" (No guesses.)
BANG!
(Hang on. How many shots in a shotgun?)
BANG!

I dared to open one eye and glance up. Dextrose had his revolver out, cursing under his breath; Hilda was reloading. Everyone was still alive.

BANG! Dextrose fired again, but his hand was shaking and

his entire body gyrated unsteadily on its feet.

Back down the road I saw Hilda cock the shotgun. She held it out and looked vaguely down the barrel, more myopic than markswoman. Dextrose began shuffling towards her, pistol raised.

Burying my face in the road, I covered my head with my hands and let the smell of the wet tarmac return me to England.

BANG!

Then:

BOOOOM!

I sensed something flying over me.

After that, debris started raining down, clattering about the road around me. I did not dare open my eyes, waiting for something painful to hit me, knock me senseless or shatter a bone. Nothing did. For those few seconds, someone was looking after me, and he did not wear a tweed overcoat in the sunshine and he did not stink of booze.

When the unnatural shower had ceased and only the rain remained, I opened my eyes, removed my hands from my head and rose to my feet.

Devastation.

Lonely Bush Gas Station had simply vanished, replaced by the sort of crater a modest meteorite might have made. My father lay further up the Nameless Highway, blown there by the explosion. My concerns for him were allayed when he struggled to his feet and began wandering around looking perplexed, which was normal.

For her part, Hilda, the aged murderess, had been deposited some distance onto the sandy scrubland opposite her former residence, and lay bundled and unmoving nearby her upended wheelchair. I remembered Importos' dying expression; her demise did not trouble me.

We had lost everything bar that which we carried on us. The bike was gone, Importos was gone, my luggage was gone... But we had survived, Dad and I.

It was all too much. The shock, the fear, the dicing with death, they all collided inside my stomach. I bent double and was sick among the slew of rubble that littered the scene.

When I had finished, by chance the cursed rain stopped too.

"Mink me! Eh?" went Dextrose as I approached him. He was sitting in the middle of the road supping from a bottle of beer. Where he had found it, I had no idea.

He held the bottle out to me. It was the first time I had ever seen him share his booze. I took it, tipped my head back and gulped down the warm, frothy brew, savouring the liquid and the numbness it promised.

"Alright! Stop! Mink me! That's enough!" he gasped, motioning urgently for its return. He snatched the beer back, drained it and lobbed the bottle away.

I sat down next to him.

"Thanks," I mumbled.

"What for?"

"For saving us."

He was barely recognisable. A deep graze obscured his left cheek, seeping blood among the sand and grit, and his hair was matted with blood, no doubt the result of his crash-landing. The other side of his face was no worse than before, which was still shocking. His tracksuit bottoms were ripped at both knees, fantastically stained, and his overcoat was losing a sleeve.

"I'd forgotten you had a gun," I said.

"Us too," he replied.

"So how…"

"Went into me pocket to find that beer. Found that instead. Decided us might as well take a pot at the old cobweb on wheels. Couldn't take no chances – another day or two an' she'd have been in danger of hitting one of us!" He chuckled throatily to himself.

It was too early for me to find any of it funny. "Why are you laughing?"

"Well, I'm no marksman meself. Must have missed her and hit the petrol pump. What a minking bang! Eh?"

I shook my head.

"Ah come on, lad!" persisted Dad. "Harrison Dextrose has been through worse than this!"

It didn't seem possible. "But you've just wiped off the map…" – quick mental arithmetic – "16 per cent of the landmarks on the Nameless Highway. Lonely Bush *no longer exists*."

He shrugged. "You heard the old mink. They'll plant another one."

"You're forgetting that the 'old mink' is dead."

He nodded thoughtfully and we sat there in silence for a while.

I was stunned at how he had come to the rescue, having seemed so screwed up and lost within himself. Granted, his primary concern was doubtless his own safety, and his rescue had been all luck and no judgment… Yet, thinking about it, that's how he had come across in *The Lost Incompetent*. Good fortune fell into his lap, whatever the levels of his womanising and debauchery, and his complete disregard for the conventions of preparation and planning. He sort of explored by default.

What drove him? Surely not purely the chance of fame and/or

notoriety? Or even the whoring? I simply couldn't work him out.

Harrison Dextrose was such a mass of contradictions. And I couldn't help feeling some admiration for him seeping back.

"Why are you helping me?" I asked.

"Is I?"

That's what I'd thought: my own safety was a mere by-product of his. Or was that the old braggadocio? The bluster he concocted to obscure his sensitive side? Because he did have one, I felt fairly certain.

"Alright," I said. Let's see how deep he went. "What have you been thinking. While we were quiet just then?"

He shot me a queer look. "What's this? Lady-talk?"

I said nothing.

"Oh alright," he conceded. "I've been thinking I wish I'd saved two minking bottles, not one!" And he laughed.

This time I joined in. Our eyes met, his far from sparkling, but I dared not lean in for the family hug, not with one so determinedly macho.

The gaiety petered out and we fell silent.

I reached out for a nearby shard of metal. It was turquoise on one side, unpainted on the other; I suspected it had come from that old petrol pump. I began passing it between my hands. "So, what are we going to do?"

"Well," he said, exhaling. "We're minked!"

"Do we just sit here?"

He shook his head, shrugged.

"That heat's gone, at least," I said. I looked at my watch. "Nearly five o'clock. We could always walk a bit?"

"Where to?" There was nothing to be seen in either direction, just that never-ending road, straight as a stiff one. "How far to Mlwlw?"

Ah. That old chestnut. And we'd been getting along so well. Should I come clean? He was in no state to throttle me, after all.

"Actually we weren't heading to Mlwlw."

His neck stiffened.

I continued: "We were heading to Pretanike, to find your wife. Mrs Dextrose."

No response.

"My mother."

He placed a palm on the road surface and pushed out a creaking leg. He put the other palm down and heaved himself onto all fours. Gradually, groaning, he pulled his torso upright and stood up. He dusted off his hands.

"Yer coming, then?" he said.

And we started trudging, away from the setting sun, off towards Pretanike.

Nameless Highway, Tuesday, 6:25pm:

It had soon become clear that he could not trudge and talk at the same time. The former took too much effort. But I was happy: any progress was progress, and it took us further away from the nightmare of Lonely Bush.

Without control, I replayed Importos' death over and over again in my head. So brutal and swift. That sweet-seeming old lady and her hard-of-hearing husband. Tea, cake and homicide.

I kept wondering whether there was anything I could have done, and was relieved to conclude each time, no matter how I twisted it, that there was not. He had been opposite me, across the table, and it had all happened so quickly.

Detritos gone, and now his brother, each time with the same star witness: myself. What would their parents think? I trusted I would never find out.

Imagine their heartbreak. Both sons, outlived. No parent should have to experience that.

Importos' distraught visage came back to me and I dry-heaved.

The fact that his passing also alleviated my retribution concerns kept surfacing and I had to repeatedly batter it back down, fearing for my own morality. How could my mind even countenance such dirt? Yet, like a guilty past, it would not go away.

I was feeling exhausted and couldn't begin to imagine how

Dextrose must have felt. That pensioner with his habits. He wheezed and muttered, shuffling along, like the one at the back of a chain gang.

At one point he tripped and fell. I was a little way ahead at the time – my subtle way of compelling him onwards – and I heard the stumble and turned around. He was lying on his gut, limbs splayed out, as if he'd been run over in a Hanna-Barbera cartoon. As I approached him, he rolled onto his back and lay there staring at the sky. He grinned at me ruefully.

"Want a hand?" I asked.

He lifted his right arm; I grabbed him. And something strange happened.

Something... almost magical.

His hand was soft, far softer than I might have expected for one so coarse by nature, and it felt so much larger than mine, though in reality it was not. It was the first time I had held him, touched his skin, and I became lost in imaginings.

I saw myself as a young boy; the colours were washed out and the movement flickered, with odd flares of white light, as if I were viewing the scenes on an old cine projector. I was wearing shorts and a T-shirt, bare feet on a lawn, very blond-haired, skipping around a paddling pool.

The scene switched. Dressed as a cowboy now: plastic chaps, felt hat, waistcoat, sheriff's star and a silver pistol, hiding behind a tree and emerging to fire at an unseen assailant.

Another switch: a swimming gala, myself in too-tight trunks, lined up against competitors, ready to dive off the edge of the pool.

Again: birthday party, wearing a paper hat, eleven lit candles on a cake, preparing to blow. I stare into the camera eye, a child smiling, expression frozen in time.

Then I realised there had been adults in each montage, lingering on the periphery. A man and a woman, not Father and Mother.

Mr and Mrs Dextrose?

The visions disappeared and I was back on the Nameless Highway.

I looked down at my father and saw that he was crying.

Tears rolled down my own cheeks.

I lifted him to his feet.

Some while later, Dad announced that he was "minking done" and toppled over into the side of the road. Though we had stopped for several rests, I sensed that this would be our last of the day.

Would he be able to continue tomorrow, I wondered? Would there even be a tomorrow?

We might die of the cold, or thirst, or hunger, or be eaten by one of the monsters that lurked out there, hidden from view. The odds were stacked against us.

I sat down beside him and shuffled closer so that I might share with him some of my body heat. The light was fading. The sky had turned red again.

Red sky at night... But there were no shepherds out there. There was no one at all.

We had previously passed just one other vehicle – that crappy old farm truck – having travelled almost halfway along the Nameless Highway. What were the chances of another appearing, to whisk us to safety? Slim. And if we weren't rescued, we would surely perish.

In a rising panic, I checked my pockets and was delighted to find, besides my wallet, that second bag of Sheep Shavings I had saved.

"Look!" I exclaimed, holding it aloft. "Food!"

My father glanced at the bag and raised an eyebrow, breaking a crusted scab in doing so. "Well done," he said, half-heartedly. "Let's see what I've got on us..."

He laid what he retrieved before him, naming each item as

he did so.

"Lighter... string... pocket knife... torch..." He checked it worked, playing the beam on my face and chuckling when it did. "Boiled sweets... compass... haemorrhoid cream. Hehe... sticking plasters... wallet." He did not open that in front of me. "Notebook... pencil..."

I was gobsmacked. He'd reminded me of Tom Baker in *Doctor Who*, and I was disappointed when he did not produce a paper bag of Jelly Babies.

But he hadn't finished. "Hang on, I were sure I had..." Patting around his chest area, he held up a finger and delved into an inside pocket. "Knew I'd packed a bottle of mink somewhere! Never had need of it before..."

And he produced a plastic bottle of water. It had stagnated and turned slimy green, but that did not matter. It was liquid and we would live.

For the time being.

The least I could do was go on a recce for something to burn – the cold was beginning to bite – and our fortune held when I spotted, some distance up the highway and off to one side, a broken wooden crate. It had fallen off a lorry, I imagined, and I saw that someone had scrawled

CHICKINS

along one side; however, the poultry was long gone. Mutated by now into something with a beard and fangs, I didn't doubt.

The wood was so wet that it wouldn't light, until I split it into smaller pieces to expose the dry inner layers. Once Dad's lighter generated a flame among those, we were in business, piling them before us, the fiery glow warming our hearts while steam hissed off them.

Above us, the clouds had vanished and the darkened sky's

galactic denizens watched our preparations with mounting interest. We took a long slug of slimy, foul-tasting water each, even my father for whom the substance was tantamount to treachery. It slipped down my throat like a length of snot. Then I shared out half of the Sheep Shavings, carefully replacing the remainder in my pocket, and we ate those in a reverent hush, broken by the noisy crunches on the unhealthy grossness.

Finally – since our rations were sparse – Dad and I sucked one boiled sweet each. His was purple, my favourite flavour, though I didn't complain, and mine was a twist of amber, sugar-coated on its edges. Cough candy. It brought back happy memories: a quarter-pound for tuppence from the school tuck-shop, and all mine because no one else liked them.

This wasn't the life – we could have been far better off – however it was the very best we could manage under the circumstances.

I stared at him, illuminated in shades of orange, saw past the fact that he looked as if he had been cut barely alive from farm machinery, and so many questions flitted around my head.

Why had I been adopted? Why had he gone travelling? How much of the machismo was a façade? What about his own parents? My real grandparents. They hadn't even crossed my mind. What was Mum really like? I had only seen that one photograph, and she looked so lovely and alive. I didn't even know her first name. I could hardly keep calling her Mrs Dextrose.

I chanced it. "Dad, what's…"

But he cut me dead. I think he'd seen me lost in thought, and there was only so much he was prepared to give away so soon. "I'm minked, boy," he said. "And that fire won't last long. Here, move in next to old Dextrose. Mind yer don't touch me old…" He remembered who I was and caught himself, before the innuendo could slip out.

Nameless Highway, Wednesday, 2.13am:

The bottom of my foot had been kicked and there was a voice, somewhere above me. My closed eyes registered light and I could hear a deep, rattling hum. An engine?

"Wakey wakey! Bet you boys are glad to see me! *Thunderbirds* to the *rescue!*" Hold on, what had he said? *Rescue?*

I was on my feet in an instant.

The sky was mauve. Before me on the Nameless Highway was an old truck, tinny looking and dented, cream-coloured with a tarpaulin covering the rear. Its engine was running and there were spotlights at the bumper and above the windscreen. That cyclical guttural thrum, cutting through the silence of the early morning, felt both eerie and exciting.

In shadow against the vehicle's glare was the figure of a man: short, with bow-legs and a brimmed hat.

He repeated himself: "Bet you boys are glad to see me!"

"Yes," I said. "Yes we bloody well are!"

He held out his hand. "Charles Tiberius Snipe, at your service!"

I threw myself at him, sending him almost off-balance, and enveloped him in a bear-hug. "Thankyouthankyouthanyou!"

His hat came up to my nipples. The hug began to feel awkward and he pushed me gently away.

"No worries, mate. Don't mention it. My friends call me

Charlie," said our saviour. "At least they would if I... anyway! What's yours?"

"I'm Pilsbury. This is my Dad."

Despite the racket, Dextrose remained curled up and unconscious. I couldn't bring myself to wake him.

"Is he alright?" asked Charlie. "He looks terrible."

"Yes. Yes, he's fine. How..."

He put his hands on his hips and swaggered a bit without moving his feet. "You're lucky I spotted you there, down at the side of the road. Chances of another vehicle passing this way in the next 24 hours are slimmer than a... slimmer than a... shit! No, hang on, I'll think of something!"

I waited patiently while he tapped his temple.

"I've got slimmer than a person who's on a diet, but that's not one of my best... hang on..."

My patience waned. "So, can we have a lift?"

"That's why I stopped, dummy!"

Were saviours meant to be punchable?

I shook Dextrose gently, then much harder when he would not wake up.

"Wh? Hnn? Quench?" He blinked and looked up, shading his eyes from the lights. "You again."

I tried not to let it affect me. "We've been rescued. We've got a lift."

He cleared his throat disgustingly and spat out the results. "I'd have survived," he said. "But if it's here..."

Charlie bent down to shake his hand. "I'm Charlie! But you can call me Virgil from International Rescue... no, call me Scott – he's my favourite!"

"Mink off, twot," snarled Dad, who couldn't have had enough sleep.

Thankfully, Charlie was not put off. "I've got another surprise for you guys," he said, his voice barely containing his excitement.

What could he mean?

"What minking surprise?" growled Dad, clearly in concurrence.

"Guess who else I picked up?"

Neither my father nor I spoke.

"Alright, here's a clue: she said she was looking for you boys!"

He began biting his fingernails in anticipation.

It couldn't possibly be. My face drained of all its life.

"Asked me to keep an eye out for you, she did! And I found you! She's gonna have a right surprise too, and no mistake!"

I had to force out the words. "Where is she?"

He motioned towards the tarpaulin. "In the back... you don't exactly sound delighted."

When we didn't say anything, he burbled on: "I, I couldn't get her wheelchair in the front. Cos of the seats. That's the only reason I put her in the back. But I tied her down OK!"

I looked at Dad and he looked at me.

"I've done my bit," he said. "You sort it." And he sat down.

The air was perfectly still, the lights from Charlie's truck made the Nameless Highway seem ghostly, and tiny insects cavorted and glowed in their glare. All the while the engine idled, a constant, undulating mechanical moan. All I felt was a sense of evil present. Hilda the murderess was just a few yards away, concealed only by a single layer of material.

I had thought we were rid of her, had assured myself that she was dead. But old people can be terribly resilient.

The horrors of Lonely Bush came flooding back to me in a whirling vortex of nightmarish imagery. Eustace in the rain, drenched and despondent; that room with its photographs, its tea and cake; that thing she had said about the upper floor... what was it? "We keep that for the visitors". What atrocities lurked up there?

The knife and the blood. Poor Importos' face and that horrific, gaping wound. "Stick him, Eustace, stick him!" The relentless pursuit by the witch...

Dad's voice broke through my fearful thoughts. "Oh mink it! I'll do it me minking self!"

I can't pretend I wasn't relieved. "Be careful," I urged him.

"Minks," came back.

He limped past me, flicking on his torch. Its beam danced around as he disappeared to the back of the truck encased in near-darkness. I saw him flick up the tarpaulin flap and disappear inside the vehicle. Not a word did Hilda utter and I wondered why, fearing the worst.

"Sound a-minking-sleep!" called out Dad. "Hold on."

There came sounds of movement then the torch beam shone from the rear of Charlie's truck, back towards Lonely Bush. In it suddenly appeared a figure in a wheelchair, pushed off the back and landing with a clatter and a thump.

"Ooooow." Hilda's voice, weak but not defeated.

Charlie finally clicked that something was awry. "Hey, now hold on, boys! What's this all about? That's no way to treat your mother!"

I could see that one of her arms was bent backwards at an interesting angle and her black dress was in tatters, exposing her skinny, wrinkled, pale midriff. Her bun had come undone and her white hair looked like an explosion at the surface of water. Her face was vividly bruised and her glasses were missing. She squinted into the light of Dad's torch.

"That's not my mother," I said. "That old woman murdered my friend."

Charlie laughed without feeling. "No way, guys! You're having me on! *Her*?"

I could only shake my head. He stared at me, his eyes dancing over every detail of my face, seeking the truth. Then he knew.

He whistled. "Jesus. If I'd..." His voice trailed off.

Dad eased himself down from the truck and began walking

towards the vehicle's cabin. "Right, we're off. You, get in the front of the van," he ordered Charlie.

Hilda's voice emerged from the shadows beneath the taillights. "That you boys? It is, isn't it?"

It was an old lady's voice. A broken, bent old lady. I had to remind myself what she had done.

Still I couldn't help myself. In the dim haze of the taillights I righted her wheelchair. Then I took hold of her beneath the armpits, picked her up and placed her gently in the chair, rearranging her dress as best I could. I felt her wince and she muted a grunt, but she did not cry out.

It was a spontaneous action. Had she secreted away a knife, she might have stabbed me; in that moment it was a chance I would have taken.

All the while, I could not look into her face. But our heads were close and when I was preparing to take my leave she whispered into my ear, "Thank you."

As I turned to walk away, she spoke more loudly, battling for defiance. She said: "You know I'll follow you to the ends of the earth, don't you?"

As I reached the passenger door Dad was beside it, waiting. "You can get in first," he said. "I'm not sitting next to that mink."

I pulled myself inside. The passenger seat was two bums wide, in ripped brown leather with extruding foam. Charlie stared at me – I noticed straggly red hair tumbling from beneath the hat, and his freckled cheeks were sunburnt. In his mid-twenties, he looked like a little boy, a farm-boy, battered by the weight of the world. He looked nervous and put-out.

Nameless Highway, Wednesday, 3.20am:

No one spoke for a while, lost in an aura of unease. At least we were putting miles between ourselves and the past. The cab was warm and our top speed was a dizzying 55 mph, though the old crate's workings mithered.

Then Charlie said, "So, er, what exactly happened back there?"

Dad slid down in his seat and hunched his shoulders.

"Long story," I said.

"Well, I'm all ears! Haha!" He paused. "I'm not, of course. All ears. That would look stupid! They'd have to call me… no, hang on… got it! Ear-ic! Eric – geddit?" He really was very nervous.

We did owe him an explanation. I told him: "We stopped at the Lonely Bush Gas Station. The old woman killed our friend there."

He fidgeted in his seat. "Hell. I wondered what had happened back there. Saw the big hole and the debris, then I spotted the old lady, seen her occasionally, though it's the old man who fills up the truck. She was pretty beat-up, but I helped her up, and she said, 'My boys, I gotta find my boys. Will you help me?' What could I say? So I kept me eyes peeled and then there you were in me headlights, down by the side of the road." Charlie turned to me. "So who was this friend of yours? A good friend?"

I thought about it a little too long. "Yeah." It didn't seem right to speak ill of the dead.

"What did she do to him?"

"I'd rather not talk about it."

"Did she blow his head off with a shotgun? I saw a gun back there."

A thought struck me. "Are there any police around here?" That'd put a stop to her psychopathy, once and for all.

"There'll probably be one in Flattened Hat. That's where I'm headed. I'll drop you boys off there."

"How far's that from Pretanike?"

"Last town before it. Well, only town before it!" He nudged me and winked. I had no idea why.

At least our luck was shaping up. After all the perils, we seemed to be landing on our feet.

Charlie asked, "So what happened to the gas station?"

"You'll have to ask him," I replied.

A little louder, aiming Dad's way, Charlie repeated, "So what happ…"

"Mink off!" snapped Dextrose.

"Alright, I'll tell you," I said. "He shot it and it blew up."

Charlie whistled a long whistle.

"By accident," I added.

"Nevertheless," he said.

Nevertheless? "What do you mean, '*Nevertheless*'?"

"Well, you can't go around blowing up people's livelihoods."

"*She killed our friend!*"

He shrugged. "Like I said: nevertheless. Cops might not see it that way."

I was gobsmacked. "Is that what passes for justice around here?"

"Pretty much," he replied.

I would reconsider involving the police.

Nameless Highway, Wednesday, 3:55 am:

Charlie sat very close to the wheel due to his lack of height, head extended, alert, ostrich-posed. Dad had fallen asleep and was gently snoring. At regular intervals he would blow off, moist-sounding with a steamy, rainforest vibe, the stench tangible. We wound down the windows.

I felt so very tired too, but couldn't sleep. Instead I watched the road ahead, illuminated only so far by all those headlamps, and felt comforted as the sands to either side flowed past.

Charlie told the occasional lame joke.

"What did Batman say to Robin before they got in the Batmobile?"

I didn't know.

"Robin, get in the Batmobile!"

At other times, the young driver and I would bat around pitiful conversation.

"How long you had the truck?"

"Ten years. No, maybe eleven. No, ten. D'you like it?"

"Uhuh."

But generally I gave in to my thoughts.

The recent bonding with my father was playing on my mind. Drawn together in adversity, we had perhaps begun to understand a little of one another. I had felt a warmth from him that a son is entitled to feel. My concern was whether it would last. Doubts hovered. He had been roughly sober of late, which could surely not continue indefinitely. And then what?

Already he had seemed crotchety since meeting Charlie. Could he cling to that gentler side of his nature? Something in my gut suspected otherwise. No other person I'd met had been so obstinate, obdurate, melancholic and tough to endure.

If I could only keep him off the booze until we found Mrs Dextrose, perhaps he would see what he had missed and we could all live together as one happy family? I wanted to picture her delight when we found her, our embrace, but the only photograph I'd seen of her was so dated I couldn't imagine what she might look like these days.

How incredible if we could find her... A cold flush enveloped me and panic set in. Where was Dextrose's sketch? And that map of Pretanike given to me by Quench? Did I have them on me? Or were they among my luggage, toasted back at Lonely Bush? They were key to our search.

Furiously, I patted my pockets, causing Charlie to quip, "Got ants in your shirt?" Then I remembered discovering a secret pocket sewn beneath the safari suit's collar – and there they were, tightly furled.

My relief was tempered, however, by the realisation that I had not found my battered old copy of Dextrose's book. *The Lost Incompetent* had accompanied me not only throughout my travels, but since the age of 18, since I had become a man, of sorts. As I racked my brain, I remembered with a shudder that I had packed it carefully into my rucksack. The rucksack tied to the bike.

It was gone. My old companion.

I doubted there was much call for it in the bookshops these days, not 25 years since its publication. Nor with a readership, one suspected, smaller than the average Dead Vole Fan Club AGM. So that was that.

I slumped down beside Dextrose feeling very sorry for myself, and looked across at his unconscious head with its weeping sores, scabs and pustules. Then I thought to myself: why worry when I have the real thing?

Nameless Highway, Wednesday, 5 am.

Conclusively bored.

"So what do you do, Charlie?" I asked.

He turned to me and pulled a stupid boggle-eyed expression, waggling his tongue and going, "Wlwlwlwlwlwlw!"

"I do that!" he said.

I could not bring myself to humour him. "I meant for work."

"Yeah, I knew."

"So what do you do, then, Charlie. For work?" By then I didn't even want to know.

"I tune bagpipes."

It was the first funny thing he'd said, and I chuckled despite myself. I'd expected him to work on a farm.

Charlie looked hurt. "No, I was serious."

"Jesus," I said. "I didn't even know you could tune bagpipes."

"Course!" said Charlie. "You can tune anything."

"Rubbish! You can't tune..." I plucked something from the ether, "beetles."

He thought for a bit. "No. But that's just one thing."

"Alright. You can't tune biscuits or gravy or the name Gavin..."

"You're just being stupid. They're not instruments. I tune bagpipes. OK?"

"OK. How's business?"

"It's fine."

I could tell it wasn't.

"How many bagpipes have you tuned?" I asked.

He performed some mental arithmetic out loud. "One... two... thr... no, one. No, two. Two if you count me Pa asking me to tune his bagpipes, but then not paying me anything."

"Who was the other customer?"

Dad snorted. (A sarcastic reaction or some part of his sleep process, I couldn't tell.)

Charlie chose to ignore my question. "In Flattened Hat, where we're headed, they have a big theatre, so I'm pretty sure there'll be some work there."

"Because all the plays are big on bagpipes?"

"Yep."

I felt a bit sorry for him and wondered whether I could steer his career in another direction. "What did you do before you tuned bagpipes?"

"I sold hair products."

That sounded more lucrative. "What, like hairdryers and curlers and stuff?"

"Well. It was more hair product, really."

"Gel and sprays?"

"No, I meant hair product as in just the one hair-related thing."

I was lost.

"I sold combs, Pilsbury. I sold combs, if you must know. But there was no money in it. Here." He pulled a plastic blue comb out of his top pocket, the prongs laden with browning gunk feasted on by nits. "You can have that. I'm done with combs. Fuck combs. Combs are shit."

I held it by one corner and dropped it into my deepest safari-suit pocket.

"So what do you boys do?" asked Charlie, with a hint of antagonism.

"We're... we're explorers," I said, monitoring Dextrose's

reaction in my peripheral vision. He didn't stir.

"Wow!" said Charlie, unable to help himself. Then added, "So where you been?"

"All over, really."

"Anywhere special? Cos I've never seen the point of explorers."

I heard Dad mutter, "Minker," under his breath. So he was awake.

"Take Captain Cook," our driver continued. "What use was he?"

"Well..." was all I managed.

"Anyone could have done what Cook did. If they had a boat. Or Christopher Columbus! I've never even been to America! So I mean, what use was he?"

That seemed to be an end to the matter, and I was grateful when the conversation dwindled in the aftermath.

Nameless Highway, Wednesday, 6.15 am:

As the fat old sun lofted its jaundiced, balding bonce above the horizon, tendrils of light pierced the windshield and I realised I must have fallen asleep. Before us now I saw flocks of birds and vegetation in clusters. We were closing in on civilisation.

Most amazingly, in this bizarre flat land, where not even a mole had dared to raise a hill, I spotted ahead on Charlie's side of the road, an actual protuberance. "What's that?" I asked excitedly, pointing.

"Oh, that? That's Call-That-A-Hill? The indigenous people used to worship it. Before they all got killed. Wanna stop and have a look?"

Sightseeing. Actual sightseeing, like normal tourists did. I couldn't wait. Wash away with something worthy some of the degradation I'd been forced to endure. I only wished I had brought a camera.

"Have you seen it up close?" I asked Charlie.

"Why would I want to do that?" he replied.

Call-That-A-Hill?, Wednesday, 7:05 am:

Our driver turned off the Nameless Highway and followed a stony trackway that ended in a square of sand marked out with logs. A sign read:

Call-That-A-Hill?
Car Park
Fee: 2 dollars
(Place fee in honesty box)
No Overnight Parking

"Fuck!" exclaimed Charlie. "You have to pay to park here! You sure you wanna see it? It's just a shit rock."

As he turned off the engine, Dad became fully conscious. He was sweating profusely, though the morning was cool and the windows were open.

"Gob like a rattler's minkhole. So dry," he moaned. "Need booze." He groped at me. "Got any booze?"

No. No-no-no. I had to keep him off the booze. It was my only chance – and his, I felt convinced – to maintain our burgeoning relationship. At least the truth offered him no opportunity. "No, it all blew up, if you remember. But Dad, you don't *need* it.

You've been fine without. You've been *better* without."

He leaned across me to get at Charlie, which placed his head next to mine. His breath was fetid, swamp-smelling. "Got any booze, you?" he demanded.

"Who, me?" But Charlie could tell he was in no mood for play. "Er, no, sorry, don't drink. Teetotal."

That set him off. He launched himself at our hapless driver, raging and all out of self-censorship. "Why you little life sapping, gut wrenching, turkey basting, copulating, peach fuzzing, tool gripping, tit wanking, shit sieving, low living, pot pissing patsy!"

Then he slumped back into his seat and broke down in tears.

The final precious molecules of alcohol must have been soaked up into his system while he slept, and he had entered withdrawal. Whatever, we had no booze, with zero chance of procuring any, and that was an end to it. He would just have to push through, and I could only imagine the practice would do him some good.

There was nothing I could do to help him and, anyway, I was pretty keen to get going on the sightseeing.

With Dad blocking the door my side, hunched and juddering, Charlie had to let me out of his side. I stretched my limbs and exhaled noisily, wondering why they had built the car park a good 100 yards from Call-That-A-Hill?

I could understand the name, at least. It wasn't much of a hill, more an exaggerated mound, flattened on top. It was the only noticeable bump for perhaps hundreds of miles around, which presumably afforded it the celebrity. Under the rising sun it assumed an alluring red blush colour, of an embarrassed lady's cheeks, or a smacked bottom.

I didn't have any dollars so I pushed a tenner sterling of Quench's money through the slot in the pay-box. Why did I pay? Call it decency, call it what you will; I also had a fear that in this land anything was possible, and that a parking inspector might have been lying in wait nearby, disguised under camouflaged sheeting.

Close up, the rock was bulkier than I had expected. Call-That-A-Hill? was at least three times my height and perhaps 50-feet wide, roughly square-shaped in cross-section. Its surface consisted of wide, shallow grooves, running vertically from top to bottom. How it had become flattened off, I had no idea.

It felt like sandpaper to the touch and when I scraped at it with my fingernail a few grains came away. Sandstone. Had I had the time and inclination, I reckoned I could have whittled it down to a nub within a decade.

I tried doing the proper tourist thing of wondering how long it had been there, and what had formed it, but was clueless. Instead I decided to circumnavigate the block, stroking my chin thoughtfully.

I was amazed to discover, on the far side, a door. A wooden door made from a single sheet of hardboard, attached to the face of the rock with hinges, cracked and bleached. It was short for a door and above it someone had scratched into the sandstone:

THE HERMITAGE

Next to that was a small bell on a curved strip of metal, employed as a crude spring, and attached to that was a length of string.

How bizarre! Were there actually people inside Call-That-A-Hill??

I had to find out. But did I dare ring the bell? Did I? What if someone irate appeared, armed or otherwise? Old me, the Glibley version, would have baulked at the idea, would have sneaked quietly away and dismissed the notion of regret, that I had never satisfied my curiosity.

I pulled hard on the string a few times. The bell rang, tinny and hollow.

The door did not open and there came not a sound from within.

I rang again.

Nothing.

I was debating whether to try the door myself, when it suddenly opened just a touch. Then a touch further and a head poked out, blinking in the daylight.

It was a disturbing little head, white and smooth, so thin-faced it might have been a skull on a stick, someone's idea of a prank. I had to double-check for eyeballs to be sure that it wasn't.

"What do you want?" went the head, snuffling and grouchy. The sort of voice an actor might use to portray one of the meaner characters in *The Wind in the Willows*.

"I. Er, I," I stammered.

A wizened grey arm appeared and pointed upwards. "Can't you read?"

Having regained composure I said, "Yes."

The arm disappeared inside. "Don't you know what a Hermitage is?"

Actually, I didn't. I knew there was a Hermitage museum, though I didn't know where, and imagined this might be something like that, offering a pictorial history of the rock, perhaps with the odd diorama. "Is it a museum?" I guessed.

He screwed up his face, and I think I heard a foot stamp petulantly. "No! No it's not! It's where a hermit lives. Do you at least know what a hermit is?"

"Yes, I do" I said. "It's someone who lives on their own."

"So shit off!"

The door slammed.

I was rather lost for words.

"You're not going to believe this," I said, clambering into the cab.

My father was trying to sulk while in the grip of *delirium tremens*. Although I felt sorry for him, it seemed best to remain stoical on his behalf.

I went on: "There's a hermit living in the rock. And he has a bell over his door! Why would a hermit have a doorbell?" The thought had struck me on the way back to the truck. It was most curious.

Dad perked up. "There's some mink out there?"

"Yes, a hermit."

He began clawing at the door handle.

"I wouldn't go there if I were you," I warned. "He's not very friendly."

"Minks!" went Dad. "Anyone that lonely must have minking crates of booze!"

He flung himself out of the cab and began staggering towards Call-That-A-Hill?

Charlie spoke. "Can we leave without him? He gives me the creeps."

We watched my father's return. He didn't seem to have been at the Hermitage for very long and he wasn't carrying any crates.

When he returned to his seat I noticed he had a black eye, to add to his litany of facial wounds.

"What did he say?" I enquired politely.

He didn't reply.

Nameless Highway, Wednesday, 7.50am.

It wasn't long after we left Call-That-A-Hill? that a dot appeared on the horizon and grew and grew. Too large to be a single structure, it had to be an actual settlement. At last.

Charlie pointed at it. "That, boys, is Flattened Hat. Last stop on the line, where I make me fortune." He flicked his hat brim.

Dad stirred from his slump. "They got bars there?"

"Sure," said Charlie.

That cheered him up no end, and filled me with dread.

I shifted the subject off alcohol. "So you've been there before, Charlie? To Flattened Hat?"

"Plenty of times. Used to ride the Nameless Highway selling me combs. Back and forth, back and forth. Know Flattened Hat well."

"What about Pretanike?"

He looked at me as if I'd just propositioned a moorhen. "No way!"

"Why not?"

"Cos it's rubbish. Nothing to do there."

"But it's vast. A city?"

"So they say."

"You mean you've never been?"

"Wouldn't go."

"Why not?"

"I told you, cos it's rubbish."

"How do you know?"

"*Cos everyone says so.*"

"Who's everyone?"

He was becoming exasperated. "My *folks*. My *friends*."

"Small town, is it, where you live?"

"How'd you guess? You must've pass Socks 'N' Sandals, right?"

"Mmm." I didn't elaborate.

"That's me local. There's a dirt track behind that leads to me hometown. Glow Coma, it's called. Nice place – small, but nice. You should come visit."

"I'll do that," I lied.

"Me Pa, Kai…" – I nearly choked on my epiglottis – "he runs a farm there. Used to work with him, till I went out to seek me fortune."

Jesus. "Hence the combs and the bagpipe tuning?"

"Hence the combs and the bagpipe tuning."

He took a hand off the steering wheel and held it up for a high five. Tinged with self-loathing, I obliged.

Flattened Hat, Wednesday, 8.45 am.

Pedestrians – actual other people – a grocery, street-lighting, residential housing, a school (if pokey, at least serving education), burger joint, trees (with green leaves), roads with kerbs... All of these we passed as Charlie turned off the Nameless Highway into Flattened Hat. Not that we had spent ages apart from what might be termed 'normality', just that the events of the previous 36 hours or so had taken quite a toll on my psyche. The familiar sights were such a blessed relief. It felt as if I had escaped.

For starters, I couldn't wait to lie down on a bed with a mattress, linen and pillows, the sort of thing I once took for granted. I was knackered. My eyelids kept closing; I would dream something bizarre for a split second, then a movement of the vehicle would jolt me alert. My limbs felt heavy, I was filthy and dishevelled, and my mouth tasted of drains.

As we drove down the main street, Charlie pointed out the theatre where he planned to ply his trade. It was the size of a church hall, wood-built and painted light green, with an art deco arch over its front door and two signs: one depicting the name of the joint ('Flattened Hat Theatre') and the other advertising the current act ('TONIGHT: THE SUICIDE POETS'). The Suicide Poets sounded like an indie band so I made a mental note to consider checking them out. I had missed hearing decent music. Might be just the tonic: a *soupçon* of culture.

Frankly, I was looking forward to some time off, though hilariously I was supposed to now be on holiday. Pretanike, I estimated, was barely a couple of hundred miles away: a few hours drive. Yes, I had earned a break.

"I'll drop you at a B&B I know, OK?" said Charlie.

"Will you be staying there?" I asked.

I needn't have worried. "No, 'fraid not, boys. I know some people, they let me kip on the sofa for free." He added hastily, "I'd ask if you could stay too, only they're, er, their spare room caught fire."

Dad, who had become increasingly antsy as we neared the town, drumming his fingers and staring intently forwards, mouth open, butted in, "Mink the minking B&B! Where's the minking bar?"

It was what I had dreaded but had figured inevitable. Could I talk him round? Charlie stopped the truck.

"Dad. Look at me."

Though the sweating had stopped, the liquid had undermined various of his scabs, which were now peeling off, and his few patches of proper flesh had become wrinkly. His hair was flat and unkempt, hideously greasy with terrible loose ends, and his beard looked like something the North Pole plumber had pulled from Santa's plughole.

He glared.

What could I say to him that had not already been said? He had got this far without me, still breathing, if hardly unscathed.

"Nothing? Right then." He stuck two fingers up to me then Charlie. "Mink you. And mink you."

As he was about to close the door, I blurted out, "You're only hurting yourself."

He turned. "You think I don't know?" And walked away.

Had I misheard him?

"Wait…" I called after him, but he did not stop.

Charlie nudged me in the back and pointed. "That's your B&B," he said.

Unfortunately, next door to the B&B was an establishment with this lettering beneath its eaves:

JIMMY'S TOPLESS BAR

Dextrose was making for it like the parched heading for an oasis. At nine in the morning.

Back to square one. I shook my head and felt like weeping.

Desert Rose Guest House, Wednesday, 9.00am:

Charlie had a parting joke – "Two elephants walk off a cliff. Boom boom!" – which it took me a while to get.

I shook his hand. "Thanks," I said. "You saved our lives."

"True," he said, polishing fingernails.

And it probably was. We had not passed a single vehicle since he had picked us up and nothing had overtaken us, least of all Hilda in her wheelchair. Had Charlie not spotted us at the roadside in the dark, our tongues might now have been doubling as sandpaper and we'd have been all out of Sheep Shavings. A complete stranger – Kai's son, to boot – he had put himself out to help us.

I felt for my wallet. "Could I pay you something? For the petrol? Gas?"

He shook his head. "I was going this way anyway."

"Well, just in case you…"

"Got the business, remember? Keep your money, mate. Maybe one day you'll get me to tune your bagpipes?"

"Sure," I replied.

The Desert Rose Guest House was a two-storey, pink-washed, detached house, with white window frames and red roses growing around the door. I sniffed a bloom as I stood on the doorstep and realised it was plastic.

Once inside I was faced with a staircase and, running beside that, a corridor. To my left was a window in the wall, with a shelf and a bell. 'Ring for service', said a sign, so I did.

Ping! It was the sort of sound holidaymakers were accustomed to hearing. The sound of imminent service.

The carpets were crimson and black, floral designed, heavy on the eye. Behind the window was a small office featuring desk and chair, obsolete-looking PC and paperwork along the opposite wall. On the desk were plastic roses and framed prints of further roses nestled among the paperwork.

The office door opened and a middle-aged woman walked in. She wore a pleated grey skirt, white shirt with pearls at the neck, and thin red cardigan. Her hair was brown and loosely permed. She pulled the window across and sat down. I could see the powder on her cheeks.

Then she smiled and I noticed her teeth were stumpy, blackened and rotten, like a mouthful of mixed raisins and peanuts.

"Welcome to the Desert Rose Guest House," she said. "My name is Rose. How may I help you?"

I couldn't get past the teeth.

She repeated herself, with emphasis. "How may I *help* you?"

"I'd like a room, please!" I over-trilled.

"What's the name?" she asked, picking up a pen.

Could she not afford dentures? "Dextrose," I said. "Pilsbury Dextrose."

When the forms had been completed, monies paid in advance – Quench had been indecently generous, so there were pots still to spare – and I had been informed of meal times and the key and shower situation, she rang the bell herself.

Ping! It made me want to press it again.

"My daughter will show you to your room," said Rose.

A young woman appeared as if from nowhere. A vision. She

was not conventionally beautiful. But she did something to me.

"I'm Clemmie," said the vision. "Can I take your bags?"

In her mid-20s, she wore denim dungarees over a white T-shirt and her brown hair was tied in bunches. Her cheeks were flushed, she was quite stocky and wore horn-rimmed tortoise-shell specs, popular in the Fifties. Her thin smile and the way she'd leaned her head to one side when she'd asked about my bags – so coy. I was entranced.

I realised I hadn't spoken. "Oh, yes, uh, sure! Thank you so much!"

She brought her head up to vertical and raised her eyebrows. "So?"

"So, er, what?"

"So where are your bags?"

"Oh. Sorry! Hahaha! I don't have any."

"You're a funny guy," said Clemmie.

It was then that I spotted something awry among her teeth. No, please. No.

"Do you…" I stopped.

"Sorry?" she said.

Braces! She was wearing chunky metal dental braces!

"You're wearing braces!" (I narrowly avoided adding, "Phew!")

"Yuh. Er, sure."

"Cos your mother…" Erk.

"Yeah, she has bad teeth. You're not the first to point it out. It's OK. You should see my Dad's mouth."

"No thanks! …I mean, er, sure, why not? I mean…"

"Follow me," she cut in, saving my blushes. "I'll show you to your room."

"This is the Rose Room," said Clemmie, unlocking the door at the top of the stairs and ushering me inside. As I entered I heard a subtle hiss beside my right ear and felt a fine spray envelop my head. It smelled of fake flowers, went right up my nostrils and I choked violently.

"Sorry about that," said Clemmie. "Motion sensor. It sprays rose-scented air freshener when you enter the room. Mum's idea. I hate it. That's why I let you go in first."

The tease.

I sat on the bed and bounced a few times. Boy, did it feel good. Actual comfort.

The room was terribly rose-themed. Rose wallpaper, a white wardrobe with painted pink roses climbing up its sides, pink ceiling, and walls covered with rose prints.

"How many rooms do you have?" I asked.

"Two," she said.

"What's the other one called?"

"Also the Rose Room."

"Then I shall take this one!" I declared, all jaunty.

"I know," said Clemmie. "You'd already booked it."

I smiled at her and she smiled back.

"So…" I said.

"Well, if you need anything, just ring the bell downstairs." She turned to go.

"No, wait!" What to say? "Er. I was planning to take the day off."

"Oh right, so you're working here?"

"No, no," I chortled. "I'm on holiday."

She wrinkled her nose; her glasses slipped down and she pushed them back up with a finger. "So you're taking a day off – on holiday?"

"It's a long story."

"OK," she said, once again turning to leave.

I had to keep her talking. "So I was wondering. What's worth doing in Flattened Hat? Entertainment-wise?"

Clemmie shrugged. "Not much."

"There must be something!"

"Well, I'm going to see the Suicide Poets tonight…"

My in! "Great!" I said, too quickly. "That sounds great. I'd love to see them too."

She looked at me askance. "You like poetry?"

The Suicide Poets weren't an indie band? "Sure. I love poetry! I wandered lonely as a cloud and all that."

"OK," she said. "Maybe I'll see you in there." And she was gone.

I had a date!

I gazed out of the window, set on the rear of the property and facing out over a newish-looking red-brick housing estate. People were heading to work, or out shopping, on foot, by car; it all looked so… normal. This was precisely what the doctor had ordered: everyday relaxation, untroubled by psychotics.

Flinging myself flat on my back onto the soft mattress, pillows behind my head, I savoured the soft linen while trying to ignore the cloying smell of air-freshener. It was only a single bed, but I was pretty sure I could squeeze in one more…

Desert Rose Guest House, Wednesday, ⑦.④④pm:

When I woke it struck me that the room, which had been flooded with sunlight, was now dark and illuminated by artificial light filtering in through the window.

Night-time. Surely not? I looked at my Timeco Z112.2 XG. It read 19.41. I'd slept for almost ten hours. Hardly surprising, I supposed.

But wait. Clemmie. The Suicide Poets. What time would they be onstage? I dared not miss them.

Launching myself off the bed, I immediately felt dizzy.

Any self-respecting lothario would have taken a shower. I was too nervous of missing the performance, and so my date, to spare the time. Instead I peeled off my safari suit – wishing I had a change of clothes as I did so – and slooshed myself down from the sink. The cool water felt like a balm.

As I dressed again I pushed out creases and brushed off dust with a hand. This is what explorers looked like, I decided. Clemmie would surely trade my exotic tales for a little wear and tear.

As I left the Rose Room that pesky sensor hit me with another squirt of atomised old-lady. Hardly the aromatic effect I was after. Then again... it was a scent of sorts. So I shimmied back in and out for a further brace of blasts.

Good to go.

I wondered whether to ring the bell for Clemmie on the way down the stairs, but the house was very quiet so I assumed she must already be out. Plus, I definitely didn't want to have to talk to her mother or father. They might demand to know my romantic intentions while their teeth fell out.

The reception was dark and unmanned. I opened the front door and closed it gently behind me.

Flattened Hat Theatre, Wednesday, 7.55 pm:

The night air was soothingly warm, the perfect antidote to the itchy heat of the Nameless Highway. It would be just a short walk back up the main drag, the route Charlie had driven in on, to my goal. (And my girl.) Thoroughly refreshed and brimming with hope, I felt like I was bouncing on air.

A young boy cycled towards me.

"Evening!" I called out.

He stared at me on the way past. "Paedo!"

"I'm not a paedo," I felt obliged to point out.

The incident would not flatten my mood.

Then I remembered Jimmy's Topless Bar and Dextrose.

There it was, the lettering now lit up and surrounded by white lightbulbs, only half of which were functioning. The windows were blacked out and no discernible noise came from within. Might he still be in there, arseholed and besotted? Frankly, I'd have been amazed if he weren't. But he wasn't going to spoil my night. Not tonight.

I turned left and headed for the theatre, whistling a classical tune. Bit of sophistication.

It was almost eight o'clock when I tripped up the doorstep into the Flattened Hat Theatre, having jogged a bit to make up time.

I needn't have worried. The place was all but empty.

A tatty desk and chair immediately inside the door, incorporating an ancient bloke dozing, comprised the box office. At the far end of the room was the stage, before which rows of perhaps 100 seats had been set up (wishfully, thus far). Suspended above the stage, three coloured lights – red, blue and green – flashed on and off. Along the right wall was a perfunctory bar.

The place smelled of age and dust, of the ghosts of Thespians and erstwhile punters. The seats were red velour, the wallpaper flocked, the woodwork dark and the once-white ceiling attractively corniced but nicotine-stained. It was like wandering into the psyche of a Victorian gin addict.

Expectantly, I looked around for Clemmie. But there was only one woman in the joint, hunched under an unfashionable hat, knitting in the third row. Not her.

Elsewhere: three figures onstage, all male, setting up five standing microphones; one old codger, bald with waistcoat, behind the bar; a tall, flamboyant-looking chap in a dark velvet frockcoat, seated at it, staring into a glass.

Poetry, I thought, and shivered.

The dozing box-officer had not stirred and it seemed a shame to rouse him, so I walked straight in and made for the bar.

It was better stocked than Socks 'N' Sandals, though only just. Three optics and two hand pumps, plus a selection of bottles on unrefrigerated shelves. The barman, stout with comb-over, wore a long-sleeved shirt with those garter things around the upper arms. I could not imagine what use they were. He was smoking a cigar and his pitted face suggested he had suffered from terrible acne in his youth.

"Yes, sir?" he said. Smoke drifted into his eyes and he winced.

"I'll have a pint, please," I said.

"Lager, lager or lager?" he asked.

"Lager, I guess."

"Yeah, which of the three?"

"The middle one?"

"Wise," he said.

"And four bags of peanuts, please."

I felt a tap on the shoulder. It was the flamboyant-looking chap: dark, flowing locks swept back from his face, pointy-nosed and haughty. His eyebrows had been plucked and his eyes were piggy. Beneath the frockcoat he wore a frilly shirt, opened to the chest.

"From whence does one hail?" he asked in rich, upper-crust tones. He was English.

I grinned at him, despite suspecting him of poetry performance. It was heartening to hear a familiar accent, made home seem nearer. "I'm English," I said. "You are too."

He held his arm at waist height and bowed over it. "One is apparently in the presence of genius. Did one travel here purely to see we Suicide Poets? Is one a…" he could barely bring himself to say it, "*fan?*" He was so posh, the 'fan' sounded more like 'fayen'.

I pointed at myself. "Who, me? All the way from England? To see the Suicide Poets?"

He looked down his nose at me. "Yeeees."

"No, from the Desert Rose guest house, actually. Five minutes walk away." That told him, the flouncing twot.

He took out a lace handkerchief from his top pocket and waved me away with it. "Heathen," he said, and returned to his stool.

"One pint of lager," said the barman, plonking the glass in front of me. Under his breath he added, "He's a right wanker, in'e?"

I downed a half-pint in one go, followed by a bag of nuts, then looked around for Clemmie, however there was still no sign. A new customer pulled up a stool beside me. He was wearing a red leather three-piece suit with shiny blue winkle-pickers. Dyed black, his hair had been cut into a mullet, and his face was caked in make-up.

He stared at me. Metallic-blue eyeliner, green eyes.

Another bloody poet, I didn't doubt.

The flouncing twot to my other side called across to him: "That chap's from England. Came all this way to see little old us!"

"Ohmygod!" gasped his colleague, slapping my knee. "Are you an interviewer? Which paper do you work for? Better not be *The Stage*!" His voice was twangy and nasal, highly camp.

Time to make my excuses. A break for the toilet would suffice. "Any idea which way the loos are?" I asked.

He stood up. "I knew it! Questions, questions, questions!" Raising his right arm and pointing down at himself, he performed a little twirl and announced in a loud, sing-song voice to those present, "Pay attention, everyone. I'm being *interviewed*!"

I was rather taken aback.

"Do close your mouth, honey," he said. "You'll have spiders crawl in there in this place!" He looked around the theatre and mock-shuddered.

"I..." I began.

He put an arm around my shoulder and steered me towards the right of the stage. "You come backstage with me and you can ask me anything you want! I'm all yours!"

"But I..."

He held a finger to his lips. "No buts, honey."

'Backstage' turned out to be a room little larger than a cloakroom. Indeed, it possibly was one. A single lightbulb illuminated the space, containing just two benches opposite one other and a mirror on the wall. Clothing was piled on the floor and there was make-up and sandwiches on one bench.

"It's not much but we call it home!" trilled my new friend.

He sat down, ushered me opposite, crossed his legs and put his hands on the uppermost knee. "Right!" he said. "I must tell you *all* about myself!"

"I'm not a journalist," I pointed out.

"That's what they all say, honey."

"No really, I'm an explorer."

"Journalist, explorer. Explorer, journalist. What's in a name? Now, where's your pen and paper? You're going to need to take this down. Just you wait – I give dynamite quotes; you'll be able to sell this anywhere." He wagged a finger at me. "But if you sell it to *The Stage* I will *hunt you down*, honey! OK?"

"I don't have a pen and paper," I said.

"And you're a professional journalist?! Whatever next? Here, have mine." He produced a bundle of pens and several pads wrapped in an elastic band from his red leather jacket pocket, selected one of each and handed them to me. "Right, fire away!"

"Er, well, em," I stammered.

"OK, so I'm Bish-Bash-Bosh. Like Percy but with more *balls*, you know?"

I didn't, which didn't stop him. "Then there's Esteban, who you've met at the bar. If you print that we're lovers, it's libel. Isn't he just *adorable*, though?"

No, I thought, he's a complete bastard. "He didn't sound very Spanish to me."

"Well, there's a story there."

I wished I hadn't said anything.

Bish-Bash-Bosh continued: "His mother, right? She once crawled all the way from Canada to Spain in an underground sewage pipe! Can you *believe* that?"

No.

He went on. "Then there's the identical twins, Romulus and Remus. They were up on stage just now, setting up. Did you see them?"

"I hadn't noticed they were identical twins."

He raised an eyebrow. "Hmm. Between you and me, they're bitches. And their names aren't really Romulus and Remus. They're Keith and Kevin." He shuffled delightedly on his bench. "But swear to me you won't print that."

"I swear," I swore. (It was true.)

He winked. "Good. And finally there's Nooooooo. He was on the stage too."

Come again. "Sorry, Noooo? There's someone called Noooo?"

"Honey, which century are you living in? Of course there's someone called Nooooooo. And please, promise me you'll spell his name with seven o's. If people spell it was fewer or more, he goes *men-tal*! He really does."

I looked at the door willing someone, anyone – preferably Clemmie – to come in and interrupt us.

No one did.

Bish-Bash-Bosh proceeded to interview himself, perhaps unimpressed by my efforts. "When did I first realise I was a poet? Well, I wrote my first poetry in the womb, so you do the math. My mother was a *slave* to the Threepenny Opera, she really was. I suppose you'll want to know why we call ourselves the Suicide Poets? It's so *obvious*, honestly. So *boring*. But don't worry, I like you so I'll answer your question."

He paused. "Are you writing this down?"

"Er, yes, sure," I said, and scribbled on my pad:

I WISH I WAS DEAD

"Right, OK. So we're called the Suicide Poets because we are prepared to *die* for our art, honey." He clawed theatrically at his heart. "We are."

"Prepared or intending to?"

"Good question!" Bish-Bash-Bosh furrowed his brow. "Both. Either. One or the other. Actually, it's rather a silly question!"

Alright. "Have any of the Suicide Poets ever killed themselves?"

He looked at me as the teacher might study an errant schoolchild. "Now now, honey! Don't you start coming over all investigative on my ass!" He stood up and pretended to look at a watch, though he wasn't wearing one. "Time's up! Lovely to meet you."

He blew me a kiss and off he skipped.

When I returned to the auditorium, my heart missed a beat.
Clemmie was there.

She hadn't stood me up! (I had never doubted her.) She was sitting in the back row wearing a sleeveless black dress that showed off her upper arms. Her hair was down and she wore bright red lipstick. She was *gorgeous*. I waved at her but she didn't notice. The theatre was woefully low-lit.

I sneaked up behind her and playfully covered her eyes with my hands. She shrieked and jumped out of her seat.

"Oh. It's you," she said, panting and holding her chest. "What did you do that for?"

"Sorry, I didn't mean to startle you." I was hopping from foot to foot.

Someone tapped on a microphone, which echoed around the all-but-empty hall. I glanced towards the stage. The five Suicide Poets were on-stage, looking arty and middle-aged. Bish-Bash-Bosh blew me another kiss.

I waved. "I just interviewed him," I told Clemmie.

"Oh," she said, retaking her seat.

I sat down next to her and she shuffled slightly away, the seats being rather too close together to allow adequate personal space.

"Do you come here often?" I asked, already regretting the cliché.

"Hello, good evening! We are the Suicide Poets!" announced the five poets in unison.

Then Bish-Bash-Bosh said: "We tour nations bringing culture to the masses. Consider it our duty, laying wordplay on your asses."

Besides myself, Clemmie, the old knitting lady (still knitting), and an earnest-looking young man in a corduroy jacket, the audience comprised three young men in adjacent seats in the front row. They were jostling each other and spilling their pints.

"Get on with it!" heckled the middle one of the three.

Bish-Bash-Bosh shot him a withering look.

The heckler persisted: "If you're the Suicide Poets, kill yourselves!"

"Brilliant," retorted the lead poet. "How many times do you think I've heard that?"

Clearly a rhetorical question, it seemed to confuse the heckler. "Seven? Twelve? One?" he flapped, then shut up.

"I didn't introduce myself," I said to Clemmie.

"No," she replied.

"I'm Pilsbury."

"Hello," she said, eyes firmly on the stage.

Three of the performers had departed, leaving only the identical twins. They wore pinstripe suits and had donned bowler hats; each stood under an open umbrella. They were thin-faced yet fat-bellied. One wore big red spectacles, the other wore blue.

"We are Romulus and Remus," said one.

Through the corner of my mouth nearest Clemmie, I told her, "Actually, their real names are Keith and Kevin."

The other twin said, "This is a poem called *Turbulence Inside*

Our Heads. We wrote it for Trevor."

When no one clapped, they removed their microphones from their stands and each took a step backwards.

"AAAAAAAAAAAAAAAAAAAAAAAAGH!" bellowed one, bent double but still holding up his umbrella.

"AAAAAAAAAAAAAAAAAAAAAAAAGH!" bellowed the other, ditto.

(After that, they alternated lines, which went...)
"AAAAAAAAAAAAAAAGH!"
"AAAAAAAAAAAAAAAGH!"
"AAAAAAAAAAAAAAAGH!"
"AAAAAAAAAAAAAAAGH!"
"GGGGGGGGGGGGNNNNNNNNNNNNN!"
"GGGGGGGGGGGGNNNNNNNNNNNNN!"
"AAAAAAAAAAAAAAAGH!"
"AAAAAAAAAAAAAAAGH!"
"AAAAAAAAAAAAAAAGH!"
"AAAAAAAAAAAAAAAGH!"
"SAVE US!"
"SAVE US!"
"Save us!"
"Save us!"
"NO!"
"WE WILL *NOT*!"

They bowed and left the stage to stunned silence.

Well, I thought. The old knitting lady had packed up her wool and left halfway through. It had been kind of *a capella* death metal. The best I could think to say of it was that it had sort of rhymed until the last two lines.

I checked to see that Clemmie hadn't left and was relieved to see her still seated next to me, if looking a little on edge.

Next came a godawful noise, as if a disorientated bluebottle's repeated battering against a window-pane had been amplified. Again it came, and again. Then all five Suicide Poets took the stage, each cradling the same musical instrument.

I couldn't quite believe it.

"This next poem is dedicated to Charlie, who tuned our bagpipes this morning. Without him, we couldn't have performed this for you," said Bish-Bash-Bosh.

I was filled with quiet amusement and horror.

"This is called *Five Open Letters to Paul McCartney Concerning Mull of Kintyre*," the lead poet went on. "We haven't performed it since 1994, so we may be a little rusty. Please forgive us." He bowed.

Rusty – *on the bagpipes?* I sunk down into my seat.

Each Suicide Poet created a discordant, infernal racket that might have been heard in space. Then they took it in turns to recite – at least reducing the number of bagpipes played from five to four – at hollering volume.

It went like this:

Bish-Bash-Bosh:
"Paul McCartney.
Please don't start me.
No, it's too late now.
I've started."

Esteban:
"Paul McCartney.
'Mist rolling in from the sea?'
Only waves of nausea
rolled over me."

Romulus (or Remus):
"Paul McCartney.
It was you, Linda McCartney,
and Denny
Laine. The shame."

Remus (or Romulus):
"Paul McCartney.
What would John-ny
Lennon have said?
Did your lame song make him dead?"

Happily we never got to hear Nooooooo's open letter to Paul because the heckler from earlier launched himself onto the stage and started wrestling the bagpipes out of Esteban's arms. His mates joined in and a fight broke out.

Turning to Clemmie, I said, "Bet the last verse would have mentioned the Frog Ch..." But she was leaving.

"What did you think?" I asked when I caught her up outside.

"I'm leaving, aren't I?" she said.

We walked in silence in the direction of the Desert Rose.

Desert Rose Guest House, Wednesday, 9:35 pm:

"OK, well it was nice to meet you again," said Clemmie, making for the downstairs hallway, somewhere along which her room must have been.

I had to act fast or I would lose her.

"Erm," I said in a raised voice, aimed at her retreating form. She turned. Pursed her lips. Mmm... lovely lips.

"Yes?" she said.

"I could murder a coffee!"

She paused. "I'm sorry. Hot refreshment's only available nine to five. But there's a kettle in the communal kitchen upstairs."

Moment slipping away. "No, you've misunderstood me. I was hoping to have a *coffee*."

"Yes, I heard you the first time. Hot ref..."

"No, I didn't mean..."

"Orange squash?"

"Sorry?"

"Cold drink? Orange squash?"

"That's not..."

"Iced tea?"

"Oh dear."

"Milk?"

"Actually, I'm not feeling that thirsty any more."

"Oh. Oh well," she said. "If you change your mind."

Had to be more direct. "In England, where I come from, 'coffee' is a euphemism."

"Is it?" She frowned. "So what do you ask for when you want a coffee?"

It wasn't going at all well. "Look, I'll get to the point," I said. "Would you..."

Suddenly there came an almighty banging on a nearby wall. A man's gummy-sounding voice shouted, "Whatf all vat wacket? Get to beb!"

Clemmie looked abashed. "My Dad. Gotta go," she loud-whispered. "Night."

And that was that.

How near and yet how far?

The way I saw it, I had three options:

1. Head up to my TV-less room and fall asleep through boredom.
2. Head back out into Flattened Hat, maybe find a bar and grab a bite to eat.
3. Save Dextrose from himself.

Option 2 stuck out like a sore thumb, and even 1 was preferable to 3.

But then, what price loyalty?

Jimmy's Topless Bar, Wednesday, 9.50pm:

I wasn't sure what to expect as I pushed on the door of Jimmy's Topless Bar. My single – vain – hope was that Harrison Dextrose would not be inside.

"Minking marvellous!" were the first words I heard.

He was seated on a stool, elbows on the bar, chin in hands, staring at a 50-something barmaid engrossed in a book, wearing no top. Her breasts were voluminous and she was using them as a rest. She wore reading glasses and had a chestnut perm (possibly a wig: it didn't look quite real).

The room was dingy, with plain walls like chalkboards, and whiffed of stale sweat (there was another note in there, which I hoped never to identify). All of its windows had been blacked out. A dartboard hung in one corner; beside it a jukebox barely audibly played *Stand By Your Man* by Tammy Wynette.

There was only one other customer, seated next to Dextrose, though they were paying each other no attention. He was a wizened little old man with a bent back and trousers that were too big, held up by braces.

"Heehee! Oi love them dirty pillows!" announced the little old man, apropos of nothing.

The barmaid looked up and tutted.

Dextrose slapped him on the back, spilling his own drink as

his elbow slid along the bar surface. The glass rolled off and smashed onto the floor.

"Another one, boys?" sighed the barmaid, putting down her book.

No one had even noticed me in the doorway.

All out of enthusiasm and loyalty, I reverted to option 1.

Desert Rose Guest House, Wednesday, 1.1.5.0 pm:

I lay on the bed and allowed my mood to sink. Drizzle pattered its downbeat rhythm on the window-pane and somewhere a dog howled a forlorn siren song to other lonely, horny mutts.

I couldn't sleep.

A glass of milk and a ham sandwich had been left on the bedside table, by the lovely Clemmie I hoped, and were a brief but welcome respite from the overwhelming sense that everything was going wrong.

I felt so badly let down.

Why had I kidded myself that Dextrose might change? I'd read his book: that was him. The alcoholic skirt-chaser, hedonist, deviant. His world revolved around him.

That I had seen a softer side to him, at least verging on the paternal, only made his return to the dark side worse. We were supposed to be on a mission, to find his abandoned wife. He'd understood that, I knew. Although I doubted he would ever admit it – immaturity, misdirected pride – he did want to find her.

I had become swept along with the lame-ass plan, based on a childlike drawing made under the influence of hallucinogens, and on the claims of a charlatan, with Dextrose's memory of places and times key to our hopes. How stupid had I been?

Chasing shadows.

At least I'd *had* a mother and father. Physical presences. They had even managed to live in the same house as me. For years! They had communicated with me, had acknowledged my existence, catered to my needs and comforted me when I was ill. They'd shown responsibility. Of parents, that was hardly too much to ask. And they had only been my guardians.

Why on earth had I been so in awe of Dextrose?

It made me wonder whether I had been too hard on Mother and Father? It was all too easy to remember the tougher times, the claustrophobia and the irritation of being brought up. But it hadn't been all so bad. It really hadn't.

When I was a young boy in buttoned-up pyjamas, Father used to tell me bedtime stories. I would lie bound in linen and he would ask me to pick a character and setting, then he would weave a fantastical tale around those, off the top of his head. He'd been very good at that, and I had always looked forward to his tales, the sense of safety and the escapism.

And every night, before he turned off the light, he would pat me on the head, as tenderly as his own evidently repressed upbringing would allow.

I'd forgotten that.

Another incident sprang to my mind. There had been a boy at boarding school who had bullied me during my early teens. He made me fear break-times, would tease and taunt me, sometimes punched and kicked. I hated him.

It was his power trip and my pathetic impotence, and the taunts of my classmates riled and upset me. I never dared offer a physical response because the bully was stronger than me. So readily downtrodden had I been.

Neither would I have told Father, volunteer my weakness, though he noticed one weekend when I had become especially withdrawn and had coaxed the story out of me.

He listened quietly and, when I had finished pouring out my

woe, for once he did not recommend a stiff upper lip, his solution to so many of life's problems.

That Monday, he drove me to school for the week as usual, before heading back to teach at Glibley Secondary. Unusually, when he parked the car he got out too. The boys were kicking balls around the playground, killing time before assembly.

"You're going to point this bully out to me," he said.

I was mortified. Eyes were upon us.

"Come on," he commanded. "I don't have long."

So I did it. I pointed to the boy, feeling like Judas, and the boy saw me doing so.

I could barely watch as Father strode across the playground, stopped at my tormentor and spoke to him, for no more than a few seconds. When he returned to his car he said nothing to me, did not even look my way. Then he was gone.

The retribution never came. The bullying just stopped. The boy actively avoided me afterwards.

Only a couple of weeks later, once my embarrassment and trepidation had subsided enough for inquisitiveness to kick in, did I steel myself to ask Father what he had said. He tried to brush the query aside, but I persisted.

Eventually he told me: "I just said to him in a vaguely threatening manner, 'Remember what happened to Pythagoras'."

I was bemused. "Why, what did happen to Pythagoras?"

"No one really knows," he replied. "But I was darned sure that young bully wouldn't. A maths-based threat!"

Though Father never had much of a sense of humour he laughed that day, and I could not help but join in. It was one of those moments.

Perhaps I had been too hard on him?

I had certainly given Dextrose too generous a ride. So I made up my mind, as a clock outside chimed midnight: I'd get him back for his solipsism, for his disloyalty, for his wanton ways. Maybe I should just abandon him, as he had me? That'd sure slap my message across his swollen face.

   Yes, why not?

   Sorted.

Desert Rose Guest House, Thursday, 6:25 am:

It had been a night of fitful slumber, punctuated by nightmares featuring Importos, Hilda and Eustace. All too real. I had woken up several times, shaking, almost feverish, and when I drifted back to sleep the terrible visions had continued precisely where they'd left off.

I recalled feeling, even in my subconscious, an enormous sense of relief when the cavalry had finally arrived in the form of a fleet of police cars, rolling in convoy down the Nameless Highway and into Lonely Bush, sirens blaring.

When I woke up, the sirens were still blaring.

Immediately I guessed what was going on.

Red light travelled in pulses along the walls of the stairway, beamed in through glass. Which emergency service – services? – they belonged to, that was debatable, but I knew full well which establishment they would be attending.

The sirens ceased as I descended the stairs. Rose was at the bottom in a floral nightgown, heading for the front door. I shimmied past her, reached the latch, then had to stand aside while she found the key for the lock.

"I'll bet it's that damned titty bar again," she muttered to herself. "Always trouble. The lowlife they get in there."

"Indeed," I replied.

"What are you doing up, anyway? Is this something to do with you?" she demanded.

"What's going on, Ma?" Clemmie's voice, muffled by walls.

I couldn't let them know the truth – that my father was a lecherous drunk whose face was falling off – so I was forced to think fast. And it just slipped out: "I'm an undercover police officer. Stay inside and leave this to me."

"Oooh," she went, practically swooning. "You should have said so before, officer."

Pushing Rose aside, I swung open the door and stood on the step. Swathed in flashing red light, which felt seedy, I turned and held my palm up towards her. "Go back inside, ma'm. Let me take care of this."

That was when Clemmie appeared in her jim-jams. Pale blue jim-jams, probably cotton. Her hair in sweet disarray. Rubbing bleary eyes.

As I closed the door I caught her say the words, "…must have been pretty deep undercover…"

A single police car, white with a green stripe along the side, was parked outside Jimmy's. The drunk being bundled into the back seat by a copper in a hat was instantly recognisable.

The barmaid I'd seen earlier was standing in the bar doorway, ranting and shaking a fist while her boobs wobbled in sympathy. "Get him out of here! Dirty old sod! You throw the book at him, officer! Never in all my years…"

The drizzle had stopped, leaving that nostalgic, heady aroma of dampened grass. I sucked it in, looked around to see Clemmie and her mother's noses pressed against the guesthouse window, ogling, and dived into the crime scene.

"Excuse me, officer," I said, keeping a respectful distance. "Can I help?"

Dextrose lay sprawled across the rear seat of the cop car,

attempting to right himself in the manner of an upside-down beetle. His tracksuit bottoms were soaked in what I trusted was beer, and I could smell the alcohol fumes even from a safe distance.

The officer addressed me. "And why might you be able to help, sir?"

I swallowed dry nothing. He had the disposition of a sergeant-major, all chest and chin. His khaki uniform – shorts, short-sleeved shirt, long socks, blunt pointy hat with four dents, such as a scoutmaster (or an eccentric German) might have worn – was immaculate. His buttons were polished and his expression scared me.

"Iyav neverseenthad man inmylife, orifice," slurred Dextrose.

I had no way of telling whether he was trying to protect me or had forgotten who I was again.

"What's he done?" I asked.

"And why would that be any business of yours? Sir?" the copper persisted.

Should I confess? "He's my father, officer."

He eyed me suspiciously. "*That's* your father?"

"Yes. *He* is."

The copper glared. "You realise I am at liberty to arrest you also, for consorting with a known criminal?"

I didn't, but felt the concept was best sidestepped. "What's he done, officer?"

He pointed towards Jimmy's. "According to Miss Venetia Williams, the beverage dispenser at said establishment, the accused proceeded to place his penis in her lime juice and soda water at…" he consulted his notebook, "5.57am, while requesting of her in a 'leery' manner, 'Do you fancy a quick mint?'"

"Actually, it's 'mink'," I pointed out, as he slapped shut his book.

Sadly it didn't surprise me at all. More than once in *The Lost*

Incompetent had Dextrose documented himself doing precisely the same: dunking his private part in a lady's drink then asking her out. It appeared to be his chat-up technique when exquisitely drunk, and it had never occurred to him that it didn't work.

Instead, I said: "That's most unlike him, officer. Are you sure it isn't a case of mistaken identity?"

Dextrose, I noticed, had fallen asleep sucking his thumb.

The copper pushed out his shiny shirt buttons. "Sir. Besides Miss Williams, the accused was the only human personage in said establishment. Now, if you do not wish to become incarcerated also, I suggest you stand aside and desist from asking questions." He opened his car door and slid in.

"Wait, please, officer. Where are you taking him?"

He donned a pair of sunglasses slowly, while staring at me, savouring his role. "Pretanike Jail. Now disproceed from the crime scene, sir. That is your final warning."

He slammed his door and turned on his flashing lights and siren, though there was no other traffic in sight. I watched the car disappear up the road, flustered and bereft. Now I would be looking for both Mr and Mrs Dextrose in Pretanike: a disconcerting burden of responsibility, suddenly thrust upon me.

Quite sensibly, I could have stayed in Flattened Hat, married Clemmie following a whirlwind romance and lived happily ever after, expunging any memories of the Dextrose clan from my mind. Just let it go. Get on with my life.

But I couldn't.

I wished I could have done, but I couldn't.

Rose's gaze followed me as I returned to the guesthouse and she was waiting on the doorstep as I arrived. Her daughter had disappeared. Probably overcome with admiration.

"What happened?" she asked eagerly. "Did he ask for your help?"

"Out of my jurisdiction," I replied.

"So what happened?"

I tapped the side of my nose conspiratorially. "Police business. You understand, I'm sure, ma'm?"

"Ooooh!" she gasped. "You can tell me, you know..."

"No time, I'm afraid. I need to follow that police car to Pretanike Jail."

But how?

I needn't have worried. "Clemmie! Clemmie!" Rose called back down the hallway.

"What?" her daughter replied.

Rose said, "I've told this charming young policeman you'll give him a lift to Pretanike. He needs to get there urgently."

Brief silence. Then: "Why me?"

"Because I have to stay here to run the guesthouse and your father has to..." The landlady glanced at me. "You know what your father has to do. Now get a move on, young lady!"

"Do I have to?" Slightly whinier than I might have anticipated.

"Yes! You do!"

Nameless Highway, Thursday, 9.55 am:

I will confess that my ardour for Clemmie was cooling slightly by the time the dark needles that were Pretanike's skyscrapers appeared on the horizon. There is only so much information one person needs concerning another's grandparents, unless one is addicted to genealogy.

Boy, could she talk about family.

I learnt that her paternal grandparents were called Reg and Edie, that Reg died two years ago, aged 82, of lung cancer, and that Edie (87) lived a short walk away, in Lavender Close. Clemmie visited her every Thursday afternoon, they watched the daytime soap (*Hoi, That's My Wife!*) while eating fig rolls, and Edie habitually pressed a penny coin into her palm as she left.

"It's not a lot, I know, but it adds up when you've visited as often as I do," Clemmie explained.

Reg had wheezed a lot, though he had never once in his life smoked. No one could explain this. The consultant at the hospital (Dr Beverley) suggested he might have unwittingly worked with asbestos in his younger days. However, since Reg had owned a confectionery business until his retirement (12 October 1979; 32 family members had attended his retirement party, pointedly not including Reg and Edie's son, Jake, with whom they had fallen out once he began dating and later married Sharon Probert, "a bitch") that had been deemed unlikely.

Having a father who worked in sweets had been the root of Clemmie's father Arthur's – and later Rose's – dental problems. Reg and Edie had tried interesting him in vegetables, even banned him from eating sweets, but he would sneak into the backroom of the shop as a child and steal the stock. White mice and strawberry bonbons were his favourites. Even into adulthood, Arthur had been unable to kick the sugar habit, leading to all of his teeth having fallen out or been extracted by the time he was 27. Rose was the first and only woman he had courted.

And so it went on, through Grandma Nesta and Grandpa Deke (RIP – natural causes), aunties Vi, Val (RIP – motor-vehicle accident) and Vera, uncles Rich, Stevo, Terry and Jeremy (gay – source of a family rift), cousins Willy, Bill, Eric (at catering college), Jake (aforementioned), Sylv, Dashiell, Lydia, Nancy (dangerously overweight) and Tiff, nephews... I can't go on.

Clemmie, on the other hand, could.

I did try to interject, however it proved hopeless.

When, for instance, Clemmie mentioned that her cousin Bill had once left Flattened Hat to go travelling, I spotted my opportunity and pounced: "I've been travelling!"

She paused only long enough to note, "That's nice," before going on to tell me how cousin Bill had been "God knows where," and had not returned home for "a good 72 hours," before riffing on cousin Dashiell's dislike of cheese wrapped in wax.

Ironically, for the first 20 minutes of the drive, she had silently sulked and I had had to coax her into talking.

Unaccustomed to female company as I had been, I did understand the importance of listening in the dating game. It's not what you reply, it's what you're prepared to absorb.

So Clemmie's four-on-the-floor verbosity dampened my

enthusiasm only slightly and, as she nattered on, all the while with her eyes on the road, soaking up the Nameless Highway, I was able to take in her profile.

Her chin was quite rounded; loose flesh drooped from beneath it like snow overhanging eaves. Her cheeks were plump and reddened, though she was bare of make-up, and her lips were thin. She tended to drive with her mouth open and her tongue-tip out.

Her forehead was convex, wrinkle-free, with evidence of flaking skin. She had a very cute nose, small, button-ended and curving upwards. Her tortoiseshell spectacles were pushed back up to its bridge and her eyes were golden-brown. More brown than golden.

Thick, mousy-coloured hair rippled down over her ears, like ice cream over oysters.

The only time she ceased her monologue was when she turned towards me suddenly and snapped, "Stop staring at me! You're giving me the creeps!"

I laughed and she said, "No, I'm serious." Obviously joking.

How did Clemmie compare to 'the goddess', Suzy Goodenough?

Suzy was sexier, there was no denying that. But Clemmie was homelier. The girl-next-door to Suzy's girl-several-streets-away.

Suzy was an inveterate tease. Clemmie… She was a tease also. Suzy…

Actually, the comparisons didn't really matter. The fact remained that I was hopeless with women. I'd spent years trying to wheedle myself into Suzy's affections, yet she had always fulfilled her carnal desires elsewhere, among the worldlier boys with the haircuts and the banter. All that investment for no return.

What earthly chance did I stand with Clemmie?

*Pretanike outskirts,
Thursday, ①①③⑤ am:*

We had driven into sprawling commerce. The once arid, barren swathes of land either side of the Nameless Highway were replaced by stores and eateries in warehouses the size of aircraft hangars – grey in colour, gaudy of logo – the closer we drew to the city.

Yummy Burger, Scrummy Burger, Best Pizza, Piece-a-Pizza, Pizza Piazza, Fashion Barn, Booze Barn, Shoe Barn, Cut That Barnet!, DIY Town, Toy City, Sofa World, Honest John's, Pistol Pete's, Shirley's, Garrison's, Levy's, Buy A Pet… And on it went.

Advertising billboards lined the road.

EVERYBODY LOVES THEIR BANK
(It says so here so it must be true!)

DINSDALE MOTORS – THE BEST YOU CAN BUY
OR YOUR MONEY BACK*
* subject to terms & conditions, see website

ALL-NEW 447-BLADE SWISH RAZOR
– one more blade than the 446!

LARD IS GOOD FOR YOU †

We drove past too fast to read the smallprint on the last one.

There were people everywhere now, milling, mingling, in melees, buying, buying, buying, and vehicles of all descriptions, sweeping past us, honking and jostling in their anxiety to deliver, to collect, to consume.

I felt like Neil Armstrong, dropped from the moon into the ticker-tape parade through New York City, and wondered how unsettling all that humanity must have seemed to him.

"You're not really a policeman, are you?"

I believe it was the first question Clemmie had asked me since we had set off.

"No," I said, having only briefly entertained the idea of fibbing.

"Why'd you say you were?"

I couldn't really remember.

"Who's in the cop car?" she asked.

"My Dad," I told her. "He was a bit drunk."

"So what happened? Why the cops?"

This time I threw a marquee-based party for the idea of fibbing. "He got beaten up by some guys in the bar. Got blamed for it – mistaken identity."

"So where'd the guys go who did it?"

"Dunno," I said. "Must have done a runner."

"Too bad."

"Yeah."

"What you gonna do?"

I'd lost count of the number of questions she'd asked me! "Bail him out, I guess."

"That'll cost."

"Will it?"

She didn't reply.

I didn't blame her – it had been a crap response.

At least she seemed to be warming to me.

Pretanike now loomed before us: ostentatiously high buildings, too many windows, choppers in the sky and a sense of electricity. Something clicked as anticipation coursed through me. Suddenly anything was possible. The prospect of the city felt thrilling.

This was the end of the road. So much to achieve.

I made another mental list:

1. Get Clemmie to fall in love with me. (Or at least hang out for a while – sufficient time to let nature take its course.)
2. Free Dad from jail.
3. Find Mrs Dextrose.

It did seem daunting, but I was positive. No, more than that, I was tingling. Pretanike had brought me to life, urged me to expect the unexpected. No holds barred. To dare is to do, my friend! To dare is to do!

Clemmie turned to me, sunlight glinting off her tortoise-shells. "Nearly there. Worked out your plan yet?"

"Free Dad, then find my Mum," I said.

"Find your Mum? Where is she?"

Tricky one. "Somewhere around the Statue of Charles Partridge?"

"Your voice went up at the end."

"So does yours. Even when you're not phrasing a question."

"Whatever. You mean you're not sure where she is?"

"No, no, we're pretty sure."

Distracted by the conversation, her foot had eased off the pedal. The driver behind honked. "Fuck you!" she shouted at her mirror, flicking a finger backwards. "Hang on, so you're telling me you *lost* your *mother?*"

"I didn't lose her!"

"Then who did?" She wasn't finding it amusing.

"Really, it's not my fault," I said. Then I made my play: "Will you help me?"

"Woah!" she exclaimed. "That wasn't part of the deal. You're lucky I drove you all this way. And it'll cost you. Plus my return fare."

But I didn't want her to return. I had to show willing. "Sure, no problem. How much do you want? I can pay you now. With tip! You've earned it, hahaha!" (Bit over-willing.)

When I had handed the notes over – an agreed amount that seemed a tad over the odds – and she had stuffed them into the front pocket of her dungarees, Clemmie said, "So you want some help?"

My heart palpitated.

A shadow slunk across the bonnet and enveloped the car. Skyscrapers on either side, buffeted sounds of life, caged heat.

We had entered the city.

Clemmie pulled into a car park and stopped the engine. "I'm famished," she declared. "I need a burger. Do you want one?"

I spotted a Yummy Burger over on the far corner, between Sharpshooter Sporting Guns and Timmy Loves Toys. "Yes I do!" I replied.

"Give us the money, then," she said, holding out a palm.

"Sure!" I almost dared not tempt fate. "You're going to help me then?"

She opened her door and stepped out of the car. "Maybe." Half-smile. And away.

I could barely contain myself. My plan was only bloody working! How unlikely was that? Pretanike: theatre of dreams! The longer I could keep Clemmie in my company, the more she would get to know me, the greater the chance I stood of...

A man in a black uniform wearing a peaked cap was standing in front of the car, writing in a notebook while peering at the registration number. My neck stiffened.

Although I stared at him, he studiously avoided my gaze.

He slapped a ticket on the windscreen, flicked a wiper over it then grinned at me broadly. He wore unruly, dark stubble and bottleneck glasses. The cap was too small for his head, causing it to sit at a jaunty angle.

I leapt out of the car, shouting. *"What do you think you're doing?"*

"Correction," he said. "You mean: what have I done?"

It was true. "Yes, but... You can't do that!"

"I can, sir. And I have." He grinned again. His magnified eyes were giving me the fear and his voice sounded nasal, as if a bigger boy were holding his nostrils closed.

I reverted to pleading. "Look, my friend's only gone for a burger. Over there." I pointed at Yummy Burger, but he didn't look. "We'll be gone in a minute, I promise."

"Yes," he said. "You will be. With a parking ticket for non-payment."

We'd only been stationary for 30 seconds, tops. Bastard must have been crouching behind a nearby vehicle. "I bet you love your job," I said.

"Yes, sir, I do. If you would like to appeal the fine, the council's Licences & Appeals Office is two blocks away, right out of the car park, 21-27 Shelby Street. But I wouldn't bother, if I were you. Now, if you'll excuse me..." The git turned to go.

"You speccy tosser!" It just slipped out.

He turned back. I noticed his trousers were too short. In fact, his entire outfit seemed to have shrunk in the wash. "Sticks and stones may break my bones, sir," trilled the tosser. "But names will never hurt me."

As he walked away, I dearly wished I'd had some sticks and stones.

When Clemmie returned I was unable to contain my outrage. "Look!" I blurted out. "You've been given a parking ticket!"

She ripped the offending documentation out from under the wiper. "What the fuck?"

"I know!" I agreed.

"No way, José," snapped Clemmie. "I came here for you! So that's *your* parking ticket, not mine!"

She screwed up the ticket and threw it across the bonnet at me.

Then she got in the car and drove off.

Clenching my fists as Clemmie's bumper departed the car park, I shouted at no one in particular. "BOLLOCKS!"

How the hell had that happened?

I snatched the crumpled parking ticket up off the ground and launched it into space, then threw myself to the ground, beating my fists on the tarmac. Seconds later, I noticed a pair of shiny boots beside my head.

"You seem to have dropped this, sir," came the nasal voice.

I looked up. He was straightening out the ticket.

"I think you'd better come with me," he said.

20-24 Shelby Street, Thursday, 12.50pm:

I was frogmarched to the Licences & Appeals Office, a dreary, concrete-and-glass building with no appeal of its own.

Inside, members of the public were queuing at windows, behind which were seated drones wearing joyless expressions. I joined the queue at the 'PARKING FINES' window, building up a head of steam. Eventually, it was my turn to be served.

"Hello," I said, thrusting my ticket through the gap beneath the window. "I'd like to appeal a parking fine."

The man behind the counter wore a beige corduroy jacket with a shirt and tie. He had flat black hair that swept over his forehead from a right-hand parting, and a dark, brief moustache. His head was very long. It looked like a stretched version of Hitler's.

He ignored me, pretending to write something in a notebook.

"I'd like to appeal a parking fine," I repeated, a little louder.

He put down his pencil very deliberately, though continued staring at the book.

I peered at him.

After several seconds he deigned to notice me, adopting a supercilious grin. "Yes?"

"I'd like to appeal a parking fine."

"Would you? Would you now?" he said.

"Yes, I would."

"Fine not quite right for you, was it?"

"How do you mean?"

"This fine you'd like to appeal. Not quite right for you? Not to your tastes? Somehow offended one's *delicate sensibilities*, did it?" He enunciated 'delicate sensibilities' very annoyingly.

I put my hands on the counter. "It wasn't even my vehicle."

"Do you have *any idea* how many times I've heard that one?"

"But it wasn't! I was just a passenger and the driver had gone to get a burger."

"Oh," he said. "How tremendously convenient." He rubbed his hands together and smiled that supercilious smile again. "Went to get a burger, did he, this driver of yours? Bit peckish, was he?"

I was quite taken aback. "Yes! *She* was!"

"A lady? I see. No matter. Answer me this. Whom would you say was in charge of said vehicle, while this *lady-driver* was appropriating her repast?"

"Well, certainly not me! I was in the passenger seat!" My voice had become a little too high-pitched.

He was pretending to take down what I was saying in his notebook, moving his pencil across the page without actually writing anything. "The... accused..."

"What do you mean, 'The accused'?"

He ignored me and continued. "The... accused... claimed... he... was... in... the... passenger... seat... while... the... driver... comma... a... lady... comma... had... gone... for... a... burger." He looked up. "Beef or ham?"

"I'm sorry? What?"

"Beef or ham? The burger?"

"What does that bloody matter?"

"I'll put beef," he said. "Not that it matters really." Report concluded, he hammered the pencil into the page for the final full stop, breaking the lead, then glared at the broken point as if it were the pencil's fault.

"Forget it," I snapped. "I thought you'd just hand out forms here?"

He shook his head violently as if waking himself up. "Yes, that's right!"

"Then I would like the form for appealing a parking fine."

He pointed to his left. "Two windows down," he said. "I revoke dog licences."

"But it doesn't say that above the window! It says 'PARKING FINES'!"

"Yes," he said. "Yes, it would."

I was dumbfounded. "What?"

"This is the parking fines *window*, but I'm not the parking fines *officer*. No. We like to swap about a bit, you see? Gets very boring sitting in the same seat every day."

He'd lost me.

"See Darren there, two windows down, he's in charge of parking fines." He went on: "Darren's in my seat, I'm in his. We swapped seats. At lunchtime. Change of scene." Supercilious smile. "So if you wouldn't mind queuing at that window, I'm sure Darren will cater to your every whim."

"You're kidding me!" I snapped. "I've been queuing here for..."

"Goodbye!" he said, and pulled down the roll-blind over his window.

"I know you're still there," I said.

He didn't answer.

Dutifully, meekly – pathetically – I joined the other queue, which was naturally the longest in the building, and waited there seething. When the fat bloke in front of me was finally finished and I heard the "Next!" I walked up to the window.

It was him – the same idiot who had served me at the previous window.

"It's you!" I said.

"Yes," he said. "Darren got rather bored with that seat, so we swapped again. Perfectly reasonable, don't you think? Do you enjoy a change of scene in your work?"

"No I don't! What am I supposed to do now?"

"Up to you, sir."

"Do you have any idea how long I've queued at this window?"

He studied his watch then looked at me. "About 20 minutes?"

"Yes, that's right. And now what am I going to do, since you're in charge of dog licences?"

"To be fair, it does say 'DOG LICENCES' above the window." He pointed upwards.

"Yes. I. Know. That. But *you* told me to come here!"

Innocent expression. "Did I?"

"Yes, you did."

No reply. Just a look.

I went on: "So what am I going to do?"

He slapped his hands on the desk and peered at me incredulously. "It's all me-me-me with you lot, isn't it? I've noticed that. Do you have any idea how very, very tedious it gets, handing out the same forms to the same shower of ingrates, from the same seat, day in, day out? *Do you?*"

I shrugged.

"See?" he said, in the manner of one who has proven a point. "That's what I mean: not an ounce of concern for *my* welfare."

I'd had enough. "Can you give me a form for appealing a parking fine?"

"No," he said, adding in a helpful voice: "But if you've had trouble with any dangerous dogs?"

"Right then, I'd like to speak to the manager."

He tilted his head. "My service not good enough for you?"

I was incredulous. "*No, it isn't!*"

"Because I've never had any complaints before."

"I don't believe that for a second."

"Very well!" he snapped, and stood up. He rapped on the window with his knuckles and stood on his tiptoes to look over my shoulder.

"Excuse me! Excuse me! Yes, you, the lady behind this git." (He mumbled 'this git', but I heard it.)

I turned around. The old lady was pointing at herself, mouthing, 'Me?'

"Yes, you," he said. "Would you say you've had received perfectly reasonable service here?"

"Who, me?" she said.

"Yes, you! Are you deaf?" He enunciated very slowly. "Would... you... say... the... service... here... has... been... very... reasonable? Dear?"

"Certainly," she said, in an eager-to-please voice.

"But she hasn't even been served yet!" I pointed out.

He took his seat. "She might have been here before."

This was ridiculous. "I'd like to speak to the manager."

"Right!" he snapped, and stormed off muttering to himself.

I waited a full ten minutes while the queue behind me became restless, and I had to avoid catching anyone's eye – as if the situation were my fault.

Finally, the same man returned, sat down at my window and put his hands on the desk. "Yes?" he said.

"I wanted to speak to the manager!"

"I am the manager," he said.

"But you're the same idiot I'm trying to complain about!"

"I'm afraid we won't tolerate that sort of language." He was trying to put on a different, more authoritative voice.

"What? *'Idiot'*?"

He glared at me. "If you use that word again, I shall have to call Security."

"I've told you, I want to speak to the manager!"

He replied through gritted teeth. "And I've told you. I. Am. The. Manager."

"But you're the same..." I had to check myself. "You're the same *person* who served me, about whom I am trying to complain."

He sat there looking pointedly confused, before a huge grin broke out across his face. Dawning enlightenment! "Ah, I see! I see what's happened here! Yes, we often get confused, me and him, him and I, that person and this person who is myself. People quite often mistake one for the other. Because, you see, we often wear the same jacket." He pushed his collar forward, so I could inspect it more closely.

"You're the same man!"

"I assure you I'm not. I'm the manager." Supercilious grin.

"You're an idiot," I said.

He pressed a button beneath the counter. Two uniformed security guards appeared from nowhere, put a hand under each of my armpits and carried me away.

Security Control, 21-24 Shelby Street, Thursday, 1.30pm:

I found myself alone in a small, airless office, seated at a bare table. An angle-poise lamp had been plonked in front of me and turned on, interrogation-style; however, since the room was bathed in daylight, its effect was lost. There were pages pulled from magazines pinned to one wall, each featuring some form of law-enforcement officer puffing out their chest in a pristine uniform, with the title: '*AREN'T COPS SEXY? MAGAZINE – THIS MONTH'S PIN-UP*'.

One of the security guards who had carted me away from the Licences & Appeals Office entered the room carrying two Styrofoam cups, sat down opposite and placed one in front of me. He wore a black uniform with a black-and-white cap ('SECURITY' written around its band) and had eaten too many pies. His head tapered outwards from his temples to his shoulders, as if a small child had fashioned it from slowly melting butter. There was a large sweat patch on his white shirt, hovering over his chest region, and I could tell, despite the hat, that he was bald.

"Are you aware of your crime?" Security Lunk asked, in a voice that was thick and gloopy.

"No, I'm not," I said, wondering whether he needed a decongestant.

He snatched back the cup previously given to me and downed the contents in one. "I'm not here to play games," he said.

Neither was I. "As far as I'm aware, I haven't committed a crime."

"I'll be the judge of that," he said. "What's your name"?

I sighed. "Pilsbury Dextrose."

He narrowed his piggy, dark eyes. "Trying to be funny, are we?"

"No," I said. "That's my name."

"Alright, where's your ID card?"

"I don't have one."

"Everyone in Pretanike has an ID card," he said. "That's the law."

"I'm not from Pretanike."

"Not from Pretanike?"

"No."

That seemed to stump him.

He heaved himself up and began pacing the room, thoughtfully rubbing the area where his chin should have been.

"Can I go?" I asked.

"Not until the police arrive," he said.

I couldn't believe it. "The *police*? What have I done to involve them?"

The door swung open and a uniformed, 30-something woman walked in, wearing a face chillier than a Yeti's toes.

"Ask them yourself," said Security Lunk.

The police officer sat down opposite me.

"Would you like a cup of tea?" the lunk asked her. His voice had risen a couple of octaves, all smarm, though still gloopy.

She ignored the question. "What's the charge?"

"While appealing a parking fine, ma'm, he twice referred to a licensing officer as an 'idiot'."

"Leave!" she snapped, waving him away with a hand and

eyeballing me.

Her lips barely existed. Her face looked as though it had never experienced laughter; it was pointy like a ferret's, and she wore her bleached hair tied back in a bun beneath her police hat. She sat with both hands on the table in front of her, leaning forwards, ready to strike.

She stared at me, never blinking.

"*CALLED-A-COUNCIL-OFFICAL-AN-IDIOT-DID-WE-SIR?*"

It was a high-pitched shriek, emitted so quickly that the words rolled into one. I nearly fell backwards over my chair in a bid to escape it.

"Christ!" I yelped.

"*DO-YOU-HAVE-ANY-IDEA-OF-THE-PENALTY-FOR-BEING-IDIOTIST?*"

I didn't. Even had I done so, I wouldn't have been able to speak.

The officer stood up, walked to the door and peered through its little window. When she returned to her seat, she looked different. Less tense. She picked off her hat, reached back and pulled out the bun, shaking her head to let the hair fall. She replaced the hat.

"Sorry about that," she hissed.

What the hell was going on? Good cop/bad cop featuring just the one cop?

She leaned forward. "Sometimes they listen in."

"Sorry?"

"Don't be," she said. "I'm Halo," she added, holding out a hand.

I was too shaken to shake.

"It's OK, I won't bite," she said.

Pulling a pack of cigarettes from her pocket, she offered me one and lit her own. "I hate being a fascist," she said. "But we're in a recession so I took what work I could get. Soon as there's a vacancy at the garden centre, I'm outta here. So, what's your plan?"

I accepted the cigarette even though I didn't smoke, choked on it and stubbed it out. I explained how my plan of sorts had already been ruined by the parking-ticket fiasco.

She listened intently, then said, "I'm guessing you're something to do with the tramp they just brought into the station."

Tramp? It had to be. "Drunk old man, face messed up?"

"That's him."

"Well... yes. How did you know?"

"You have the same eyes and nose."

I didn't. "He's my father. Can I see him?"

"They're deporting him. Next flight out."

"*What?*" I yelped.

Halo leaned forward and clamped a hand over my mouth. "Shhhhh!"

"Bllwn?"

She released her hand.

I tried again. "When?"

She looked at her watch. "On the 17.50 flight to London, England. He's sobering up in the cells and being driven to the airport at 15.40. You want to join him?"

"Well. Yes. Please. I suppose I have to. But I have to find my mother first."

"Why? Where's she?"

I explained as succinctly as possible, interrupted only by her sharp intakes of breath. "Your father's a moron," she said, and I nodded. "The Statue of Sir Charles Partridge is about a dozen blocks away. You'll make it in ten minutes in a taxi."

"Can I call one from here?"

"You got an ID card?"

"No."

"Then you can't get a taxi."

"What? You can't get a taxi without an ID card?"

"You want me to write it down for you?" She sighed, flicked her cigarette butt onto the floor and lit another. "You gotta move. If you run you'll just have time to look for your mother. But be back at the cop station next door by 15.15. I'll make sure we get you on the flight with your father."

"What if I find her?"

Halo raised an eyebrow. "You really think so?"

"I have to try."

"Let's cross that bridge when we come to it."

"Thanks," I said, and got up to leave.

She began tying her hair back into a bun. "Aren't you forgetting something?"

"Am I?"

"Parking fine," she said.

"Do I have to?"

"No way round it."

As I was about to shut the door behind me, a thought struck me. I leaned back into the room. "Is there such a crime as being idiotist?"

"Sure," she said. "How do you think the people making the laws protect themselves?"

Streets of Pretanike, Thursday, 2.05pm:

Having feverishly studied the map of Pretanike torn from Quench's book, I attempted to memorise the route and ran.

The pavements were teeming with people, many dolled up for work, others ambling with shopping bags. I zigzagged between them as fast as I could, breathing noisily. I was trying to stay calm, planning my next moves like a chess player, estimating speed and direction of those heading towards me, shimmying this way and that. It reminded me of my rugby-playing days at school. How I had hated that game.

Always at the back of my mind was the thought that I was wasting my time. For so many reasons:

1. Harrison Dextrose had forgotten where he had left his wife.
2. And how long ago he had left her there.
3. However, he had revealed the location, via his subconscious, in a sketch that was at best open to interpretation.
4. Having drunk a supposed truth serum called demon juice.
5. According to a deranged shaman, the sketch resembled an area on a map, which is where we had assumed Mrs Dextrose would be.
6. Yet there was no proof that my father had even been to Pretanike.

7. (And I had omitted to ask him.)
8. (Then again, I would hardly have been able to trust his answer anyway.)
9. In the unlikely event that Dextrose's sketch and the Shaman's interpretation were accurate, what were the chances of Mrs Dextrose having remained around that spot?
10. Would she really trust or expect that old fool to come back and find her?

If only she knew she had her son back.

"I'll find you, Mum," I gasped under my breath, running, running, running.

Who was this woman? I didn't even know what she looked like. I didn't even know her name! She was 'Mrs Dextrose'. That's what everyone called her – even her own husband. But what was her first name?

Delia! I bet that was it. Delia Dextrose. Had a ring to it. Seemed to fit her era. If her husband were in his early-seventies, she'd be there or thereabouts... although knowing him as I did, I bet he had married someone younger. She might even be in her fifties, having had me in her early-twenties.

Why did I know so little about her? My mother.

At least I had tried to quiz Dextrose, that night we'd bonded beside the Lonely Highway, but he had said he was too tired to talk. Why hadn't he wanted to tell me about her? Was he hiding something?

Generally in *The Lost Incompetent* he had portrayed her as the battleaxe at home – typical bravado, I had taken it with a pinch of salt. Yet there were moments...

He had dedicated his book, "To the wife". And once he'd admitted to missing her during his travels, recalled how she looked after him during his umpteenth night of shameful behaviour. He had sounded almost contrite.

Mrs Dextrose must have had the patience of a saint and the loyalty of a batman.

What would she look like? I had seen just that one photo. Her on the yacht, headscarf and summer dress, swinging from the mast, looking so contented – boy, that must have been taken a while back. Would she be a little old lady now, with a cardigan and stoop, or upright, strident and vital, with blood in her cheeks and a gleam in her eyes? What colour hair would she have? What lipstick would she wear? What would she sound like? Would she have an accent?

How often had she thought about me since the adoption?

How much did she care?

What if I actually found her?

What on earth would I say to her?

I stopped and bent double, wheezing violently, my mouth drier than a sand sandwich. Though I was fantastically thirsty there was no time to find liquid. I scrabbled for the map again, used my recuperation time wisely.

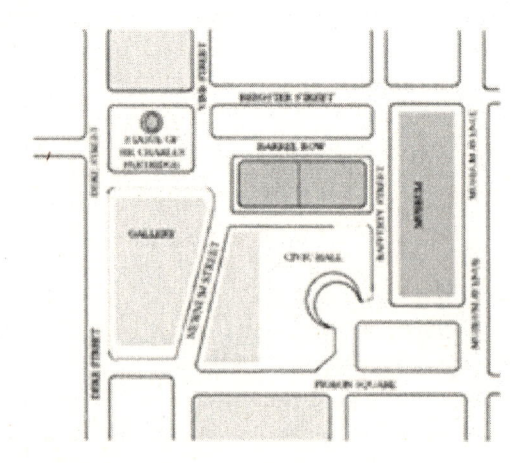

At a crossroads, I looked up and around for street signs. Pigeon Square and Museum Avenue… so close! Rather than head into the complicated maze of roads that might have offered the shortest route from A to B, I plumped for the least confusing: straight up Museum Avenue, left onto Beegster Street.

14.26. Had to move, body unwilling.

The museum loomed before me on my left: a great block of sandstone with ionic columns, tourists milling about outside (they had to be tourists, since they were going to a museum). Several times I had to sidestep into the road, oblivious to the nose-to-tail traffic, then skip back to safety. More than once my fatigue caused my ankle to give and I toppled dangerously before, more by luck than design, regaining my balance.

What was I going to do when I got to the statue?

Mrs Dextrose wouldn't be there, having waited dutifully beneath old Charlie Partridge, tapping a foot impatiently, on the off-chance that her husband might finally remember her and return to sweep her off her feet. Still, that statue had to be the key. Had to be.

At the junction of Beegster Street I swerved left, arms flailing outward under momentum. Passers-by stopped and stared. My face was burning up. Every breath felt like razors scoring my throat. Every muscle burned. 14.29.

I didn't bother waiting for the traffic lights on the junction of Beegster and Rafferty. I didn't check for cars. I just ran across. Horns honked, someone shouted ("Wanker!"), tyres screeched, I paid them no heed. I remained unscathed. Good fortune. Hell, I was owed some.

Shops on the ground floor of an austere building to my left were blocking my view of the statue, but I knew it was up ahead, could sense it.

And then what would I do?

A few feet from the kerb, on the corner of Beegster and Vine, it came into view, perched on a plinth in a rectangle of green surrounded by railings: the Statue of Sir Charles Partridge.

The road was clear. I charged across. A park gate before me. I swung it open, flew across the grass. Stumbled and fell at the feet of Sir Charles, gasping for air like a mountaineer above the clouds, yet aware, incredulously, that I had made it after all the tribulations.

This was it: my physical goal. But not the emotional one. No time to water the ponies.

Pulling myself to my feet, I looked around. Wrought iron benches were lined around the lawn, each unoccupied. Not a single old lady in sight, who might have piqued my hopes.

I turned 360. Across the roads on every side were tall, architecturally ostentatious old buildings: ornate window frames, pious figures carved into the stone, marble and gold touches, the settings of high society. I scanned the pavements around their bases. Nothing stood out. But what was I expecting? Mrs Dextrose waving a handkerchief – "Coo-ee!" – lofting herself on tiptoes?

14.32. It had taken almost half an hour to reach the statue; the return journey would take longer on my quaking limbs. At what time must I be back? 15.15? Left me less than quarter of an hour to search.

No chance. Not a hope in hell.

The statue. Five stone steps led up to the plinth, a wilful block of polished granite bearing an inscription:

SIR CHARLES PARTRIDGE
1866-1927
AIR ACE
'STILL FLYING'

I looked up. The bronze full-figure, twice a man's size, towered overhead, silhouetted against a canvas wash of ozone blue. I had failed to notice what a lovely day it was.

Taking a few steps backwards, I could fully appreciate Sir Charles' heroic stance. He wore breeches, high boots and a leather flying jacket with its collar pulled up around his neck. His hands were on his hips, chest puffed out, gazing from beneath an old flying helmet with an expression of beatific superiority. So extensive was his moustache that I could have pulled myself up on it and perched on his head, like a vulture, or a wise monkey.

Don't ask me why – because I couldn't tell you – but that's what I decided to do. I climbed the Statue of Sir Charles Partridge.

Mounting the five stone steps, I heaved my chest onto the plinth and dragged my legs up and over. One hand in the crook of his arm, a foot on the top of his boot – another heave. Other hand on his shoulder, tight grip around one handlebar of that moustache, same on the other, the soles of my trainers scrabbling for purchase...

All the while, my mind could not help drifting back to my childhood comics, in which errant tykes with catapults were chased off flowerbeds by park keepers known as 'Parkie'.

But no one shouted, no one saw, and suddenly I was sitting – precariously – on Sir Charles' polished helmet many feet above the ground, gazing out at what he had surveyed for all those frozen years.

There was no one fitting a possible description of Mrs Dextrose, just city gents prowling the pavements and families on the stroll. I had to be proactive. Had to prove to myself that I had tried.

Then something struck me: something I'd been staring at but not seen. A large sign above the double doors on the ground floor of the building directly across the street. 'Victoria Hotel'.

A hotel! Had Sir Charles been trying to tell me something?
14.38.

It was a chance slimmer than a lady's personal cavity – but it was a chance. It was all I had. Instantly enlivened, I considered throwing myself to the ground, make time, until vertigo rang the bells of good sense.

Victoria Hotel, Thursday, 2.02pm:

I flung myself up the red-carpeted marble steps and through the gilded glass double doors. I was in an atrium. To my right, reception desks, staff in maroon, acting occupied; ahead, further glass double-doors with restaurant tables behind; to my left, a corridor leading towards a heavy dark-wood door; beside that, red-carpeted stairs curving upwards.

My mind was spinning. The foolish thing had begun entertaining the idea that Mrs Dextrose might actually be found. That she had resided here ever since the abandonment by her husband. Live in the lap of luxury, bill him afterwards? Perfectly feasible.

What on earth was I going to say to her?

The back of my head tingled.

Calm down. Think. How to find her? No sense careering headlessly around the hotel, banging on doors, shouting her name.

The receptionists.

I ran across to the nearest uniformed young chap at the desk, who was tapping at a computer.

"Excuse me!"

He did not look up. His uniform was gold-braided though his tender age made such trimmings feel rather pantomime.

"Excuse me!"

"Yes?" Professional smile, acne.

"I'm looking for Mrs Dextrose," I blurted out. Even as I was voicing it, the futility flooded back. What had I been thinking? Idiot. Stupid, delusional idiot.
"First Floor, Helena Suite."
I started. "What?"
"First floor. Helena Suite."
"Mrs Dextrose?"
"Yes." Unprofessional raised eyebrow.
Fuck.
Incredible.
I'd only bloody found her.

The staircase wound upwards in a spiral. I took its steps three at a time, prancing like a sprite, temples pounding, and found the first-floor landing. Left or right? I'd been too hasty to ask.
Intuition? Left.
I was in a wide corridor, doors on either side, some distance apart. I ran. On each door was a nameplate.
'Edward Suite'...
'Alice Suite'...
'Alfred Suite'...
'Helena Suite'.
'Helena Suite'.
My mother... behind that door? Could it really be possible? What should I do?
Suddenly I was stumped. A little boy confronted by a situation beyond his experience. Eight years old again. The door in front of me grew to the size of a giant's, like something from Alice's Wonderland. I stood there, dazed, until I heard a knocking.
When I followed the sound I saw my own knuckles rapping on the varnished wood.
"Yes, come in!" A man's voice, from behind the door.
A *man's* voice?

It had never entered my head that I might not like what I found.

I pushed down the door-handle and felt as if I were floating; everything seeming unreal.

Inside was not as I might have anticipated.

The Helena Suite was no boudoir. There wasn't even a bed. Inside, at the far end of an airy, expansive room was a stage, on which were standing, in one long line, a number of ladies of middle-age and above, wearing swimsuits. Before them were arranged more rows of chairs, though these were only sporadically occupied by small groups of generally younger individuals.

Sunlight flooded in though four vast picture windows bearing creamy linen drapes.

Silence fell and everyone stared. At me.

Was one of these ladies my mother?

A young woman near the door, blonde-haired, in a light grey business suit and clutching a folder, addressed me. "Can I help you?" she asked.

"I... I'm looking for Mrs Dextrose," I said. Although I spoke the words timidly, they echoed around the room, gathering gravitas.

Silence.

Then a silver-haired old lady on the stage, wearing a polka dot swimming costume and turquoise swimming cap, clutching a handbag as if her life depended upon it, stepped forward.

"I'm Mrs Dextrose," she said.

My mouth fell open. I couldn't stop it. My heart was beating like a jack-hammer.

Then another of the women on the stage stepped forward, then another, and another.

"I'm Mrs Dextrose!"

"I'm Mrs Dextrose!"
                   "I'm Mrs Dextrose!"
"I'm Mrs Dextrose!"
"I'm Mrs Dextrose!"
          "I'm Mrs Dextrose!"
"I'm Mrs Dextrose!"
         "I'm Mrs Dextrose!"
                "I'm Mrs Dextrose!"
"I'm Mrs Dextrose!"
           "I'm Mrs Dextrose!"
"I'm Mrs Dextrose!"

The blonde-haired young woman with the folder was now in front of me. "Can I help you?" she repeated.

My eyes were unfocused. "What is this place?"

"This is the Dextrose Marketing Board 'Ladies of a Certain Age' beauty pageant," she said, bubbly-voiced for no good reason.

I shook my head. Nothing would compute.

She went on: "We promote dextrose in Pretanike and decided this year that our promotional figurehead should be an old lady. You know, likes baking and sweet tea. So we're choosing our 'Mrs Dextrose'! It'll be great! She'll appear in the press and will be a fun new character for our TV advertisements. Would you like a leaflet? Did you know that dextrose, also known as glucose, provides a valuable source of energy in…"

I closed the door behind me.

Streets of Pretanike, Thursday, ②.⑤⑧ pm:

There was a bicycle leaning against the railings outside the Victoria Hotel, no lock on it. I picked it up and pedalled away. If idiotism were a crime in Pretanike, heaven knows what they'd have made of bicycle theft. I didn't care. I was in a hurry. I had a flight to catch and a father to be with. If I couldn't have both parents, I was damned sure I was going to hold on to the one.

What was I thinking as I cycled back down Beegster Street?

That it was funny feeling so disappointed when I had never really expected to succeed.

Pretanike Airport, Thursday, 4.00pm

Officer Halo had been true to her word. When I presented myself at the Pretanike cop-shop, a note from her informed me that a ticket had been reserved in my name at the Pay-Loo Airline desk. No mention of my mother.

Officer Halo apologised, but she hadn't managed to find me a seat next to my father. Had she been there in person, I would have hugged her.

Airports are vacuum-packs for the soulless. Sterile nodes on a route-map of adventure. Terrible places filled with trolleys, toddlers and unsmiling officials who feel up your inside leg. I couldn't wait to get out, to move on.

Killing time before boarding, and following the deprivations of the previous days, I stuffed my face with all manner of foods and downed soft drinks, then treated myself to a new outfit. Nothing snazzy, just a T-shirt and jeans, denim jacket, new underwear (bliss), some cushioned trainers. I allowed no quarter to fashion. Believe me, when you've squatted beside the Nameless Highway having narrowly avoided being shot up, some branding oik ticking your shoe is your final concern.

The change of clothes was about more than comfort and hygiene. It was symbolic. I was going home, back to my old life – though not to my old ways; no way – and I was done with exploring for a while. I just needed time for it all to settle in.

I left my smouldering safari suit in the changing room. Let it terrorise the next poor bugger in there.

I did spot Dextrose from a distance at one point, being escorted through customs by a pair of police types. He'd been eased into what looked like blue-and-white-striped cotton pyjamas, with that overcoat slung over his shoulders. They must have given him a shower, because his hair and beard had dried comically fluffy. He looked as though he had his head in a raincloud.

That he was audibly lambasting his captors gave me heart. He'd be fine.

The remaining time before my flight dragged like a corpse across tar. I took a seat at a plastic café table, in limbo, my head a whirl of contradicting emotions. Loss and gain. Adventure and misadventure. Life and death. I struggled to find a balance.

It was all over. Everything I had been through. Livingstone Quench, the Shaman, his son, Gdgi, Hilda and Eustace, Kai, Si, Bri and Duane, Charlie, Clemmie... Importos, RIP. All of them now memories: chemical reactions among the faintest of electrical currents.

My mind could hold on to them, or it could discard them. And though I would happily have banished a few by choice, they had all shaped the person I had become. The man I had become.

I had changed and there could be no going back. No longer would I be prepared to fritter away the days on my back, growing bacteria in crevices. No longer would I be pushed around. No longer would I consider the term 'local' a badge of honour.

How my father would fit in at home, I did not know. That would reveal itself in time. I only hoped that it would work out between us.

ENGLAND

I waited for Dad before the red and green channels at Customs, aware that if he wandered through the former without thinking, his entire body might become impounded, or secreted away by government scientists for vivisection.

When I caught sight of him, being pointedly avoided by the family to his right, he looked more bewildered than even I was feeling. The nine-hour flight, added to his time in the cells, had no doubt sobered him up properly, and the sensation was not suiting him. One of those flimsy airline blankets was hanging by its corner from the neckline of his prison shirt, like the posh wear their napkins. He was taking short, shuffling steps and he kept glancing around with paranoia in his eyes. He must have fallen asleep with the back of his head against his seat, because his hair had become squashed and splayed out, resembling a ludicrous head-dress.

I was in charge of him now. It should have been the other way around, but it wasn't. And I knew, as might the errant child, that he could easily scuttle away. These first moments on home soil could prove key.

I waved as he neared me. He stopped and stared, wide-eyed and sockless.

I smiled, nervously. "So. Dad. What's your plan?"

"Where is I?" he replied.

I was going to have to start with the basics.

"We're back in England," I said. "Do you know who I am?"

"Course I minking know who yer is! Yer me boy, Pilsbury. Minking cheek!"

I could barely conceal my delight.

"Alright, don't get ideas above yer station," he grumbled. "Just cos I know who yer is."

"So what's your plan?"

"Plan?" He screwed up his nose, which was finally looking less red.

"Fancy coming with me?" I spotted suspicion flit between his eyes, so hastily softened the threat. "…for a bit?"

"Mm," he went, more yes than no.

I pulled the blanket out of his shirt. His startled look suggested he hadn't been aware of it.

"You won't be needing that," I laughed.

"Oh won't I?" he replied.

The idea that I was back in my own country was disorientating, though I had only been away for a few weeks. It wasn't as if I would have to learn the customs, speak a different language, or be made to wear a certain sort of national costume with bells on its socks; it was just that I had been away.

Once I opened the airport door to the outside world, reality hit. Whoomph. Cars, noise, fumes. England.

I had tried to hatch a few plans during the flight, however uncertainty and a desperate desire for sleep had not proved conducive. Indeed, the list I had made ran like this:

1. Hire car at airport

It didn't help that I had no clue where Dad lived these days, or if he even had somewhere to call home. Would he want to come and live with me? Should I go and live with him? (That option felt a touch too much like home-help/carer, and conjured up images of me wrestling with his bottom in a toilet.)

There would be easily enough room for us both in my mock-Tudor house in Glibley (inherited following Father and Mother's passing). Four bedrooms, two reception rooms, two bathrooms, one... anyway, I'm not an estate agent. And I hoped I wouldn't have to sell the idea to him.

I wondered what Suzy and Benjamin would make of him. Just as importantly, I wondered what they would make of me. I had changed inside; would my outward appearance have altered also? I hoped that all the exercise and the starvation diet might have knocked off some of the post-puppy fat, made me hunkier.

I couldn't wait to see them, to catch up. How envious they'd be of my experiences, those two who had remained glued to Glibley, where nothing happened and no one noticed. Perhaps I'd consummate my relationship with Suzy at last? Maybe I'd aim higher? Boy, would it be delicious to turn her down.

But I was letting my imagination run away with itself. This was the time for practicalities.

"Dad, where do you want to live?"

"In a house," he said.

Not that picky. My place, then...

It began slowly to dawn on Dad during the drive along the motorway what "We're back in England" meant – and its consequences. His reactions veered from denial and anger to depression and acceptance, with bargaining – "Take us back to the airport and I swear yer'll never see us again" – in between. It only dawned on me later that they were the five stages of grief.

If I felt like a fish out of water, he was Thomas Jerome Newton.

At least he was free from toxins, which would help him to cope. And though this return home had been thrust upon us, I was beginning to consider it fortuitous.

My original plan had been to complete Dextrose's Quest, take the call from Suzy Goodenough and fly home to her forthwith, to claim my libidinous prize. I had only extended my adventure to try to find Mrs Dextrose, though my efforts had ended in failure... I realised I really ought to tell him about that.

"Dad, you remember we were looking for Mum?"

He snuffled in the passenger seat. "Take it yer didn't find her?"

That would have explained her absence, yes. "At least I tried."

"Could have told yer yer wouldn't."

"Really?"

"That minking never-ending road we was on..."

"The Nameless Highway?"

"If yer say so."

"And?"

"Well, I ain't never seen it before in me life – so she can't have been at the end of it. Can she?"

"Are you sure?"

He scratched an earlobe. "Course."

I wasn't convinced. "Then why didn't you tell me?"

"Never gave us the chance, did yer?"

Cantankerous old sod.

He fixed me with a brooding stare. Most of his scabs had fallen off, I noticed, leaving shiny pink wheals. "Where yer taking us?" he asked.

The sky was overcast, clouds the colour of battleships hovering overhead in fleets. As we passed the 'SURREY' sign just after two in the afternoon, it began to drizzle. Dad had fallen silent.

I turned on the radio to alleviate the gloom and, though any music should have been a welcome respite from my stretch of life without soundtrack – the Walkman I had taken travelling with me having been lost, stolen or destroyed, I forgot which – the stations I tuned through churned out such frivolous, gutless pap that they only weighed down my mood.

Having become increasingly grateful that I was back home, I had begun to wonder: what if nothing changed?

As I reached familiar sights and landmarks, however, nostalgia kicked in and I could not help but cheer up.

Turning off the motorway we passed first through Little Upshott, where I used to throw bread for the birds on the duck pond and bought my first gobstopper from Christie's the Newsagent (now an estate agent, I noticed). "That used to be a newsagent. I bought my first gobstopper there," I told Dad, pointing.

He looked but said nothing.

Under the old railway bridge, part of the Buttercup Line – now disused – on which they once ran steam trains, we drove downhill into Framingham, best known as the home of the late local author, Greta Hildred. Mother had read all of her books, their covers invariably featuring swooning maidens in bonnets melting into the arms of frilly-white-shirted gentlemen named Red with dark hair and cheekbones.

"Greta Hildred's house," I duly noted. "She was a local author. Mother... I mean, my other mother, she read all her books."

"Mmph," went Dad.

Past the triangular Miller's Green, where I occasionally kicked around a football if I could find a spontaneous playmate, and down through the leafy boughs on the approach road to Glibley. To our left was the path into the woods, where I had spent much of my childhood, when allowed out to play.

I had made camps in there, formed from dumped carpet

and dead branches, and there was an abandoned old house, broken and foreboding, if you dared walk far enough into the wilderness.

I tried again. "I used to love that wood."

"U-huh?"

"Yeah, I was always in there. Every summer."

"On yer own?"

That caught me unawares. I laughed uneasily. "Not always!"

"Well," he said. "I'm sorry about that."

"I did have friends!"

"I know," he said.

I ceased the commentary after that, since we were nearing my house. There I would be obliged to form a bond with this man, whose moods were so unstable, and his demons.

By the time we reached the end of my road – there was the sign, where I had left it: 'Cherry Tree Drive' – I was having second thoughts. Wouldn't it be easier to turn around and fly away abroad again, escape all the responsibilities? Dad would have been happier, that was almost certain. Perhaps I would too? What if I weren't cut out for the family-life lark? My foot faltered on the accelerator.

"This is my road," I announced. "We're up the end, number 72, on the corner of Laburnum Close. You'll have to excuse the tweeness. It's all rather floral."

He fidgeted.

I knew something was wrong when we reached Denholm and Marcia Graham's house, and I couldn't see my roof. It had always come into view at that point: those black eaves and red brick tiles...

Not there.

Perhaps the Grahams had grown some foliage?

Was our house further down than I remembered?

I put my foot down for the last 100 yards.

All that came into view was an ugly, unpainted wooden hoarding, on which had been scrawled in white paint: 'DANGER – KEEP OUT'. The hoarding may have been half a dozen or so feet tall, but there was no building appearing over the top of it.

Number 72, Cherry Tree Close, formerly two storeys high, plus attic space, had simply vanished.

Driving up onto the pavement in my panic, I yanked on the handbrake, leapt out of the car with the engine running and flung myself at the wooden screen, hooking fingers over its top to pull myself up. Head over the parapet…

It was a scene of destruction. All that remained of my home were the foundations, vast piles of blackened bricks, and one small wall, formerly housing the fireplace, standing resolutely amid the devastation, like the last chap alive on a battlefield. The flowerbeds were trampled into oblivion, the garden shed had lost its roof and was leaning crazily; only the trees remained apparently unharmed.

It reminded me of documentaries I had seen about the Blitz.

Charred and crushed effects from within the house had been piled high in one corner. Half of my green leather sofa, now black; a melted video recorder; the desk at which I used to do my homework, legless; half-burnt books; a kettle, smashed plates; that Delft vase Mother used to covet, scattered in shards…

I could not bear to look any further.

What the hell had happened? There had been a fire, that much was beyond doubt, but how? When? *Who?* A terrible sensation appeared in my gut, and swam around like a trapped eel. *Was this my fault?*

Dad was sitting on the bonnet of the hire car, looking expectant. "When we moving in?"

Not now. "This… was my house," I mumbled, in shock,

barely able to believe it myself.

"What?" he said. "Behind there?"

"Mmm."

I had another look, hoping my eyes had played tricks on me. They had not.

"I've got to find Benjamin," I said, and scrambled back into the car.

There was a ringing in my ears as I headed up the road towards Benjamin Grebe's house, as if I had witnessed an explosion and my head had gone numb.

Fortunately, given that state of mind, he lived only two streets away, in Hollyhock Lane. His parents had left the place to him after they retired to the seaside. Suzy Goodenough used to live next door with her mother, but had since moved into the estate at the top of town.

Surely one of them must be in and could tell me what had happened.

When I reached my friend's house, having ignored the speed limit, I was delighted to see a car in the driveway. Benjamin had followed in his own father's footsteps and become a travelling salesperson; if the car were there, chances were he would be too.

I parked behind his motor, tyres screeching and barely missing his bumper, and sprang towards the doorbell.

'*Bing-bong!*' So suburban.

I strained my ears to hear inside. Yes, footsteps on stairs. He'd tell me what had happened.

The door opened.

Suzy Goodenough!

Suzy Goodenough?

"Bloody hell!" she exclaimed. "Alexander bloody Grey! You're a sight for sore eyes!" She stopped herself. "Hold on. Don't tell me: you want to know what happened to your house, right? Shit. Yuh?"

"What are you doing here?" It wasn't the question I had intended to ask.

She still looked great – all sleek curves and occasional chicanes, with those deep-blue eyes set against her long, bronze hair, and pouty-lipped. Though not quite as great as I had remembered her. Her face was curiously orange, her dress sense a little stiff, and as for those pearls...

Suzy dropped her head and regarded me through her upper eyelashes. "Yuh, it was all rather sudden, but I think it was happening before you left. I did ring you to tell you, but you didn't answer. In that funny little bar in... Moo-Moo? Was it? You know?"

I shook my head. "You're *going out* with Benjamin?"

She bit her lower lip. "Mm. Yuh... you saw your house burnt down, right? The local paper said someone left the gas on." She sucked her teeth. "*Whoops!*"

"Whoops?"

"I suppose you've got nowhere to stay?"

Dad appeared beside me.

Suzy shrieked and made a posh shooing gesture. "Go away, you horrible tramp! Alexander, there's a tramp on my doorstep – make him go away! Shoo! Shoo!"

"Actually, that's my Dad," I said, suddenly enjoying myself.

She peered at me. "Are you sure you're alright?"

"Trust me, he's my Dad."

"But he's... he's wearing some sort of prison outfit!"

"I know. Can we come in?"

Suzy looked Dextrose up and down, wearing an expression like a llama's. "Well, I... you see, we've only got the one spare bedroom and that's being redecorated..."

I'd been inside Benjamin's house countless times. He had three bedrooms. "It's OK, forget it," I said. "But thanks for your help."

She became flustered. "Look, honestly, I would. Right? Help, you know? It's just that... when we..."

I put my arm around Dad's shoulder and turned him back towards the car. "Come on, Dad. Let's go."

Suzy called after us, "Come back in a couple of days, maybe? OK? When the paint's dry! Alexander!"

As I drove away, I was trying to remember what I had seen in her.

That, I decided there and then, was the last I would ever see of Glibley. Once the decision had been made, it actually felt like a weight off my shoulders. I almost managed to convince myself that I was lucky my house had blown up.

If you're going to make a clean break, why begin back where you started?

I couldn't believe Benjamin and Suzy were together. I hadn't had an inkling. Or only a tiny one. (That time I had caught him sucking her finger; she'd snatched the digit away and claimed to have had a bee sting – until I offered to have a go, when miraculously it had stopped hurting.) And what a snob she was! Although I guess I'd noticed that too. It's funny what one is prepared to overlook when one's choices are limited.

Fuck the house, fuck Benjamin and... balls to Suzy. New life.

I should have been suicidal; instead I felt rejuvenated.

Just the one glaring snag to overcome. I had been driving without thought for destination, which would not do, what with the afternoon wearing on. We could have checked into a B&B – I still had some of Quench's cash left even after paying the airfare, plus access to my own still-sizeable inheritance – but if I had been set adrift by fate then I needed to lay down some sort of root, or face the possibility of drifting further and further until... well, until I started to become my Dad.

He had increasingly withdrawn into himself since departing

the ruins of my house. Now he seemed vulnerable: the antithesis of his usual bullish demeanour. He was out of his comfort zone – a boozer, anywhere that responsibility did not exist – and it was taking its toll. He was toying absent-mindedly with the cord on his pyjama-style bottoms.

"Dad?" I said. "Where do you live?"

"Minked if I know," he mumbled.

"Because we're going to have to go there. Right now."

He sighed deeply.

"Are you alright?"

I touched his shoulder. He whipped it away. "Don't touch us!" He banged his head on the window under the sideways momentum. "Ow! Mink!"

The vehemence took me aback. "I was only trying to help."

"Well don't."

"What's the matter?"

"Stop. Minking. Asking. Us. That."

"But I'm your son. You're my father. And I only want to help."

"Gah," he went.

I continued driving southwards on the motorway, heading for the sea. In his book Dextrose had mentioned settling on the south coast, so it wasn't completely arbitrary.

The drizzle persisted as the 'thhhhkt-thhhhkt' of the windscreen wipers over the engine's drone became hypnotic. The light was poor, though it was only late-afternoon, and my headlights were on.

Unexpectedly, my father spoke. "If you must know," he began, impatient-sounding, "I'm having trouble with me booze."

I knew he'd keep talking if I stayed quiet.

"…Only it's hard.

"…Us not drinking."

Though I wanted to butt in, I dared not break the spell.

"...See, us want to. Drink, yer know.

"... And then again us don't want to."

"Really?" *Just let him talk.*

"No," he said. "Because of what yer said. I knew what yer meant."

"How do you mean?"

"That guff yer said."

"What guff?"

He turned to look out of his window.

"You mean the stuff about us being father and son?"

"Mm."

Amazing – the old softy(ish) was coming around! "So let's sort ourselves out and find somewhere to stay. Let's get this show on the road!"

He slapped his thigh, causing a faint urine odour to permeate the vehicle. "Mink it, boy! Let's do it!" And he smiled at me.

I'd seen him cackle, chuckle and roar with laughter, but I don't believe I had ever seen him smile. It was quite unnerving; that basic expression of contentment somehow upset his face. It was like watching a politician feigning sincerity, or a gameshow host commiserating with a thick contestant. It didn't suit him.

I tried again. "So where do you live?"

"I told yer. I. Don't. Minking. Remember."

We would narrow it down, then. "Was it by the sea?"

He thought for a while then exclaimed, "It were! How d'yer know?"

I told him it was in his book.

"Were it?" he said.

But where by the sea? "Can you remember any landmarks? Any famous hotels?" – He shook his head – "Funfair?" – Same reaction – "Theatre?" – He screwed up his face – "Pier?"

"That's right! There were a pier! We got minked on it some nights and Dan Panorama fell into the briny! The mink."

The south being my area, I knew a few of the resorts with piers.

"Brighton?"

"Nope."

"Worthing?"

"No."

"Hastings?"

"Nah."

Eastbourne?"

"Mink off! How old d'yer think us is?"

That exhausted my pier-based knowledge.

Or was there one more, at the back of my mind? That quaint little town we'd visited a couple of times, way back in my childhood...

"Dritt-on-Sea?"

He practically leapt out of his seat. "THAT'S IT!"

We arrived in Dritt-on-Sea shortly after seven. It was already dark but the rain had stopped. I had quizzed Dad further about where he lived, but he had grown restless like a child overburdened with sums. For light relief, I had switched on Radio 4 and we'd listened to a documentary about women who made bras for the outsized lady. That had settled him down.

My own memories of the coastal town extended not much further than its name and the fact that it boasted a pier. And there was a funny little train that ran through the town, which I recalled finding both odd and exciting. I guessed I must have been aged five or six when we had visited those couple of times, so during the early Seventies. I'd been treated to an ice cream and there were donkey rides on the beach; I'd wanted to have a go, but Father had told me that donkeys carried diseases.

I wondered whether Father, Mother and the Dextroses had

met up – in my company, even – or was that a conspiracy theory too far?

I tried to drive into town but the place was heaving, so we parked just outside. The streets were thronged with families, who seemed to be gathering for an event. They ate chips from paper cones and children sucked on ice-lollies, though the moon was out. Flags had been tied between all the lamp-posts lining the promenade and coloured lights added a festive glow to our route. Out across the sand the waves slurped over shingle and moonshine sprinkled magic dust out at sea.

Dritt-on-Sea was buzzing. That definitely wasn't how I had remembered it.

As we wandered down the main street into town, I heard a sound that took me right back. 'Ting-ting!' – it came from behind me, and when I turned I saw that train I had remembered from all those years ago. It was a tram. Of course: a train driving through the town. A tram! Not the biggest of trams, more a tourist attraction fit for a couple of dozen passengers, boxy and blue, with its headlights on. At my feet was track laid into the tarmac.

'Ting-ting!' went the tram again. I could have listened to that sound all night, floating among the least troubled memories of childhood, reliving moments when I was carefree and my socks came up to my knees.

Dad still shuffled rather, and I had to button up his overcoat over that prison garb, lest people mistake him for some sort of criminal.

"Have you recognised anything yet?" I asked.

"Too many minking people," he grumbled, though I failed to see how that affected his memory.

Tapping the nearest adult male on the shoulder, I said, "Excuse me. Is there some sort of event tonight?" It struck me that, not so long ago, I would never have actively spoken to a stranger.

"Don't you know?" he replied. He had a long face, was bald and looked like a vicar. "It's Moren Day..."

He studied me expectantly, as if I might suddenly exclaim, "Of course! Moren Day!"

When I didn't, he explained: "The Moren's a mythical sea creature that eats fishing boats. On Moren Day the Dritters banish it from the waves with flaming torches – not that there's been a fishing industry here for 20 years." He paused. "You're not a local, then?"

"No," I said.

He smiled. "The torchlight parade starts at eight. Don't miss it," he said. "You won't be allowed a torch if you're not from Dritt, though."

We followed the flow of human traffic heading into the centre of town. While enjoying the atmosphere, I was also aware that we had nowhere to sleep and time was marching alongside us. Dad was proving no help at all.

Then a brainwave hit me. Why take Mohammed to the mountain? If Dad were unlikely to recognise anyone, perhaps someone else might recognise him? And where better to enquire than in a place that sold alcohol? He must have been once known in every hostelry in town.

There was the obvious and major snag: dare I take him into a pub? Then again, dare I try to leave him outside?

We passed into a narrow street, inadequate for the number of revellers, shoulders everywhere and a back-pack in the face. I had to keep checking behind me, that Dad hadn't been dragged backwards amid the sea of people, and downwards to ensure I didn't tread on a small child. Claustrophobia began setting in. When I spotted diamond-shaped lead lights to my left, a mass of bodies behind the glass, knowing it must be a pub I made a snap decision.

Grabbing Dad's collar, I pulled him inside. If the scent of hops hit me, it must have assaulted him.

His eyes grew very wide and he was gritting his teeth. His face had gone white, even the scar tissue.

"Are you alright?"

"No," he managed.

I reached for his hand, which was shaking. He pulled it away.

"I'm going to ask at the bar, see if anyone knows you. You can wait outside if you want."

He stiffened. "I minking will not!" He began parting drinkers on his way to the bar, like Moses through the crimson-nosed.

Clutching on to his coattails I was dragged along with him. The three bar staff, all wearing 'Moren Day' T-shirts featuring a sea-serpent drawn by a small child, were working on the edge of panic. Nearest to us was a woman furiously chewing gum, in her early-twenties with straight blonde hair pulled so tightly back she looked like she'd had a facelift.

I got in before Dad could order, pointing at him: "Excuse me! Do you know who this is?"

She surveyed me oddly. "Why don't you ask him yourself?"

I hadn't phrased it right. "No, no, I know who he is…"

"You're weird," she said, and turned her attention to Dad. "Yes?"

Time stopped. It was as if I were observing the bar from up among the old rafters, and everyone had turned to stare, anticipating his response.

He took a breath. "Ah, what the mink," he blurted, on the exhale. "I'll have a minking… what d'yer call it? Cooler?"

Cola? Cola! *He wanted a minking cola!* As I slapped his back, embarrassingly happy, a voice came: "Harry? Harry Dextrose?"

A porky chap in his sixties, belly bursting from an old-bloke shirt, slacks and comb-over, was standing in a doorway behind the bar. Sweat ran in rivulets off his forehead and his cheeks resembled a well-spanked arse.

Judging from Dad's expression, he was none the wiser.

"It is!" exclaimed the porky chap. "Harry Dextrose! I'll be damned! We thought you'd left us for good. Where you been?" It dawned on him that Harry had no idea who he was. "Robin Botham, landlord – remember?"

That did it. "Well mink me! Lord Rubby-Bottom! How is yer?"

Lord Rubby-Bottom lowered his voice. "Yeah, listen, keep it down, Harry. That's not for the customers, eh?" Then he added: "Here, I know someone who'll be keen to see you!"

Dad shrugged.

"Mrs Dextrose!"

I was stunned. "Mrs Dextrose?" The nape of my neck tingled. "You mean she's here?"

The landlord waved a thumb at me. "Who's this, Harry?"

But Harry didn't speak.

"I'm his son," I explained hurriedly. "Mrs Dextrose – is she here?"

"Yeah. But. You're his *son*?"

Dad remained frozen in time, saggy-gobbed.

"Where is she now?"

"Might be upstairs."

"Upstairs? In this pub?"

"Didn't he tell you?" said the landlord. "They couldn't afford the rent on the old place so I let them use our spare room."

"How long ago was that?"

He shrugged. "Three years? Maybe a bit less?"

Hang on. "So you're saying that Mrs Dextrose didn't travel with him, on his last 'expedition'?" I couldn't help the quote marks.

"Like I said, they moved in upstairs, then he left soon after without a word to anyone. She was hopping mad! We started to wonder whether he'd died, but she wasn't having any of it. You are in for an earful when she gets hold of you, Harry!"

I pushed Dad with the palm of my hand. "You bloody old fool. You never lost her! She never even went with you!" I was laughing despite myself.

He winced.

"So she's here now?" I asked the landlord.

"Hang on, I'll call up..."

He went out back and I heard: "Mrs Dex-*trose*? Mrs Dex-*trose*?"

I could barely contain my excitement and trepidation. I was to be reunited with my mother!

Robin Botham reappeared. "Not there," he said. "Must be out at the parade."

Dad and I exchanged glances.

"You lads care for a quick one, then?" said the landlord. "On the house!"

We didn't look back. Not even Dad.

The melee in the lane outside the pub had calmed down. As I sought my bearings I noticed for the first time the sign hanging up on the wall: The Dog and Duck, featuring a painting of a brown-and-white hunting dog and a duck, craning its neck. Something clicked in my mind's eye.

That wasn't a cow and the moon – it was a dog and a zero. The cricket version of zero: a duck. The Dog and Duck!

So the demon juice had worked after all. Somewhere, way at the back of Dextrose's mind, among the stacks of detritus, the empty bottles and the used prophylactics, he'd been aware of his wife's situation all along. If only his drawing skills had been better, we might have made the connections.

But this was no time for recriminations. They could come later, at the reunion.

Grabbing Dad's hand, I pulled him along with me in the direction the crowd had been heading, trying to force some impetus into his frustrating gait.

We emerged shortly into a square, humming with massed, expectant voices and lit up on all sides by the orange caress of flickering flames. The torchlight parade was starting. A clock struck eight.

How the hell were we going to spot one particular old lady among this mess of people?

"Dad, what does Mum look like?" It seemed an odd question to be asking.

"Long silver hair," he offered. "And a woman's face."

Heart racing, I scanned the crowd seeking out women of a certain age. It was all I had. Mostly there were families with children in tow, whom I could discount, though there were sufficient oldies milling about to make the task a nightmare.

The flaming torches comprised long, pus-coloured wax candles, held in a cardboard tube with a circular hand-guard, so they looked like toy swords. Indeed, some of the children were using them as such, play-fighting with siblings and friends, while parents tried to wrestle the weapons off them, citing health-and-safety. I could sense the St John's Ambulance folk licking their lips.

In the back of my mind was the knowledge that, if we did fail, we could track Mrs Dextrose to the pub later. But I wanted to find her now. I had to. Already I could imagine the warmth and amazement of a reunion among those tiny real fires.

As we turned a corner of the square the crowd was funnelling down one particular street, presumably heading for the sea to confront the Moren.

"Anything?" I asked Dad.

He shook his head.

"What about her?" I asked, pointing towards a nearby bent old lady wearing a bobble-hat, whose face resembled a sultana.

"Minking cheek!" he shot back.

We followed the flow out of the square, shuffling along the edge of the parade, as the river of contented souls in rainwear and thick jumpers, revelling in the community vibe, made its way towards the ocean. I was too tense to share their enjoyment.

As we crossed one junction Dad suddenly gripped my arm.

"Mink!" he hissed through clenched teeth.

I followed his gaze, my pupils flitting over the scene, taking snapshots then moving on, until they alighted upon the likeliest candidate.

She was wearing a blue, rubbery-looking mackintosh, and a bright-yellow waterproof hat, such as trawlermen wore. Hanging down over the back of the mac was a ponytail of silvery-blonde hair. She was shorter than the average promenader, and I had only glimpsed her briefly when the people around her shifted positions.

"Blue mac, yellow hat?" I asked.

"Think so. Me eyes..."

When I looked back among the crowd, she had disappeared. I scanned for the yellow hat, but it had become submerged among the flesh and clothing.

On impulse I threw myself into the throng, leaving Dad behind, and spent several minutes pleading, "Excuse me!

Excuse me!" pushing people aside and spinning frantically, searching for that hat. Hemmed in and pestered along I became disorientated and lost any sense of where I was in relation to where the woman in the sou'wester had been.

One man, old enough to know better, actively pushed against me to block my route, as if getting to the front of the parade might be some badge of honour.

"I'm looking for my mother!" I told him.

"Aren't we all," he snapped back.

Frustrated, I headed once again for the sidelines, where I found Dad looking distressed. "Where'd yer go?" he demanded.

"Where do you think I went?"

I pulled him along until we neared a junction where the parade had stopped, giving me a chance to rediscover my bearings. As I once again flitted my gaze over the sea of heads, there, at the front of the queue, I spotted the yellow hat.

Its owner was no more than ten yards away, but with a sardine-packed scrum of people between us.

I shook my Dad's arm, pointing. "Look, there she is! There she is! Call to her!"

He did not. Guilt and fear had visibly gripped his troubled mind and though his mouth opened and shut it made no sound. He shook his head.

So it was down to me. I wondered whether it would always be thus.

"Mrs Dextrose! Mrs Dextrose!" I called out, waving my arms.

The people nearest me turned to stare; the woman in the yellow hat did not. The background burble must have drowned out my calls.

I tried again, louder.

"MRS DEXTROSE! MRS DEXTROSE!"

No reaction from her, though people further into the crowd

glanced at me curiously. It crossed my mind that the woman in the yellow hat might not even be Mrs Dextrose.

"*MRS DEXTROSE!*"

The yellow hat turned. It turned towards me and I saw its owner's face for the first time. Keen-eyed and small, fresh complexion, little or no make-up. Vibrant-looking. The sort of face that enjoys watching trees in a storm.

I heard Dad say, "Mink," just above a whisper.

That was her.

My mother's face. *My mother's face*. Younger than I had expected, certainly plenty younger than Dad. Mid-fifties?

Her gaze alighted just to my right. She had spotted him. Her eyes widened and narrowed in a moment, her lips pursed and she shouted something that I could not hear but which caused those around her to see where she was looking, while one parent covered her daughter's ears.

I watched as she pushed aside the few people in front of her and started moving quickly – in the opposite direction from us. Mrs Dextrose was getting away.

I couldn't let that happen. Whatever she thought of her feckless husband, I was sure she would want to see me.

"MUM! *MUM!*" I began pushing my way through the crowd. This time they pressed themselves aside.

The yellow hat stopped moving.

Once again her head turned, but this time her eyes rested on mine.

That was when I heard it. '*Ting-ting-ting-ting-ting-ting!*' So much more urgently than the previous time I'd heard that little bell ring.

I read my mother's lips – "Pilsbury?" – that was what she said – as the tram came into view from behind the buildings on the far side of the road. It caught her a glancing blow on her shoulder, spinning her round and sending the yellow hat flying into the air. A gasp rose from the crowd. I saw the tram driver's face, inches from his windscreen as he stood up and leaned forward, screaming silently, arm still pumping the bell-pull as he drove on past.

'*Ting-ting-ting-ting-ting-ting!*'

I lost sight of her when she went down.

People had gathered around, encircling her, like children do at a playground fight. But there was no chanting, only an eerie hush. I broke through them.

One man was placing a rolled up coat under her head; a woman standing above him was speaking urgently on a mobile telephone. Everyone else just watched.

There was so much blood on the road.

I threw myself down beside her prone form. "This is my mother," I told anyone listening.

This wasn't how it was meant to happen.

She must have gone down on the back of her head, because her ponytail was engorged with blood, unrecognisable as hair. It looked like a trail of gore. Her blue mackintosh had fallen open. She wore a tatty old striped V-neck jumper – red, black and blue horizontal stripes – over a lacy white collared shirt. A silver locket hanging from a fine chain rested at the base of the V of the jumper.

Her eyes were closed.

Beauty and grace, dressed for comfort not for effect.

Was this how I was to remember her?

As I gazed at her face, I felt for her hand and found it. It was small and warm. I closed my fingers around hers and gave them a squeeze. She did not respond.

This is your mother, I told myself.

So how had it come to this?

I studied the lines and contours of her face. Delicate crows' feet around her eyes and at the corners of her mouth. Her cheekbones were high and her chin narrow, she had small, pouty lips, unpainted. Elfin. Her eyebrows were very dark, in contrast to her silvery hair, and she had a small, dark mole above her left eyebrow.

Although I'd tried to picture her recently, many times, I had never arrived at an image I was happy with, which I felt might tally reasonably with the reality. What I had expected was a careworn woman, tired, with shadows under her eyes. Bitter and abandoned.

I had been wrong.

"Mum?" I whispered. "*Mum?*"

A splatter of blood marred one of her cheeks and I wiped it away. As I was doing so, someone arrived beside me on their knees, put their arms beneath her and lifted her torso off the ground.

Harrison Dextrose.

Her arms and head flopped backwards as he did so.

As he cradled her limp form against his chest, burying his head into the crook of her neck, he kept repeating over and over: "Frankie. Frankie. Frankie. Frankie…"

She looked so fragile there.

*****

Francesca Dextrose's funeral was so well-attended that the little crematorium outside Dritt-on-Sea had a speaker in the grounds, with seats arranged so that those who could not fit inside could listen to the service. To do so they had braved a chill northerly wind. I'd been asked whether I wanted to say a few words by the lady in charge, but had declined.

I mean, what would I have said? Nothing I could think of would have suited the occasion.

Dad spruced himself up and it was quite a transformation. He lived out of a metal trunk at the end of his bed, from which he'd dug out an old suit. Although it was khaki-coloured and creased in all the wrong places it showed willing, with a nod to his personality. He cut chunks off his beard, slicked down his hair and donned what I imagined was his one and only tie (brown).

Most of those who turned up seemed to know him – once they'd seen past the cleanliness and sobriety – and offered condolences; however, he courted few conversations, preferring to remain in his seat up front with his head lowered. I left him to his thoughts and hung around on the periphery, wondering what I had lost, secretly, guiltily grateful that I did not know. All I had was what might have been, a series of ifs and buts, intangibles, as impossible to grasp as a shadowplay in mist.

What if she had been – as her appearance had suggested – a sprightly, effervescent, joyful woman, who grabbed every one of life's opportunities? Perhaps her husband's lengthy absences were a relief to her, rather than the burden I had imagined? Would she have loved her son, had circumstance not dragged him away from her?

And what was that circumstance? Why had they abandoned me?

I had never known my birth mother and now she was in a wooden box. A waxwork, a puppet separated from its puppeteer. A cadaver.

I thought – feared – I might remember her face in death, that immobile expression, captured forever in my mind's eye. But I didn't. By the morning after her accident, it was like a half-completed jigsaw puzzle, and the pieces only disappeared, leaving me with a mere photofit. Mrs Dextrose had left me with more questions than answers, and I could not help but wonder whether I would be better off trying to forget her, as if I had never chased that yellow hat that awful night.

No one at the funeral asked who I was or why I was there, and Dad can't have mentioned me to anyone. I doubt he could have coped with the complication. There was no wake, everyone simply drifted away.

Although I had worried that he would hit the bottle immediately after his wife's death, he had proven me wrong. Instead, he had spent the four days prior to the funeral sitting on her bed in their twin room above the Dog & Duck, sifting through her effects, stopping often and staring into space. (I supposed it was inevitable they would have slept in separate beds, although the circumstances above the pub had left them no choice.)

At night I tucked myself into her bed and he into his own. I don't think I could have done that had I known her. Her smell lingered on the pillows, a floral aroma I matched to a perfume on the dressing table. I sprayed a little onto the back of my hand and, having checked that Dad wasn't looking, dabbed some of the evaporating liquid onto my neck. Immediately afterwards I felt weird and rushed to the bathroom to wash it off, fighting off nausea. That was the last time I touched her perfume.

It was a very old room, with a wooden floor so solid it made no sound when trodden upon, and beams in the ceiling, all original features. (Robin the landlord told me the Dog & Duck had been built during the late-16th century, back when Dritton-Sea had been a haven for sea-faring folk and their whores.) A two-bar heater plugged into the mains provided the only heat. We existed with both bars on.

A sewing machine had been left out on her bedside table, which she must have worked at while sitting on her bed, as there was no chair; a pair of trousers she had been mending were folded beside it. Her bedspread was very colourful and patchwork, and I felt certain she had made it herself.

Her bookshelf was so crammed with books that others had had to be piled in front of it. Historical biographies, of politicians, writers, poets, artists, warmongers, peacemakers, romances and the classics, plays and plenty of detective fiction, and, I suppose inevitably, explorers – but no copy of *The Lost Incompetent* (though there were a couple of dozen pristine copies stacked beside Dad's bed). She seemed to have a thing for Inspector Morse.

What little wall space there was, not obscured by shelving, the dresser or the wardrobe, she had filled with pictures, photographs and postcards. The pictures and photographs were of fishing vessels, tall ships, lobster pots set at arty angles, salty types with pipes and nets, as if she had taken a keen interest in the local area and its erstwhile industry.

It was the postcards that intrigued me the most – three of them, picturing 'Sunny Barbados', 'Weaving in Lanarkshire' and 'Welcome to Basingstoke' – and I peeled off the Sellotape attaching them to the wall to read the backs when Dad had excused himself one time. Had I been expecting anything from him to her, I was to be disappointed. Auntie Milly, Cedric and Lilith, respectively, had signed those cards. I wondered who they were, but did not ask.

There was no clock, or timepiece of any description, in the room. That had surprised me.

Only on the afternoon before the funeral, when Dad had left to buy some provisions, did I pluck up the courage to look in the wardrobe and drawers. Despite my misgivings, I had longed to look through her private things. She was dead, so what harm could it do? Besides, perhaps, to myself? In the end I could not help it; I had to satisfy my curiosity.

The large drawers at the bottom of the wardrobe were a disappointment: just some sheets, blankets and bulky woollens. I flicked through the clothing hanging up: a modest collection. It was all functional wear, suited to days out rambling or chilly evenings in the open, bar one slinky, sequined dress tucked right at the back. I tried to imagine her in it, but failed. Likewise, the footwear on the shelf below: two pairs of clumpy shoes, one pair of wellies, and a delicate pair of patent leather strapless high-heels with golden buckles. When had she last been treated to a night out, I wondered?

The four small drawers in the dressing table contained underwear – I opened and closed that one quickly – skirts and shirts, a plastic carton containing make-up and a cheap velvet box of jewellery. The make-up collection was small but the items were well-used. Two lipsticks, a box of eyeshadows (beige tones), tube of foundation, some blusher and an eyebrow pencil. I opened one of the lipsticks, a shade of pink, and saw the indentation her lip had worn into its edge.

It didn't require an expert to know that there was nothing worth stealing from the jewellery box. Beads and brooches, a couple of silver rings, a silver locket, oval-shaped... I realised – at least, I was fairly certain – it was the one that had been hanging around her neck. Should I open it? I sat staring at it for many minutes, until I became convinced that Dad would return any moment and that he would not like what he saw.

Then I prised it open quickly, fingers fumbling. It was him: a tiny head-shot crudely cut from a larger photograph, black-and-white, taken at a time when his hair was still in check. He was smiling. It was such a relief, I nearly cried out loud with happiness.

I could never have defended his dereliction of her – the tawdry bits of which I was aware – but I had to know that she still cared, despite him. Because I was certain, however much he huffed and bluffed, that she meant plenty to him.

Contented on that front, one gaping hole in our family saga remained, which I had tiptoed and pussyfooted around – buried, frankly – and which I could not let lie any longer. So when Dad returned to our room clutching shopping I blurted it out. "Dad. Why was I adopted?"

He dropped the bag and stiffened. A melon rolled out across the floorboards, its ridges playing out an uneven beat.

Seconds passed.

"Sit yerself down," he said.

"Us had no money," he began. "Simple as that, son. Had no roof over us heads. Had no food for us mouths."

"Why not?"

Sitting opposite me on the edge of his bed, he looked down at his feet. "That'd be the rub," he said.

"Well?" I wasn't going to let him squirm his way out of it this time.

"If yer must know, I'd bought Dextrose I, just a week 'fore yer mother tells us, 'I's preggers'. Were bad timing."

Dextrose was his yacht. He'd used it on several of his expeditions. "You mean you'd spent all your money on a yacht?"

"That's about it."

"So you were broke when I came along?"

"Mm." He had the grace to look uncomfortable.

I just didn't get it. "Why?"

"Why what?"

"Why buy a yacht when you obviously couldn't afford it?"

His face flushed a little. "Harrison Dextrose is an explorer, son – that's what he does. I were going to make us money. I had plans for that boat."

"Which were?"

"Single-handed around the world. That's what I were going to do! Make history, coin in the cash!"

I trawled my trivia knowledge. "Didn't Francis Chichester make history by sailing single-handed around the world?"

"Hmm," he went. "Can't say I'd heard of the minker, till someone mentioned his name."

"Alright. You said you had *plans* for the boat – what else?"

"Remember, Pilsbury, this were the mid-Sixties – men was heading into space. It were a time of great exploration. No barriers, no boundaries."

"So what else?"

"Find the North West Passage sea route?"

"Wasn't that discovered in the 1900s?"

He smiled weakly and nodded. "Someone else pointed that out, just 'fore us set off. Lucky they did! Minking cold up there!"

I didn't laugh. "What a mess."

"Sorry, son."

"Couldn't you have just sold the boat?"

He looked at me, incredulous. "I told yer: I's an explorer! That's us job! Without me boat I were grounded."

"Couldn't Mrs Dextrose have got a job?"

"No missus of mine is going out to work! I has some

principles, yer know."

"And because of your *principles*, you abandoned me."

He said nothing, but stared at me, hands clenched together between his legs, hunch-backed. He looked like a little boy.

"Who were those people who adopted me?"

"Ah, see! The missus's sister knew this couple, Humphrey and Mildred, and she wanted a baby but couldn't. Respectable folk. Folk with money. We knew they'd bring you up right..."

That was it. "I was fucking *miserable*, Dad!" I shouted. Then more quietly. "I was fucking miserable." A tear escaped my lower eyelid. I felt its progress down my cheek and tasted its saline sadness as it trickled between my lips.

The mattress beside me sank down considerably, then an arm curled around my shoulders.

"Come on, son," he soothed. "Come on." Whiskers tickled my face.

His voice was higher-pitched than normal. "We met them a couple of times, when you was a bit older. Down here in Dritt. Yer probably wouldn't remember it. We was trying to get you back, but they was having none of it. Said it weren't fair on you, that you'd settled there and wouldn't know who we was. In the end we all agreed: they was right. But it broke yer mother's heart."

I was sobbing uncontrollably, shaking, taking juddering breaths.

"Broke mine too, truth be told. We was fools, son. I were a fool." His voice brightened a little. "Yer know, one time I decided to kidnap yer back! Drove round to their house and staked the place out. Two days I were there, sitting in that car, stinking to high heaven, waiting for the chance to snatch yer back."

"So?" I managed to blurt out between heaves.

"Wrong house. I'd got the digits wrong way round. What was yer? 27? And I'd sat outside 72. Or were it the other way round?"

I just started laughing. There was snot running into my mouth, slimy and gross and I couldn't help myself. The laughter turned into hysteria.

The man was a fucking liability. I simply couldn't believe how useless a human being he was. I could have hated him – should have hated him – but it wouldn't happen. What would have been the point? His ineptitude was all part of his not inconsiderable charm. No more backward steps. There had been too many of those in my life already. Far too many.

Dad did not join in the hysteria, perhaps he didn't see the joke; he just held me as I let it all out.

When I had finally calmed down, he said, "I'd understand if yer couldn't forgive us."

I studied him through sore, bleary eyes, that man with his blackheads and his scars, his brow furrowed, his expression all nerves.

"Water under the bridge," I said.

"Really?"

Snorting up enough phlegm to fill an eggcup, I wiped my eyes with the back of my hand and smiled. "Course."

He smiled back. "I love yer, son."

"I love you too, Dad."

The morning after the funeral, he shook me awake.

"I can't live here no more," he said.

He sat on his bed holding in his hands a small tin box, black-painted and dented. He unlocked it, extracted a leaflet and handed it to me.

It was headed:

THE SERIES OF GENTLEMEN HOME FOR RETIRED EXPLORERS

Its cover depicted a gothic building in grounds with tall

trees with, inset, a small photograph of an old chap in a wheelchair attempting to raise a smile.

"That's where I'm going," he said. "Don't worry, it's a charity. It won't cost yer a penny."

"It's not about the money, you old goat," I chided him.

"It is to me," he said. "Anyhow, it's what I want. Me travelling days is over."

*****

The door was large and heavy, with wrought iron fixings and a gargoyle for a knocker. I pulled on the gargoyle's tongue and let it fall back. 'Donk.'

It didn't sound terribly loud so I repeated the action. 'Donk.'

Dad, who was wearing his funeral suit and had once again attempted to slick down his hair, though unruly tresses had sprung back up, looked nervous. I heard him suck his teeth. Rather him than me, I thought.

"You're sure this is what you want?" I asked.

Before he could reply, the door creaked open.

A fearsome looking woman in a starched white nurse's uniform stood before us, glaring. Her coal-black hair was arranged into a beehive and a funny little folded hat sat on top of that. It would have been comical, had I not been so perturbed.

"*You only needed to knock once!*" she bellowed, at a volume more suited to addressing people 50 yards behind us. "*You will wake the residents!*"

It was 2.33pm.

"*Hmm,*" she went, still sounding like a foghorn.

I hoped that introductions might break the ice. "I'm Pilsbury Dext…"

"*I know who you are!*" she thundered. "*And that is your wanton father. I've heard all about him. We shall have none of his funny business here… well, come in! Don't just stand there, like lepers at the gates of Heaven!*"

Only once we stepped over the threshold did I realise how

short she was. She barely came up to my chest and was built like a barrel. It was her face that did it: square and mean. Her tight lips curved downwards and her flabby cheeks followed them, her expression set at permanent displeasure. She had the beginnings of a beard: thick, wiry black hairs, poking sporadically from around her mouth.

"I am Nurse D'eath," she said, quieting down at last, and eagle-eyeing my reaction.

I didn't dare move a facial muscle.

"Welcome to the Series of Gentlemen Home for Retired Explorers," she added.

Her manner put me so on edge. I don't know why, perhaps I was trying to endear myself to her, but I put a hand on her shoulder. A gesture of affection? I guess it was meant to say: 'Please like me, I mean no harm'.

"*That*," Nurse D'eath bellowed, "*is the last time you will ever touch me.*"

"Thank mink for that," I heard Dad mutter.

She glared at him. "*What. Did. You. Say?*"

"Nothing," he mumbled, the schoolboy.

"*WHAT?*"

"Nothing." Louder.

"*Nothing, Nurse D'eath!*"

"Nothing, Nurse D'eath."

"Good. Now come and meet the residents."

Nurse D'eath led us down a gloomy, high-ceilinged, wood-panelled hallway lit by candles set into alcoves, like something out of *Scooby-Doo*. I expected a ghostly hand to emerge from a false panel at any second, to swipe at my departing back. To our right was a large hatch and behind that an old bloke wearing a white coat, seated at a desk, holding a broom in one hand. His face was ghostly pale and thin; bruised bags seeped from beneath his eyes in ripples. He was slumped and looked decidedly bored, but straightened upright on seeing Nurse D'eath.

"Afternoon, Nurse D'eath," he called out.

"You said that not one minute ago, as I was answering the door, Cedric. Do not repeat yourself," she boomed. *"This is our new guest, Mr Harrison Dextrose. With him is his son, Pilsbury. You will remember their faces. That is Cedric. He is our security guard and janitor."* Her voice cannoned down the corridor and bounced around in a series of diminishing echoes. It sounded like a haunting.

Through the door at the end of the hallway, we entered a vast communal lounge, painted white top to bottom. There was no natural light; a large, dusty chandelier from another time and place hung from the ceiling, only half of its bulbs working; there was a door in each of the three walls. The room contained six armchairs, five of which were occupied, each by an old gentleman. They were all asleep, one in front of a television.

The nurse clapped her hands, instantly jolting them from their slumber.

"Our newest recruit to the Series of Gentlemen!" she announced, then motioned towards the empty chair. *"Mr Dextrose, please take your place."*

He looked at me and raised an eyebrow.

"You sure this is what you want?" I hissed.

"We will not have dissention here!" shouted Nurse D'eath.

Dad nodded to me and did as he was told.

I had never taken him for a masochist. It puzzled me.

"Here," Nurse D'eath pointed to three men whose chairs were arranged next to each other, like seats on a plane, "are Mr Reculver, Mr Hoath and Mr Chislet."

Reculver waved, Hoath smiled, Chislet did not react.

Each in his early-eighties, I guessed, they wore matching outfits: tweed jacket and plus-fours, long green socks and shiny brown-leather shoes, with matching tweed caps. Each had a tartan blanket draped over their lap.

Reculver was an imposing sort of fellow with fingers the length of prize runner beans. He was so pale he was almost translucent. His flesh clung to his bones and he had a collection of interesting growths on his enormous ears.

Hoath had a bulbous, deep-red nose, on which was balanced a pair of black-rimmed spectacles, and wisps of ginger hair hung down from the back of his cap. He regarded me with a tangible sneer.

And Chislet... I wondered whether he might be paralysed. A short, fat, white-bearded, bald-pated fellow wearing half-moon glasses, he never moved, though you'd begin to notice his eyes follow you around the room, as if he were a portrait in a haunted house.

"That," the nurse pointed at a chap facing the door in the far wall, "is Mr Wilmington-Hovis... *Mr Wilmington-Hovis! Stop staring at the bathroom!*"

Very slowly, with a shaking hand, Mr Wilmington-Hovis reached down, gripped what I realised was a wheel and swivelled himself around. It was not an armchair at all, but an old-fashioned meerschaum bath-chair.

His ancient head was resting on his chest, as if he did not have the strength, or the inclination, to lift it. He wore a white vest and pale blue pyjama bottoms. His muscles had wasted away, his arms were covered in liver spots, his eyes were hollows and his chest sunken. So old and wizened was Mr Wilmington-Hovis, he looked like the sort of thing an Egyptologist might discover beneath bandages.

Nurse D'eath snapped, "*Mr Wilmington-Hovis, sulking does not become you! Any more of that and you will go to your room!*"

His hand twitched but he said nothing.

"*Mr Peel! Mr Peel!*" the nurse called out to the old man in the corner watching television, though it appeared he had fallen asleep again. "*MR PEEL!*"

Mr Peel jumped as if he had sat on the live rail and landed back in his chair clutching his chest.

"*Mr Peel, come and greet our guests.*"

He grabbed a walking stick and tottered towards us methodically, stooping and smiling. I decided that I might like him the most.

When he eventually reached me, he bowed. "Kenneth John Peel," he said. "They wrote a song about me."

His voice was very soft and his handshake surprisingly firm for a dodderer, though he did have more meat on him than the rest of the bunch. He was wearing a tight red tracksuit better suited to someone a quarter of his age. I'm afraid I couldn't help but notice the banana-style outline of his aged penis.

"I'm sorry," I replied. "Which song?"

He tutted jokily. "You know!" And he began to sing, pausing in the wrong places: "Do you, ken John Peel, at the break of day? Do you, ken John Peel, with his coat so gay? Do you, ken John Peel, when I'm far, far away... Got it now?"

I did. (And I knew that 'ken' meant 'know' in the Scottish dialect, rather than 'Kenneth'.)

"Yes. Yes I do," I replied, not wishing to hurt his feelings. "By the way, that's my father, Mr Harrison Dextrose."

Kenneth John Peel spoke. "Harrison Dextrose, eh? I've read your book," he said. "Didn't believe a word of it."

Nurse D'eath clapped once again. "*Good! Now everyone knows everyone else! Mr Dextrose, I shall now tell you the Rules. Commit them to memory.*"

Good luck with that, I thought.

She recited: "1. No drinking." – He didn't even blink – "2. No smoking. 3. No shouting. 4. No swearing. 5. No comfortable bedding of any description to be brought in. That one is particularly for you to remember, the younger Mr Dextrose," she added, wagging a finger. "6. No talking after lights out. 7. No using the toilet after lights out – a bucket is provided in your room. 8. No females other than blood relatives or spouses. 9. Visitors only between the hours of two and three. And lastly, number 10. No leaving the home without permission. Are we…"

Mr Wilmington-Hovis piped up unexpectedly, "We're explorers – and we aren't allowed out!" His voice was weak and hollow-sounding, as if it were its own echo.

"*Right, that's it!*" barked the nurse. "*Off to your room!*"

She grabbed the back of the meerschaum bath-chair as he tried feebly to kick her, and began wheeling him off towards the door to my right.

"*I forgot to mention, Mr Dextrose,*" she called back. "*This door leads to the bedrooms. I shall show you yours later. As you should be aware, the far door leads to the bathroom. Use it wisely. The other door leads to my office and quarters. You must never – ever – use that door.*"

I stood shell-shocked.

"*One last thing, Mr Harrison Dextrose. You were very lucky to acquire this place at the Series of Gentlemen. Your application arrived on the day we had a death.*"

When the door shut behind her, I said urgently in a lowered voice, "Dad, we've got to get you out of here."

"No, son. This'll do us fine. Don't you…"

Kenneth John Peel cut in: "What have you been up to, Dextrose? Eh? Ever killed a grizzly with your bare hands and washed down its still-beating heart with a rough tequila?"

Dad shook his head.

Peel sensed blood. "Ever climbed the Herringbone Glacier and made love to a lady at the top?"

"As if he has!" mocked Hoath.

"I bloody have!" said Peel.

"I was going to say…" I began, but they talked over me.

"We, however – that is, Mr Reculver, Mr Chislet and I – have climbed the Herringbone. Indeed, we have been all over Antarctica." Hoath paused for effect. "And we never saw you there."

"No doubt I was there at a different time!" snapped Peel.

"Why, when were you there?" demanded Hoath.

"You first."

"No, you!"

Reculver clicked his fingers to gain my attention. "They always have this row," he said, raising his eyes to the ceiling.

Peel heard him. "Reculver think he's above the debates," he said to me. "But he's not. He and I once argued for three days over who was first to ascend the Matterhorn on one leg."

"Hopping, really," Reculver explained.

"Yes, who first had hopped up the Matterhorn," said Peel.

I couldn't help asking, "*What's the point of that?*"

It sounded as though everyone in the room had drawn a breath. "'What's the point of that?' Mr Chislet?" Hoath said to Chislet, who was yet to speak.

"What a curious question, Mr Hoath," Reculver agreed.

"The boy's green," said Peel, for once on their side.

I noticed that Dad remained silent. I had never seen him so overwhelmed.

"Yes, what's the point?" I reiterated.

Peel guffawed falsely. "You clearly know nothing of exploration, young man. Exploration is all about firsts. He who is second makes not a footnote in the history books. Tell me, who was the second man on the moon?"

"Edwin 'Buzz' Aldrin," I replied, having boyishly devoured the Apollo missions.

"Ah," went Peel. "Bad example. Alright, who was the second man to travel around England with a turbot?"

That one got me. "I've no idea," I said.

"Precisely my point," he said. "I, on the other hand, was the first."

"Really?" I went, knowing it would wind him up.

"He makes them up!" scoffed Hoath.

Peel ignored him. "The boy's an ignoramus!" he spluttered, and began ranting, counting off the exploits on his fingers: "I was the first to slide on a tea tray down Nanga Parbat; the first to circumnavigate Grantham on a spacehopper; the first to survive being forcibly defenestrated from an ice breaker in Antarctica; the first…"

As he rambled on, Reculver addressed me once again. "You know, we call her *Nurse Death*."

"Yes, I thought that might be the case."

"Oh," he said, and looked downcast. "That's a shame. That was one of mine."

"*WHAT IS THIS NOISE?*" Nurse D'eath was standing in the doorway that led to the residents' bedrooms, surveying the scene, simmering.

Everyone fell silent. Kenneth John Peel tottered back to his chair in the corner.

"*Visiting time is over, the younger Mr Dextrose,*" she announced pointedly. "*And you… heathens will go to bed early. With no supper.*"

I shook Dad's hand formally for some reason.

"I'll be back," I told him.

I had arranged with Robin Botham to take the room above the Dog & Duck. It was mutually beneficial and I had never believed in ghosts: as far as I was concerned, Mrs Dextrose would not be coming back, not in any shape or form. It was time to move on.

When I arrived back there, I was shocked to discover that the lodgings had been cleared out. The bookshelves and wardrobe were empty, the sewing machine gone, the pictures and postcards, too. The walls were bare. The beds had been stripped down to their linen and the top of the dressing table cleared. I checked the drawers, knowing that I would find nothing.

Dad's wishes, no doubt, though the sparseness, the sudden removal of all that personality, made me feel very alone. There had always been someone around, barring loo breaks, during my recent travels – whether I had desired the company or not. Now it was just me.

I would have to make the place my own, I decided, and made a mental note to find some sea-faring scenes for the walls.

The next day I visited Dad again, worried for his sanity in that gothic asylum. As it turned out, he seemed fine. Chipper, even. He'd just had his lunch – "Minking pasty and minking chips" – and that morning had attended his first therapy session with Nurse D'eath, which he said had helped him release some of the tension accumulated over the previous weeks.

The old boys then argued over which of them had undertaken the most death-defying adventure; Dad felt settled enough to join in occasionally and, to my mind, won with his tale of shark-baiting with a gangrenous big toe off the Lesser Barrier Reef. Not that I'd ever heard the story before, which made me doubt its veracity.

Hoath then tipped Wilmington-Hovis out of his meerschaum bath-chair and everyone laughed – bar Chislet, who seemed to exist in a trance. (An odd cove, I wondered what on earth use he had been to Reculver and Hoath on their expeditions.)

It was all rather jovial, until the nurse appeared and demanded to know who was responsible for depositing Wilmington-Hovis onto the floor. The mood in the room changed, as if blanketed in frost. Nerves tautened. When no one owned up, Nurse D'eath advanced upon Hoath and he cowered in his armchair, holding up his forearms before his face.

I left soon afterwards.

Back home I began writing up my own travels, longhand in a

notebook – following in Harrison Dextrose's literary footsteps for a change. The process went so well that I decided to invest in a typewriter – which felt more romantic than a word processor, better suited to the spirit of my words – and headed out shopping. I found one eventually, an old Remington, the size and weight of a small pig, in a charity shop.

Afterwards, the noise of seagulls squawking lured me to the seafront: a shingle beach, stretching out either way as far as the eye could see, dotted with hardy folk dressed up against a meaningful wind, staring at the breakers. One fool was out swimming, their white bathing cap being eyed by a floating tern.

I also saw the pier for the first time in more than a quarter of a century. The design of it rang no bells, not even a tiny tinkle, perhaps because it was so bare and uncommercial; no candy floss nor amusements. It was, however, very, very long: an awful lot of planking raised a few metres above the sea surface, with a construction much like a bus shelter at the very end. A sign beside it on the beach read:

England's Second-Longest Pier

No doubt Kenneth John Peel's pier had beaten them to it.

I took a walk along it, to pass some time and to plan the coming weeks. It would be propitious, I decided, to settle down for a while after my recent travails. Take it easy. That would also keep me close to my father, who needed me. Although I could afford to live off my inheritance for a good while to come, I planned to ask for part-time bar-work in the Dog & Duck, which should help endear me to the locals. (And hopefully find a girlfriend.)

As I sat sheltering on the end of the pier, all alone and transfixed by the motion of the waves, a familiar sound drifted to my ears across the white horses.

'Ting-ting!' it went. 'Ting-ting!'

In the coming weeks I developed a routine, visiting Dad on Mondays, Thursdays and Sundays, writing up my travels during my spare time, and working in the pub on Friday and Saturday nights. The locals gradually took me into their confidence with tittle-tattle, and I began to feel at home in Dritt.

Most rewarding, I found, was getting to know the old gimmers in the Series of Gentlemen Home for Retired Explorers. What had initially looked like the near-death branch of one of John and Yoko's bed-ins, became more intriguing as my visits wore on.

Mr Reculver had the best sense of humour and was the most self-aware. He, Hoath and Chislet had teamed up back in the day when a tweed sock was deemed the Acme of snow-wear technology, and had specialised in exploring the unknown nooks and crannies of the frozen Poles. Until one year their publisher bought them tickets to Benidorm as a treat, and they never looked back.

"Pilsbury, never explore Antarctica," Reculver warned me. "It is perishing down there and penguins smell worse than you think."

I assured him that I wouldn't.

Hoath was rather the wind-up merchant, and the most boyish of the residents (which must be taken in context). He'd be the first to jump on one of Kenneth John Peel's outrageous exaggerations and, though it made me feel awkward, was the ringleader of the regular bullying of Mr Wilmington-Hovis.

Poor Mr W-H. He didn't really say much – though still considerably more than Mr Chislet – and seemed to foster a persistent sense of injustice, trapped in his meerschaum bathchair, scowling at the walls. Rarely would he join in with the arguments over who had been the first/bravest/sexiest, and when he did so he was too easily shouted down.

Hoath told me that Wilmington-Hovis had until recently been visited by a grandson and three great-grandchildren, until one afternoon the youngest had asked when he was planning to die, because Daddy was bored of waiting for Great-Granddad's money. I noticed when that story finished that no one laughed.

Peel was the only resident I ever saw with a visitor: a painted blonde woman in heels and fur, in her late-sixties, whom he claimed was his wife. Except I overheard them arguing about her 'fee' and he palmed her some notes, looking considerably put out. I supposed he was so used to being surrounded by the half-deaf and two-thirds-blind that he'd let his guard slip in my company. He really was a rubbish liar, which is perhaps why I couldn't help liking him. (His history was also very poor, so he'd claim to have explored alongside the likes of Vasco da Gama, Ferdinand Magellan and assorted Vikings.)

The others, I gathered, had over the years been abandoned by former loved ones. In contrast to their readiness to elaborate upon expeditions and erstwhile derring-do, it was nigh on impossible to get them to open up about their private lives and how they had ended up in the home. Decrepit as they were – even Dad began to look more frail in my eyes, as if guilty by association – the testosterone lingered, and they were gentlemen of a certain era who avoided discussing the touchy-feely.

This much, however, was obvious: no matter what air of independence they might like to project, and in the face of the constant bickering and one-upmanship, they relied upon one another for companionship and support. They were a gang.

I thought that out loud once, which somehow ended up with me composing a rap for them. It went like this:

Don't got knives.
Or wives.
We barely got our lives.

We're old.
Got no gold.

With the heating on we're cold.
We've explored.
Now we're bored.
But don't take us yet, oh Lord.

There was a middle eight:

Reculver, Hoath and Chislet
Wilmington-Hovis, he's the business
Don't fuck with Ken John Peel
Or broken you will feel
Harry Dextrose
He's the…

I couldn't finish it so we dumped it.

It was shit but it made them happy. We were going to perform it *a capella* (Peel having offered the services of his human beatbox, which we politely turned down), but none of them could remember past the first line, and then Nurse D'eath burst in from her office, demanding to know what was so funny.

Wilmington-Hovis gave her some cheek – well, he said, "Nothing, Nurse D'eath" – and she slapped him hard across the face then wheeled him off to his room.

She was a bastard, there's no easier way of putting it, more cruel dominatrix than carer. She'd been merely snide with them during my early visits, but as she grew used to me, and the fact that I was as scared of her as the residents were, she grew bolder, nastier and more physical.

Once, she put a stale éclair on Mr Chislet's armchair and when he sat down told him he'd defecated himself, then stoked up the others' derision. He looked genuinely upset – as did she when I picked it up and ate it. That turned the tables. I saw her mists descend, but she knew I could escape at three o'clock.

Sadly, that was as daring as I got.

I said nothing when she 'accidentally' kicked Mr Peel's walking stick out from under him, after he'd regaled her with his tale of ascending Saltoro Kangri by emu; likewise, when she pretended to get her daily horoscope mixed up with her medical notes, and told Mr Reculver he had cancer. For a man with four toes touching the bucket, it could have been the *coup de grâce*. Fear then resignation overtook his demeanour, and he glanced at me, a piteous glance. When Nurse D'eath admitted her mistake in a music-hall voice, slapping her corpulent thigh, I thought he might go for her. But it would have taken him too long.

The dreadful woman was always talking down to them, treating them like children. They were better than that, deserved much more. I genuinely looked forward to my visits, despite the depressing nature of the place. It felt like I'd gained a bunch of eccentric granddads.

Nurse D'eath never picked on Dad while I was there. He'd been a different person since joining the Series of Gentlemen: his manner was subdued, he seemed almost pensive. I put it down to his being the relative 'new boy' – the others treated him as such, being sticklers for hierarchy – and assumed that he would in time rediscover his usual bombastic self.

On Sunday, some six weeks after Dad had joined the home, I felt comfortable enough with them to bring up their cowardliness in the face of the Nurse D'eath. Wilmington-Hovis was snoozing at the time and Dad was watching telly in the corner, but Chislet's eyes slid left to glare at me, Reculver nodded ruefully and Peel pretended he hadn't heard (perhaps he hadn't).

Hoath exploded. "How dare you! How dare you! You're not too old to put over my knee!"

"He is, you know," said Reculver, adding: "How old are you, Pilsbury?"

"I'm 33," I told him (for the umpteenth time).

"What a nice age," he said.

Then Peel chipped in with some garbage about being best man at Chris Bonnington's wedding. That was the trouble with trying to start a serious conversation in the Series of Gentlemen Home for Retired Explorers: one couldn't.

I tried again, having first apologised to Mr Hoath, who had begun to sulk. "I just don't get it," I said. "There's one of her and six of you, yet you never even talk back to her. She treats you like shit and I hate seeing it. Why don't you react? When are you going to stand up for yourselves?"

It was a reasonable speech, I thought, though I did check over my shoulder halfway through to see that Nurse D'eath hadn't entered the room.

Wilmington-Hovis woke up and mumbled, "I'm hungry."

"You've only just had lunch, you old fool!" snapped Hoath.

Peel tried again with his Chris Bonnington tale.

Then Wilmington-Hovis added: "I hope it's not broccoli."

As I sighed, Reculver piped up. "You know, Pilsbury, your visits make me sad," he said.

I regarded him quizzically.

He went on: "Not because I don't like you – *we* don't like you – because we do. It's just that you make me feel so bloody old." He laughed to himself and wiped his nose with a finger. "You know, you remind me of me. I imagine it's hard for you to look at an old fool like me, in this silly, rotten shell, and picture me as a young man. You must think my stories as ridiculous and unlikely as Peel's..."

Peel opened his mouth, ready to splurge indignation, but Reculver continued: "I was your age once, you know. Many years ago! And in many ways I still am that age, sad as that may be. Only the fight has gone, Pilsbury. Only the fight has gone.

"Old age suffers us so many indignities. I'm 87. You wonder how something can creep up on you over a period of 87 years. You think you'd notice it. But you don't. One day I was seven, and now I am not. And here we are. I have my friends with me, and we get by, on fading memories and stewed tea. Nothing Nurse D'eath can do can either improve that, or make it heavier to bear. We are what we are. It is what it is."

Everyone was rapt by his little speech, bar Dad who was still wrapped up in *Neighbours*. I wanted to hug him.

"But I won't lie to you Pilsbury," concluded Mr Reculver. "There are times when you walk out of that door that I envy you."

That night, something woke me. I had no idea what and, when I checked the illuminated display of my Timeco Z112.2 XG, it read 03.58. The room was in near-darkness and there was no sound, no seagull pattering along the roof, a noise that had woken me on more than one occasion. Yet I had a sense of being watched.

Fear gripped me and I lay stock still, listening. So heightened did my hearing become that after a while I was convinced I could hear the ticking of the clock in the town hall tower, way up the road. Still nothing stirred in the room.

After a while, when my terror had subsided and I was certain enough that I was alone, I dared to reach across and switch on my bedside light on the dresser.

I screamed.

Sitting on the end of my bed was the Shaman's dummy, staring at me with its beady eyes. Its nose was broken off, its dinner jacket was ripped and dusty, and its monocle glass was missing though the frame remained.

There came a banging on my door. I pulled the covers over me, fearing for my safety as well as my sanity. My hands were shaking.

"Pilsbury!" Robin Botham's voice. Dear old Robin Botham! "You alright in there?" he called thought the door. "I thought I heard a lady scream?"

"Robin, please, come in," I called back weakly.

How desperately I needed company.

"Christ, what's that ugly thing?" he said, spotting the wooden boy.

"You don't know how it got here?" I asked. "No one's been up here? No strangers?"

He thought for a bit. "None that I can think of. You alright?"

No. "Yes, sure. I'll be fine, thanks."

After he left I kept the light on, waiting for the dummy to make its move. Eventually convinced that it was inanimate, I lunged at it, wrenched open the window and flung it out into the night. I heard its wooden head land – 'ctnth' – on tarmac.

Then I sat there, sheets pulled up to my chin, bolt upright, terrified, wondering how the fuck that abomination had got there, when I had left it discarded at the side of the Nameless Highway weeks ago.

Words rang in my ears. These words: "You know I'll follow you to the ends of the earth, don't you?"

It couldn't be her. Just couldn't be.

Could it?

The following morning I didn't leave my room until gone ten, when the sun was fully up and the light through the window allowed me some comfort. I dressed quickly and crept out of the pub, peering around corners before entering corridors and inspecting the bar for signs of life. But the Dog & Duck was closed and the chairs and stools were unoccupied. Dust floated around the room, sparkling in the winter sunlight.

Outside the back door, the alleyway and car park were likewise silent. When I reached my car – a second-hand banger purchased primarily for the 15-minute drive to and from Dad – I checked the footwell of the rear seats before unlocking the doors. No killers there. I flipped up the boot. Nothing. Then the bonnet, though there was barely enough space under there to swing a hamster.

Satisfied, I yanked open my driver's door, dove in, slammed the door shut, hit the door lock and checked the back seats once again. Then I started the engine and drove away, checking in my mirrors to be sure that no one was following. Satisfied, I breathed out such a sigh of relief that my halitosis bounced back off the windscreen and I spluttered.

For the first time since 03.58, I felt safe.

At 10.33, I parked in a lay-by just around the corner from the Home for Retired Explorers, switched off the engine, and waited there until visiting time began, whilst remaining fully vigilant. I was too scared to grow bored.

At 13.59, I walked up to the Home for Retired Explorers and pulled back the gargoyle, as I had done so often in the past.

"*Young Mr Dextrose! Not one of your usual visiting days!*" bellowed Nurse D'eath when she answered the door.

"No!" I replied, as jauntily as I could manage. "Thought I'd break the habits of a lifetime!" I'd practised that reply out loud a hundred times in the car, so often that I almost stumbled over it.

She poked her head outside. "No car in the car park, I see…"

"No, broken down, I'm afraid. Had to catch the bus." I'd practised that lie too.

Her piggy eyes glinted with suspicion. "Just so long as you've no funny business in mind…"

"Haha! As if, Nurse D'eath!" I chirped, convinced I reeked of guilt.

At 14.48, having sat through a succession of Mr Peel's bloody stories and Hoath moaning about the bread rolls at breakfast time, while I was a bundle of nerves, I finally allowed myself to reveal my brilliant plan.

Gathering Dad, Reculver, Hoath, Chislet, Peel and

Wilmington-Hovis in a circle of chairs, I first checked that the nurse's office door was tight shut, then leant in and motioned for them to do the same.

"I'm taking you to the seaside," I whispered as loudly as I dared.

"You'll have to speak up!" blared Wilmington-Hovis.

"What did he say?" Reculver asked Hoath.

"He said he's taking Ruth up the backside," replied Hoath. "I think."

"That's me boy!" said Dad.

I had to start again.

Eventually, I hoped, everyone understood. That night I would be taking the six of them to the seaside: Dritt-on-Sea. How I would fit us all into my car, I wasn't sure. Cross that bridge when I came to it. No sense in over-planning. I would drive them to the pier, we would sit and watch the waves, and after an hour or so I would drive them back to the home.

"If anyone wants to stay in Dritt, do a runner, I'm happy to turn a blind eye," I told them.

Mr Chislet whistled. "Fuck me!" They were his very first words in my presence.

Dad stood up and slapped me on the back. Wilmington-Hovis and Peel looked petrified. Hoath didn't seem to have taken it in. Reculver beamed.

I returned the grin and hoped I would not let him down.

Truth be told, my 'brilliant' plan hinged upon one crucial factor. At least I did not need to trouble the old gimmers with it; I simply needed them to be dressed and ready by midnight.

"If you do not hear my knock on the door to your bedrooms…" I rephrased that: "If I do not open the door to your bedrooms by five minutes past midnight, go back to bed. My plan will have failed."

At 14.59, certain residents – I shall not name and shame them – could barely contain themselves and were fidgeting in their seats like small children. We had fallen unnaturally silent, too pent-up to speak, though eagerness patrolled what remained of our muscle groups.

The door to Nurse D'eath's office opened and she entered the room. She must have sensed the tension because she all but sniffed the air.

"Anything the matter?" she asked, lower-volume than usual.

She was on to us and we would have to hold our nerve.

Wilmington-Hovis twitched.

Peel raised his hand.

What the hell was he doing?

"*Yes, Mr Peel?*" bellowed the nurse.

Peel's stare bounced around the group. His mouth had fallen open and I noticed, to my horror, that he had developed an erection.

I shook my head at him as minimally as I could, gritting my teeth, desperately attempting to master ESP: '*Say nothing, Mr Peel! Please, don't blow it!*'

While Peel's indecision reigned, Nurse D'eath walked across the room and into the centre of our circle of deceit. There, she folded her arms.

"*Well, this is all rather conspiratorial!*" she announced. Then suddenly she lunged out a hand and flicked the head of Mr Peel's upstanding cock.

"Ow!" he squealed, as his ancient member instantly deflated.

"*Visiting time is over, the younger Mr Dextrose!*" bellowed the nurse. "*Be gone with you!*"

And so it began.

At 15.02, having closed the door to the communal lounge behind me, and having made sure that I was not being followed, I stopped at Cedric's window. This was the crucial part of my plan.

"Hello, Cedric," I said.

"Afternoon, Mr Pilsbury," he replied, tipping his cap. "Can I help you?"

I will confess, my heart was beating like a woodpecker's beak. "Yes, Cedric," I said. "I was wondering. Could I bribe you to conceal me beneath your desk until midnight?"

I swear he chuckled. "How much?" (I'd banked on that.)

"Will 50 pounds do?"

From his expression alone I assumed that it would. "See your money?" he went.

I thrust the notes, previously counted out, at him. He kissed them and folded them into a pocket.

"Open your door ready," I hissed.

I walked to the front door, opened it, waited a second, and closed it loudly. If she were watching from a window, monitoring my walk down the driveway, I was scuppered. But there was no time to dwell on that. I slid silently back across the floor, slunk into Cedric's office and crawled beneath his desk.

He was laughing to himself again. "You OK down there?" he whispered.

"Fine, thanks," I whispered back.

At 15.56, Cedric, who I'd have sworn had been snacking on pickles, from the sounds he had made, dropped the first of several silent but brutal blow-offs. The stench subjugated the air beneath his desk, like Nazis marching into Poland, and seeped into my clothing. I didn't have the gall to ask him to desist, and anyway, all too soon I failed to notice it.

At 16.22, he bent his head down and said, "I reckon you could come out from there if you wanted. Nurse D'eath's so fat, you could be back under there before her she'd squeezed her butt through the door."

I didn't dare chance fate. I did, however, run hastily through the next stage of my plan with him: shortly after midnight, when I had gathered together the troops, I would need him to let us out of the front door.

"No can do," came the reply. "At 11.30 I lock that door and switch on the alarm. If that don't happen, *on the dot*, she will be down on me like... well, like a ton of Nurse D'eath."

I hadn't foreseen that. "So how do I get us all outside?"

Cedric pondered for a while, then said: "Well, the front door's alarmed – but that big window in the bathroom ain't. You could climb out there. It's on the ground floor."

I passed him up another tenner.

At 23.27, there came a sharp kick in my ribs.

"Shh!" hissed Cedric. "You snore any louder, you'll bring the ceiling down!"

I'd been long enough asleep that I could feel dried saliva along the side of my cheek and gunk had gathered in the corners of my eyes. Uncomfortable and cramped as it was beneath the desk, I'd had so little sleep on account of the Shaman's dummy that I could probably have drifted off among hedgehogs.

"I gotta lock the door now. After that, she'll come down to check everything's OK. That's when you'll need to be real quiet, or we're in the shit. Got it?"

I had.

Next, I saw the bottoms of Cedric's legs depart his office, and heard his padding footsteps head for the front door. Keys rattled, one turned in a lock, there was a brief silence, then I heard the electronic beeps of the alarm being set. His footsteps returned.

Moments later I heard the heavy wooden door at the end of the corridor creak open. Nurse D'eath was coming. Curling myself into the tightest possible ball, I tried to slow my breathing. When that proved impossible, I closed my eyes, clenched my fists and prayed.

"Everything alright, Cedric?" came her hushed tones, saved for the dead of night.

"No problem, Nurse D'eath."

"Good. Then I shall wish you goodnight."

"Night, Nurse D'eath."

Footsteps padded away along stone floor. The door closed.

Cedric's baggy-eyed face appeared beneath his desk. "You're on your own now, fella."

At 23.58, having given the nurse long enough, I dearly hoped, to wash, change into her jim-jams, climb into bed and ideally fall asleep, I crawled out from my hiding place.

"Thanks!" I hissed at the security guard cum janitor as I slid away on all fours, but he seemed to have lost interest in the operation. That, or he was planning to deny any knowledge of me.

At the end of the frankly spooky, candlelit corridor I stood, gulped, leant on the door handle and pushed. To my paranoid ears, I had unleashed the operating sounds of Satan's rusty hell-hinges; the reality must have been less spectacular, because no nurse came bowling from her quarters.

The lounge was in pitch darkness, to which my eyes were unaccustomed. Amazingly, given the paucity of thought that had gone into my plan, I had brought with me a pocket torch. However, with the windowed door to Nurse D'eath's office only yards away, it would have been too risky to use it.

So, with tiny, sliding steps, eyelids wide apart to create the greatest possible aperture, I shuffled towards the residents' door, hands out before me, feeling for obstacles, trying to remember where all the chairs had been.

"Is he here yet?"

"Stop saying that!"

"What time is it?"

"How do I know?"

"I've never trusted him."

"Minker."

I'd caught those exchanges a good while before I even reached my goal – and through solid wood. As escape parties went, they had all the subtlety of toddlers on sugar.

I flung myself the remaining distance, yanked open the door and went, "Shhhhh!" as quietly yet urgently as possible.

"Hurrah!" came the barely muted cheer, then I had to stop them singing *For He's a Jolly Good Fellow*.

We were going to have to move fast.

"Quick, follow me!" I hissed, feeling for the nearest body, finding its hand and pulling. My night vision was at least improving and I could just make out the bathroom door.

"Where are we going?" came Peel's voice.

"To the beach, you fool!" said Hoath.

"Please! Shhhhh!" I urged them.

"Is he here yet?" (Wilmington-Hovis.)

"Stop saying that!" (Hoath.)

"Will I need a spade?" (Peel.)

The only positive I could find was that we were at least moving.

For a glorious couple of seconds there was absolute silence. Then came a squeaking. Wilmington-Hovis's meerschaum bath-chair. Unnoticeable during the day, at night, with the senses on high-alert, it wheels sounded like vigorous frottage occurring on a trampoline pulled from a canal.

That did it. I stood to one side and windmilled my arm in the direction of the bathroom. "Everyone! Go! Go! Go!" I hissed.

When any body came within range, I shoved its back onwards. I didn't care who it was, or what its state of decay, I just shoved. When I made out Wilmington-Hovis's seated figure, bringing up the rear of the queue, I grabbed the handles of his bath-chair and ran.

Dad was holding the door open as I skidded through. Assuming – hoping – that we were all safely inside, I turned and shut it behind us. And waited. Even the old gimmers held their tongues.

We waited. We waited some more.

Silence.

How we had pulled that off without getting caught, I could not begin to guess. Either angels had been watching over us, or Nurse D'eath was a heavy sleeper. The latter seemed likelier.

Bowing my head, frazzled and shot through with adrenalin, I allowed myself to succumb to the sense of blessed relief – but briefly. We were not done yet, not by a long chalk.

Avoiding switching on the bathroom light, as that would have floodlit the outside, instead I made use of my pocket torch.

When I swung its beam over the residents, I couldn't quite believe what I saw. Dad, Reculver, Hoath, Chislet, Peel and Wilmington-Hovis, all in their pyjamas with their top buttons done up. Standing before me wearing the expectant expressions of good boys come Christmas. (Reculver, at least, had had the sense to also wear his dressing gown.)

It was heartbreaking.

"It's freezing outside!" I hissed.

"Is it?" went Hoath.

"What month are we in?" asked Peel.

"Do you know, I've forgotten what the cold is," said Reculver. "Blessed central heating. Never off."

"Perhaps we should ask her?" suggested Peel. "To turn it off, I mean."

"Don't be stupid!' said Hoath.

"I want to go home," wailed Wilmington-Hovis.

Blocking out their to-do, I shone my torch at the window to the outside world. It was a large double sash, heavy in construction, with a lock attached to the bottom frame. I tried it, desperate that it would open or I would once again reach an impasse.

No dice.

No bloody dice.

"I have a plan." It was Mr Reculver.

"Really?"

"I've already thought this through, Pilsbury," he said. "Because I have tried to escape before." – That stunned the natives – "And I believe there is only one method that might work."

I was all ears. "What's that?"

"Well," he said. "That's a strong, well-constructed window. So it'll need something heavy to break it. And the only thing in here that's suitable is the sink."

OK. "So your plan is: to throw the sink through the window?"

"That's right. Except it's attached to the wall and the floor."

U-huh. "But you think you can shift it?"

"Well," replied Reculver. "I've tried on and off over the past 23 years and I haven't managed it yet."

Brilliant.

He continued, undaunted: "But tonight I feel I may succeed."

"Why tonight?"

"Because you have inspired us, Pilsbury."

The big man squatted down, wrapped his sizeable, yet unconditioned arms, around the base, clenched his teeth and... "Hhhhhhnnnnnnnnnnnnnnnnnnnn."

Everyone was silent, expectant. Willing Reculver to succeed.

The sink did not budge.

"Hhhhhhnnnnnnnnnnnnnnnnnnnn."

Nothing.

"Hhhhhhnnnnnnnnnnnnnnnnnnnn."

That went on for a while, during which time I played my torch around the room. I was appalled to see that the bath had no screen around it, not even a curtain, and that the toilet cubicle had no door. Was there no privacy afforded even here?

As I shone the beam around the window one more time, I spotted a red box high up on the wall, with writing on. It read: 'In case of emergency break glass with hammer'.

"Hold on..." I said.

"Hhhhhhnnnnnnnnnnnnnnnnnnnn."

"Has no one noticed this before?"

"What is it?" asked Peel.

"Hhhhhhnnnnnnnnnnnnnnnnnnnn."

"A red box, minkbreath!"

"How did that get there?" asked Hoath.

"What's it say on it?" (Peel.)

"Hhhhhhnnnnnnnnnnnnnnnnnnnn."

"I want to go home!" (Wilmington-Hovis again.)

I tapped Reculver on the back. "Yes?" he said, straightening with difficulty. I squiggled the torch beam over the box.

The penny dropped. "Good Lord," he exclaimed. "You know, when an object becomes over-familiar, one somehow fails to notice it."

Just then, the bathroom door burst open and a great bulk in shadows loomed there like a black hole hovering.

"*WHAT IS GOING ON HERE?*"

I heard at least one whimper.

The bathroom light came on. Backs of hands shot up to cover sensitive eyes.

"Look at you all!" sneered the wretched nurse. "*What do you think you look like? And you, the younger Mr Dextrose, did you really think you could get this lot past me?*"

I had done, yes. "No," I said.

D'eath snorted. "The moment I didn't see you on the driveway, when you were supposed to be leaving, I knew something was up. My suspicions having already been aroused when you gormless lot acted like kids planning a tuck-shop raid. *Pa-thetic*. Incidentally, I have sent Cedric home. His employment has been terminated."

We stood there, we grown men, taking her derision. Peel and Hoath, staring down at their shuffling feet. Reculver, rubbing a hand over his face. Wilmington-Hovis, chin on chest as usual; his pose never really altered. My father – *looking shameful?* What on earth had come over him, these past few weeks? Only dumpy Mr Chislet, staring back at Nurse D'eath, offered any semblance of defiance.

"*What in God's name were you thinking, the younger Mr Dextrose?*" she bellowed, revelling in the victory, milking it for all its worth.

"I was taking my friends to the seaside," I said. Someone had to stand up to her.

Faces turned towards me.

"*They're not your friends!*" she spat. "*Look at them!* Feeble, simple-minded, pitiful creatures."

That did it. "Oh, piss off you sinister old goat," I snapped.

Her gob fell open, revealing a tongue like a pink toad.

And I was on a roll. "These gentlemen have put up with your bile for far too long. Mr Reculver, Mr Hoath, Mr Chislet, Mr Peel and Mr Wilmington-Hovis, Dad – my offer still stands…"

Nurse D'eath's slow handclap started, echoing around the tiled bathroom, muffled by the plumpness of her mitts. Clap… clap… clap… clap.

"Very good, the younger Mrs Dextrose. Very good. Well, be my guest. If your 'friends' have the temerity to leave. Be my guest – I'll hold the door open for them. So. Who's going to the beach with young Mr Dextrose? Who's first?"

Feet shuffled. With my gaze I sought each of them in turn, first laced with expectation then, when each avoided my eyes, with pleading. Even Reculver bowed his head.

"Actually, I don't want to come." It was Wilmington-Hovis.

I walked over to him, his frail old frame in that wicker chair. "But Mr Wilmington-Hovis – *Mr W-H* – it was your righteous indignation that shone the brightest. You're part of the reason I did this. Surely you can't…"

"Sorry," he said. "I have to go home." He swivelled his chair and turned away.

I could not bring myself to look at Nurse D'eath. I could already picture her face.

"Ahem." Kenneth John Peel this time.

Not him, too? Surely not? "I'm… I'm not going either. Actually."

"Why not?"

"Because. Well."

"Because well what?"

"I'd rather not say."

"Oh come on, Mr Peel! Kenneth John Peel! *Ken John Peel!* The man they wrote the song about!"

"Well, you see, I'd miss the place."

"Sorry?" I was dumbfounded. "You'd *miss* this place?"

"Alright. Not so much the place. I'd miss the therapy."

I'd heard it all now. "Surely you're cured by now!"

"Hmm. Well. It's not quite like that."

"So what is it like?"

Hoath butted in: "If you must know, Nurse Death wanks us off every morning. I'm tempted to stay myself."

Nurse D'eath stood aside, arms folded, smirking, while Peel wheeled Wilmington-Hovis out of the bathroom. Those squeaking wheels made the only noise.

The game was over and I had lost. They were institutionalised, hopelessly ingrained in the system. I'd been wrong to push them so far, so quickly, the fragile old souls. I felt a surge of guilt. "Look, I'm sorry, I…"

"Mink this! I'm with the boy!" came Dad's rallying cry.

Reculver glanced at Hoath who glanced at Chislet, the three old friends in their polyester-cotton night attire, with their veins and their growths. As one, they nodded.

The team was back together.

We were going to the seaside!

Nurse D'eath merely watched, a supercilious grin slapped all over her chops. When we were gathered together in solidarity, she led us to the front door and held it open. Her parting words were: "They'll crumble. You'll see. *And don't you think you've got away with this.*"

Dad stuck two fingers up to her.

It felt good to have him back.

With my father in the passenger seat and Reculver, Hoath and Chislet in the rear, we bounced along on full throttle while the engine complained, beneath a sky the colour of squid ink.

No one spoke, as the three long-term inmates discovered the outside world anew. Past the church and Martin's the butcher's, down Oak Tree Hill where the cows were sleeping, past the village green and the duck pond, out onto the roundabout and the main road. A car passed us going the other way; its occupants pushed their heads out of its windows and youthful jeering careened away with them.

"The young scallywags!" cried Hoath, unaccustomed to the contemporary vernacular.

"What a set of minks," muttered Dad.

After we passed through Little Dritt, its stone cottages with their thatched roofs and its local shop, the sea appeared to our left, across untended grassland.

I heard Reculver gasp, "Oh my."

It was a particularly beautiful night. A pair of lumbering cumulo-nimbus clouds drifted either side of a near-full moon, radiating its intense light and casting it over a casually undulating sea. White and red lights blinked on and off out there, scattered about the water: vessels on the hunt for fish.

The sand appeared silver, a strip of precious metal. As we approached Dritt-on-Sea, passed the tram unlit and stationary at the end of its line, the pier, our destination, came into view.

"That's where we're heading," I told my boys.

"I don't care where we go," replied Reculver. "Just make it last."

A couple were just strolling off the pier, arm in arm, as I parked at the roadside ignoring the double-yellow lines. I checked my watch – 00.47.

A hefty breeze was blowing in off the sea, which blew my jacket open as I stepped out of the car. I wrapped the fabric tightly around me with one arm as I opened a back door with the other.

Reculver, Hoath and Chislet stared at one another.

"Come on, out you come!" I cried over the blustery wind. "The world won't bite!"

Hoath was out first, fine strands of red hair flailing crazily; then Reculver, beaming once again. Chislet emerged finally, bouncing himself along the back seat like one of Barnes Wallace's bombs until he could flip out his legs.

When he righted himself, he clasped my hand. "Thank you, son," he said. "You've done us proud."

"Why. Er. Thank you, Mr Chislet."

But he was already gone.

It was bitterly cold and I – the youngest and therefore the likeliest to survive – was the only one wearing appropriate clothing. I couldn't keep those old gentlemen exposed to the elements for long or they would literally catch their death.

They were standing, huddled together, waiting for me. The old guard. Heads bowed against the wind, hair – on those fortunate enough – dancing, pyjama trousers pulled up to belly buttons, slippers (and socks, in Chislet's case), and brushed cotton tops. Their teeth were chattering, but I could see it in their eyes. Alive. Eager.

The scene brought a lump to my throat. "Come on, boys!" I called out. "There's shelter at the end of the pier! Last one there's a sissy!"

I led the way. The wind blew right through us, howling, whistling past the pier stanchions, as our footsteps thudded on the boards and we gripped tightly to the railings.

"Sorry about the weather!" I quipped when we had finally made it, and the five of us gratefully threw ourselves into the shelter at the pier's end, the wind having only increased in intensity the further we staggered out to sea.

It was effectively two open-fronted, green-painted wooden huts with glass panelling, set back to back, each featuring a pair of wrought-iron benches. Though the wood rattled and the glass shook, the shelters did at least function as intended: they were little havens. Once inside, it were as if someone had turned the volume down.

Hoath and Chislet were shivering and Dad, whose teeth were chattering out meaningless Morse code, looked as if he might throttle me. I could see in Reculver's face that he was trying to hide his discomfort – and he had the dressing gown – but there was pain in his eyes and his pale skin had turned a shade of alabaster.

I apologised once again, this time sincerely.

"Please, Pilsbury," said Reculver, squeezing my knee. "The last thing you need to do is be sorry. You've set us free out here, my boy. If I died now, I'd die happy."

I smiled at him and hoped he wasn't tempting fate.

Hoath added: "You seem to forget: we've explored the Poles. This feels like the Tropics!"

Chislet nodded.

Bless them.

"How much longer we got to stay here?" demanded Dad. "Minking freezing!"

Reculver looked back down the pier and said, "Here, someone's coming."

He was right. A tall, lean figure, male in outline, was heading towards us. I wondered why on earth anyone would be braving these elements at this time of night.

When the approaching man was no more than 20 yards away, the moonlight started to pick out some of his features. He had dark hair, cut into a bowl haircut, was wearing jeans and some sort of casual jacket. He looked… sort of familiar.

When he was very close, I recognised him.

It was Tk-Tk.

The chief Gdgi's son from the Q'tse village.

The chief I gave the cigar to. The poisoned cigar.

The chief who almost certainly died.

If he'd come all this way to find me, I was a dead man.

I couldn't run back to land because the pier was too narrow to get past him, and there was nowhere else to go other than downwards, down into the briny. Before I could make Hobson's choice, Tk-Tk was upon us.

"Hello Pilsbury. Do you remember me?" He positioned himself in front of us, back pressed against the railing to steady himself against the wind. I could only just make out what he'd said.

I would have to talk my way out of this. Make the lad see sense. "Yes, I do remember you," I called back. "You know, the Shaman tricked me into giving that cigar to your father. I had no idea it was poisoned."

He looked unconvinced. "If that is true, then why did you flee?"

An awkward one.

Thankfully, Dad cut in. "Who is this minker, son?"

Tk-Tk heard this. "Son? Then this is your father?"

From behind him and beneath his jacket, the young man pulled out a knife, about a foot long with a serrated edge. The moonlight travelled up and down its blade as he waved it. "Old man, come over here!"

"Oh mink," groaned Dad.

Keep him talking, I thought. Play for time. "You put the doll in my room?"

He smiled. "Yes. A nice touch, I think." Impatiently he grabbed my father, who had been dawdling on the hostage front, and dragged him out onto the pier, out among the elements.

Dad's greasy, stringy hair whipped around his blanched face. Fear had overtaken him. Even he couldn't cope with this one.

Devoid of any better ideas, I ploughed on. "Why did it take so long? For you to find me?"

"To find you was easy. I am a hunter. To fly here was much money. I washed dishes for many weeks to earn this. It will be worth it."

"Will it?" It was all I could think of.

He flashed his teeth, waving the knife point in my direction. "Yes, it will, when I have revenge!"

I heard the words, "Sod this," and spotted something bright yellow, about the size of a penny, head for Tk-Tk, then become caught by the wind and divert towards my father. A moment later, there was a feathered dart hanging from his left cheek.

I turned to see Mr Chislet holding a wooden pipe, about a foot long, to his lips.

What the hell was going on?

I watched Dad feel for the dart, hold it between two fingers and pluck out it. As he stared at it, lost in disbelief, his knees went. He dropped then fell forward.

"*DAD?*" I yelled, and rushed to his aid, with no thought for Tk-Tk and his knife. Why hadn't I reacted sooner?

I put my arms around him and lifted him up, as he had done to his wife so very recently. "Dad?"

From above me came Tk-Tk's voice: "It is done. My father's life for your father's life."

Harrison Dextrose's pupils were drifting in and out of focus. He held a finger to his dry, chapped lips. "I don't have long, son. Let me speak," he said weakly. Tears were already spilling from my eyes, landing on his poor, scarred cheeks. I could see the pinprick of blood where the dart had gone in, and wiped at it with a finger.

He spoke: "Pilsbury, son. Listen. I've a secret... you've a half-sister. You'll find..." His voice trailed off. His eyelids flickered. Closed.

I didn't care about his secrets, didn't care about anything but him. The father I had fought so hard to keep. "Dad! Dad! *Dad!*" I shook him. "*Dad! Please don't die.*"

"Mink," is what he said.

I buried my head in his chest and screamed blue murder.

I felt a tap on the shoulder. "There's no poison on that dart."

Chislet.

Even in my trauma, it registered.

I looked up at him, misted eyes sore in the wind. "What?"

"Yes," he said. "It's just a dart. There's laws against poison in Great Britain."

Reculver stood beside him. "Did we mention he was blowpipe champion of Western Npala five years running. Weren't you, Mr Chislet?"

His friend nodded.

I looked back down at Dad.

One eye opened. "Did I hear that right?"

The other eye opened. "Is I still alive?"

Yes, he was! "*You fucking bastard.*"

"Don't be mad at us," he implored. "I really thought I were gone when I saw that dart. Scared the living mink out of us. Seriously, me life flashed before me eyes."

I started thumping him repeatedly on the chest with the sides of my fists, laughing and crying at the same time. "Short film, was it?"

"Here, that stuff I said…"

"Already forgotten," I lied.

He winked and I noticed that his face had turned blue, but not from the cold; this blue disappeared then reappeared. I sat on my haunches and looked back towards the shore. A police car had stopped beside the pier and two coppers were getting out.

Dad propped himself up. "Here for that little mink with the knife," he said.

But Tk-Tk was nowhere to be seen and the coppers were coming our way.

"They're here for us," I said.

"Right," said Reculver, ripping off his dressing gown and handing it to Hoath. "I'm not going back to that place. Goodbye Mr Hoath, Mr Chislet. New boy. Pilsbury – thank you." He smiled and ruffled my hair.

With a final wave, Reculver dived, gracefully for an octogenarian, off the end of the pier and into the turbulent waves. We watched his ghostly white arms flash in and out of view, the froth of his kicking feet in their wake. By the time the boys in blue had reached us, he had been swallowed up in darkness.

Pilsbury and Harrison Dextrose will return in:

Pilsbury Dextrose and the End of the World

BIBLIOGRAPHY

Death-Defying Places in Which to Make Love to a Lady – Kenneth John Peel, 1962

I Climbed the Matterhorn On One Leg Before You (And Other Firsts) – Kenneth John Peel, 1948

You're Cold? I Thought it was Summer! – Kenneth John Peel, 1947

Three Men on a Goat – Chislet, Reculver & Hoath, 1967

Taming the Yeti & Other Adventures – Reculver, Hoath & Chislet, 1955

Big Game Recipes – Hoath, Chislet & Reculver, 1951

Don't Let it Snow! Don't Let it Snow! Don't Let it Snow! – Reculver, Chislet & Hoath, 1937

Idea for a Blockbuster Movie: Jaws – Royston Wilmington-Hovis, 1976

Very brief sample from:

In The Footsteps of Harrison Dextrose

How It Began

It was my 18th birthday when I chanced upon Harrison Dextrose's *The Lost Incompetent: a Bible for the Inept Traveller*, little knowing that it would one day lead me to kill a man with a dead penguin.

I regularly visited Second-Hand Books in Glibley, my hometown, being a voracious reader of anything from fiction to manuals on making furniture (though I never actually made any). Each time, I would rifle discreetly through the vintage pornography tucked into a hidden corner – dog-eared copies of Girl Illustrated and Lost in Bloomers, their covers featuring demure girls with dark curls and wry smiles who had forgotten to wear any clothes.

It was while flicking through the familiar magazine covers, as a birthday treat to myself, that I found Dextrose's book. Perhaps someone had changed their mind about buying it and had dumped it there, or they'd had insufficient funds and All Gussets and Garters had won.

I picked it out, realising that fate had meant me to read it. Fate did not let me down.

The edges of the pages were brown and gently undulating. On the cover was a black-and-white photograph of the author's head. Harrison Dextrose stared defiantly into the camera, eyes alive with rancour. What manner of man was this? A full, dark beard festered around his jawline and encroached on his cheeks. His hair was a mop of curls, greased down in a futile attempt at neatness. Tiny broken blood-vessels coursed between the blackheads on his nose. Flaunt the imperfections – I loved Dextrose on sight.

The back-cover blurb read:

Harrison Dextrose is the last of the great British explorers. This is his first book, a cornucopia of strange incident, concerning his journey from Blithering Cove in England to Mlwlw in Aghanasp, tracking down his former acquaintance, the philanthropist Livingstone Quench. Dextrose names this his Dextrosian Quest, a justly grandiose title. It will take him through lands rarely written about, because they are considered unfashionable. However, the author never ceases to find colour, even if he must inspire it himself. Which he often does.

Dextrose had clearly lived. The eyes said 'early 40s', the features said 'add ten'. Stuff the Walter Raleigh of history books, who returned to these shores fawning and proffering root crops. Here was a real sea-faring hero, ravaged by alcohol and sexually-transmitted disease, who probably couldn't remember the name of the ruling monarch. Were his parents alive, I felt sure they would have long since disowned him. Was there anything of me in him, I wondered? I liked beer and had always been an embarrassment to my parents...

With thanks to:

Tom, Lucy and Lauren at Legend Press.

Robin Wade at Wade & Doherty.

Ian MacEwan (reading), Neil Newnum (drawing), Mr S (rainforest vibe).